FATE & FORTUNE

FATE & FORTUNE

A Hew Cullan Mystery

SHIRLEY MCKAY

ISIS
LARGE PRINT
Oxford

First published in Great Britain 2010
by
Polygon
An imprint of Birlinn Ltd.

Published in Large Print 2011 by ISIS Publishing Ltd.,
7 Centremead, Osney Mead, Oxford OX2 0ES
by arrangement with
Birlinn Ltd.

British Library Cataloguing in Publication Data
McKay, Shirley.
    Fate & fortune.
    1. Lawyers - - Scotland - - St. Andrews - - Fiction.
    2. Murder - - Investigation - - Fiction.
    3. Scotland - - History - - James VI, 1567–1625 - -
    Fiction.
    4. Detective and mystery stories.
    5. Large type books.
    I. Title
    823.9'2–dc22

ISBN 978–0–7531–8892–7 (hb)
ISBN 978–0–7531–8893–4 (pb)

Printed and bound in Great Britain by
T. J. International Ltd., Padstow, Cornwall

for mum and dad
with love

Grateful thanks to Lance St John Butler, who, like Hew, is both a scholar and a player of the game of caich. He was kind enough to read through parts of the chapter entitled "A Game of Chases" and advise on its complexities. The mis-hits there are mine, not his.

If in my weake conceit (for selfe disport)
The world I sample to a Tennis-court,
Where Fate and Fortune daily meet to play,
I doe conceive, I doe not much misse-say.
All manner chance, are Rackets, wherewithall
They bandie men like balls, from wall to wall:
Some over Lyne, to honour and great place;
Some under Lyne, to infame and disgrace;
Some with a cutting stroke, they nimbly send
Into the hazzard placed at the end

William Lathum
Phyala lachrymarum. Or a few friendly tears . . .
1634.

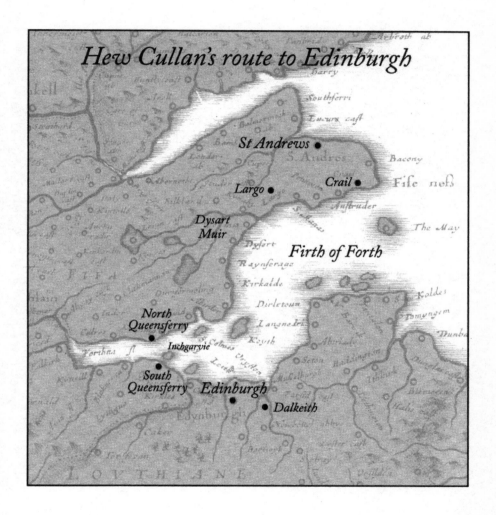

Hew Cullan's route to Edinburgh

Lenten Fare

St Andrews, Scotland
March 1581

In St Andrews, it began to snow, soft at first, insistent, blowing white upon the market place. The wind dropping back, as though tired of its game, allowed the snow to settle on the buiths and stalls, where shopkeepers hurried to withdraw their wares, brushing the flakes from the sills. From his house on the Castlegait, the physician Giles Locke looked out upon the white-rimmed cliffs, gloomily rubbing his beard. A single gull swept from the wall of the castle, circled once and dipped into the salt waves out of sight. Giles watched it in disgust. Five weeks into Lent, and bleak as winter still. He felt his wife's departure keenly. Only Meg could lighten endless days of fish and coax a hint of sweetness from the rankest kale. Yesterday, in an attempt to cheer his palate, the servant had roasted a herring gull over the fire. The doctor's belly lurched in recollection. The oiled clumps of seaflesh, tasting of fish, had marked its lowest ebb. In retrospect he thought he would prefer to eat his candle, and for all the light it gave, he might as well. Doctor Locke was out of humour. For how could a man be sanguine, in this raging wind and cold, without the proper comfort of good meat?

In the midst of this melancholic self-diagnosis — wet and windy, he decided, with a surfeit of black bile — he perceived his servant urging at the door, "Do you not hear me, professor? There's someone here would speak with you."

Mournfully, Giles shook his head. "Ah, not today. We must be gone within the hour. Advise him, Paul."

The servant stamped impatiently. He blew the chill from his fingertips. "Aye, and I tried. But yon will not be swayed. A man of means, no doubt. He's sick, for sure, and draggle damp wi' snow."

His master groaned. "As we will both be, presently. Bid him call again tomorrow, if he must."

"I did not think, sir, you would leave him in the cold. I have him here, withal."

"I told you, *no* . . ."

But the protest came too late. For Paul had admitted the stranger and the doctor had observed at once, despite himself, that the man looked sick at heart. A man perhaps of thirty-five, dressed for the cold and the fashion, a little tight and pinched about the face. He brought with him a flurry of snow. His cheeks were flushed, and though he stood trembling, Giles hazarded the cause was not the cold.

"Professor Locke," the stranger whispered. "Thank the lord!"

"I pray you leave your name upon the morrow," said the doctor brightly, hope in the ascendant, "I have business out of town, and do not consult today."

"For pity, though," the signs were inauspicious, for the man was on his knees, "I have come across the Tay in hope of seeing you."

The doctor sighed. "There, there. You come across the water, in this season, sir? And I see you have an ague. You had better stayed at home."

The stranger had rallied sufficiently, noticed Doctor Locke with sinking heart, to settle in the doctor's favourite chair. Open-armed, a gossip chair, well plumped and padded with pillows, placed precisely to capture the last of the light, the full of the warmth of the fire. Giles conceded the advantage with reluctance, while the patient gave a deprecating cough.

"A little fever, aye, a chill about my bones. I lay at the ferry port last night. Yet I must return today. I beg you, sir, a moment of your time."

The cheeks below their blush were blotched and scabbed. The throat throbbed damp with sweat.

"Sit closer to the fire," surrendered Giles at last. "I warn you, I may not delay for long. But my servant here will pour you something hot. A caudle, Paul! What ails you, sir, that you consult so far from home? Are there surgeons none across the Tay?"

"Surgeons, aye!" the man said bitterly. He took the cup from Paul. "Need your servant stay?"

Doctor Locke considered this. Then he remarked briskly, "Indeed, he need not. Paul, you may prepare our cloaks and blankets for the ride. Pray God, the skies will clear. You see, we are embarking on a journey, sir. Ah, well, a moment, then. Why are you come to me?"

The man replied faintly, "I have heard your reputation, and have means."

"I do not doubt it," Giles said dryly. "You are a burgess, perhaps?"

"A merchant, aye."

"How long have you been troubled with this fever?"

"A week, perhaps ten days. It comes and goes."

Giles tutted. "Aye, for sure. What ails you else?"

"A roughness in the throat, an aching in the bones. It is a common rheum, I doubt, no more," the man replied.

"I doubt there is more," Giles said severely, "else why did you come to me? Have you suffered this before?"

"Not that I recall."

The doctor turned to scrutinise him, curious in the firelight. "You say your throat is sore; then will you show your mouth? Come here, that I may see you better in the light. You have not noticed lesions on the tongue? And there," Giles prodded gingerly, "you do not feel a pain?"

The stranger shook his head.

"Your forehead is a little warm; you sweat, not overmuch. The fever is light. But the cold air, I protest again, can scarcely help you here."

The man appeared to brighten. "Aye, I doubt tis unseasonably raw," he answered eagerly. "You recommend the fire?"

"Indeed I do."

There was an odd note in the doctor's voice that served to sink the patient back in gloom. But Giles continued cordially, "Will you not remove your gloves, and warm them on the coals? Your journey's long. You came on horseback, I presume?"

"Fine horse, aye. Came across the water. Nor jibbed to cross the ferry, in this wind."

Giles raised an eyebrow. "Fine horse, indeed. No discomfort in the saddle? Sores, contusions in the fundament?"

The man shifted a little, self-consciously. "What's that? A pain in the arse? Well, you know," he answered uneasily, "Tis a rough enough ride from the ferry."

"For sure," the doctor soothed. "Well, sir, you'll take off your gloves. Else, as my mother used to say, you will not feel their benefit. I see you have the scab upon your hands."

"What scab?" the man asked, alarmed, inspecting the backs of his hands. "I see no scabs."

"Here, on the palms." Giles turned them round. "Tis slight enough, for sure."

"A little chapped and chafing from the cold. It's nothing," shrugged his patient.

Giles persisted quietly. Once resigned to consultation, his relentlessness was thorough. "May I trouble you to remove your boots? Ah, yes. We see the same here on the feet."

"Why are you washing your hands?" the merchant demanded.

The doctor had withdrawn discreetly to the corner of the room, where washing cloth, tin jug and basin were assembled on the board. He set down his laver and smiled. "Tis a habit I acquired from my young wife. We are not married quite the year, and already I am trailing in her ways. She says I reek of physic, when she wants me soft and sweet. You see I am in thrall to her. Ah, this water's cold! And yourself," he made pleasant inquiry, vigorously drying, "are you married at all?"

"Aye, I have a wife," the stranger said suspiciously.

"Children?"

"Four."

"Four children? Then you're blessed." Giles hung the towel on a peg. "And you're a merchant, well-to-do, and have a buith or shop. And doubtless you must venture overseas at times, in search of foreign markets or to fairs?"

"At times," the man conceded.

The doctor nodded thoughtfully. "Then you must miss your wife."

"What of it, then?" Some hidden inference appeared to cause offence, for the man rose abruptly, and began to pull on his boots. "Thank you; I take up your time."

"You have not had what you came for," Giles informed him gravely. "Was it not a diagnosis you required?"

The man sat down again. "The ague, a light fever," he repeated. "It will pass."

"Aye, it will," agreed the doctor.

"*Well* then?" the merchant countered desperately.

The doctor stroked his beard. "When were you last abroad?"

"Four months ago. But that can hardly signify."

"I fear it can. Four months ago you went abroad, and now you come to me with fever and a raging throat, with lesions and contusions in the mouth — you have not felt them there? Tis no surprise; they cause no pain, in the present stage. You may observe them in the glass. And you have scabs upon your palms, for which you put on gloves."

"For the unseasonable cold," the patient protested.

Giles continued unperturbed, "And on the soles of your feet. These afflictions are externals, and the province of the surgeon's art, not mine. Nonetheless, since you consult me, you permit me see the place where this began?"

"I do not understand," the merchant whimpered. Unconsciously, perhaps, he had drawn his thighs close in their cushion. His breech was padded, in the fashion, with a mat of hair.

"Ah," the probe was penetrating, "but I think you *do*."

There was a moment's silence, before the stranger fumbled with his hose and opened up the buttons at his crotch. "Tis nothing," he said hoarsely, "and has healed."

The doctor glanced, and then he touched his blade upon a callous nestling on the hairline like a stone. "That does not hurt?"

Wordless, the man shook his head.

"But there has been a chancre, on the pintle shaft. And that, I think," the doctor prodded softly, "could not escape your notice after all. And while the pustule here was putrid, or in this last fever, did you lie with your wife?"

The patient whispered, "*No*."

FATE & FORTUNE

Giles smiled at him approvingly. "Good man; you may do up your breeks. Do not bed her awhile, throughout your present sickness. Or any body else," he said in afterthought. "While the lesions fulminate, I pray you will not deal."

"My present sickness?" The patient looked up at him. "There is still hope, then? It may be cured?"

"Well, we may treat your symptoms for the while. But as I say, the fever will abate, without the need for physic."

"I have money here for medicines," pressed the merchant, "and your time . . ."

The doctor shook his head. "I will not prescribe them. What you suffer from is not within my sphere. I will write you a recommendation to a surgeon here in town, and he is most discreet, for I see your fears and apprehend them. The treatment for your ill is blister, fire and mercury. This is not rooted in the humours, and it cannot be amended from within. Tis not a moral cause," he added gently, "that I must refuse you. But I will not take your money, where I cannot make a cure."

"Then you are alone, sir. For I know of no other, who would not judge or profit from my pain," the patient answered miserably. "If it were spoken in our town, that I had caught the Spanish fleas, I should be turned out from my business and the kirk. The symptoms will subside, you say?"

"Aye, but for a while."

"And you recommend the surgeon? Tell me sir, for I have heard such savage things about the pox, the curing

8

some claim worse than the affliction. *Tell* me, is it as bad as they say?"

"Well," Giles cleared his throat. "It is true that some of what you may have heard is spoken unkindly, to punish the afflicted for their sins — from a sense of moral outrage, people do exaggerate the cruelty of the cure. But then again, the surgeons sometimes blunt their knives and heat their irons more fiercely than they need to, in self-righteous self-appointment, as the crueller cure. To speak plain, they see their role to punish as they heal. Nay, sir, I see that I frighten you; that is not my intention. Be assured, the surgeon to whom I recommend you is not one such as those, but curious and gentle as his trade permits. I say this but to serve your question, whence the rumour comes. For, I must confess, I know no better course than mercury. I do concede it rigorous, and not always well effective in remitting the disease."

"Then there is no hope," the man concluded wretchedly.

"Come, now, there is always hope," Giles consoled him kindly. "Find yourself an inn in town, a dinner and a bed. Tomorrow, you may brave the surgeon, while the day is fresh. Good luck to you. Have courage, friend. But now I must be gone. Did I not say? I'm going to a funeral."

The track to Kenly Green had all but disappeared, and they made a hard journey of it. The doctor's stone-dark mare, Grey Gillat, had grown slow of late, for reasons that were lost on him. The marschal had pronounced her sound, alluding somewhat cryptically to cruel excessive loads. Which was a patent nonsense, Giles protested, for she was a trotting palfrey, nothing more. "What loads does she carry?" he had roared at Paul, who had shrugged and smiled. For Paul himself, he hired an ancient roan, whose going was unsteady when the path was smooth. Therefore, with the white wind in their faces and the promise of a storm, their progress was a little slower than it might have been. To make matters worse, the servant objected, "I do not think, sir, they will have the funeral today. The ground is frozen hard. I think we should turn back."

"Since when were you required to think?" Giles retorted crossly. "Be grateful that you do not walk."

"Twere quicker," Paul said reasonably.

Giles shot him a look. "We do not go only for the funeral," he answered, a little more graciously, "but for your mistress' sake. Take courage, then."

Paul nodded dubiously.

"Besides, there will be bakemeats," his master enthused.

They rode on awhile in silence, as Giles pondered the question of Paul's new-discovered opinions. He did not doubt their source: they came from Meg. The doctor's wife was skilled in natural lore and medicines, and with his greater learning they had made a practice of a sort. Mostly, they were complementary; sometimes, though, they felt at odds. It had been her idea to share a little knowledge with the servant, Paul, and gradually she taught him to prepare her simples and receipts. Her reasoning was sound, for ignorance, she claimed, bred fear, and Paul already had suspected them of magic, with alarming consequence. Better then to teach him basic truths. The downside, though, was this emboldened insolence; at times, as Giles suspected, neither of them quite allowed his full respect and mystery. He half expected Paul to set up as a quacksalver himself. Now, as if he read his mind, the servant said, "So what was it wrong with him, then?"

Giles reined in the horse, which at her present pace could scarcely make her slow, and turned full in his saddle to glare at him. "You allude to what, precisely?" he demanded coldly.

Unabashed, the man continued, "Yon sick merchant, frae Dundee. I'll warrant twas the pox."

"And why would you think that?"

"Man disna cross the wattir in this weather jist to see your face, as famous as ye are."

Giles fell silent, spurring on the horse, and Paul sensed that he had crossed the line. "Though doubtless, sir, you *are* well kent," he ventured timidly.

"There are many things," the doctor deigned to notice, "which you do not know. You made mistakes before, which cost us dear. I bid you, be aware of it."

The servant flushed. In truth, though, it was not the slight that troubled Doctor Locke. His outrage was more feigned than deeply felt. The thought of his last patient preyed upon his mind. Giles considered all with an open circumspection. He was often sceptical, but seldom proud. He followed his convictions where they led, and was prepared to ask for help wherever it might come the most effectively. Even if, he reasoned wryly,

11

that ran counter to reason and sense. Meg was the case most to point. And yet this particular case he was scarcely inclined to discuss with his wife. This was not the first man he had seen in recent days with syphilis, nor, his instincts told him, would it be the last. And aye, of course, Paul had guessed right. For such a man would not care to be treated close to home.

"Well, well," he said at length. "Even these old nags have found their way at last. Take them, Paul, seek out the groom, and I'll walk on before you to the house."

The house at Kenly Green had always welcomed him. Coming through the gate he saw the flare of candlelight, the warm and smoky comfort of the hearth. He walked through Meg's walled garden where the light snow dulled his step and ice congealed the bare, ungiving earth. Below, he knew, the pale shoots sheltered; another month would pass and they would flower. The present sad affair did not unsettle him, for Doctor Locke knew death in all its forms. He walked the brittle earth towards a blaze of light.

But something else had caught his eye that did provoke a frown. In the corner by the wall he saw a figure standing, whiter than the snow, frozen still and desolate as any cast in stone.

"*Hew! My dear friend!*" The doctor's arms went round him fiercely, clutching with the warmth of his great heart.

Hew Cullan smiled a little foolishly and came to life. The wind laced his cheeks with salt tears. "Is it too late, Giles?" he whispered.

He had come across the sea, and through a white storm, discarding one by one his comforts, horses, friends, through sheets of ice and fog too sheer for ship or horseback, still he came, discarding them, intent upon his coming, through the ice and storm. And now that he was come, he could not enter there, but found himself left stricken in the garden, frozen out, for fear.

"Oh, my dear friend!" And the bulk that was the doctor, warming and protecting him, whispered through the tears, "Dearest, he died a *grand* death."

Prayers for the Dead

They were not mourners, most of them, who came to fill their cups at Matthew Cullan's funeral. The great hall, with its vast beaming hearth and cluster of candles, closeted and cheered the little crowd. The lure that had attracted them was set out on the board: Lenten salmons green and cured; haddocks fried in butter in sweet herb and caper sauce; coddled eggs in chafing dishes, flummeries and flans. Flanking all were four curd tarts, white and green and blue and yellow, almond, spinach, plum and saffron, coloured like the sun. For drinking there were mellowed ales, or gascon clarets dark as blood, set like jewels in pewter cups. And for those who had ventured in late from the snow, there were fire-breathing waters, syrups and cordials, possets and caudles in great foaming pots. These detested confections were pressed on Hew Cullan, as he was brought shivering in to the hearth. "For pity, give him air!"

Hew felt an aching sharper than the pricking of his fingers, waking up too quickly from the numbness of the frost. His sister Meg had hold of his hands, rubbing them briskly, pulling him back from the heat of the

14

flames. "He must be warmed more slowly, or the frost will bite."

The grey dogs napping by the fire had had their fill of fish heads, and forgot their master as they slept. Hew drew in his breath. The air felt hot and raw.

"We had no hope of you. However did you find a ship?" he heard his sister ask. The colour had returned into his palms; his fingers stung relentlessly, yet she did not relinquish them. He had crossed the sea from France, on the one ship, the last ship, before the white storm, for week on week through waters vast as winding sheets that billowed upwards to the masts, where he had almost died, yet he could not remember it.

"I came too late," he answered, foolish, inarticulate. From weariness and cold, perhaps from grief, he could not shape the words.

Meg held him close to her, breathing his coldness. "We were to bury him today, but the ground is frozen hard, and the beadle has sent word the grave is not prepared. Therefore he must lie another night, and God has willed that you are here to watch him with us. Tis providential, Hew."

He glanced towards the oak stand bed that occupied a dark place in the room, the heavy curtain drawn. Meg shook her head. "He is not there. The wright came in this morning and made fast his kist. We placed it in the laich house, where it's cool."

Hew longed for escape from the heat and the crowd. He lit a lantern from the fire, and made his way down to the laich house, the low vaulted cellars below the great hall. The space was a warren of chambers, each large enough to form a separate dwelling place, that served as Matthew's stores. Hew held the lantern aloft, looking in to each room in turn. The outer vaults were stripped bare, but as he ventured further he found casks of ale and wine and grain sacks, lightly dribbling, where the mice had nipped. Deeper still were bottled fruits and rows of apple racks: last year's pippins wrapped in paper, wizened and soft to the tooth. The place had a leathery sweetness that brought back his childhood. And in the very centre of the vault, in the room adjoining this, he found his father's dead-kist, lit head and foot by candlelight. As Hew approached, he heard a low voice singing, and a stranger by the coffin turned and smiled, sketching vaguely with his hand. He did not pause to speak, but disappeared into the apple room. Hew stared after him a moment, before he knelt upon the earth, a little awkwardly, and set down his lamp in the dust. Not since he was the smallest child had he come into his father's house without asking for his blessing, and he tried to ask it now, but could not find the words. The kist was draped in velvet cloth, the sombre fringe brushed against the dust into a deeper darkness still, beyond the reach of candlelight. Hew fingered the drop of the velvet, committing its touch to his heart. A little mud fell crumbling through his fingers, remnant of the mire of other deaths. But he found nothing of his father there. He was relieved when Meg came down to find him, pressing her hands into his.

"A man was here praying," he confronted her. "Was it a priest?"

16

She would not confess it, even to him. Her eyes opened wide in a gesture of surprise. "You know it is not proper to say prayers before the dead."

"Aye, and so do you." Unexpectedly, he grinned. "He always had his way. So too in death."

Then he whispered, desolate, "I thought to ask his blessing, Meg."

"You had it, always," she consoled him. "Will you lift the lid?"

He shook his head. He felt unable to express himself, as though he were still in the garden, frozen out from grief or fear, from neither of those things, but a curious remoteness. Meg was talking still. He forced himself to listen.

"What matters is that you are here. The pity is that we did not expect you. The house is full tonight, and I have given up your bed, to Master Richard Cunningham, an advocate. Do you know him, Hew?"

"I know the name. No matter. I will sleep by the fire in the hall. A blanket will serve well enough." Weariness had overcome him. He could barely speak.

"I cannot think it will," she answered doubtfully. "All this is yours now. This is your house."

He stared at her, startled, and cried out in anguish, "It *cannot* be, Meg! Do not say that!"

It was coldness, after all, that affected Hew so strangely, for on his second cup of wine, he began to feel revived, and prepared to face the crowd. Giles Locke was talking with a stranger and Hew's cousin Robin Flett.

"What irks me," Giles expostulated, through a chunk of cheese, "is that ministers reforming of the kirk did *not* reform the fish days."

Robin Flett assented. "Rather than to divorce the fast from Lent, I hear the parliament is minded to extend it."

Giles, who was swallowing, spluttered at this, while the stranger laughed. "Not this year, I hope. But when you have a wife that cooks as well as yours, the fish days cannot hurt so much."

"Aye, that's true," Robin Flett leaned forward and poked Giles in the midriff. "For all her flaws, she feeds you well."

"What do you mean, her flaws?" demanded Giles.

"Well, you know, her *flaws*," Robin waved a hand, a little vaguely, in the air, "I do not mean that she has many, save the one she cannot help."

"What *do* you mean?"

The stranger interrupted quickly, catching sight of Hew. "Master Cullan, I presume?"

Giles recovered his composure. "Hew! Are you thawed? Do you know Richard Cunningham? He is a procurator in the Edinburgh courts."

"By reputation only, sir." Hew addressed the advocate, grateful for the show of tact. "I'm glad to see you here."

Cunningham, Hew judged, was in his early forties; tall and pale-complexioned, sober yet discerning in his dress. His hair was dark, a little grey about the temples, neat and closely cropped. He wore a true black coat, buttoned to the neck with a score of silver buttons, cut in velvet cloth, and his white gloves were slashed at the fingers, showing off his rings.

"There I have the advantage," the advocate observed politely, "for I knew you as a child. Your father made me welcome in his house."

"I'm afraid I don't remember. But your name is not unknown to me; nor, I doubt, to anyone who kens the law."

"You flatter me." The lawyer bowed.

"Perchance you could do with a lawman, Hew," Robin leered unpleasantly. He had been drinking heavily of Matthew Cullan's wines, and a livid purple smear had spread across his throat. "Your father was a rich man, and his legacies are vast. Have you thought how ye might manage them?"

Hew stared at him. "I am returned from France this afternoon to find my father dead. Wherefore I confess, I had not turned my mind to it."

"Aye, well, ye should. When better than the present, when there's expert help to hand?"

"My father's man of law is based here in the town," retorted Hew. "When the time is proper to address affairs of business, then I have no doubt that I can call upon his services. I should not presume upon Master Cunningham."

"What, say you, yon is too grand?" his cousin snorted. "I've yet to meet the lawman who's o'er grand to grasp at money, and let me tell you, there's a deal o' it in sight."

The advocate ignored this. Mildly, he remarked to Hew, "It is the case, I practise from the tolbooth of St

Giles, though I do from time to time receive instruction to attend the circuit courts, which is what brings me to Fife. The disposition of wills, and the rest, is, alas, out of my sphere. I have no doubt that your father's man is sound, for I would ever trust his judgement. Nonetheless, it must be said, my door is always open to you, should there be some service you require."

"What did I tell you?" winked Flett.

"I am not disposed," Hew addressed him coldly, "to approach these matters now. But when I do, I full intend to call upon old debts. Tell me, Robin, how's your ship?"

Robin choked into his cup. "Lucy is with child again," he changed the subject hurriedly.

Hew raised an eyebrow. "Another expense? And so soon?"

"Not so soon as you think." The merchant had recovered. "The twins are grown to lusty lads.

"Have you sons, Master Cunningham?" he challenged the lawyer. "Men must have sons, think you not."

"Indeed, I have two, and a daughter, besides. My older boy is placed here at the university, in St Leonard's college, where I do believe that you were lately regent, Master Cullan." Cunningham had turned again to Hew. "We were sorry not to find you there."

"It's true, I taught there for a while, to help out a friend," Hew answered enigmatically. "The college has a new regent, and I understand, another principal, appointed by the king. I've heard nought but good of them. How does your boy?"

"I thank you, well. At first he found the grammar hard, but your father's secretar, Master Nicholas Colp, was of help to us there."

"That man? I would not have him near *my* sons!" Flett snorted. "I could tell you scandals to disgust you, sir."

"No doubt," the lawyer said, "but I decline to hear them."

"What! You balk at scandals! I should think you lawyers thrive on them!"

"Then you are mistaken, sir. They are the greatest nuisance, for they prejudice the case."

"Ah," the merchant leaned over and prodded him. "But what if they were *true*?"

The lawyer allowed a faint smile. "In court, sir, truth is of no consequence. What matters there is argument.

"Excuse me. Master Cullan, I believe I see your sister. I must speak with her."

"Well," the merchant tailed off lamely, "as I think I said, tis proper to have sons. Tis high time you gave that wife of yours a child!" He nudged the doctor. "Doctor, heal yourself, I say . . . but when you come to see us, Hew — Lucy will insist upon it — you will not know my fledglings, fine and fat as any bairns you'll see. George has four new teeth, and taken quite amiss with it, and Lucy most alarmed, until your good doctor with one of his potions settled it sweetly."

"It was Meg's doing," Giles replied brusquely. "I had none of it." Abruptly, he turned on his heels.

Hew caught up with his friend at the lang board, pouring a goblet of wine.

21

"Robin is rude, and the worse in his cups. But you do not usually rise to it," he commented.

"I care nothing for him," asserted Giles. "Yet he has injured Meg; he calls her *flawed*."

"His wit is dull and pointless; do not let it prick. He means the falling sickness. That was blunt indeed, but not unkindly meant. Her illness is a flaw," Hew reasoned gently.

Giles coloured, but conceded, "Aye, you may be right. His pinpricks are not worth the flinching. In truth, I am too raw where childbed is the question, for I know the risks. I cannot still my fears. I *love* her, tis the rub."

"What do you mean?" queried Hew. "Is Meg with child?"

Giles shook his head. "No, not that."

"Then why should you fear? Is she not well?"

The doctor sighed. "She is quite well. I do confess, my fear defies good reason. Yet we have been apart some weeks, perforce of your father's last sickness; and in that time . . ." He checked himself hurriedly, "Well, it is foolishness. She has been well since Michaelmas, and free from fits, for which we must be thankful."

He did not seem reassured, but before Hew could probe deeper, he had changed the subject.

"Well, well, enough of that. How was Paris? Have you found your vocation at last?"

Hew grimaced. "I might have had a living there. And yet I could not settle. I was not disposed to stay."

"Ah," Giles prompted gently, "Meg thought you had found a lass."

"Did she? Little witch!" Hew laughed. "Aye, I do confess it then. There *was* a lass. It turned out sour."

"I'm sorry for it. These things happen. It was not to be."

"In truth, I thought it was. But she construed it differently. She played the coquette, and was true to her kind."

"By which I understand you do impugn her race, and not her sex," protested Giles, "else I should be afraid she broke your heart."

"Aye, but for a while," Hew answered ruefully, "I think she did. No matter, though, tis mended now. But I have done with France, and without my father's death, I should have come home anyway."

"Tis easy to be cozened by the French. They are most inventive in their love. And they can cook, of course," reflected Giles.

"You need not make me out as such a gull," his friend objected. "I do not doubt the strength of her affections. Only that the pity was, she shared them liberally."

The doctor patted him "Well, well, tis as I said. The girl was French. The loss of that pert temptress is our consolation, since you are come home to us. We'll find you a Scots lass, sober and constant."

"Not yet awhile, I hope!"

"You might think of it though. You are what, twenty-six? Hew, I hardly like to ask you this, but as your man of physic I presume that I might mention it . . ."

"Ah, now that sounds ominous. This will hurt me, I can sense it; don't put on your doctor's cap!"

"I'm serious, though. You say your lass was apt to share her close affections . . ."

"Aye, to be more blunt, she spread them thin."

"Then she has left you nothing, I suppose, that should concern you? No boils or pustules, sores? You have been in health these past few months?"

Hew stared at him in astonishment, and then broke out laughing.

"And I did not know you better, Giles, I should take offence! What then, do you take me for? Colette has wounded nothing but my pride."

"Ah, I am glad to hear it. Still, if I examine you, twill only take a moment, and you let down your points. It will set your mind at rest."

"It does not need setting at rest. Giles, I am astounded that you ask this at my father's funeral. I assure you, there is nothing of the sort that should concern you. I am well; Colette was well, and we have not consorted for the past six months. Though wherefore I should tell you this, as doctor, friend or brother — shortly to be none of those, if you pursue this course — is far from clear to me."

"Forgive me, Hew, I have forgot myself. In truth, I have forgotten *you*, which is the worse offence. The fact is I have seen so many cases of the Spanish fleas of late that it has fouled good sense."

"Ah, the *Spanish* fleas! Therein lies your error, for the lass was French."

24

"The Spanish fleas is but a name, tis known here as the verolle or the grandgore, or the Spanish pox; the Spanish call it the Italian disease, the Frenchmen call it *espagnol* and the English call it French, the *morbus gallicus*. In Italy they know it as the maladie of Naples, save in Naples where . . ." Giles postulated seriously. Then he caught Hew's smile. "You're teasing me, my friend. It's good that you are home."

"Aye, tis well," Hew clapped him on the back. "Tis well you take my word on it, and do not bid me draw my pistle at my father's wake. Let us leave the subject. How is Nicholas?" Hew remembered his old friend. "Is he not here tonight? Why then, is he worse?"

"In one sense, he is worse," Giles answered cautiously. "In truth, not *wholly* worse, though not improved. He is frail still, quite frail. For want of good warmth and sunlight, his humours run cold. Since you saw him last, it may be said, in some respects, at least, his health is worse. And yet he is not dead. And since he is alive and has survived the winter and the winter oft does carry off the weakest and the sick, and since he was disposed to die the last time that you saw him, then you might conclude him somewhat better now. Aye, he is quite well. And will be glad to see you."

"And I him," Hew muttered, too baffled to smile.

A Winter's Tale

As the party began to disperse, some to find a bed, and some to drink and gossip through the night, Hew found himself alone before the fire. He was closing his eyes and was almost asleep, when a slight cough disturbed him. The lawyer, Richard Cunningham, smiled apologetically. "Forgive me, Master Cullan, I did not mean to startle you. I had hoped to offer my condolences, apart from present company. Yet you look so peaceful here. I'll leave you to your thoughts."

Hew struggled to his feet. "I pray you, stay a moment," he answered wearily. "My cousin Flett was rude to you. I hope you will excuse him. You are welcome in this house."

"His words are of no consequence. I meet many men like him. But I wanted to say to you simply, and privately, how much I regret your father's death. He was — though I should hesitate to say it to his son — almost a father to me. Years ago, when first I did come to the bar, he oversaw my steps. I might say, he shaped me. I have felt his loss."

"You were his pupil?" Hew was moved by the simplicity of his expression. There was a gentleness in the man's manner that appealed to him, reluctant as he was to be drawn in conversation.

"I could have had no better teacher."

"Thank you, sir. Your words bring comfort. I have thought, these past hours, how little I have known him."

"You were always in his heart."

"Has my sister seen to your needs here?" Hew changed the subject abruptly. The advocate bowed.

"She has been too kind. Your bed is soft and clean. And yet I must confess, it troubles me to take it from you; you have travelled hard, and through the snow, and you have lost a father; and for all its comforts I may not rest easy while I take your place. Will you not share it with me?"

Hew waved a hand. "Certainly, no, I shall sleep here. The lamps are lit, the fire is warm; I shall not want a bed. I pray you, sleep easy, as I shall."

He would not want for sleep; he felt beyond exhaustion, longing to close his eyes.

"Here, with the servants and dogs?" the lawyer looked sceptical. "You are master of this house. Besides, if I might mention it, you look ravelled to the bone, and your cousin Flett is like to drink into the night. The clamour will disturb you. Come with me, rest in the quietness; or, if you will not, then share a private drink with me, without these distractions. I will not trespass on your thoughts."

"You are kind, sir." Hew felt the waves of weariness consume him, and he allowed Richard to lead him out like a child into the stillness of his room.

"Your servants have been good enough to lay a fire in here. Come, sit by the brazier. You're shivering."

The lawyer called for drink, settling Hew in close beside the fire. With the solace of good wine, Hew felt refreshed.

"Shall I leave you to sleep?" Richard asked politely.

"I think I will sit awhile. Stay, if you will."

"In truth, I should prefer to. For I'm weary now myself." Richard loosened off his collar. "Ah, these clothes! I know not what they starch this with, tis stiffer than the jougs! The servant has arranged your room most prettily. Do I detect your sister's touch?"

Hew acknowledged it. For there was lavender among the rushes on the floor, and petals on the sheets, that scented fresh and sweetly; and the water in the bowl that bubbled by the fire was seasoned with dried flowers and fragrant herbs. Two candles were lit in their cups on the wall, not tallow but beeswax, dimpled and new, and on the fresh-laid sheets his mother's crimson counterpane turned back upon their crispness made him want to weep, so achingly familiar in the candlelight. His books were there, brought from his boyhood, his laver, his inkstand, and pens.

If the lawyer had observed how all this had affected him, he chose not to remark it, rinsing his mouth in the warm scented water, wiping his beard on the cloth.

"Your father," he reflected, "might have served the Crown, if he had stayed. No doubt your mother's death affected him. And yet we never understood why he retired."

"My sister was unwell," Hew answered woodenly. "We came here for her health."

"So I have heard." The lawyer let the question drop unasked. He sat upon the counterpane, tugging at his shoes. Presently he ventured, "You'll permit I call you Hew? I knew you as a child."

Hew nodded warily.

"I wish to ask you something. Now, perhaps, is not the time, but tomorrow . . . well, we shall be occupied, and it is the nature of my business, that I may not linger long. Tis only recently that I renewed my old acquaintance with your father, since my boy was come here to the university. And I was sad to find him in decline. Nonetheless, I was fortunate enough to spend a little time with him before he died, and as fathers will, we discussed our sons."

Hew had stiffened. If the lawyer noticed this, he chose to pass it by.

"And we were both proud fathers, I am not ashamed to say. It will embarrass you, no doubt, as it would do my own boy, to hear how we indulged ourselves. Yet you will permit my saying, for tis meant as a kindness, that your father was most touching in his pride for you. He hoped that you might follow in the law."

"I know it," Hew said heavily, "and I have tried the law. That much my father knew. I am not disposed to like it." He stirred in his chair, setting down his cup.

"I understand. Perhaps I ought not to presume to put my case. No matter, though. The fact is this: If you were to consider the law as your profession, then nothing would please me more than to take you for my

29

pupil and to oversee your coming to the bar. You are, I understand, full learned in the civil laws, and ripe for your probation. None would be more welcome in my house."

Hew was silent a moment. His eyes were low, upon the fire. Quietly, he said, "You are too kind."

"Do not speak of kindness. I may not pretend that I am half the man your father was. Yet if I could impart to you, the half I learned from him, I might serve you well. In modesty, I hesitate to mention this, but my regard has influence. The position of king's advocate is not beyond my reach."

Cunningham's tone was earnest, unaffected, and Hew softened his response. "I know your reputation, sir. The honour you impart is undeserved. I would not, for the world, have done you a discourtesy. But I must protest again, I am not suited to the law."

The lawyer nodded. "Your father thought otherwise. But there again, we may be blind to our children's predilections. All too often, it would seem, we cast them in our moulds. Now there's my own boy begged to be a cabin boy," (despite himself, Hew smiled), "and here I've gone and put him to the university."

"Ah, but then you knew he would not care to be a cabin boy," Hew objected shrewdly.

"Did I though? But how? No matter, now. I am resolved, I shall not try to sway you, nor take offence if you decline. Do not make your answer yet awhile. Only, may I ask you, why you are so set against the law? You have spent many years in study. Was it all for nought?"

"I cannot readily explain it, sir, without I prick old wounds. I once had a friend indicted for a crime, a heinous crime, that he did not commit. I knew my friend was innocent, and I had proofs, and knew the law, and yet I could not prove it by the law, wherefore I do hold it in contempt."

The lawyer was listening intently. Urgently he asked, "Your friend was hanged?"

Hew shook his head. "I set the whole before the king, who pardoned him."

The lawyer smiled. "Which tells me you have wit, and may well serve the law, when you well understand it. I wish I had had your insight, when I was your age. Yet we are alike. For something of the sort befell me too, some twenty years ago. I was a probationer, working with your father, in the tolbooth of St Giles. I was an arrogant lad, subtle, I confess, and I had learned the law and all its tricks. I could not wait to play them for myself. I saw the law as sport, and took delight in it, like racquets in the caichpule, batting back and forth. Your father had his chamber in the close among the notaries; I work there still, though in those days I shared lodgings in the low shade of the kirk, and now my house looks down upon it from the hill. But then, the world ahead of me, I was proud and eager, and ambitious for success. The first case I defended on completing my probation was almost, I might say, a *friend*. He was one of the writers who worked in our row, who prepared our papers and made notes for us. And he was privy in this role to rare and secret documents. We knew him as a meek and modest man,

31

whose life consisted solely in the functions of his office, and a sober, fond devotion to his wife and child. Well, there was at this time a great lord taken for a spy, imprisoned in the castle at Blackness and due to stand his trial. You will permit I cloud the details; they are secret even now. But on the day before the trial, documents were brought before his gaolers that sanctioned his release, a pardon in what seemed our queen's own hand, that bore her signet seal. He was released unto his friends and thence to England, where he pursued his plot against our Crown. The pardon was a forgery, the gaolers tricked; and the signet seal was traced to an old letter in our writer's rooms. He had trimmed it with a knife and stuck the seal afresh to calculate his forgery, and it was neatly done."

"But he was guilty, then?" concluded Hew. "Why did he do it?"

"I can only guess for profit. He would not confess. And to the last, he did protest his innocence, which made it all the worse. He begged us to defend him. This modest little man, who spelled our writs so patiently, with whom we shared our drinking on a quiet afternoon, came begging to our chambers, pleading for his life."

"But was my father there? What was his part in this?" Hew pursued uneasily.

"He was otherwise engaged, and could not take the case. And so it came to me, the wretched man so grateful it was touching to behold. He fell upon his knees and kissed my hand. And standing up alone there for the first time in that court without your father's counsel . . . I confess that I failed him. I did not argue well, I could not make a case; in short, the man was hanged."

Hew shook his head. "Consider he were guilty, then it was not your fault. And if the man was innocent, then that must prove my point about the law."

"I did not consider it. I knew that I had failed him. For I had been afeared and flustered in that court. I was afraid, in truth, I should be tainted with his crime, who must defend the *man*, and not the fault. The charge was treason, after all. And yet there were no proofs, for he did not confess, no witnesses came forth, another could have found that seal, and stole it from his room. I should have made his case, and I could not. Then afterwards . . . Afterwards I went to your father and I told him what had happened. He spoke to me with such understanding, with such kindness, that I swear it made it worse. But that was not the worst, for he insisted we attend the execution."

"My *father* did!" exclaimed Hew. "That was not like him!"

Richard regarded him gravely for a moment. "I believe it was," he contradicted quietly. "For Matthew said, if we would know the law, then we must know the whole of it; and see the consequence of what it was we did. And while your father was most gentle, yet he was severe, and I was half afraid of him. He took me to the mercat cross and made me watch that poor man die, nor suffered me to look away until the last. I wish I might tell you, he died cleanly and bravely. But it was not so."

Shaken, Hew murmured, "And yet you went on in the law?"

"At first, I was resolved to leave it there and then. Your father did convince me I might turn my rage to good. And I did, though I fear not in the way he intended. Matthew thought an advocate might also have a conscience. In personal life, I would agree. But in the court, it's different. The lesson I learned there, was not to fail."

"You do not persuade me to pursue you in the law," Hew said bluntly.

The advocate smiled. "It is the devil's tale, I do confess. I know not why I told it. You are the first to hear it these past twenty years. The lateness of the hour, your father's death, have moved me to break confidence. Let us blow out the light."

He lay in his shirt beside Hew on the bed, and drew the thick curtains to close out the draught. The small fire beyond burned down in the darkness. The water in the basin had begun to ice and crack.

Human Remains

Matthew Cullan was buried in the kirkyard of St Leonard's on the last day of the old year 1580, on the 24th March.[1] It was also Good Friday, a coincidence that surely would have pleased him as he made his final journey underground. Dying, he had scornfully declined the burial ground most proper to his person and his means. He would not lie within the audit of that kirk, but stayed a papist to the last beyond the stubborn outcrop of its walls.

Matthew would have liked the bells to ring. But in the wake of the reformed kirk, his children had to settle for the mortbell swung before the kist, their only consolation that the bellman sulked and shivered in the absence of his hat. The purpose of the bell was purely practical: it did not serve to mark the passing of the dead, but to summon tenant farmers from their scattered cottages to assist the coffin on its progress to the grave. The kist was carried from Kenly Green, at

---

[1] According to the old style, Julian calendar. In Scotland, the new year began on March 25 until 1600; 1599 was a nine-month year.

the outskirts of the parish of St Leonard's, to the little chapel in St Andrews, a distance of almost four miles. The clatter of the handbell was unwelcome in the fields, where the black ewes dropped their lambs into the bitter sunshine, and the shepherds turned their backs, pretending not to hear. And so the bulk of the burden was borne by Hew Cullan, by his sister's husband Giles, by Matthew's ageing steward and his son, by the lawyer, Richard Cunningham, and by Nicholas Colp. Robin Flett was sick, and begged to be excused.

Nicholas appeared, as wan and frail as ever, to insist upon his place in the procession, with a fierce intent of purpose that put the rest to shame. Giles had nodded calmly, "Aye, for sure, he'll walk with me." And Hew observed the doctor hoist the bier upon his shoulder, where his cheerful bulk took on the greatest weight, and, wheezing surreptitiously, he braced his other arm across the back of Nicholas and bore the brunt of both, the living and the dead, in one consoling stroke. Thus strengthened by the force that walked behind him, Hew began their slow procession through the slush.

The pale salted sunshine had dampened the track, the snow dissolved to mud, and the fringe of the mortcloth was trailed in the mire. No one spoke; there was no sound save the gulls, the distant rush of sea, the coarse discordant jangling of the bell, and they were glad enough to come into the town, borne eastward by the seagate, when the scholars of St Leonard's came obedient to the bell to take their burden from them to the quiet earth. The bearers' arms hung slack as

Matthew Cullan's kist was dropped into the ground. There, without comfort of psalm, the last frozen clods were thrown over him.

Once these rites were done, a quietness descended on the tower house, as the visitors departed one by one. Richard was the last to leave. He had business with the coroner, and intended to remain in Fife for several days, returning to the capital once the skies were cleared. He left Hew with assurances of goodwill and welcome, if he ever changed his mind. Then, at last, Hew found himself alone, to dispose of the remains, and consider his father's affairs. Matthew had died well in every sense, leaving behind a great deal of money. His property and land accrued to Hew. The fabric of the house, their mother's linens, drapes and plate, was left to Meg, and taken down accordingly. Hew felt its inner life disintegrate, wrapped and boxed and carted down the narrow lane. This was not his childhood home. He had grown up in Edinburgh, in the shadow of St Giles, and remained there at the grammar school when Matthew had retired to Kenly Green. His education both at school and at the universities had long ago eclipsed all family life. His sister Meg was sensitive to this. "One day, you will bring your wife here. She will want her own things," she told him, rolling up the tapestries. She declined her father's standing bed, its drapes and feather mattresses. So great a bed would dwarf their little house, scarcely worth the cost of carting it, dismantled, down the muddy track to town and up the winding stair. She also had refused their mother's crimson counterpane that had lain on Hew's bed since childhood. The colour did not please her, she had claimed.

Matthew's legacies stretched far beyond the tower house, as his man of law explained. "Your father owned land and properties in Leith, and a small house in the Canongate, somewhere near the water port. Those are let out to tenants, and the rents accrued — they now must be considerable — collected by an Edinburgh goldsmith, your father's man of business there, George Urquhart. His buith is on the north side of the hie gate, close to the kirk of St Giles. I recommend you go to him, when this weather clears. I will write you letters that will prove your claim. There are also" — he frowned a little, squinting at the document — "large sums of money paid on account to a printer, Christian Hall, residing near the netherbow."

"A printer?" Hew was interested. "Paid out for books?"

"I think not. Over several years, sums of several hundred pounds have been ventured there. Whether as a loan, it's impossible to say. But more than enough for the whole press entire. Tis likely that George Urquhart can explain the terms to you, and if there is a debt, you may recover it."

"Perhaps I own a printer's shop," suggested Hew, amused.

"It's likely that you do."

There were bequests also for some of Matthew's servants, and for Nicholas Colp, who remained to look after the library, and immediately embarked upon a catalogue of books. Hew found the servants difficult,

38

puzzled by the maid and her uncertain little courtesies; the darkly sullen deference of the cook. He spent an afternoon with his father's old steward, the factor, Jock Chirnside, learning the extent of his estates. Chirnside was polite but wary. Most of the properties were let, and he made careful reckoning of the rents. The farmland closest to the house supplied its basic needs, which had been few in latter days. Meg's gardens, roots and herbs were kept up at her request. Hew was impressed at the depth of his knowledge; he knew all the farmers well, their skills and circumstances. The rents were collected, the monies well stocked. Yet he seemed ill at ease. The reason came apparent when he ventured at the last, "Shall you keep on the house, sir?"

Hew wondered this himself. "I'm not decided yet."

The man nodded gloomily. "Aye. Only for the men about the farm . . . tis hard to find work at this time of year. If you should wish to sell, or to manage things yourself . . ."

Hew realised to his dismay that their lives were linked with his, and that like the house and land, they were left at his disposal. He hastened reassurance, with a sinking heart. "You may tell the men that none of them will want for work. Whatever I decide, I will not see them starve."

"Tis good of you," the man said doubtfully.

"As for managing the land, I hope that you may stay, as long as I have need of you. For myself, I should hardly know where to begin."

"Tis true eno' *that*," Chirnside agreed.

Hew felt overwhelmed by these responsibilities. He took refuge in the library, where Nicholas was working on his catalogue, perched high on a stool behind a tower of books.

"I know not how to deal with servants," Hew complained. "I was not born to this."

"In truth though, you *were*," his friend pointed out. He scratched his face with the tip of his pen, and a trickle of grey ink ran down his nose. Absently, he wiped it with his sleeve, setting down the quill. "Though if you want advice, I'm not the man to ask, since I am a servant here myself."

Hew snorted. "You, a servant? Has the world gone mad?" He drew up a chair and flopped into it fretfully, seizing a book from the top of the tower.

"How goes your catalogue?"

"It *was* going well," Nicholas said pointedly.

"Aye? Well and good." Hew did not take the hint, flicking idly through the volume he had lifted from the pile. "My father possessed some rare books," he observed. "*This* is the poem that gave our regent, Master Davidson, so much trouble when its printing caused offence to the earl of Morton. I know not how we come to have a copy."

"Aye, all those are controversial," Nicholas replied. "That is why I picked them out. I wondered whether it would not be politic to miss them altogether from the inventory. Or put them in a different one. What do you think?"

"Oh, I do not think so. If the list is made in full, then at least I know of what I stand accused," Hew answered, more cheerfully. "In this little pamphlet, there can be no harm, now that Morton has fallen from grace. Aye, put them in. And let us fill the gaps — Buchanan, for instance, whose philosophies could never please my father, except he did concede the fineness of his *Psalms*. Dearly, I should like to have his *De iure regni*. And *that* I think, would not endear me to the king." He glanced through the poem. "I cannot think this verse was worth its trouble, to speak truth. But Davidson was a good man, and well missed. Do you recall him having in his class a most prodigious child, James Crichton?"

"Aye, for sure. That your friend Walkinshaw called the *abominable*. But he was at St Salvator's."

"That's the one. He was younger than the rest and braver than the rest and fairer than the rest and brighter than the rest . . ."

". . . and spoke eleven languages."

"You lie, sir. It was twelve. Did I ever tell you that I met him at the College de Navarre? He challenged the professors to a match of wits, on any question they should choose to put to him, in whatsoever tongue, and none of them could best him. It was the talk of France."

"That's marvellous."

"Marvellous, indeed. Contentious little shit."

Nicholas looked faintly shocked. "I think you are a little out of sorts today."

"I confess it. Out of humour, tedious and vexed," Hew confirmed. He tossed the book aside and took another from the pile.

"It's hard to make a catalogue while you dislodge the books," Nicholas objected mildly.

"They are dislodged already," Hew retorted.

"It may look so to you, but there is method in it."

Hew returned the volume, sighing heavily. "I am restless, Nicholas. I don't know what to do."

"So I can see."

Hew began to pace the room, prying into corners, turning over books. At length he came upon a small wooden writing box, and began to leaf through its contents. "What's this?" He had drawn out a letter, unopened, the seal still intact.

Nicholas looked up again. "Oh! I had forgotten that! It arrived some weeks ago, when your father was too ill to read it; so I put it in the writing desk. Then, of course . . ."

"He died." Hew had cut the seal with his pocketknife, and was frowning at the contents. "Here is something strange." He read aloud:

We are ready for the work when you may choose to send it,
Your devoted servant, always,
Christian Hall.

"Christian Hall, the printer," he reflected. "Aye, it must be that. Here is his mark."

He showed the page to Nicholas. It was marked with the printer's device, a black bird in the branches of a tree. Beneath this was a cross, entwined within the letter H.

"The tree of knowledge, I suppose. But what's the bird? Some sort of crow or corbie?"

"Something of the sort," Nicholas concurred. He looked uncomfortable.

"And what is the *work*? Do you know about this?"

"I know something of the matter," Nicholas confessed. "Though I cannot think that in your present humour it will please you."

"If it proves a diversion, then it pleases well enough," Hew answered lightly. "What does it mean?"

"Your father has for some years now been preparing a book for the press. When he became too frail to hold a pen, he dictated the last words to me, and I transcribed them for him. The manuscript is now complete, and in a closet here in the library."

"A book? What sort of a book? Why did I not know about this?" Hew demanded.

"He wished to have it kept secret until it was finished. As to the kind of book, it is a legal textbook, based on his account of his old cases, on which he kept most careful notes."

"And he did not think to mention this to me?"

"He trusted me to tell you when the time was ripe," Nicholas explained uneasily. "And I did not judge it ripe. I fear you will not like it, Hew, for the book is directed to you. It is a treatise from a father to his son, to persuade him in the study of the law. The last words he spoke were a letter that I took down for him." Nicholas opened another box, and removed a folded paper, handing to it Hew. Without another word, he went back to his catalogue. The library fell silent, but for the faintest scratching of his pen, as Hew began to read.

My own dear son,

It is many years now since I came to the bar, and since I had to plead my case. My eyes are grown so frail I must ask Nicholas to make my letter for me; that is to say, to act as my scribe, for I am content that the years have not dulled the wit, nor blunted the intent of what I write to you. You will, I know, forgive the breach of confidence, that Nicholas, your friend, whose tribulations you were privy to so recently, must mediate these words. He understands us well.

My dear, I write this letter, as I wrote the work to which it is prefaced, to persuade you to the practice of the law. To which I know you are not readily persuaded, yet your natural disposition recommends no better course. You are possessed with wealth and fortune, graced with art and wit. You have lands and books enough to furnish endless lifetimes, were you but content enough like Nicholas to lose yourself in learning, or to play the landed gentleman who struts about the town. Yet I know, my son, that with this pleasant solitude you cannot be content. You have a vigour, a restlessness, that learning cannot satisfy, that has not been requited in your journeys through the world. Your wit demands a keener end. You were born an advocate, and though you will dispute it, I assert that very force of argument must prove it.

You will make your case against the fact, most prettily, I know, for it was always so.

When you were the merest child, nor more than four or five, your uncle had a garden wherein you were wont to play, and in it stood a ruby pippin tree, of which he was inordinately proud. You had a fondness for red apples, and he teased you with their promise, that he never did fulfil. He was a greedy man. And as they grew ripe, his apples were harvested, shored against the winter months, baked into puddings, that never were shared. The next year, though, the yield appeared much smaller than before. The apples he had counted as they ripened on the tree were disappearing ere they could be plucked. Your uncle was convinced that someone had been stealing them, and he resolved to keep a closer watch upon that tree. And so it was he found you in his garden underneath the bower, a ruby pippin plump between your hands. Wherefore did he drag you in before me, pippin in your hand, declaring he had caught his apple thief. He held you roughly, that he must have hurt you, yet you did not cry, but set your lip at him, and calmly said he had "no proofs of that."

"No proofs!" roared he, "Did I not catch you redhand, with the apple in your hand?"

To which you did reply, "For that I have the pippin in my hand it does not prove I stole the pippin. Where are your proofs, your witnesses, that say I climbed the tree? Look, it is not bitten."

And you placed the perfect pippin on the board in front of us.

"Well then," I implored you, "if you did not steal the pippin, tell me how it came into your hand."

You shook your head. "I will not," you said stubborn, "and I need not, sir. For you say, that the burden of the proof rests with the prosecution. Wherefore, let my uncle prove he saw me take the fruit."

Your uncle was enraged, yet I confess, the boldness of your answer pleased me well. I doubt that some will say I have been lax in my affections, that I have always given audience to your pleas; but I have known you, always, to be most skilled in disputations, most alert and suited to the law. Wherefore you were put to school, and to the university, where you excelled in argument.

And yet, while from childhood were apparent your skills in disputation, I saw another side to your character, which did appear at odds with them. You had more depth of feeling than your friends; cruelties that were commonplace did haunt you. You were prone to nightmares, you saw horrors everywhere. I sensed in you a real and human sympathy, a kindness, wherefore I did shelter and indulge you, and your education cloistered you. You were not prepared, perhaps, to follow through the rigours of the law, its bluntness, its relentlessness. When your skills were called upon, you felt too deep the harshness and injustice of this world, and vowed to turn your back on your vocation. You condemned the law, that it might fail an honest man. And the horrors and injustice that the world inflicts, you blame upon the law, that was designed to right them.

In this you are mistaken. You may reconcile your scruples, and serve the better for them, in the role of advocate. Therefore I commend my book, and dedicate to you, my dear beloved son, my own defence of law, in hope that as you read it, you may find your place. Know that each account is drawn from cases close to me, dearest to my conscience, closest to my heart.

Hew folded up the letter and glanced across at Nicholas, who stared down at his page. Hew cleared his throat. "This story of the pippin is mere stuff and sentiment," he said at last.

"For sure," murmured Nicholas. "I took no notice of it, and in truth, I have forgotten it."

"It is an old man's foolishness, and since it is a trick, to play on my affections, I may disregard it."

"Aye, for sure."

Hew began unfolding and folding up the paper, and at last he blurted out, "Is it churlish to be angry with a dead man, do you think? Because he has died, and has had the last word?"

Nicholas put down his pen. Though his friend spoke lightly, he saw the real hurt behind it, and he answered sympathetically. "Though it may not be reasonable, yet it may be understood. What will you do with the manuscript? Will you have it printed?"

"I know not. I suppose that I must see it."

Nicholas nodded and produced a key that opened up the closet. Evidently, Matthew had construed his book to be a precious thing. It was written in a score or more folded tablebooks, each of twenty sheets, the whole thing comprising a very large volume of closely wrought text. The title page read "In Defence of the Law."

"The last part I transcribed," Nicholas was saying, "but I have not read the rest. The principle, I understand, was to explain the criminal and civil courts, by means of illustration, to illuminate and show the process of the law."

Hew opened a page at random. "*On Spuilzie, that is commonly a crime against the person, notwithstanding which, in divers cases criminal I do recall . . .*" He closed the book again. "Ah, no. For I am done with spuilzie, and the rest. It is a law they do not have in France, that is the better for it."

"No doubt there is another in its place," suggested Nicholas.

"Oh aye, for sure. I am done with them all. I can see no sense in it," Hew continued, setting down the manuscript. "Why would he want to put it in a book?"

"That is plain enough. Your father missed the law. He relinquished it too soon, and in his prime. His heart remained with his old cases, and it pleased him to remember it. In my poor way, I feel the same, for while I cannot teach, I while away the hours in writing texts I hope may serve the grammar school. And I have dreamt of a treatise on Ramus," Nicholas added wistfully, "that I would call, *The Ram's Horn*, though I could never hope to see it through the press."

"I can see the point of that. But not of this."

"It has its purpose too, for students of the law."

"For the education, I infer, of one student in particular," Hew concluded grimly.

"The letter to you was not meant for the press. There is nothing in the manuscript that refers to you. It is merely a textbook."

"Then for that I must be grateful. But why was he intent on publication? I cannot think that any good will come of it. And the press is not without risk."

"There is nothing in a law book to offend," Nicholas demurred. "And since it is contracted, then no doubt it has already passed the censor. This is a textbook, for sure, that has no sinister intent."

"I must take your word for it, or else be forced to read it," Hew said dryly. "I may be my father's instrument, and take it to the press, but rest assured I shall not be converted by his argument. Look how crabbed the letter is! How could he write so small?"

"Crow feather quills."

"That wretched bird! My father has invested a small fortune in this press. I cannot think, that if he undertook to pay the whole cost of the printing of the book himself, it could cost so much. Do we have any books that bear this mark — a cross, no doubt for Christian, and H, for the Hall? I know not what might signify the crow."

Nicholas shook his head. "I have taken note of printers' marks in making up the catalogue. And I do not recognise this."

"All that money paid, and not a book to show for it. It is a mystery."

"The bird is a raven, perhaps; that signifies wisdom," Nicholas suggested.

"In whose philosophy? The owl is wisdom, that's Minerva," Hew retorted, "but the corbie, beyond doubt, is an ill-begotten bird."

The Senzie Fair

April broke fair, the bitter sheets of wind collapsing in the sunshine, and the grey slush and mud were dissolved into spring. Walking to St Andrews in the first week after Easter, Hew found himself among a throng of people. The track was worn smooth by the rumble of carts. "Where is everyone going?" he asked a young farmhand.

"Why, the senzie fair!" The boy stared in astonishment.

"I had forgotten. Aye, of course."

The senzie was the largest of the annual fairs and markets, lasting fifteen days. Coming to the market as a boy, Hew had thought it was the fair for *sinners*, with its open brawls and squabbling and its powder courts and thieves. His father had explained that it was named after the synod house, and for the place the bishops once had held their council, in the cloisters of the abbey where the fair was held. For sinners after all, then, Hew concluded privately. The fair had marked the end of winter and the final surfeit of the lean dark days of Lent. A thousand foreign merchants opened up the world, far beyond the cloisters of the little town. Hew had heard the pipers piping in the crowds, watched the fights and races on the green, and had his fill of sweets and gilded gingerbread. There were jugglers and tumblers, and once a small monkey, a sad little death's-head, hiding its face in a green velvet coat.

It felt strange now to be coming in a crowd, and as they came towards the bay he broke away, crossing the burn a little downstream and avoiding the vast fleet of ships that were tethered in the harbour, stretching out to sea. He approached from the south, and crossing to the west port away from the fair he made his way up to the Swallowgait, and on to the Castlegait, where Giles and Meg had taken a house. His sister welcomed him, and showed him round the upper rooms, two or three large chambers, with a kitchen to the rear, where the familiar savour of her cooking warmed and cheered the hearth.

"You don't mind, if we sit here, Hew? I should keep an eye on the pot."

"No, indeed," he assured her. "So this is your new home? It's grand."

Meg smiled, a little wanly. "There is not much of a garden, and what we have is too close to the sea. But I have kept the physic garden up at Kenly Green. I hope you do not mind it, Hew."

The flatness of her tone surprised him.

"How can you think to ask it?"

"Everything is yours now."

"Heartily, I wish it were not. But this is a pretty house, Meg, and the tapestries sit well here. I envy you your views."

"Aye, but for the wind," Meg answered listlessly, "Giles says if the castle is besieged again, then our house will be the next to fend the cannon balls, if the wind has not yet swept us down into the sea."

Hew laughed. "That's cold enough comfort! Is Giles at the university?"

Meg nodded. "He is with a patient. Since we came back from Kenly Green, he has scarcely been at home. He spends his hours between the college and his old turret tower that he calls his consulting room, where half the time he locks himself with patients, and the rest he sits and reads. And often he will strain his eyes to fret and squint by candlelight, and does not come to bed till dawn. And I confess . . . it was not what I expected." She dropped her eyes low, and Hew felt a growing concern.

"He is a busy man," he ventured cautiously.

"Aye, he is," Meg sighed. "And once he would discuss his business. We shared the practice, Hew, and I dispensed the remedies. He asked me for advice. Now he makes his own prescriptions, sees his patients privately and does not break their confidence. He shuts me out."

"Then they are private matters, that he may not talk of, even with his wife," suggested Hew. "Or else he does not want to trouble you, when you are grieving still for father's death."

His sister shook her head. "I know what it is that preoccupies him. There is an outbreak of the virol in the town. The wives of those poor wretches that consult him come to me for help; he cannot think me blind to it. Yet he will not discuss it. The subject is too delicate, the matter is too coarse, to speak of to a *wife*. He has become my father, and he treats me like a child," she answered wretchedly.

Hew sensed something deeply amiss. He was conscious that his sister had no mother to confide in. Yet he could not talk to her about the marriage state. Decorum, and a natural reticence, together with a want of relevant experience, were strong inhibitors. "If you are unhappy you must talk to him," he urged.

Meg shook her head. "He will not hear it. He is careful to avoid it. And when he does not work, what little time he has," she went on hopelessly, "he has embarked upon a course of healthful exercise. He has a mind, he says, to take up golf. There upon the peg you see his golfing doublet."

"I see it, aye, the lozenged silk," Hew frowned.

"And here set out for warming are his golfing hose and garters, and there behind the door, his golfing cap and slippers."

"Well . . ." Hew felt at a loss. "'Tis strange. But if he's fixed on sport, then why not play it too?"

"Giles says the unaccustomed air would bring on fits."

"And you were swayed by that? I do not think it likely. When were *you* likely, to take such advice?" Hew exclaimed.

"Of course it is not likely. Don't you see? He does not want my company. And I am loath enough to force myself upon him." Meg was close to tears. "I sometimes think it was for pity that he married me. I am a poor enough wife."

54

"That is foolishness, Meg. You must talk to him. It vexes me to see you brought so low."

"It's nothing," she smiled at him weakly. "You were right; it's father's death that has affected me. Giles is a good man. I should not begrudge him his play."

"I hope you may resolve your differences," Hew told her seriously, "for I am sad to have to leave you in this state."

"Are you going away?" She looked up in alarm.

"Aye, I must go south; but not for long. It is some business Father left. By the by, did you know he wrote a book?"

"What sort of book?"

"A book of his old cases. Very dull and dry. Perhaps he spoke of it to Giles?"

"Aye, perhaps he did." She had turned her attention back to the pot, as though the business held no interest after all. "You will find him in his tower. Go now, fetch him home. Tell him there is beef for dinner."

Hew walked briskly past the castle to the Swallowgait, turning left at Butt's Wynd to the college of St Salvator. On the north street, west of the chapel, stood the provost's lodging house, where Professor Locke kept on his rooms in clear and frank refusal of the married state. Hew climbed the stairway in the turret tower, rapping lightly when he reached the top.

"Come in, come in!" the doctor called out briskly. "Pray undress behind the screen, while I make warm my hands."

"I pray you, do make warm your hands," Hew answered pleasantly, "though, if it please you, I shall keep on my clothes." He pushed open the door and went in. The room had changed little, though a few more jars and bottles had appeared upon the shelves among the rows of curios, instruments and books.

"Hew!" The professional glance of welcome broke into a smile. "Ah, forgive me, I mistook you for a patient! But perhaps you *are* a patient, and have reconsidered?" Giles ventured cautiously. "Then you need not be ashamed. It will only take a moment now, to set your mind at rest."

Hew flopped down on a cushion on the window ledge and groaned. "Peace, will you never give up? I have not come as a patient. Aye, and I will swear to you, that I will never loosen off my points to you, while I live and breathe."

"I take your point. You need not drive it home," said Giles, a little hurt. "Well, I am glad to see you, nonetheless. Have you been to the house?"

"Aye," Hew admitted. "And there's beef for dinner. But I found Meg in low spirits."

Giles, who had brightened at the start of this remark, looked a little thoughtful at its close. "She is a touch melancholic," he acknowledged. "That is to be expected, since your father died. I should perhaps have noticed it. I will prescribe her something. And, if she will have it, I will take her to the surgeon to be bled. I fear I have neglected her."

"You may be sure she will not have it," Hew replied severely. "And you have neglected her. It is your company she wants, and not your physic."

Giles appeared stricken. "What has she said?"

"She thinks you do not care for her, since you spend so little time with her."

"She cannot think that! For the reverse is true."

"Then show it. For, in truth, it grieves me that I find her so despondent. What is the matter, Giles?"

"You cannot doubt I love her," Giles retorted desperately. "It is this cursed sickness comes between us, Hew. I do confess, it vexes me."

"The falling sickness?" echoed Hew. "Yet you were full willing when you wed . . ."

"Ah, not that! I do not mean Meg! Peace, you must know, I do not mean Meg! You know full well, her sickness is no hindrance, save I am afraid . . ." the doctor checked himself. "It is the wretched grand-gore that distracts me."

"That I had noticed," Hew replied dryly. "But is it so bad?"

"The pox runs rife throughout the town . . . like the very plague. In truth," Giles said earnestly, "it is worse than the plague, which terror strikes swift and kills quickly."

"The kirkmen say the virol targets the corrupt, and is the most discerning scourge of sin," Hew remarked judiciously.

Giles snorted. "Aye, they do, and turn their backs on countless wives and bairns. The grandgore wreaks its havoc through the generations, ravaging and maiming over many years. It is a most insidious disease, and dearly, I would like to find a cure for it. For what the surgeons presently propose . . ." he shook his head, "well, those are horrors dreamt in hell. You cannot conceive what the poor wretches suffer."

"But for a gentler remedy, might you not look to Meg?" persisted Hew. "And share your apprehensions? She has wit and skill."

"And shall I speak to her, of foul, polluted congress?" Giles blurted fiercely. "Or of suppurating pustules, on the privy member? Dear God, she is your *sister*, Hew! She is my *wife!*

"Perhaps Meg has told you," he changed the subject abruptly, "I am embarked on a most healthful course of exercise. I recommend it to you, as most beneficial."

"That I infer is part of the problem," Hew retorted. "She tells me you have taken up the golf."

"Golf, oh aye," Giles said dismissively. "But that is a winter game, and now that it is spring, and the grass begins to grow, it is difficult to play. In truth," he frowned, "it proves a costly sort of game, for the balls are made so hard, they crack the clubs."

"That must be vexing," Hew observed.

"It would be, if I often hit the ball," conceded Giles. "No matter, for I am resolved in *giving up the gowf*."

"Meg will be relieved."

"And taking up the caichpule," Giles went on stubbornly, "to which end I have set my heart upon a purchase from the senzie fair. There is a man there has for sale a pair of tennis drawers. Then you and I will take *our* turn upon the caichpule at the priory, for I know you played in Paris, at the *jeu de paume*. Shall we play racquets or hand?"

This last question startled Hew. He replied, a little nonplussed, "You were thinking of playing with me?"

"Aye, and why not?" enthused Giles. "You play well. And since I am a novice, you shall point out the rules."

"Giles . . . you do not think that you may find it . . . somewhat hot and straining?"

"What of it? For though a chafing heat may stir the blood . . ."

"I fear it might."

"Yet I am stout enough to brave the storm."

"Aye, so you are," Hew sighed. "In truth, though I should like nothing more than teaching you the catchpole, yet I am afraid that it will have to wait. I am about to leave for Edinburgh, on some business. And I may be gone a while."

"Ah, then that's a pity. Still, the weather is perhaps a little chill," Giles conceded. "We shall try our racquets later in the spring. What business have you in the capital?"

"Debts owed to my father. And another strange affair, that perhaps he mentioned to you? He has left a book of his old cases in the courts, with directions to a printer, Christian Hall."

Giles shook his head. "I never heard of that. It's strange he did not mention it. Though not so strange, perhaps, that he should leave a casebook. I have often thought that I might publish one myself. God willing, aye, a treatise on the pox," he added thoughtfully. "When I came here to take up this place, it struck me as singular, in this time and age, not to find a printer. In a university of such renown, I quite expected it. Yet it turned out our theses are sent off to Edinburgh, that has printers, but no university."

"Aye, it was not always so. When Nicholas and I were boys in St Leonard's college, some six or eight years ago, there was a printer in the town, who came to grief."

"How so?" Giles looked interested.

"One of our regents, John Davidson, wrote a poem that was printed without his consent, that caused great offence to the Court. For which the printer, Robert Lekprevik, was sentenced to ward in Edinburgh castle, and remains there to this day for all I know, or else is dead."

Giles tutted sympathetically. "Then what became of Davidson?"

"That is a sad story, and one that does no credit to your college. Davidson was called before the Privy Council. He appealed to the Kirk Assembly for support, who called to witness one John Rutherford, then provost of St Salvator's, whose office you now hold. Now this man wrote a refutation of the poem in question, that later he retracted, saying that he had no quarrel with its substance, only that he had inferred, that Davidson *called him a goose*. This Davidson denied, and said he had imagined it."

"And was he called a goose?" Giles inquired archly.

"There was a cleric in the poem, and he was called a goose. No names were named. But you will understand, the substance of the charge, and the Crown's complaint, was not whether Davidson called Rutherford a goose."

Giles chuckled. "Let us both be thankful we abjure such petty squabbling. The retraction, surely, was a help to Davidson. The University must have supported him?"

"They might have done, had the Assembly had the courage to defy the Crown. But Davidson could not be sure of their support. And so he took advice, and fled to England, and we lost a good and worthy regent, and an honest man."

"Then I'm sorry for it. Was he your regent?"

"Not ours, though we knew him well. In our first year as students, he was still a magistrand. And these events took place when I was gone to Paris. It was Nicholas that told me of them, in a letter. I doubt my father knew of it, for strange to say, he has a copy of Davidson's poem in his library. Nicholas has put it in his catalogue."

"Your father had a keen eye for controversy," Giles smiled. "Aye, well, a cautionary tale. Let us hope that Matthew's law book will not get you into trouble."

"I think it very likely," Hew said solemnly, "that this strange affair is doomed from start to end."

"Well, then, Christian Hall, you say?" Giles peered at his shelves, "I do not know the name."

"The device is a crow in a tree, with an H and a cross," Hew replied. "You have not seen such on your books?"

"Not that I recall. The corbie's an odd enough choice," remarked Giles. "That signifies, I think, a false or tardy messenger. Or like the carrion crow, brings with it thoughts of death." He sang a brief snatch from

the ballad, "The Twa Corbies", "*over his white banes,
where we lay bare, the wind shall blow forever mair.*
No, there's nothing here . . . Now here's a book to
interest you, returning to our theme, that has been
lately Englished from the Latin, directions for the
health of magistrates and students. Tis pertinent on
exercise. The author says of tennis, that all parts and
members of the body may be moved — save that it may
be harmful to the head, which must be held aloft, like
so . . ." Giles stuck out his neck and pitched a phantom
caich ball to the roof. "Tell me, Hew, is this the
stance?"

"Aye, something like," Hew answered doubtfully.

"Then it will prove more wholesome than the golf,
and likewise beneficial. I look forward to beginning
with our lessons. Meantime, for your printer, have you
thought to try the fair? There are bookstalls there a
plenty. Tis likely they have heard of him. In fact," he
nodded, "since there is no time like the present, let us
go together; you shall help to strike my bargain for the
tennis things." He set down the book, and pleased with
this plan, began to button up his coat.

"Fair enough," Hew grinned. "Shall we take Meg?"

Giles frowned at him. "The fair is most busy and
noisome. It could do her no good. But we shall bring
her gingerbreads, or ribbons for her hair."

"If you treat her like a child," objected Hew, "it is not
like to please her."

"As her man of physic, I could not assuage my
conscience, if I had encouraged her to walk among the
thrang. It would precipitate a fit, you may be sure of it.

Aye, you're right, no gingerbers. The fair is a source of concern, I confess," Giles reflected seriously. "So much of this prevailing sickness comes from overseas. A thousand foreign sailors and their whores compound our present fears."

"You see demons everywhere!" Hew protested, as they stepped into the clamour of the street. Stalls had spilled out from the cloisters of the priory to line the three main thoroughfares; in the marketplace, they jostled with the usual buiths where hawkers cried their wares. The odours hung heady and cloying. They fought their way through to the cathedral, where foreign merchants had set out their wares, silverware and silks more precious than the petty toys and trinkets in the street. The town pipes and drum that had called in the fair were sitting idle on the grass, and the piper himself in yellow and red leant against the far wall eyeing up the lassies, biding the time he was called for a tune. A troupe of tumblers staged their act upon the centre of the green, and Giles relaxed a little as he paused to watch. Playfully, Hew tugged his sleeve.

"Don't think on it! For you have *not* the build!"

"Think you not? Tis pity," Giles allowed a smile. "Ah, well, never mind!"

A Game of Tricks

Beneath the cloistered penthouse, sheltered from the wind, they found stalls selling sheets of French paper, folded into quires, as well as books and pamphlets and an assortment of penners, inkhorns and inks. "A table-book, gentlemen?" the stationer called out.

"Perhaps," Hew murmured absently. He declined the proffered notebook, and picked up a small volume, bound in brown calf. "Buchanan's *Baptistes*," he said aside to Giles. "Nicholas will like this. Have you *De iure regni?*" he inquired of the bookseller.

"Have a care," cautioned Giles, "the book is frowned upon."

"Not yet proscribed, I think," Hew whispered. "Dearly, I should like a copy for my library."

The bookseller made a show of examining his stock. "I doubt I sold that one this morning. Here are Buchanan's *Psalms*, that always proves most popular."

Hew shook his head. "It was the laws of kingship I required."

"Aye. Well then," the man conceded defeat, "I doubt it can be had from Henry Charteris, his buith upon the

64

north side of the high street, just above the tron. All these books are his."

"Are you from Edinburgh, then?"

"I am, sir. Here's a Latin grammar, *Roodiementya* . . ."

"No grammars please," Hew told him firmly. "Tell me, do you know a printer by the name of Christian Hall?"

"Hall?" The man looked dubious. "Ye perhaps mean Arbuthnot?" he suggested.

"Tis *Hall*, and his mark is like this, an H with the sign of the cross, inside a black-feathered bird." Hew sketched the mark with his fingertips on the cover of the book.

"*That* I have never seen. Charteris, now, his mark is an *H* and *C*. You wouldna be mistaking him?"

"There's no mistake."

The bookseller shrugged. "Aye, like as no'. There's printers come and go, I do not ken them all."

Hew bought the book for Nicholas. "This Christian Hall," he said aside to Giles, as he counted out the coins, "is something of a mystery." But Giles appeared distracted.

"Aye, but what's that there?"

A crowd of college boys were clustered round a stall.

"What do they there?" Giles worried. "Who gave them leave to go about the fair?"

"Ah, let them be!" Hew grinned, "they are but boys!"

"And they are my concern," his friend replied severely. "Though you may treat your own concerns more lightly, I must bear the weight of mine. Let us at least see what attracts them."

Hew snorted rudely. "I recall, that it was your idea to come out to your fair. You should start as guilty as your charges, truant as you are."

"But since I am their principal, I must be their guide," insisted Giles. "They are green and young, and ripe for their corruption. What *is* it they are looking at?"

As Giles approached, the students gasped and scattered, adding weight to the suggestion of their guilt. The stallholder called out, "Ah, gentlemen, I doubt you must be cats that chase away my gulls."

"Then do you gull them, sir?" Giles quizzed him sternly.

"I, sir? Not at all. Come, see for yourselves."

He gestured to his wares, laid out across the surface of his stall, and Hew saw that what had drawn the student customers were rows of playing cards. Some were in their wrappers, tied with threads and overprinted with the manufacturer's mark, but several packs lay open on the counter in a fan, with queen and knave and king, block printed and hand coloured, stencilled in yellow and red.

"Card games, sirs," the seller caught Giles' eye. "These I have printed myself, and are yours for a very fair price. And for a gentleman like you, sir," he said, winking at Hew, "something finer, perhaps: a game of tarock? You know it, sir? It is a game of tricks." He produced a pack of cards with a flourish and in a sweep of hand displayed them on the counter like a fan, for Hew to see their pictures edged with gilt. "*Trionfii*, from Italy."

Giles interrupted, "We have no wish for *Tarrochi*. I see now why the boys have scattered. Gaming is prohibited, of course. Follow, if you will . . ." he instructed Hew, and wandered off.

"A moment, aye," Hew answered absently. He picked up a trump card, edged in gold leaf. "These are very fine. This is the Traitor, some say the Hanged Man. And here is the Devil himself."

"Yes sir, *Il Diavolo*."

"Are you come from Italy?"

"Not I. I come from Flanders, sir, and bought those on my travels. By trade I am a pressman."

"Indeed? You speak perfect Scots."

"My mother was a Scot," the card seller explained, "and I was born at the Scots house at Campvere. As a boy, I was prenticed to a printing house at Antwerp, but when the Spanish came I made my way north west, to Middelburg. Will you take the cards, sir?"

"Indeed, I think I shall." Hew felt for his purse. "Are you a Lutheran, then?" he asked astutely.

"A Calvinist, as my mother was before me. My master, a playing card maker, died after the auto-da-fé."

Hew stared at him. That there were horrors there, beneath the quiet tone, he had no doubt. "Then I am sorry for it," he said gently. "What has brought you here?"

"As I say, I moved northwards to Middelburg, where I hoped to establish a press. But the costs of such a venture cannot be imagined. I found myself in debt. At length I took up my stock to Campvere, and boarded the first ship that sailed from the harbour; and, as luck would have it, it was coming here." The card seller looked around fearfully, dropping his voice.

"Here, at least, you are free to follow your faith," Hew encouraged him. "And you need have no fear of the Spanish."

He had sympathy for the man's tale, that hid behind the facts a dark sense of desperation and of loss.

"When the fair is over, what will you do?"

The card seller shrugged. "As my wares must show, I'm skilled in printing colours. There's an art to laying red on black. I will find a press and beg for work. I hope to stay in Scotland, though I may go north or south."

"Then I wish you well," Hew pocketed his change. "And thank you for the cards. What is your name?"

"Marten. Marten Voet."

"Aye? Well thank you, Marten, and good luck."

"What have you there?" Giles had returned with a parcel.

"A pretty thing. A game of tricks," Hew answered thoughtfully.

"Truly? Then I'll warrant you're as bad as all the bairns, whose heads are turned by tricks and toys. I dare not leave you for a moment," snorted Giles. "Well, now, tis the dinner hour. I have made my purchase, and the students all are fled. Let us walk through the harbour and up the kirk heugh."

As they came through the seagate, they heard a voice cry, "Doctor Locke!" Giles gave a groan. "It is the coroner," he muttered to Hew. "No doubt you will remember him. He and I have had some dealings since you left.

"Sir Michael!" he called out, pleasantly and pointedly. "Are you come here to the fair? We were there ourselves, but presently, and now it is the dinner hour, we go home for our dinner."

"There is no time for that," the coroner said cryptically. "The tide is coming in."

Giles looked a little puzzled. "We are not having fish," he offered, as a reasonable response.

"Did you not receive my order, sir? I sent word to your house."

"As I said, we have been to the fair."

"No matter, you are here now. Come quickly. And you, sir," he looked closely at Hew, "you are Hew Cullan, I remember you, and have heard of you but lately. Well then, well met. You shall come too as a witness."

"What have you heard?" Hew demanded. The coroner was not a man whose acquaintance he had hoped to make again.

"The advocate Richard Cunningham informs me that you are to be his pupil at the bar. In that you are most fortunate. He is an excellent man."

"In that you are deceived, sir," Hew said, rather churlishly. "No such arrangement was made."

The coroner stared at his rudeness. "Then I am misinformed. We will not stay here to argue the point." He turned again to Giles. "The body is in a cave on the shore, betwixt the harbour and the castle, and once the tide is in, the place becomes impassable. We must go straight away."

"Then there has been a death?"

"Of course there has, man! What have I been saying?"

"Ah, then, no, not I," protested Hew. "I cannot help you here."

"You can, sir, and must. Pray you, bear witness. Do not refuse the Crown."

"Aye, Hew, come along," Giles colluded briskly, "for the sooner we are gone, the sooner we are done."

"Let us keep our voices low," the coroner advised, as they hurried through the harbour. "I have no wish to cause alarm. It is difficult enough to keep order at the fair."

"I understood the fair to have its own court," remarked Hew.

"Aye, it does. It does not extend to slaughter," the coroner said tersely.

Giles pursed his lips. "You suspect foul play?"

"'Tis possible the poor lass drowned. But the harbourmaster says it's like no drowning he has seen, which is why I sought your advice. She's a low enough wench, of no worth. I want no hue and cry."

"Then it's a lass?" Hew said, moved. "Does anyone know who she was?"

The coroner shrugged. "As I say, she is no one. Keep your voices low, we do not want a crowd. I would be obliged, sir," he turned again to Giles, "if you could hazard how and when she died, whether she were drowned, or unnaturally killed."

"Who found the body?" wondered Giles.

"One of the fishermen. They come here with their lasses, to be secret in the caves, and tease them with the danger of the tides. There's one lad and lass that will not deal again," the coroner said grimly. "We questioned them both closely, and are well assured, they had no part in this. Now, sirs, down by the side of the pier. Be wary of the seaweed on the rocks."

They clambered down the wall at the far side of the harbour, hugging closely to the cliffs, for the tide had begun to come in. The rocks were clogged and brackish, wet and spongy to the touch. Hew began to sink a little as they made their way towards the castle beach. They walked across the narrow strip of shore until they came to a chasm cut into the cliff, where they saw a bare foot stretching, tangled in the weed. The girl was lying in the sand, like a restless child asleep, one arm thrown above her swollen face. She was wearing her cap still, a little adrift.

"Is this how she was found?" Giles asked.

The coroner shook his head. "Her dress was found over her face, and her nether parts exposed. We lifted back her skirts. The harbour master says he has no knowledge of her. That implies she is a stranger here."

Gently, Giles lifted the arm and examined her hand. "A fisher lass, though. Look at her fingers," he muttered to Hew. "See how cracked and raw they are; that comes from the herrings. The sea water hardens and thickens the skin, but these little sores never heal. She is young, sixteen, I hazard, small and badly nourished for her age. And she is very poor, though I infer that she was coming to the fair, or else had been there. Though her clothes are old, they are her Sunday best. Her dress is clean."

"How did she die?" the coroner persisted. "Did she drown?"

"Her hair and clothes are soaked, possibly from spray. Tis possible she drowned, but I do not think it likely. I would hazard, if we cut her open, we would find no water there. Tis hard enough to see, through this discolouration, but there are bruises on her face around her mouth, the pressure of a hand, that was meant to stop her cries. Do you see this, Hew? This is the mark of his thumb. Now . . ."

Carefully, he folded back her dress, and the thin thighs flopped open, willing in death. "She has been dead perhaps a day and night. There is no rigor here. And she is not a maid. And yet there is a little blood and bruising on the thighs, which does suggest, that she was recently a maid, or else she was taken by force. Though I cannot be sure, I conjecture that this lass was smothered: suffocated, that's to say. And she has been raped."

"Then it's as I feared," the coroner said gloomily. "We must hope this is a singular transgression, that will not occur again. We will leave her here till nightfall, and the next low tide, when I will have her taken to St Leonard's kirk. There is a place there will serve as a dead house, for a day or two. If no one comes to claim her, we can bury her in private, and allow this death to go unmarked. We may be thankful she is of little worth."

"How can you say so?" Hew asked, appalled. "She was a girl of sixteen!"

"My concern is to prevent rumour from spreading, and from causing riot and disorder at the fair. It takes little enough to set off the mob. But my office is to make arrests, and act on the instruction of the Crown. My jurisdiction does not extend to solving crimes," the coroner said evenly. "If you would see justice done, provide the justice with a suspect, and I will be glad to make an arrest. As I recall, you did so once before."

"What does he imply," Hew demanded as he left, "because I solved one crime, am I responsible for all? There is nothing I can do."

"I am inclined to agree," Giles answered sadly. "The likelihood is that this poor child's killer has left in a boat. The town is filled with strangers, and unless he kills again — God willing, he will not — the lass will take his secret to the grave. I am right sorry that you had to see this, Hew. I ought not to have encouraged it. Go on ahead, and say I won't be back for dinner. I will make her decent for the man who comes to bury her."

Bloodlines

Although Hew had turned his back on St Andrews, he did not forget the dead girl. As he began his journey south, he resolved to make his way along the coast, inquiring at each port and harbour whether they had lost a lass. For someone missed and mourned her, looking out each morning on the grey unfolding sea, waiting for their loved one to come home. He did not know what he would say, if ever he found them. But he hoped to bring her back among her friends.

Nonetheless, though Hew did not forget the girl, he was anxious to put the town behind him and forget his own responsibilities. The breath of warmer air upon the late spring frosts had left an early haar upon the water that the bluster of the sunlight threatened to blow off, promising a sky of cloudless blue. Hew was wearing fine new clothes, in deference to the capital, trunk hose and doublet made of cream embroidered silk, with a plum coloured coat beneath a matching gown. Clean linen shirts and nether hose were packed into his saddle bag, and a smaller backpack slung across one shoulder held his father's manuscript, folded in its wrappers and sealed with sealing-wax. In a pocket was a letter to the

Edinburgh goldsmith, proving his claim to Matthew Cullan's estate.

It was Hew's intention to keep to the line of the shore, where the paths were well worn and less hazardous, and he was less likely to fall prey to beggars or thieves. He planned to come to Largo Bay by dusk, and to stay a night there at Strathairlie, the house of an old friend, setting out for the ferry at Kinghorn the following day. The small towns and villages along the Fife coast were safe and sheltered landing places, where he meant to rest his horse. Against all odds, and the predictions of the groom, he had chosen once again to ride Dun Scottis, a sad-coloured ambler of uncertain temperament. The dun horse had mellowed in his master's absence, or perhaps was growing old, for a sweet bed of straw and persistent gentle exercise had calmed his wild recalcitrance into a placid stubbornness. Hew remained attached to him. Since his business held no urgency, he was content to amble on across the countryside. Therefore he allowed the horse to set the pace, and explored the cool awakening of the land and sea. The farmers pulled the plough across the fallow fields, and the crows began to gather at the turning of the earth, in anticipation of seedtime. Winter oat and barley crops, lately deep in snow, were blown like sheets of water in the wind. Some of the farmers were Matthew's old tenants; the fields that they furrowed were Hew's. The slow and heavy dragging of the oxen through the soil felt deeply satisfying, as the earth renewed its natural cycle, and Hew arrived in Crail contented and fulfilled, as though he had himself been labouring on the land. He paused on the Marketgate, to traffic with the blacksmith and to hear the news, while the smith hammered out a new shoe for Dun Scottis. But among the gossip and report, he heard nothing untoward. In the harbour the boats had put out to sea, and the bairns scrambled barefoot over the rocks. No one had known the dead girl.

In Anstruther and Pittenweem, the story was the same. The horse trotted on while Hew kept his eye on the track and followed the line of the shore. They made good progress, passing by the ruined kirk of St Monan's, so close upon the water's brim that Hew felt certain he would trace the fisher lass, where the world came tumbling to the edges of the sea, but the minister received him with a puzzled kindness: no lass was missing from here.

Hew hurried on through Elie and Earlsferry, and turned the corner into Largo Bay. By now, he had almost lost hope of placing the dead girl. Nonetheless, he did not take the track towards Strathairlie House but rode down to the harbour, in Seatown of Largo. Women and girls sat outside the cottages, tying hooks to lengths of cord, long lines for the white fish that lay flat on the bed of the sea. They formed a fierce and jagged group, and Hew felt shy of approaching them. He led Dun Scottis further to the shore, where two boys came by with a barrel of mussels, collected as bait from the outcrop of rocks that lined the shallow bay. He guessed they were brothers, for both had a crop of muddled red hair. Once again, he asked the question, "Is there a lass gone missing from here?" and was startled by its effect.

The older boy glowered and glared, while his brother hopped excitedly from foot to foot.

"Aye, sir, there is, Jess Reekie."

"Haud yer tongue," his brother cautioned, ineffectually. The excitement of a stranger, with fine clothes and a horse and a full fat purse, was too tempting to persuade the boy of danger, and he babbled on, "Big Rab Reekie's daughter, that was sweet on Davey here."

The boy Davey blushed. "Away and piss," he suggested, though whether to the smaller boy, or Hew, was far from clear.

"She *was* though," his brother insisted. "And she begged you take her to the fair."

"You shut your mouth."

"'Cept her daddie wouldna let her. Wee hoor that she was, ye'd take her richt enough, save you were feared of big Rab."

"*Shut* yer mouth."

"Who is Jess Reekie? Is she missing?" Hew persisted.

Davey shrugged. "And if she is, it's nought to do wi' me. You're deid, son," he informed his brother, who continued undeterred.

"That's her mammie, Jeannie Muir, jangling with the fisherwives."

There was nothing for it but to broach the women, and Hew did so with a sense of trepidation. Already, they had noticed him, and paused their gossip to admire the stranger, brave and fair and dainty in his fancy coat. As he came closer, one of them called out, coarse enough to make him blush, for though he scarcely understood her, he had caught the drift. The others stood cross-armed. They did not suspect him. Death did not come over land, bonnily clad and on a dun horse. It came from the sea, and they were used to it, focused on a point beyond the waves. Therefore Hew was a welcome diversion, a toy for them to stare upon, gross and mocking in their gaze. It did not seem likely, after all, that such a fragile girl could have come from such stock, or from anyone known as *Big Rab*. Hew's courage almost failed him. He did not want to have the telling of it, now the trail had come abruptly to its end. He did not want that lass to have her ending here, in these bitter-weathered women, their faces filled with scorn.

He cleared his throat. "Which one of you is Jean Muir?"

There was a moment's consternation, before a black-haired woman stepped out from the rest. "I am Jean Muir," she answered warily. The women stood alert and watchful. Jean stared blankly, eyes dark with dread. He knew then that he had found her, though he tried to tell himself it was some other girl.

"There was a lass found dead on the beach at St Andrews, a day or two past." Hew kept his voice low, out of reach of the fisherwives, gathering like crows. Nonetheless, they cawed in chorus, "I *telt* you, she'd went to the fair."

Jean Muir did not waste glances, she did not waste words on them, but pursed her lips tightly and pulled close her shawl. "The dead lass," she whispered. "What was she like?"

And what could he tell her? *No one, the coroner said.* He answered her bleakly, "Slender, and small. The doctor thought she might be sixteen years of age. She had on a strippit blue gown, and a white linen cap. Her hair . . ." He trailed off. He could not tell the colour of her hair, made dank and dark by the sea.

"Fifteen," Jean said, vaguely.

"What's that?"

"She was fifteen," Jean Muir murmured, walking on past. "I'll go an' fetch my bairn."

She walked as though asleep, sure and heavy in her trance. And Hew had no doubt that she could, that she was fierce enough and strong enough and proud enough, to scoop up the lass in her tight muscled arms and shake off the sea water, shaking off death, to carry her home. The crow women scattered, scowling at Hew. And one of them — sister, mother, friend? — stout and braver than the rest, called out, "Wait, it's almost dark. The men will fetch her home tomorrow in the boat."

"And lose a day's fishing?" Jean Muir scoffed. Even in grief she was scornful, thought Hew. But perhaps more especially in grief. It was a hard little core of defensiveness, gathered inside her, gathered around like a shawl, all of her close-set and weathered grimly, fierce and hard and small. She said, "Whisht, Nancy, whisht. Let me go."

"Mistress . . . it's twelve miles . . . and soon it will be dark. And likely they have buried her . . . and still, it may be possible, that this was not your daughter after all," Hew reasoned hopelessly.

"It's Jess," Jean replied, with a dull complacency, and tramped on, no longer seeing him.

He cried out, "Wait, let me help you. What can I do?"

"What you can dae," the stout Nancy snarled, "is let us alone. You telt her. Now let it be." She hurried off in pursuit of her friend.

Hew did not escape so easily. The other women circled, hungry for gossip, to pick over the scraps of his news. Digesting, they assessed and were reassured. Their own weans were safe, and their own daughters blameless, hard-working, tucked up in bed of a night. Jess had been an *unco'* lass, bonny and too trusting, wanton as a hoor, and willing as a bairn, and like as not to find herself in trouble with a man. And so she had.

When at last Hew had disentangled himself, Jean and her fierce friend Nancy were long gone. He pictured their dull trudge across the fields to a town they would not come to before dark, to fetch home their dead lass, already lying cold beneath the ground. The boys had gone from the shore, and the boats lay sombre, empty in the bay. Hew continued upwards from the beach. He followed the course of the burn to the lands of Strathairlie. The burn began to bulge and leach upon the land, flooded by the recent thaw, or perhaps it was the dam that served the mill. Hew felt raw as he approached the house, a little worn and shadowed in the gloom of dusk. The bright, congenial welcome of the country house no longer seemed to fit. His friend, Andrew Lundie, was away on business, and Hew was almost glad to find him gone from home. In his absence, he was met by Andrew's father John, as attentive a host as ever he could wish for, yet Hew felt uneasy with his hollow talk and comforts, that did not match the darkening of his mood.

"Andrew is married, did you hear?" John Lundie informed him. "And he has a son, my grandson, you know. But you, Hew, are not married, I suppose? And no sign of any heir?"

"Not yet, sir, I'm afraid." Hew admitted, smiling weakly. They were settled in the great hall, to a spring supper of boiled eggs and pullets, with white manchett loaves and sweet yellow sack. John Lundie sat toasting the bread on the fire, for sippets to soak up their wine.

"Tsk, tis a pity," he remarked, turning the toasts on their fork. "Since everything settles on you. It is essential to consider and consolidate one's property, and keep it close to home. I have hopes that our family may have possession of this whole estate before too long. Then as to Andrew, you see, and his little son John, I may settle on him, and die well. As I have no doubt, your father did, though without the solace of a grandson to ensure his line. Now then, as I understand, you are apprenticed to Richard Cunningham, the advocate."

"*Do*, *you*, *sir*?" retorted Hew, startled from his manners. "Who told you that?"

John Lundie looked nonplussed. "Why Master Cunningham himself, was it not, Agnes?" he appealed to his wife, who looked up from her cup and smiled vaguely.

"Well then, I dare say," Master John went on, "Master Cunningham was present at the recent circuit court, at which I was obliged to serve as witness, a most wretched venture, to be sure; I dare say it was then I heard it. Or was it from the crowner? Can it be a secret, though?"

Hew shook his head. "A misunderstanding," he muttered.

"Truly? How very singular."

After supper, John proposed a game of cards, and with the lady Agnes and John's second son and daughter, they made up a five at maw. Hew felt ill at ease, and could not settle to the game. At last, when he had missed his turn a second time, and lost his stake, Agnes remarked somewhat archly, "I fear that Master Cullan is too much the scholar to approve our game. I dare say tis the hazard that offends him."

"Ah, not at all. Forgive me, I am distracted tonight." Hew set down his cards, showing his hand, and John Lundie frowned. "Perhaps you would prefer a game of chess?"

"I confess, sir, my mind is elsewhere."

"Indeed?" John looked a little perplexed. It was plain, he very much wanted to pick up the cards, and conclude the game, in which he had been poised to take the third trick. He hesitated, merely, out of politeness, debating whether he must now invite his young friend to confess what troubled him. Before he could give way to better judgement, Hew confided, "Indeed, sir, there is a service you can do me, if you will."

"Aye, then?" John proceeded cautiously, "And what is that?"

"It is a wretched tale. There has been a murder in St Andrews. I pray you, send word to the coroner that I have found out the poor girl's name. She is Jess Reekie from Seatown of Largo, and her father is Big Rab the fisherman."

The lady Agnes set down her cards and let out a faint little cry. "Is it possible, John?"

Her husband frowned. "Hush, a moment, Annie. Now," he said sternly to Hew, "have a care. Speak softly, that you don't upset the ladies, and explain yourself. What's all this?" He was wearing spectacles, for his eyes were not what they had once been, and in the fading candlelight he could not tell the clubs from spades. The change in his expression had dislodged them from his nose. Impatiently, he snatched them up and put them in a pocket.

Hew continued recklessly, "It is as I say, on St Andrews shore was found the body of a fisher lass that had been raped and killed."

At the word *raped*, the lady Agnes gave another squeal, and her husband rose abruptly to his feet.

"Since Hew does not care to play cards, and the night is clear, we shall take a turn around the gardens." He placed a hand upon Hew's shoulder, with a firmness that allowed no room for compromise, and directed him briskly to the door, where he removed the lantern from its hook.

"Now, sir," he commanded, holding it aloft to light their passage through the garden, "Tell your tale."

Hew explained about the fisher lass. John Lundie stared into the blackened trees, and in the glimmer of the lamplight Hew saw him frown.

"Does this crime spell danger to my family?" he inquired at last.

"No, sir, I am sure of it," Hew assured him. "Though she came from Largo, the dead girl was a fisher lass, and her killer doubtless known to her. There can be no threat to your daughter or your wife."

"That is as I thought," Lundie answered bluntly. "Then I wonder why you thought it fitting to alarm them."

"To speak truth, sir, I did not think, and I am sorry for it," Hew excused himself. "These sad events affected me, so that perhaps I lost my sense of decorum."

"You lost your sense," John Lundie qualified. "In these lawless times, our womenfolk are fearful. It is our place to reassure them, not to cause alarm. This rape is no business of ours, and, for certain, no business of yours."

"I hoped, sir, you might think it *was* your business, sufficient to inform the coroner," insisted Hew. "Tell him he must question the fishermen, and, in particular, a lad called Davey."

"Do you not *listen*? This is no affair of ours. If harm has come to Jessie Reekie, as you say, her father will amend it. There's no need for us to be involved."

"But surely, sir, we have a duty to the Crown, to inform the coroner and uphold the law," protested Hew.

"You begin to vex me," Lundie frowned. "I would not hear this from my son, and I will not accept it from you. But, since you have lost your father, and are a guest in this house, I shall excuse it this once. You were always a hot-headed boy, I do believe, a headstrong boy; your father did indulge you somewhat. Nonetheless, you will permit that in the absence of your father I dispense some fatherly advice."

Hew felt cornered and enclosed. He stared into the garden, set out like a counterpane. They were walking through the physic beds, planted in neat, knotted squares, where the pansy and primrose in close little buds bowed their shy heads to the light of the moon. The clumps of bay and parsley, sorrel and sweet sage, were measured and constrained. These tight-nipped borders bore stark contrast to the mossy walls and wild untrammelled herbs at Kenly Green. Meg allowed her flowers to grow to glossy fullness, nature nurtured softly by her secret cultivation, a wilful, wild cacophony of colour, shape and scent. Though Hew had not responded, John Lundie took his silence for contrition.

"Well and good," he nodded. "You should know that I have presently . . . but *presently*, mind, been witness at the assize, and a most tedious and irksome business it was. And yet I did this willingly, as my duty to the Crown, that I refused to shirk."

"But surely," Hew countered stubbornly, "you were sent a summons, and you had no choice."

John Lundie fixed him with a glare. "If you believe that, then you really are green, and not at all ripe for the law. You think there is no choice? Most of those called paid bribes to the court clerk to scratch out their names, or sent others masquerading in their place. Thirteen were unlettered, three or four were deaf, one was a natural idiot, and several more excused themselves, by claiming to have died. But I, sir, did turn out, to serve the Crown, and a more flagrant piece of foolishness I have never heard. So do not speak of duty, nor of my responsibilities. If I have a duty to these folk, it is to let them go about their business as they will; as long as they do not impede my family or my property. We do not want these scandals on our doorstep and, for sure, we do not need them brought to us by strangers. This is not what Matthew meant, when he wanted you to follow in the law. If you persist in this, you will bring shame on us, and shame on your dead father."

This cut deep, and Hew exclaimed, "How can it be shameful to seek justice for a poor dead girl?"

"Look, boy . . ." John looked at him helplessly, truly perplexed, and went on a little more kindly. "You have been at school too long, and you have lost the proper sense of things. And since you have no father, then I will explain it to you. Each of us must have his place, and if we step outside that place, a line is crossed. And if we cross that line . . . well, we *cannot* cross that line. It is not done. Look at my house here. It is a fine one, is it not? And the gardens are quite grand? And our lands" — he held out the lantern — "as far as the burn, and eastwards . . ." he frowned, for a moment distracted. "When you came up past the burn did you see it flooded?"

"Aye, it was," Hew confirmed, "but I do not see . . ."

"That is the dam for the mill, and a thorn in our side, we are *damned* by that mill that saturates our lands . . . Nonetheless, now, let that rest. Do you understand what it is that I am saying?"

"Not at all," scowled Hew.

John Lundie gave a sigh. "This is where we stand, and our *place* in things," he iterated patiently. "Our place is to keep these lands, and the farmers in the fields and the miller in his mill that is their place, and if they do not cross us then we do not interfere with them. And the fisherfolk that fish the seas, that also is their place, and what they do besides is no concern of ours."

"That is a closed and narrow view," Hew answered hotly. "Surely, it must be your place to help to keep the peace."

"That is what I am trying to explain to you. To keep the peace, for sure, then let us *keep* the peace. But you would cause a hue and cry, and so disturb the peace. Tell me then, who's hurt by this?"

"A young girl, that lies dead on a beach, and her mother, that has none to speak for her."

Lundie snorted. "Ah, brave fool! Then answer *this*. When you told the mother, that her girl had died, did she seek your help, or bid you speak for her? Did she say, 'Good sir, prithee, find my daughter's killer out?'" he mimicked, mocking Hew.

Hew hesitated, "Well, in truth . . ."

"In *truth*, then, she did not. So leave it well alone. Make no mistake, you are not the king's officer, to seek out and answer for crimes. Your place, surely, is to be

87

your father's son, and to live upon his lands and produce an heir, or else your place must be to be an advocate and practise at the bar, as your father wished, and if you will do neither, then I do protest, that I am at a loss as to *what* your purpose is. Enough now. Let's to bed. And since you are your father's son, and are most welcome here, we'll speak no more of this."

The household was prepared for bed, and Hew was shown to a small chamber in the loft, at the top of a spiral of stairs. The room was furnished very like his own, with light oak kist and mantelpiece, pewter jug and candlesticks, and a posy of sweet pansies, with their cheerful painted faces, scattered to bring freshness to the sheets. The bed was feathered, soft and warm. Yet Hew could not sleep. He allowed the candle to burn almost to the quick, before he threw aside the sheets and padded to the window, looking out towards the wood and far down to the bay. He heard a fretful cry, the yipping of a fox cub calling for its mother, fleeting through the trees. He saw the moonlight cast its shadow on the distant harbour, where the fisher lass had spent her days, and felt remote and lost, as though he had no purpose and no place. His cream embroidered doublet, laid across the kist, looked yellow, soiled and tawdry in the stump of candlelight, its artifice and glitter worthless in the gloom.

Rites of Passage

Hew took his leave early the next morning, yanking at Dun Scottis with unnecessary force. The horse, as always sensitive to mood, did not take quite so lightly to the track, and they both appeared sullen and fretful before the sun began to lift. At Leven's mouth, they left the coastal path, following the river inland to Cameron Brig, where having made their crossing they turned back towards the estuary. And presently they came upon Muir Edge, a settlement that seemed to edge the world itself, by the smoking wasteland that was Dysart Muir. Dun Scottis pricked his ears and shied away. Hew nudged him, little by little, cautiously around the outer reaches of the moor. Beneath, the Dysart coal beds scorched and kindled, sparking fires that hissed from cracks and chasms in the rock and wrenched the sky at night with sudden bursts of flame. In daylight now, the moor was choked with heavy cloud that stifled and made mute the birds. Clumps of blistered heather smouldered in the scrub. Even at its edge, Dun Scottis kicked his heels against the fierce heat of the earth, tossed his head and snorted, his own breath hot and furious. Beneath its tar-clogged cloud of blackness,

Dysart Muir lay hidden from the sun, and from the bright sea breeze, and circling of the gulls, and from the shrieking winds and winter frosts; no snow had ever fallen there. Dun Scottis knew, quite clearly, here was hell.

Hew, who understood the meaning of the place, was equally unnerved, and as they approached Dysart itself, and the cleaner pungency of sea and salt pans, he was scarcely reassured. For at the entrance to the coal pit by the shore, a little group of devils had appeared, streaming forth and scattering like flies. They were small as children, those devils; or perhaps they were children, lads and lasses burned to black, their faces blank with weariness, imps of Satan spilling from the lapping flames of hell. They were all but naked in the heat, the strips of rags around their waists grimy as the writhing bodies wriggling from the seam. They trundled with them truckle carts of coal, and baskets filled with fish heads, casting green and ghostly light.

From Dysart, they came next to Ravenscraig, named for the corbies gathered on the rocks, and looked across the water from the castle cliff, where they saw Edinburgh smoking high upon its rock, the backbone of the capital squat between its hills. The skies were beginning to dim, and Dun Scottis, unnerved by the coalfields and the blackening clouds, became fickle and fey at the first gust of wind. At Kinghorn and Pettycur harbours, the ferry boats lurched into blackness, and Hew decided to continue overland, upon the coastal path. Duns Scottis was flaring his nostrils, afraid of the wind and the water, and his master had no stomach for the fierceness of the estuary. They rode on as far as Burntisland, where they declined the crossing once again, and Hew spent a restless night at the ferry inn, in damp and soiled bedding, miserable and cold.

On the third day, which was Saturday, they came at last to Inverkeithing, and from there to North Ferrie, where Hew hoped to make their crossing in the narrow part. There was no jetty as such, but in one or two places rough wooden planks were set into the mud, as precipitous launching pads into the water. All were deserted but one, where a solitary boatman lowered sacks of grain into a coble moored below.

"How long till the next ferry boat sails?" inquired Hew.

At first, the boatman seemed not to have heard. But presently he looked up from his work and scratched his head, considering Hew's question as a rare and deep imponderable. Finally he found his answer. "Other morn, I doubt."

"The day after tomorrow?" Hew interpreted, incredulously. He looked across the water, where the tail end of the ferry drifted, barely half a mile out from the shore. "Surely, it will sail again today."

"Aye, mebbe," said the boatman, in tones thick with misgiving and doubt, "But the schippar had a mind to keep her at the south side, for calfatting, for she was letting in a deal of wattir, he did say."

"She's taking in water?" Hew glanced again at the departing ferry, with a feeling of alarm.

The boatman bared a toothless grin. "She aye taks on some wattir, no enough to sink her. But the morn's morn being the Sabbath, schippar thought it would be well enough to hae her caulked the day. He didna think her fit to mak another trip."

"Is there no other ferry boat?" Hew asked, perplexed.

"Oh aye, there's another, richt enough, doon wattir here," the man said reassuringly.

"Then surely, that will sail?"

"But the crew, you ken, are on the other side." The boatman gazed across the estuary and screwed up his eyes to follow the trail of the boat. "Or will be soon enough, if she can hold."

"But this is madness! Why did the crew not take the other boat, and leave that one here to be caulked?" exclaimed Hew.

The boatman stared at him, as though affronted by the question. Finally he answered. "In truth sir, tis the best boat they have taken. The other has a wee bit damage to the hull. A *hole*, ye might best call it."

"Dear God," Hew muttered to himself. He was not the best of sailors, at the best of times.

"The ferry inn is clean," the man said helpfully. "Though, if you are in a hurry I could take you across myself."

Hew looked with renewed hope at the man's boat. Though small, it looked at least seaworthy, a flat-bottomed coble unlikely to capsize.

"If you don't mind to stop off at Inchgarvie on the way," the boatman qualified. "These sacks of flour are for the garrison there. It will not take a moment to offload them. You need not land. In truth," the boatman smiled his toothless smile again, "I think you would not wish to land. But, sir, I will take you and your horse across to the south side for twelve shillings."

"Twelve shillings?" Hew shook his head. "That is extortion. I will pay you five." It was far more than the ferry fare.

The boatman shrugged and began to untie his craft. "That is the price," he said simply. "You are a rich man, and I am a poor one. You would have the whole boat to yourself. You bid me go out of my way, the wind is wild today, and I can feel the coming of a storm. I will not cross for less."

"Aye, very well," Hew sighed. It was petty, after all, to quibble over cost; no doubt the poor wretch had little enough. And it would cost him two nights' lodging at the inn, for himself and Dun Scottis, and the unremitting dullness of an Inverkeithing Sabbath, if he chose to stay and wait upon the ferry. The horse was still fresh, and could easily complete the ten or so miles from the south side to the capital before the close of day. Twelve shillings would purchase two days' grace, and an entertaining sermon in the great kirk of St Giles. Besides, he took the boatman's point about the weather; the disappearing ferry boat began to dip and lurch amid the rising waves.

"Very well, twelve shillings," he agreed.

"Up front." The man looked on cannily as Hew took out his purse. "Have you a merk, sir? If you had I merk, then I might spare your change."

"I have twelve shillings," Hew answered firmly, counting them out. "How do I board my horse?"

93

The boatman pursed his lips. "Is he skeich?"

"Not in general." Hew eyed Dun Scottis uneasily. "In general, he is stubborn, dull, and constant. I only knew him once to rear, and that was when a friend of mine put spurs to him. He did not take it kindly."

The boatman chuckled. "Well, no spurs. With horses, it is the loading and the landing of them gives the trouble; that is not so much trouble, for if they are skeich, and jump into the water, the waters there are shallow, and they will not upset the boat. In truth, on the south side it were better to urge him out of the coble and into the shallows, that he may swim in while we find our landing place. In general, once the animal is on the boat, he will be calm. I only once did see a horse was feart of crossing wattir, that a witch had put a spell on him."

Fervently, Hew prayed Dun Scottis would not prove such a horse.

"Well, sir, ye maun dismount him, and tak off his saddle and bags, and place them at this end with the sacks of grain, then lead him down the plank where he must jump a little; that's the tricky part, then hold him steady at the head and talk to him, aye, soothe him, he will know your voice. For safeness, pray take off your sword, and lay it flat upon the bottom of the boat. Have no fear of pirates, sir; these waters are well guarded by the garrison."

Dun Scottis made the leap into the boat with little more than a stumble, and soon stood steady at its broadest point, where Hew stood beside him, holding his reins. The boatman faced them at the narrow end —

"I will sit, sir, and row, the better to balance," — and pushed off from the shore.

Facing back towards North Ferrie, Hew did not see the direction of travel, and as they pulled out of the shallows and the boat began to sway he felt a little queasy. The man remarked impassively. "Aye, tis turning rough."

The wind brought with it sheets of rain, and in its shower they soon were soaked, the dull sky ever darkening. Dun Scottis smelled damp, like autumn moulds. Restlessly, he snorted and shuffled his feet. It was cold on the water, made colder by the penetrating wind and dampness of the drizzle and the spray.

"Not far to Inchgarvie, sir," the boatman said reassuringly. "A dreich enough place, even when the sun shines."

Hew turned his head, searching for the narrow strip of land, and found the ghostly outline of its fortress, barely visible behind the driving rain. Far across the other side, flickering and pale, he saw the beacons lit to help the boatmen make their passage. Not for the first time, he wondered what mysterious watchman kept them from the rocks.

"The poor wretches there will be glad of the rain," remarked the boatman.

"Why?" wondered Hew.

"No fresh water, sir. There are barrels shipped in for the soldiers, and they have their brewery there, but for the prisoners on the island there is nothing fit to drink, save what gathers in the rain vats or the rock pools. Tis not a place a man would want to be stranded."

95

"It must be bleak indeed, to be so close to the land, and yet so far from it."

"Aye. We will drop off the grain at the landing place. The soldiers will wade out to meet the boat. For that, I do thank God. I do not care to land. They say there is a most prodigious kind of rat that's native to the island, that chews its way through iron, and gnaws the prisoners' faces as they sleep; and all have lost their noses," the man said seriously.

Hew laughed at this. "An old wives' tale, I doubt."

"Perhaps. Though old wives tales are apt to have a grain of truth in them," the boatman replied, with unexpected shrewdness. "There is upon the island too an ancient leper house, where they put the sick in times of plague. Tis likely the tale comes from that."

"Aye, likely," Hew agreed. He shivered. "Is there far to go? I do not like the colour of the sky."

"No more do I. It is not far, sir, to Inchgarvie. Here is the landing place. And here's the constable himself."

The soldiers waded through the water to the little boat, and took the grain ashore, balancing the sacks upon their shoulders, to the keeper of the castle who kept watch upon the tower, the scarlet of his coat a poppy head against the drizzle darkness of the sky. Hew could not conceive of a more bleak and dreary place. His business concluded, the boatman struck out again and turned the boat eastwards clear of the rocks.

In the darkness and the rain, Hew had lost his bearings. Presently, though, he glimpsed the faint light of the beacons far receding straight ahead. "Surely," he said suddenly, "we're heading north?"

"Aye, sir, back to land."

"There must be some mistake. I paid you for the passage to the south side."

Slyly, the boatman shook his head. "Tis as I did explain to you; I had business at Inchgarvie. The business fulfilled, I return home again."

"This is trickery!" exclaimed Hew. "You understood full well, the bargain was that you would take me to the south side."

The boatman looked pained. "Aye, mebbe," he conceded. "But the weather has turned. And it were not worth my while, to continue to the south side now, but for a mere twelve shillings, for like as not I would find myself stranded there until the other morn, with such a loss of business that would not repay my time. I have a family to support, sir, and I must consider them."

"How much?" Hew demanded shortly, understanding he had been trumped.

"Thirteen shillings, sir. Let's say, a merk," the man said quickly. "Up front."

"Turn the boat around. I will pay it at the other side," Hew said curtly.

"Pardon me, how do I know it, sir?"

"How do I know you will take me to the other side, and not turn back half way, or maroon me on Inchgarvie?" Hew retorted.

The boatman laughed. "A bleak enough fate. I would not do that, sir. I am an honest man, in truth, and yet a man has to live. You have money. I have a boat. Surely, we can come to an arrangement."

"You are an honest rogue. And that you are a poor one I sincerely doubt," Hew said severely.

"Very well. Show me the merk, and you shall have the keeping of it till we reach the other side," the man said generously. "I trust you, as a gentleman. Besides, I have your sword and saddle bag," he added pointedly.

Hew swore softly, dropped the rein and reached into his pocket for his purse. This lurching movement proved a mistake. Dun Scottis, his ears set back against the wind and his dank coat sleek and swollen with the rain, had grown impatient with the motion of the boat. He had not liked the rising menace in the boatman's voice, nor the muted anger he could sense in Hew's. As Hew released the reins, he took his chance and bolted, caring little for the boundaries that distinguished boat and waves, and leaping full into the darkness that gave way to water he undid them all, unbalancing the boat. As the rushing waters hit, Hew heard the boatman curse, before his own breath gasping drowned all other sound.

The stuffing in his trunk hose brought a certain buoyancy, and as Hew floated with the tide he had time to catch his breath and consider his predicament. He did not see the boat, or the horse, or the boatman, and no answer came to his cries. At first he kept his head, and reasonably afloat. But as his clothes became sodden the padding grew swollen and heavy, in danger of dragging him down. In panic, he struck out. Floundering beneath the surface of the waves, he found himself caught in the path of a fierce and churning engine, coursing through the water like a mill. And there, gripped in a relentless chug and grinding, his eyes and lungs began to bulge and stream. When he could fight no more, the force of a great blow dislodged him from the depths and sent him spinning back against the upper flank of the machine. Grasping wildly, his fingers found their purchase, and entwined him clear of the strange winding gear that churned the estuary below. And gradually, as he regained his breath and made sense of his surroundings, his sobbing gasps kept pace with a strange pneumatic snorting, and he understood at last that he was clinging to the damp mane of the horse. Dun Scottis rolled forward through the great expanse of tide, steadfast and relentless as a man of war. Hew tightened his grip on the mane, twisting his wrists as well as he could into the rope of the halter, and allowed himself to trail, floating alongside the horse, out of the treacherous churn of its hooves. Beyond his own hands tangled in the rope, and the dark forbidding outline of the water, he saw nothing. He heard nothing but the slow mechanic rasping of the horse. And gradually he found he lost all feeling in his hands, and the hot seat of pain in his thigh, where Dun Scottis had kicked him, dulled to an ominous thud. The rush of water in his ears drowned out the steady wheezing of the horse, he felt his fingers lose their grip and the lapping waters slacken, slipping into blackness as his eyes began to close.

The Kindness of Strangers

Hew dreamt that he had come to rest upon a drying green. Waking, he saw lines of washing hanging slack and swollen in the breathless air. The place where he had landed was sooty and enclosed, heavy with the scent of ash and fire. He lay close to the hearth on blankets and straw. He was dressed in a plain woollen shirt, in place of his fine suit of clothes, and his wrists were bound in cloth, through which a little blood began to seep. Though he felt stiff and raw, he found no broken bones. His limbs were scratched and ribboned with a score of tiny cuts, and a dull throb in his thigh disclosed a mass of livid bruising, searing to the touch. The hoofmark of Dun Scottis, clean as though the hot iron of the blacksmith had impressed it there, explained the pain.

As he struggled to stand up, he heard a faint scuffle and squeal, and found himself watched by a clutch of small girls wearing ribands of plum-coloured silk. Before he could speak, they had scattered and fled.

Hew was left alone in the strangest house that he had ever seen. Cups and bowls and spoons were roughly carved from driftwood, and an ancient, splintered sea chest opened like a flower, or like the sun-bleached skeleton of some enormous fish, stripped of all its flesh. Fragments of bone were scattered on shelves, with bright polished pebbles and pieces of pot. The rafters were strung with old rope, tackle and gear swung rusting on hooks, and propped above the chimney grate, Hew could see a masthead, holding up the washing lines recovered from his dreams. Like a ship-wrecked sailor fallen into faerie land, he felt part of the seawrack that made up this little house.

"The bairns cried ye were waking. Mind, you're unco shakit on your feet."

He jumped at the sound of the voice. An old woman stood in the doorway, gazing at him curiously. "I brought you bread," she offered. "For you have eaten nothing for the past twa days. You must be famished. I will heat some broth."

She placed the bread upon the board and moved quickly to the fire, where she ladled thick grey slurry from a bowl into a pot. She was small and lithe and nimble; not so old, perhaps, but weathered like the fisher wives. Her eyes were bright and sharp beneath her plaid.

"Faerie magic," murmured Hew.

"What was that?" She turned to stare at him. "You have had a wee dunt to the heid," she concluded kindly.

Hew felt exposed and naked in his borrowed shirt. Sensing his discomfort, the gude wife broke into a

101

smile. "You're nothing that I have not seen. Though you may be a gentleman, we're a' the same uncled."

"Madam, where am I?" he asked her, bewildered.

"Madam? Ah, what dainty manners!" the gude wife replied. "I never was called *that* before. Tis plain you have forgot your place. Do you ken your name?"

"Aye, for sure, it's Hew Cullan," Hew whispered. "The ferry was closed for repair."

"Is that what he telt ye? The limmar!" she tutted. "Yon Guthrie is a rogue and no mistake. I am Jonet Bell, an' my man is Sandy Matheson the ferryman. That quent horse of yourn harled you here across the wattir. That's a brave wee hobin that you have there. My man it was that found ye lying traikit on the rocks."

Hew struggled to make sense of this. "Is this Queensferrie?" he hazarded.

"North Ferrie. Aye, ye are back where ye began. Come lad, sit ye down, you're greener than a herring gill."

Hew sat down unsteadily upon his makeshift bed. "What happened to Guthrie? Did he drown?" If the boatman had drowned, then it was because of Dun Scottis. Hew closed his eyes. However construed, that was his fault.

But Jonet snorted. "Drooned? Not he! The devil guards his ain. I heard he fetched up by Inchgarvie, clinging to his wreck, and the souldiers waded in to pull him out. The ferrymen will let him stew awhile afore they fetch him hame. Here now, there's a cup of pottage will see you right. There's nothing in your belly but Forth mud."

She ladled barley broth into a bowl. It tasted hot and wet, and little more, but Hew drank it gratefully.

"Mistress, I do thank you, and give thanks to God that he lives still. For if my horse — what happened to my horse?" He felt a sudden rush of grief, for the foolish, faithless friend that had been Dun Scottis, lying at the bottom of the Forth.

"Your horse is well. He landed in less traikit than yersel; though he were fair forfochten, he came nimmill as a kitling," Jonet answered cryptically, from which Hew understood, *your horse is well*.

"He is stabled at the inn at Inverkeithing," she went on, "where the innkeeper thoct, if ye did not recover, fit to buy him back, he'd earn his keep. He dealt you quite a kick forby, that has left his hoofprint on your hough."

"That I had remarked upon," Hew grimaced.

"According to my man, yon would ha broke your leg, but for they stuffit brekis."

"I don't suppose you have the trunk hose still?" he ventured shyly.

Jonet shook her head. "Brekis like that were no built for the wattir. And when your brave horse harled you up upon the rocks, your clothes were cut to shreds. Be thankful that they served their turn, and saved you from a deeper hurt. What was left was only fit for scraps."

And all the ferry lasses, realised Hew, were wearing little strips of him, as laces on their gowns and ribbons in their hair. No doubt his boots and saddle bag had found another home. He had been picked over, and properly stripped, before Jonet and her man had taken pity on him, and had brought him in. Or else, they had merely come late, to all that was left.

But Jonet cut through these thoughts, with a kindness that made him ashamed, handing him a pair of woollen breeks. "These will fit. They were my son's. And you are very like him in your look. That is his shirt you wear. It suits you well."

Hew buttoned up the breeches, a little more assured once safely dressed, though he had no points or doublet to secure them to his shirt.

"I think there was a jacket," Jonet murmured. She gazed at him a moment as she rummaged through a kist. "You are like him, though."

"Then I thank him for his clothes."

"He will not want them, where he lies. He has been dead these twenty years."

"Madam, I am so very sorry," Hew told her earnestly.

She threw off his pity, shaking her head. "He drooned in that same stretch of wattir, where you tipped from your boat. When Sandy saw you lying on the shore . . ." Jonet let the sentence hang, concluding fiercely, "They are rogues and swingeours, all, and they would have had your horse, if Sandy had not stopped them. He could not save the rest. Except," she pointed to the rafters, "he found a sack still wrapped around your back. And you were clutching it so tight, he said, he had an unco' task to pull it off. There were papers inside, that we hung up to dry."

Hanging from the mast Hew saw his leather backpack, battered by the tides. The sheets of sodden washing were his father's manuscript, whose dripping outer edges had begun to fuse and blur. Inexplicably, he felt the prick of tears.

"Some of the papers were turned into pap," Jonet went on, "and could not be saved. But these had been wrapped in a clout, and Sandy thought it best to hang them out."

"Madam," Hew said, overcome, "I know not how to thank you, or your husband. My father made that book. And though those salvaged pages may be nothing worth, they are worth the world to me, and I had not realised it. I shall be forever in your debt."

Embarrassed, she brushed this aside. "Whisht, son, with your madams and your thank yous and your bonny flatterings! What daftness, to be sure! You're as saft as a bairn, and quent as your dun horse. I doubt you want the proudness of your birth, or else you lost it in the wattir with your clathes. There is no debt. For what, wee bits of paper? It is your proper life you should give thanks for, and for that to God, and not to us. Now that you are well, Sandy will give you passage to the south side. Only do not mention, what I said about our son. It is an auld wife's fancy, and it does not want repeating. For the truth is Sandy cannot bear to think of Johnnie, so we never speak of him."

"You never speak of it," repeated Hew, "after twenty years?"

"It is how it is," said Jonet simply. "Sandy took it hard, and he does not care to greet."

"And yet you kept his clothes."

Jonet forced a smile. "I kept them far too long. Tis brave enough, to see them now, upon a living back."

Hew began to gather up the manuscript. He folded the dried pages back inside their cloth and placed them in his sack. He said nothing else, for he could not find the words.

The ferryman proved as kind as his wife, allowing Hew free passage to the other side. He walked with him into South Queensferrie, pointing out the road to Cramond. "It is a hard trek, for a man that is used to a horse. I can give you bread and ale enough, to last you through the day, but more than that, I fear I cannot help you. I am richt sorry you were tret so badly at North Ferrie."

"In truth, I could not have met with greater kindness," Hew protested. "When I return for my horse, I will make good the debt."

The ferryman looked pleased. "There is no debt to us, son. You are more than welcome. I ask you, if you do come back, to call on Jonet. She has taken to you, and your passing through has brought a gladness to her heart. She will not have telt you this, for she never speaks of him, but you are the blessed image of our boy that died. You will forgive my saying," he concluded anxiously, "for you are a gentleman, and Johnnie was a boatman's son, and all."

Hew ignored this last. "You say she never speaks of him?" he queried.

"Aye, she is stubborn that way. For almost twenty years, she has not said his name. I sometimes think . . . no matter, then," the old man broke abruptly. "If you will shake my hand, I'll wish you better fortune, sir, and see you on your way."

The last ten miles into Edinburgh were more arduous than Hew had imagined. The track was steep and sodden, and he soon grew hot and tired. The stone drinking bottle leaked in his sack, its stopper no more than a wedge of damp rag, and his father's manuscript, so newly dried, again became sticky and stained. He refilled the bottle as he walked, drinking from the river and the burns. He was partially dressed, in jerkin, shirt and breeks, for Johnnie had possessed no nether hose. His legs were bruised and scratched, where Dun Scottis had dragged him over the rocks, and the reins had left cuts to his wrists. His borrowed shoes were small and tight, and his thigh throbbed stiff and sore from the horse's flailing hoof. He found the going hard. But at last he came to the Dene, and to the village of the Water of Leith, where the river ran fast and the mills ground the corn for the town. From here he could see the town itself, the castle on its crag and the high crown of the kirk, a spine of spires and rooftops falling to the east, its long tail flicking backwards to the hills. It seemed, to Hew's tired eyes, like the fair enchanted city of a traveller's tale. A north easterly wind from the estuary at Leith soon blew the notion clear, bringing with it waves of that delicate effluvium, the foul and foetid perfume of Nor' Loch.

Skirting the north loch, Hew continued south until he came below the castle through the west port in the Flodden wall. Outside this wall, a settlement had sprung to serve the town, like followers of camp beyond the battlefield, a hotchpotch of inns and small country gardens, stables and breweries, potters and craftsmen. Since they were not free to trade from buiths in town, they sold their wares at the landmarket, and Hew entered Edinburgh in the middle of a crowd, stacked high with baskets and crates. A young lass drove a flock of geese, that scattered like musket shot into the grassmarket. In the midst of this commotion, Hew was not questioned at the gate. He climbed the crooked west bow to the high street. And passing through the over bow, triumphal arch of kings, he came at last to the place he had known as a boy. For a moment, he stood dizzy by the butter tron, where the lawnmarket met castle hill. He had forgotten the exuberance, the noise and dirt and sweat, of market day. All directions seemed to chime, from the hoarse cries of the hawkers to the barking of the geese, from the ringing of the smiths to the hammering of timmermen, to the bleating of stray lambs and the squawk of flustered hens. Hew leant back against the wall. As he drew his breath he heard a tiny tinkling in the midst of the cacophony, and saw a silver penny drop beside him, rolling to a standstill in the dust. The coin was a half-merk, a good pint of claret and six wheaten loaves. He bent to pick it up, looking round to see who had dropped it.

"You, man, show up your token!"

Two men were approaching, councillors perhaps, appointed to oversee trade. One of them carried a long wooden measure or stick.

108

Misunderstanding, Hew held out the coin. "Is this yours?" he offered politely.

The bailies exchanged cunning glances. The shorter of the two, who, by way of compensation, had the stick, held up the stout badge of his office. It was clear that he meant to have the full measure of Hew. Hew felt his spirits drain. "Good sirs, what are your names?" he asked them with a sigh.

The taller man replied, "Thomas and I will be asking the questions," which at least went some way to an answer, and Thomas glanced at his friend with a faint air of reproach before he resumed the attack. "Where is your licence to beg?"

Hew felt himself flush. "You misunderstand, sir," he told his inquisitor stiffly. "I am no beggar."

"Ah," the burgess smiled unpleasantly, "then you did not pick up that penny we saw."

"No . . . or rather, aye, I did. I did not mean to keep it."

"He did not mean to keep it," the squat inquisitor confided to his friend. "What say you then, we let it pass?"

His companion gave this some thought.

"Well now, he speaks well," he conceded at last. "Perhaps he can make good account. Where are you from, friend?" he said encouragingly to Hew. "Where is your parish?"

Hew sighed conspicuously. But he had met officious types before, and knew that to refuse to answer would prolong a painful process.

"My name is Hew Cullan, lately of the parish of St Leonard's in St Andrews. I was born here, in the town. My father was an advocate, and I count myself a gentleman," he stated bluntly.

The short bailie snorted. "Ah, do you indeed! Then have you not looked in the glass?"

"I met with an accident," Hew explained lamely. He began to see himself as Thomas and his tall friend saw him. The boatman's clothes were worn and old, and though he had a shirt and breeks, the very least that decency required, he had no nether hose or proper coat. He had abandoned the boatman's boots at Leith water, when the hobnails had worked through the soles. His legs were bare and bruised below the boatman's britches, and his hair had not been combed since its dipping in the Forth. Worst of all, he had no hat; his plum-coloured cap, with its ostrich feather trim, lay sodden at the bottom of the estuary. In a last stubborn showing of pride, he had refused to accept the blue bonnet. And so he had come into the capital, bare-headed as the daftest loun, expecting to be greeted as a lord.

The milder of his twin inquisitors tugged at his colleague's sleeve. "'Tis possible," he whispered, sotto voce, "from his manner and his speech, that he may be a gentleman, but fallen on hard times. But think you, could he not be fugitive from justice? He has the look of one who has been freshly whipped."

Thomas subjected Hew to closer scrutiny. "Aye," he said judiciously, "or else the look of one who should be freshly whipped."

110

Hew answered wearily, "I was capsized at the ferry, where I have lost my clothes and papers. That is my misfortune, not my crime."

"There has been no report," the kinder bailie murmured, "of the ferry boat capsizing."

"It was not the ferry," Hew began to answer. Then he saw the hopelessness, and fell silent.

"I am come on business, with a commission to the printer, Christian Hall," he explained at last.

"On whose behalf?"

"My own." Hew tugged at his scrip. "I have a manuscript here for the printer."

"And that survived the shipwreck?" Thomas winked to his friend.

"Miraculously, it did," Hew answered shortly. "The press belongs to my father."

"Is that so?" The tall man rubbed his beard. "You know Christian Hall. Did you ken a man called Cullan owned the press?" he asked his fellow doubtfully.

"I never heard of such. Then Christian Hall will vouch for you?" the squat man questioned Hew.

"He will vouch for the book. Though I confess that he does not expect me."

Whatever he had said, he said it all, for the bailies exchanged subtle glances, which Hew could not read, and each laid a hand on his arm.

"We will see this settled at the tolbooth," Thomas said emphatically.

They did not turn, as Hew expected, to the southern corner of St Giles, but marched him to the tower of the worn and ancient tolbooth, rising gloomily to choke the narrow street. Thomas hammered loudly on the turnkey's door.

"Wait," Hew cried desperately, "there is one here who can vouch for me. The advocate, Richard Cunningham."

"Oh, aye?" Thomas smirked. "Right enough. He kens Richard Cunningham," he confided to his friend.

"Then he is the devil, and a rogue beyond a doubt. There's many men that cry upon that name before they swing," the tall man winked at Hew. "I'm afraid you can't afford him. Master Cunningham does not consort with beggars. Though he has met enough thieves, in his time." He rapped sharply once more on the door, and the gudeman appeared, gently grumbling, swinging a great bunch of keys. Hew looked around for a means of escape. A small crowd had gathered, all of them strangers: their interest ranged from scornful curiosity to fierce and frank contempt. They left no open passage to the kirk.

"Aye, what is it now?" The gudeman groaned. "Will I have no peace today?"

"Here's a beggar for you, Robert," Thomas answered cheerfully. "Put him in the ironhouse."

The gudeman gazed at Hew, sad-eyed, and shook his head. "That is not the place, as ye well ken. Besides, the tinklar and her bairns are in the ironhouse. Since she is a woman, it would not be fit."

"What, man! The Egyptian! Were ye no telt to put her in the thieves' hole?" Thomas expostulated. "She's a vagrant and a thief, and like as not a whore."

"Aye, but for the bairns," the gudeman answered lamely. "For they are but bairns, and the hole is awfy dark."

"In truth, I have no patience with your saftness, Robert! The hole is awfy dark! Tis dark enough where they are going, and the bairns had best get used to it. The lord Sinclair his man has set his claim on them."

Hew interrupted, with a sudden rush of dread, "Where are they to go to, that must be so dark?"

Thomas ignored him. "Then put him in the thieves' hole, since the whore is in the ironhouse," he iterated heavily, "it cannot be hard to work out."

Hew reached out to grasp the gudeman's sleeve. "You cannot let them do this," he pleaded. "For pity sir, I beg you." The gudeman shook him off, as mildly as he might blow off a fly. "Now do not fash. And do not fight it, sir. For if you cross these gentlemen tis likely you will hang, and that I should truly be sorry to see."

"Aye, so he would," the tall man endorsed this. "The gudeman is unco kind-hearted. He hates to see anyone hang."

The gudeman of the tolbooth deftly turned Hew's wrists behind his back with a strength and force that belied this gentleness, and held them firm in the grasp of one hand as he felt for his keys. "Now son, if you will not settle quietly I will have to chain you hand and feet, and you would not care for that, I doubt, your hands and feet so sore," he advised.

Hew tried to twist back to face him, but the gaoler's bulk behind him at his back pushed him forward to the door. "Look, now! There are steps." He felt the outside world disintegrate; the bustle of the market and the crying of the cramers receding with the sunlight as he stumbled on the stair. If Thomas and his friend remained above, they had become irrelevant, displaced by the rattling of the gudeman and his keys. His calm and placid lordship of this place entirely his allowed no trace of hope. He would be sorry, aye, beyond a doubt, to see Hew hang. He pitied and kept watch with a cool and sad complacency more chilling than the bailies' thirst for blood. At the foot of the steps, a second door was opening, and Hew knew that once behind it the last vestige of light from the street would be gone. He clung to the gudeman.

"For pity, do not leave me here."

The gudeman loosened his fingers and propelled him through the door. "I maun see to they bairns, and then I will come back to you," he intoned kindly. "You have no money, I suppose? For drink or aught?"

Hew shook his head. Though the gudeman could hardly have seen it in the darkness, he interpreted the silence, for he answered, "You may have oatbread, and water to drink, God willing, and grace of the baxter, for the bailies are right slow to pay their dues." The gaoler heaved a solemn sigh. "I'll see what I can do. They are fixed on one of their purges, of Egyptians and strong beggars and the like, and not a care to who will pay the gudeman for their keep. When the tinklar wifie hangs, there may be bread to spare."

"Is she to hang, then?" Hew pressed him. Though he did not want the answer, he was keen to keep the gudeman talking, to prolong the moment till the last door closed.

"Aye," the gaoler regarded him curiously, "she is a villain, that tells fortunes, and plies magic fast and loose. She has been here once before."

"Then what will become of her children?"

"Aye, the bairns, tis well remembered. I will see to that. I'll leave you now," the gudeman finished pleasantly, "until this time the morn. And when I come this way, I'll pass a cup of water through the grate."

"Send word to Richard Cunningham. I swear he will repay you, on my life," Hew implored.

"But you know, my dear sir," the gudeman countered mildly, "your life is not worth very much. And though you cry for Master Cunningham, I doubt your kinship to him. We cannot have him troubled, by every loun and limmar that would plead for his defence. Well, though, you speak bravely, and you have an honest face, and a certain youth and softness that acquits you well, and so for that reason I will grant you that when Master Cunningham comes next to court, I will speak to him your name and make your predicament known. He is not here at present. He is gone about the circuit court."

Hew cried, despairing, "Then what happens next?"

"Next Tuesday you will come before the magistrate. If no one comes to speak for you, you likely will be scourged and branded in the lug. Take my advice, learn from it, and look for proper work. You may find it in the coal pits or the salt pans. Do not resort to begging, else you will be hanged." With that word of comfort, the gudeman slammed shut the door, leaving Hew alone to contemplate his fate.

In that first, desperate moment, he clung to the door, as though some residue of hope might filter through its cracks. Then forcing down his fear, he turned to face the cell. Though the stench was overwhelming, he knew that he would soon grow used to it, and that appalled him more. For when his stomach had ceased to lurch and rebel, and he no longer noticed the stink of decay, he would himself be part of it, absorbed into its core. Breathing shallow as he could, he felt his way about the space in front of him. The cell was no more than five feet by seven, small enough for him to touch the walls from its centre, high enough, at least, for him to stand. As he became accustomed to the darkness, he saw a trace of light; a tiny grating opened upwards, admitting a pinprick of daylight, or perhaps, on cloudless nights, the glimmer of the moon, and through this grate the trickle of the rain had washed the squalor of the street. The walls were streaked with filth, and the straw below the grate, that once had been a bed, was clogged and moist.

Hew curled up by the door, in the driest corner he could find. The dampness of the air that seeped through to the bone did nothing to obliterate the stench. He took off his leather knapsack, which became his pillow, and drew a curious comfort from its scent. He closed his eyes and tried to picture in its place the warm flank of Dun Scottis, the earthy April showers, the sweetness of the sunshine and the rain. And exhausted, cold and hungry, in this dark and hollow place, he fell asleep.

The Devilmaster

It was the cold that woke him, creeping insidiously into his bones. He woke long before the light. Gradually, though, the sun rose in the sky and a pinkish, milky daylight filtered through the grate. Outside, he heard murmuring, as though a crowd had formed. He heard a far off hammering, and somewhere up above, a deep, metallic clang. He understood these sounds, and tried to shut them out. Then as the sun climbed higher still he heard the sounds of commerce from the luckenbooths, along the northern aspect of St Giles. He allowed his mind to shape them into flesh: a fishwife fresh from Leith, with panniers full of haddocks; limp-eyed ponies, laden, trotting over stones; the ringing of the kirk bells, calling in the day, the harrying of children late for school. He imagined the booksellers, setting up their stalls, a prayer book for the kirkman who hurried to St Giles, a thrilling piece of tattle for his wife. He heard the market criers, sweet and mournful like the gulls: *caller herring, who will buy; neaps like succar; leeks and kale.* He tried to bring to life the textures and the scents, pungent oils and vinegars, dripping from a sponge, and slabs of yellow butter wrapped in muslin cloth. Yet he could not overcome the prison vault, the dark and putrid dankness of the gaol, where he left no mark upon the passing world.

His eyes had already become focused to darkness when the gudeman came to let him out. Someone called, "God's truth! Can it be you?" And he was standing in the light, in the gaze of Richard Cunningham, who met him with an air of such amused benevolence he could have wept.

He said simply, "Master Cunningham, I am truly glad to see you, sir," and haplessly, hopelessly, held out his hand.

Richard broke into a smile, and clasped Hew in his arms in a quick and warm embrace, recoiling, somewhat briskly, from the smell.

"I should think you are," he answered humorously. "You are a little altered since we met.

"This is Master Cullan, and my friend," he confirmed to the gudeman. "There has been a mistake here, which I shall redress. Meanwhile I will take him in my charge."

He removed from a pocket a purse of gold coin, which he tossed to the gaoler intact. The gudeman retreated, well pleased with his spoils.

Richard rubbed his beard. "The question is," he said to Hew, "what we should do with you now. I have some pressing business in the court room, where I dare not take you, in your present state. I think it may be preferable to send you to my house. My clerk here," he gestured to a man behind, "will show you the way."

"In truth, I am in no fit state to grace your home," Hew admitted awkwardly.

"Andrew will explain it to my wife."

Richard drew the man aside, for a hurried consultation. Then he smiled at Hew. "Now I must take my leave, and put this matter right." He moved on swiftly to the entrance of the council house, at the south west quarter of St Giles.

The clerk spoke impassively to Hew, in a tone that suggested he had seen it all before, and would not stoop so low as to remark upon it. "Will you follow, sir?" He led Hew back into the lawnmarket, where the voices he had heard were given form and faces in the dizzy, urgent pressing of the crowd. Hew drank in deep draughts of air, with all its mingled pungency of sweetness and decay, grateful to be part of the returning world.

They had come to a stop at a tall land on a tenement that looked upon the street, with a forestair leading upwards to a wooden gallery. Only then did the servant pause to look at Hew, with a hint of scepticism. "Perhaps it would be best," he allowed at last, "if you wait here."

Hew stood a little further from the door, afraid that it would appear that he was loitering. The high street had a rough, ramshackle air, quite different from the leafy thoroughfare of South Street in St Andrews, where the merchants built their houses on neat and ordered rigs. The lands upon the tenements appeared to crane their necks towards the sun. Like plants starved of light they pushed their straggled shoots up vainly to the smallest prick of sky. Everything was pushed upwards, striving for the mountains where the air was clean, leaner and lankier, stretched towards the sun. Timber frames and forestairs sprouted ever up and outwards, until the whole town twisted like a turnpike, rising to the castle, straining round the galleries that spilled into the street. Hew kept a watchful eye out for the bailies. A fruitman stood close to the house, selling baskets of apples and wardens, long-wintered, weathered and worn, and trays of dried medlars and plums.

Presently, the clerk returned, and honoured Hew with a contemptuous smile, that flickered round the edges of his lips.

"Done," he said laconically. "Go up to the kitchen there." He led Hew to the side door in the close, and pointed to a turnpike stairway. "Second opening on the left, on the second floor."

Hew found himself inside a warm and well-lit room, as large as Jonet's cottage, that contained a roasting spit before a blazing fire. A dressing board was set with bread and butter, and a plate of mutton, thickly sliced. A low door opened to his right, and a little maid emerged, with a jug of frothing beer. She placed this on the board beside the bread and indicated through a string of squeals and gestures that he was to eat. Her duty done, she fled, as though she saw the devil supping at her hearth. Hunger overcame Hew's inhibitions, and he made short work of the meal. He was wiping his mouth with the last piece of bread, when the kitchen door opened, and a child of six or seven peeped inside. She giggled as he smiled at her, clasping her fingertips close to her mouth, and let the door slam, darting away. Hew groaned. Once again, he was a fool for maids and bairns to gawp at.

The little girl was followed in a moment by her mother, who stood calm and curious, with her daughter peeking shyly from her skirts. Hew rose abruptly, startled into awkwardness, conscious of his squalid state of dress.

"Master Cullan — Hew — you are welcome here." The mistress of the house regarded him with clear and candid gaze. She held out her hand, with a grace that he dared not return. "I am Eleanor Preston," she said softly. "The servant will send for a surgeon, to attend to your hurts."

"No surgeon, I implore you," Hew protested. "I am only scratched and bruised. I would not be bloodied as well."

Eleanor raised an eyebrow, and answered with a mother's patience for a dear but vexing child. "Well then, if you prefer, you shall have the apothecary. Come up to the loft; there is a room prepared."

Hew followed her up the turnpike stair. Richard's house appeared to be arranged on several floors, and he had lost his bearings from the street. At its very top they came into a space that overlooked the close, furnished with a writing desk and bed.

"I hope you may be comfortable," Eleanor said. "I will bring up what you need. Soap and water, I should think," she inferred discreetly. She left him on his own, to wait for the apothecary. This man was polite though perfunctory in his attentions, and Hew began to suspect that the stench of the tolbooth, to which he had in some part grown accustomed, lingered more stubbornly than he had supposed. He wished for Richard to come home, to offer him a proper conversation, and restore his sense of self. Under the apothecary's quizzical eye, he felt like one of Giles Locke's specimens, floating in a jar and of dubious provenance.

As the apothecary took his leave, the mistress of the house returned, with a suit of clothes. "Aye, you were right," Eleanor smiled. "Only bruised. The man will make up a salve."

It felt strange to Hew to be mothered in this way, for the second time in as many weeks, and he hoped she would not ask him to undress. She held out the clothes for inspection. "These will do, I think. Richard's last prentis left them behind. They are a little worn for wearing in the court, but will serve until you have new. You can throw your old ones on the fire."

"I thank you. But I think perhaps you have misunderstood," Hew answered politely. "I am not Richard's prentis."

"Oh?" she looked surprised. "But you are Matthew Cullan's son?"

"For certain, aye."

"Then there is nothing more to say." She smiled at him again. "In any case, you will be glad to change your things. Have you all that you require?"

"But for soap and water," Hew reminded her.

Eleanor hesitated. "I talked with the apothecar. I fear he is opposed to washing, as the witches recommend, in times of hurt and sickness. He believes warm water opens up the skin and makes it ripe for pestilence and putrefaction, such as is rife in . . . in the place where you most recently were . . . *incommoded*," she concluded tactfully.

Hew sighed. He wanted nothing more fervently than to rid himself of that stain, the taint of the gaol, its creeping stench and shudder on his skin.

"I have heard that argument," he pleaded, "and my brother-in-law, who is a most renowned physician, until quite recently subscribed to it, but my sister, who is wiser yet than anyone I know — though she is not a witch, of course," he capitulated hurriedly, "— has succeeded in persuading him otherwise, and now he is convinced not only does washing not cause putrefaction but a little soap and water judiciously applied may oftentimes discourage it." He spoke like Giles, he realised sadly, in this curious circumvention.

"*That* is not an argument we often hear in town. But nonetheless," Eleanor gave a thoughtful nod towards the counterpane, which did not look likely to wash well, "you may have soap and water. Richard has a bath vat in his closet," she admitted, as an afterthought, "though it takes some time to fill."

This, Hew sensed, was a step too far. "Soap and water, and some towels," he assured her, "will suffice. I thank you for the clothes. But I should like to keep the others if I may."

Eleanor stared. "You can have no further use for them."

Hew grew hot beneath her gaze, so benignly sceptical. "I mean to return them to the gude wife who lent them," he explained.

"They are noxious, Hew," she told him gently, as she might warn a child, who had simple understanding, and as little sense.

"They belonged to her son, who was drowned."

"Then leave them by the door, to be washed and aired. You shall not take them back to her, tainted with the tolbooth," Eleanor said gently.

It was pity at his tale, perhaps, that she forgot her inhibitions in the naming of the place.

"Mistress, I thank you, I cannot repay your kindness. I am truly sorry, to have brought the filth of the gaol to your house," answered Hew.

"As to that, think nothing of it. It serves as a timely reminder that that dreadful place is not so far away. Now, I will leave you to dress. Richard will be home soon. You will find us in the hall, taking supper. I knew you and your sister both when you were children," she said kindly as she left.

The timid maid returned with basin, jug and towels, and Hew scrubbed clean the remnants of the gaol. Washed and dressed, he closed his eyes for a moment on the bed, and in a moment more, he fell asleep. He woke with a start to the sound of voices below, splashed his face again quickly and combed through his hair. Now sleepily presentable, he made his way downstairs.

He found the family all together in the hall. The room opened out through high, half-shuttered windows to a timber gallery. When the windows were left open to allow the air the house looked down upon the marketplace, a light and airy loft above the noise and dust, lifted from the clamour of the street. With the shutters closed, the hall was dark and intricate, lapped in quiet lamplight and the subtle, secret stirrings of the fire. In the cool April evening, Eleanor allowed for both; she left the windows open to the last pale trace of sunlight as she lit the fire. The long meat board was set before the window, with a white-work cloth, and beside it stood the linen stand, with water bowls and washing cloths. The table had been set with pewter bowls and cups, though Richard had a drinking cup of silver, and a set of silver spoons. There were fruit dishes, bread bowls and butter plates, and saucers of pickles and salt. Besides, there was a linen press, and a French oak dresser, together with a walnut stand bed, plump with cushions, in the corner by the hearth. Eleanor had woven fabrics bright with flowers, in russet, gold and primrose, picking out the colours of the flames. The walls were coloured white and hung with painted cloths. The whole seemed light and intimate, a public and a private space, both close and distant to the town.

Richard was sitting on the settle by the fire, with his little daughter in his lap. A young boy sat reading, curled on the floor at his feet. As Hew entered, Richard smiled. "You look a little better now."

"He stinked before," the little girl said candidly.

"*That is* rude," rebuked Richard.

"True, though." Hew winked at her.

126

"Why?" The boy by the fireside closed his book and gazed at Hew with curious grey eyes. Eleanor replied, "It is ill-mannered to remark upon the smell."

"I meant, why did you stink?" The boy gazed closely at Hew, his interest implacable.

"I was in a bad place," Hew said apologetically, "and I am grateful to your parents to be out of it."

"He was in the *gaol*," the girl said unexpectedly. Then she saw her parents' warning looks, and capitulated hurriedly, "That was what my nursemaid said."

Eleanor sighed, "Servants talk."

"I have thought for some time," Richard frowned, "that Grace is too old for a nurse."

The little girl pouted. "I like her."

"We will speak of it later," Eleanor suggested. "Master Cullan, these are our children. Roger is twelve, and at the grammar school, and Grizelda, whom we all call Grace, has recently turned six. James, our elder son, is studying at St Leonard's."

"So I understand. Grizelda is a pretty name." Solemnly, he extended a hand to the child.

"I had a sister Mary, but she died last spring," the little girl confided.

"I am truly sorry to hear it." Hew looked at Eleanor, who smiled bleakly. Richard cleared his throat.

"Thank you. I'm afraid to say, we have rather made a pet of Grace, since Mary's death. Forgive my children's manners, Hew."

"There's nothing to forgive," Hew returned politely.

"Why were you in the gaol?" the boy persisted.

"*Enough!*"

Hew was surprised at the force of Richard's tone, and the boy shrank back into the shadow of the fire.

After supper, Eleanor left the room with the children, while Richard poured two cups of claret wine.

"Feeling better now?" he asked ironically.

Hew sipped the wine. "In truth, I cannot thank you enough."

"Pray, do not mention it."

"Richard, there was a woman hanged today."

"Aye, a common thief. Put it from your mind."

"But they took her children."

"So I heard. I saw the man myself — Sinclair's grieve at Dysart — coming for the bairns."

"Dear God!" You mean they are to work the pits?"

"It is the way of things," Richard sighed. "Hew, take my advice and do not waste your pity. The woman is dead, and her children are gone. To succeed at the bar, you must harden your heart. You are too soft, but I shall teach you yet."

"As to that, I have no wish to be taught," Hew replied. "For all of your kindness, I think you have misunderstood. I did not come here as your prentis, but on business of my father's."

"Now that is unfortunate," Richard answered dryly. "For you are my servant and my prentis, bound to me for a year from this day, on which terms I vouched twenty pounds before the magistrate, securing your release from the charge of vagrancy."

Hew stared at him aghast. "You bought me?"

"Aye, I had to. Don't you know the law?" Richard burst out laughing at the expression on Hew's face. "Have no fear; I will not hold you here against your will. But would it really be so bad? Consider, won't you stay? It would please me well. Can it really be so irksome to you? Try it for a week or two, and if it does not suit you, I will be content to let you go."

Hew shook his head. "I have other interests here. Forgive me, Richard. I'll repay the debt, when I restore my credit."

"Peace, there is no debt," Richard protested. "As to your credit, I can lend you what you need to make your journey home, if that is your intent. You cannot think that I would keep you here against your proper will. And for your business, perhaps I may help."

In the face of such reasoned kindness, Hew felt ashamed. "My father had interests in a printer," he explained, "called Christian Hall. The debt is somewhat large."

"Christian Hall, you say? I do not know the press."

"Also, he left properties in the charge of a goldsmith, George Urquhart. The receipts were destroyed in the Forth."

"Urquhart, now, I know. That may prove a problem." Richard stroked his beard. "Though I may vouch for you, Urquhart is unlikely to release the deeds without receipts. I suggest that you write to your lawman in St Andrews, asking him to send you letters of entitlement. I will pay the messenger. But that will take two or three weeks to arrange. In the meantime, why not stay here as my pupil, and try how it will please you?"

Laughing, Hew gave up the fight. "Aye, then, for a week or two, I thank you. Though I must conclude my business while I stay."

"Indeed you must. I shall not make too heavy inroads on your time. Tomorrow, I am occupied, and may not take you with me; you may see your printer, and call upon my credit to buy yourself new clothes. On Thursday, there's a case begins . . ." Richard broke off thoughtfully. "Well, we shall see."

"I may prove a poor enough pupil," Hew warned him.

"Time will tell." Richard smiled. "These are momentous times. The earl of Morton has been taken and before too long we may expect his trial. I do not say I will be able to take you to that; nor is it yet quite certain who will prosecute, but there is much to do here, and a great deal to be learned."

"I have been abroad, and have not heard this," Hew exclaimed. "What is the charge against Morton?"

"The murder of King Henry Darnley. That has been a long time coming."

"Doubtless, Morton's hands are bloody, yet I might suppose him innocent of that. I saw him at St Andrews," Hew reflected, "with Lennox and the king."

"Already then, his card was marked. Nemesis cares little when she strikes."

"Old wounds are apt to open."

"I suppose they are." Richard frowned a little. "You must be exhausted, Hew. It's time we went to bed. And, for your father's sake, be well assured you are well loved and welcome in this house."

It was true, Hew reflected, climbing the stair; he was barely awake. And yet before he lay down he took ink to paper, crouched in the candlelight, writing a letter to Giles. Finally, as he blew out the lamp, he felt in the closet for his battered knapsack, tucking it carefully under the bed.

Christian Hall

Hew took Richard at his word and spent the morning shopping. Many of the hie gate lands had buiths below their galleries, and he ordered shoes and linens from the soutars and the drapers at the north side of the tron. At the tailor at the cross he was measured for a suit of clothes. He bought a cloak of tufted taffeta and a matching feathered hat in gooseturd green, and a coat of black fustian, for wearing to the courts. At last he came to browse among the bookshops. Some sold Latin books for schoolmen, bought from overseas; others pawned the bric-a-brac that poured forth weekly from the press, bibles, psalms and catechisms, stirring sermons, travellers' tales, for anyone that read. The pedlars hawked ephemera: gossip, news and scandals, scores and ballad sheets. Some were shabby, second-hand, in this brave new age of print already worn and soiled. All carried frank advertisement, promising to thrill. Hew inquired for Christian Hall, and was directed to the Netherbow, where Robert Lekprevik had kept his press. On the south side near the Canongate he found the printing house.

The printers' shops had paper windows, varnished to translucency, to filter out the brightness of the sun. In

Christian's case, this seemed a mere formality; the windows looking out upon the windswept street faced resolutely north. The press was approached from the side, through a vennel dark with ink, where the lye ran freely from the printer's rinsing trough. In the absence of a sign, the paper and the ink were clues enough.

Hew pushed open the door. He found himself inside a workplace, rather than a shop. A single pressman laboured on a heavy press, pulling and beating in turn. Behind him the typesetter stood at his frame, making the best of the light. Neither glanced up, and Hew was uncertain which one was more likely to be Christian Hall, the master printer. He caught the eye of a young prentis lad, ferrying paper forwards and back from the press. The boy reminded Hew a little of the devil's imps at Dysart, for his cheeks were smudged and black. Nonetheless, he had the sense that the printer's daubs were playful, and like the paper windows were provided for effect. The hands that held the paper were quite clean.

"May I speak with your master?" Hew called out.

Momentarily, the boy appeared to hesitate. Then he nodded, dropped his papers by the pressman, and hurried to the corner of the room where the galleys were laid out. Hew saw him tug the sleeve of the compositor, who was lifting letter from a tray. The man looked down at him and frowned. Hew edged a little closer. The master seemed reluctant. "What is it now, boy? Wait until I fill the line."

"Yon man there wants you now," the boy insisted, "over by the door."

"Truly?" The printer seemed sceptical.

"Will I finish the line for you?" asked the apprentice.

"That you will not."

Composing stick still in his hands, the printer came forward to Hew. "Aye? Can I help you, sir?"

Hew held out his hand. "Hew Cullan. You are Master Hall?"

Inexplicably, the man turned on his heel, steadied the stick in his left hand, and cuffed the young apprentice with the right. "It's Christian he wants. Excuse us, sir," he bowed to Hew.

The lad reddened, but stood firm.

"Yon asked for to speak with my master," he countered stubbornly. Surreptitiously, he rubbed the corner of his ear.

"Aye. And you know, and I know, that I am not the master here."

"Aye, but you might be," persisted the boy. "One day, you will. And you will have a printshop of your own, and then you'll take me as your prentis, will you not?"

"Villain! Why would I do that?" The compositor opened a door that led through to a stair. He called out abruptly, "*Christian, you're wanted!*" and without another word returned to his composing stick. The pressman caught Hew's eye, and grinned at him. He straightened from the press and flexed his arms.

Somewhere above, Hew heard footsteps, and then a young woman appeared, with a child upon her hip, and her hair falling loosely from her cap, where the bairn had tugged at it. She was simply dressed in smock and

134

pale blue kirtle, and the stray wisps of hair were the colour of light straw. Glancing round the shop, she set the child down on the floor. The infant toddled, curious, towards the press. The woman smiled distractedly. She wore an anxious look, which disappeared at once when she relaxed. She was, Hew judged, no more than twenty-three.

"Well, sir, can I help you?" she inquired of him.

"Thank you, I was looking for Christian Hall."

"And you have found her. But I see you are surprised," she answered seriously.

It had simply not occurred to Hew that the printer Christian Hall might be a woman. He understood, at last, the bailies' cunning looks.

"Not at all." He bowed politely, masking his confusion. "I have come here as a stranger, and I must explain myself. I am Hew Cullan, son of Matthew, and I understand my father had some business here. Since his death it falls to me to settle his affairs. There were letters, signed by you, among his papers." He hesitated, reading genuine concern in Christian's face. She had large, expressive eyes, of the palest blue.

"Oh, but that's sad news! When did he die?"

"He was buried three weeks past. Forgive me, mistress. Did you know my father?"

Christian shook her head. "In truth, I never met him. Yet he was so kind to us. He was instrumental in setting up the press. He helped my husband . . . *William, no!*"

The infant had picked up an ink ball, and was busily applying it upon the heap of paper freshly stacked. The pressman looked up on Christian's cry, and came to part the child and ink, scooping William up into his arms. The infant struggled lustily. Christian ran her fingers through her hair and sighed. "Take the bairn outside," she told the prentis boy. To Hew she explained, "His nurse is sick today, and we are lost without her."

The young apprentice scowled. "I've letter to rinse out for Phillip."

"Do as your mistress bids." The pressman set the child upon its feet again and gave the lad a warning glare. Sulkily, he took the infant's hand.

"Aye, do it, Michael," said Christian gently, "I will recompense your time."

"We have reason to be grateful to your father," she continued, as the child was coaxed away. "You did not know?" She seemed surprised. "I am grieved to hear tell of his passing. Have you heard this, Phillip?" she called out to the compositor. "This is Hew Cullan, son of Matthew. He brings us grave news. His father has died."

"Matthew Cullan?" the compositor sighed as he gave up his type and returned to look at Hew, extending his hand. "Ah, sir, I'm sorry for it. Pray, forgive our rudeness."

"How so? Are we rude?" Christian asked sharply.

"A misunderstanding. With Michael."

"Tis an ill-mannered boy," the pressman chipped in — he was leaning on his press, listening in all openness — "that requires correction."

"When I require correction, I will ask for it directly," Christian replied. "And if I see you idle at your press, it will set you back you a shilling. And another sixpence, if

I hear you swear." Snorting, the pressman returned to his work.

The compositor smiled. "At risk of chastisement," he said in a dry tone to Christian, "Walter is right. You are soft with him, I think."

"Aye," she answered quietly. "And I mean to speak with Michael. But not in front of strangers."

It was clear that she thought well of Phillip, who returned to his work with a nod. Christian turned back to Hew. "Come through to the sorting house." She led the way into a little room. High up in the beams, the printed sheets were hanging out to dry, and there were piles of papers folded on the floor, about to be collated into books. The finished works were set out on a table, ready to be sold and bound. "It's quiet here," Christian explained, "and we shan't disturb their work. The printing is behind, for we were frozen out."

"What do you mean, *frozen out*?" queried Hew.

"The letter and the paper were both stiff with ice. We could not print. It seldom happens here." Unconsciously, she shivered. "For we have a good fire in the printshop, though the roofs are high. This street is always cold. But winter came so late this year. We were not expecting it."

"Indeed, it has been hard," Hew agreed politely. He wanted to forget the bleak and frozen preface to his father's funeral. "Mistress, I will come to the point. As I believe my father paid you monies . . . ."

Christian nodded, guardedly. "He did so, willingly. And they were investments, sir. We did not count them debts."

Her voice held a hint of defensiveness, short of a plea. Hew thought he understood. A widow, struggling to support her child, to maintain her husband's press, had seemed a worthy cause to Matthew. Now she was afraid the son called in the debt. To deflect from her discomfort, Hew picked up a book. "'A dire warning'. Of what?" he inquired.

"Almost anything you like." She smiled unexpectedly. "They are admonitory tracts, and always very popular. The direr the warning, the greater the thrill. We do not print them for ourselves; they are for Henry Charteris. But we fell behind, and almost lost the work." She fell silent, a little reflective, as though there was something she was not saying.

Hew leafed through the pamphlet. "Very dire indeed," he commented. "And very nicely wrought. How did you come upon the trade? I mean, to have a printing shop?"

"As a girl, I had a tutor, and I learned to read. My father was a scholar."

"Then he must be proud of you," Hew remarked politely.

"I know not, for I never knew him," Christian sighed. "He died when I was very small, and I do not remember him. He was something in the law, my mother said; I know not what. And when I turned sixteen, my mother also died, and I was left alone, except for the tutor, and our servant, Alison. They both were dear to me; and Alison remains with us as William's nurse. You see how much we miss her, when she is not here," she added wryly. "As for the tutor, he was William Hall. I married him."

"William Hall! You took his name!" exclaimed Hew.

Christian regarded him curiously. "I kept it for the press," she admitted. "His name was at the bottom of the signet blocks, and when he died, the pressman cut it off, so I might use the mark, and save the expense of having them freshly engraved. And for myself," she added sadly, "I like to keep this small remembrance, for his sake. One day, God willing, when our son is a man, the press will be William's again. The H on the block is for Hall, but the cross was put there for Christian."

"Then what signifies the bird?"

"That was not our choice. William put it there to please your father, who had given so much money to the press."

"My father?" Hew frowned. "I can't think what it meant to him."

"Nor did William, but your father was so kind a friend to us, we would not have offended him. I have never liked that bird. At seedtime, when the farmers make their scarecrows out of corbie corpses, row on row of dead black birds, it always makes me shiver."

Hew pondered this awhile. "How did your husband come to know my father?" he wondered at last.

"I cannot tell you, for I do not know. William was a scholar at St Andrews, so maybe they met there. Two years ago, when William died, I wrote to your father and he sent money through a goldsmith in the town. We promised we would print a book that he was writing. It was the least that we could do. In truth, I did not think that he would ever finish it. It seemed . . . you will forgive my candour, but it seemed an old man's foolishness."

"I thought the same," admitted Hew. "Two years since, you say? Then I was still in France."

"William was a babe new born." Christian flushed. "Your father had invested in the business. It was not my intention to beg him for money, but to warn him that without it, the press must be sold. He had the right to recover his share. Because of his kindness, and the goodwill of Phillip and Walter, we were able to keep going."

"And what is Phillip's part in this?" wondered Hew aloud.

Christian stared at him. "He works for me, and is a loyal friend. He has no other interest in the press. Why do you ask about him?"

Hew answered foolishly. "It's nothing. Only I would know the extent of the investment, that is all."

"The business does quite well," she told him frankly, "but if you wanted capital . . ."

"No, no," he assured her, "that's not why I'm here. I brought the manuscript — my father's book — for printing."

"Then it's ready for the press? I had not thought it possible!" Christian exclaimed.

"It *was*," Hew unwrapped the cloth, "but there has been an accident."

It was almost, he thought, like bringing a patient to Giles, waiting for the moment when the loose fear in the belly froze and set, and the doctor shook his head.

140

He remembered the warmth of the hand on his shoulder when he had stood frozen in the garden of his father's house, not knowing, not wanting to know.

Christian gave an exclamation, and began to separate the quires, laying out the pages on the board.

"Can it be deciphered?" Hew asked her helplessly.

"I know not, we must try. What happened to it?"

"It fell in the Forth."

"Aye? And what is the dark stain?" She wrinkled her nose. "We must salvage what we can. It will take a little time. Will you help us, Master Cullan, to make good your father's hand? We have no corrector here."

"Can it be done?" he asked. "I have the time. I mean to stay in town for several weeks, attending at the courts."

"Then you intend to be a lawman like your father?"

"What do you know of that?" demanded Hew.

"It's a law book, is it not?" Christian answered mildly.

"Aye, of course. Forgive me, I forget my manners . . . The truth is I had thought myself indifferent to the law; the manuscript itself I took for nothing, until I saw it drowned."

"I understand," she told him softly. "So often, we know only what we want, when once it's lost."

And for the sympathy, the understanding in her face, the care with which she turned the pages, he felt she read his heart, and feeling at a loss, he looked away.

"Phillip, come here a moment!" She had opened the door and called to the compositor, who groaned and

141

left his place. "Christian," he said patiently, "I will not finish these today."

"It can't be helped. Come, look at this. It's Matthew Cullan's manuscript. Can you set it, do you think? It has got wet," she added, unnecessarily.

Phillip turned the pages, frowning thoughtfully. As last he turned to Hew. "It can be done. But it will take some time to make this copy good. Are you in a hurry, sir? You may want to hire a scribe."

"No hurry," Hew insisted, reckless with relief. "I can do the work myself."

Christian said firmly. "We shall not want a scribe. With Master Cullan's help, we shall make the copy good in half the time."

Phillip conceded doubtfully, "Well, you are the master here."

"*Aye,*" suddenly, her seriousness dissolved into a grin, "I am. Remember it!"

Hew liked her, and at once he felt the manuscript was in safe hands. As if she read his thoughts, Christian smiled at him. "You and I shall work on this together. You can read aloud, and I will make the copy for Phillip to set. For the present, I must see to William. Michael is a week boy and I cannot spare him long. But tomorrow, or the next day, we shall make a start."

Hew bowed, "Madam, I look forward to it," and found that he meant it.

Hew returned to Richard's house, where he already had begun to feel at home. The forestair on the hie gate led up to the gallery, where the maid had hung out washing in the April sun. He was touched to see the boatman's breeks among the linen cloths and shirts. At supper that evening, in the great hall, he told the story of his visit to the printing house.

"A woman!" Eleanor marvelled. "However does she manage it?"

"Admirably. Though it is evident that circumstances are not always kind to her. I confess I was impressed at the way she arranges the shop."

"Is she pretty?" Grace asked shrewdly.

"I believe she is," Hew winked at her. "She is small and slight, with linen-coloured hair. Almost as bonny as you."

Grace dismissed the compliment. "Then you could marry her. And be a printer, if you did not like to be an advocate like Daddie."

Roger snorted rudely.

"Don't be silly, Grace," her mother said.

"I think that is a little premature," Hew smiled. "Yet I may well learn enough, to practise as a printer, in the hours it will take to make good my father's manuscript."

Richard frowned. "I am surprised you did not mention this before, when you spoke of your business here. When I took you in my house, I had not thought you secretive."

"Richard!" Eleanor exclaimed, "what a strange thing to say!"

"But Richard is right," replied Hew. "I did not speak of it, because, in some sense, it makes me uncomfortable. My father left a book of his old cases, analysed as an exemplar in the law, and dedicated it to me, hoping to persuade me to continue in the practick. Which course, as you know," he glanced at Richard, "I am reluctant to follow, less willing still, where I perceive myself trapped. I brought the book, in truth, in no small part resenting it. But when I saw it dripping, salvaged from the sea, I had a change of heart, and understood its worth."

"That is natural enough," Eleanor observed. "It was your father's last gift, after all."

"Have you read this book?" queried Richard.

"I confess, I have not. For in my stubbornness I have resisted it. That will make my task in deciphering the script more difficult, I fear."

"And you say it is based on your father's old cases? Truly, I might wish that you had mentioned this, and asked for my advice, before you took it to the printer." Richard stroked his beard. "It may not be fitting, to allow it in to print."

"Why, father?" asked Roger, listening intently.

"Hew's father was a gentleman . . ."

"Was he? I thought he was a lawyer."

"*Hold your tongue!*"

Hew was taken aback by the force of Richard's rebuke, to what appeared an innocent remark, but the boy gave a small and satisfied smile.

"Hew's father was a gentleman," Richard had recovered his composure, "and gentlemen do not put forth opinions in the press. It is not *done*. I fear this may do harm to Matthew's reputation."

144

"I don't see why. If learned men do not write books, then how shall we have books to learn?" objected Roger. "And if a gentleman should happen to have wit, and be a scholar too, then surely, he should share it."

"You may stay here and eat, sir, or you may speak, but you may *not* do both," his father told him icily. Roger lapsed into a sullen silence, and began to push a piece of bread around his bowl.

"For myself," Hew answered quietly, "I am inclined to think with Roger. My father, for his faults, cared little for his reputation. It was something I admired in him."

There followed an awkward silence, broken finally by Grace announcing, "I like books with pictures, like the ones in Minnie's bible."

"So do I," Hew told her. "And do you know how they are made? They cut the pictures into little blocks of wood . . ."

It seemed that Richard came to regret his outburst to his son, for at the close of the meal he inquired of him pleasantly. "I have half an hour to spare. Will you play a game of chess?"

The boy replied, "No, thank you, sir. I have something to prepare for school."

"How goes your schooling?" Richard asked him.

Roger shrugged. "Well enough." Reluctantly, he added, seeing Richard frown, "the schoolmaster was pleased with me today."

"As well he might be." Richard turned to Hew. "Roger is a subtle boy, the sharpest of my children."

"*I* am subtle," Grace protested.

"Aye, mouse, for a little lass." He chucked her under the chin. "I shall take a turn outside," he announced, to no one in particular, "and clear my head for court. Tomorrow promises to be a testing day."

No sooner had he left, when Roger closed his book and came to stand by Hew. "Do you play chess, Master Cullan? Will you play a game with me?"

Hew laughed. "Gladly. But I thought that you had work to do."

"No more tonight." Roger emptied the chessmen out of their box and began to set them on their square upon a little table by the fire. "I do not care to play against my father. For my father likes to win."

"I suspect we all do, in the end," suggested Hew.

"Aye, to be sure. But my father gives no quarter. It's the lawman in him."

"You don't seem to like lawyers much," Hew observed.

"Hush, Roger," Eleanor called out anxiously. She was sitting on the stand bed, brushing Grace's hair. "You know how it is, Hew. Fathers and sons . . ."

"Richard is the kindest father," she excused her husband, once Grace and Roger were safely in bed. "And he loves his children very much. His family is the world to him; he values nothing more. But when he has a case, he is apt to be distracted, and remote. His mood is closed and distant, and he is taut and vexed. At such a time, he is better left alone, to work the matter out. Tomorrow is a case of great importance to him. Has he asked you to go with him? I believe that he intends to. Then you should be grateful. It *matters* to him, Hew."

"For certain, I will thank him, if he asks me," Hew assured her. "What's the case?"

Eleanor stared at him. "I confess, I do not know. He does not discuss his work."

Wilful Error

The next morning, Richard's mood had changed. He appeared alert, in a state of well-controlled excitement. As Eleanor had predicted, he invited Hew to join him at the justice court. "This is a case of substance," he explained. "The chancellor has agreed that you may watch. The prosecutor is Robert Crichton, Lord Advocate, and I have been engaged to speak for the panel, who is Simon Pettigrew, a mercer in the town."

"What is the charge?" questioned Hew.

"The slaughter and cruel murder of Elspet Barr his wife. He despatched her down the turnpike at their lodging in the Canongate."

"You mean he is accused of doing so?"

"I mean he did it," Richard grinned. "And he has confessed to it. Have you seen my gloves?"

"You do not seem to mind it," Hew remarked. "I should have thought it vexing, to have lost your case, before if has begun."

"Indeed," agreed Richard. "That would be vexing. Who said the case was lost?" He found the gloves behind a candlestick, and peered into a looking glass, tweaking at his hair.

"You did, as I thought."

"I said nothing of the sort. Listen closely. I said that Simon had confessed."

"And is he not guilty, then?" Hew asked, confused.

"Beyond shadow of a doubt," confirmed Richard cheerfully. "He despatched his old wife, who was rich and ugly, and now has a new wife, who is young and fair. It is Elspet Barr's father who makes the complaint."

"Then surely, if he confessed . . ."

"Peace, now, listen closely. It is your place to sit on the bench with the prentices and students — no doubt Crichton has some of his own, even now — and to watch and learn," advised Richard. "Take note of what you see. And aught you hear you do not understand, I shall explain it in the tavern afterwards. You may enter the court, and leave it, with me, but do not come or go alone, or the macers will arrest you, for contempt. Above all, listen, do not speak."

"Surely Pettigrew will hang? You cannot offer a defence?" Hew persisted.

"I will tell you this much only," Richard laughed, "Robert Crichton, for all he is king's advocate, is growing slow and tired. This morning, you will see him bested. Now, we are ready, I think."

He was dressed in black velvet, embroidered in silver, and the same slashed leather gloves he had worn at Matthew's funeral. It was essential, he explained to Hew, to dress according to his rank, otherwise, his voice would not be heard.

★　★　★

The justice court sat in the new tolbooth, at the south-west corner of St Giles. As they approached, the kirk bells rang, and the macers at the door stood to attention, raising their wands and nodding to Richard, allowing them to pass. In an anteroom upstairs, they found their client, Simon Pettigrew, waiting nervously. Richard extended basic courtesies, before taking Pettigrew aside for a brief consultation, out of earshot of Hew. Briskly, he ushered them inside, and gestured Hew towards a narrow bench, where he had a fair view of proceedings. At the back of the room was a stage, upon which were set out half a dozen chairs and a long board covered with green cloth. Presently, behind this stage, a small door opened to admit the justices in scarlet gowns, and the whole court rose. Richard, by this time, was stationed at the bar beside his client Pettigrew, who stood dabbing at his forehead with a handkerchief. At the other end of the court, the door opened from the anteroom to allow forty-five stout men and true to shuffle in uncomfortably. From this reluctant crowd, fifteen were chosen to make up the assize. Meanwhile, Robert Crichton had appeared, in dappled dark green silks, a peacock to Richard's black swan. He was the father of James Crichton, the admirable, whose accomplishments Hew had spoken of to Nicholas. In Matthew Cullan's time, he had been queen's advocate, and had survived some twenty years to serve the king. Doubtless, Hew reflected, it was Robert Crichton who had led the prosecution of the writer hanged for forgery, losing Richard his first case. It was hard to see, under present circumstances, how

150

Richard proposed to recover the advantage. Evidently, Simon Pettigrew felt the same, for he stood weakly sweating, a peculiar, sickly shade.

The clerk of the court then read out the dittay, that the panel Pettigrew was accusit of foul and cruel slaughter of his wife Elspet Barr, that he did push her down the turnpike of their lodging in the Canongate, that he might confess or deny it. Pettigrew, emphatically, denied it. Crichton looked nonplussed. "But surely," he protested, "the panel has confessed his crime before the magistrate."

Richard said smoothly, "And now he denies it."

Crichton appealed to the justice. "You will not allow this retraction, my lord? The confession was witnessed, and the panel wrote his name to it."

The justice answered patiently, "As ye well ken and understand, Master Crichton, the panel must be tried, whether he confesses here or no. Therefore let the clerk record that he denies it, and the jury will decide whether his confession is due proof."

Crichton looked rattled, and Hew began to understand Richard's strategy. For all his experience — or perhaps because of it — Crichton had come ill-prepared. He was dependent on confession for probation; if confession was retracted, then he had no other proofs. Richard was exploiting the fact that all cases, whatever the plea, were put before a jury. But the strategy — which depended on the jury — was a dangerous one. The macers produced the list of assize, and the names of those present were read out, and objected to, by both lawyers intermittently, a process which took some considerable time. Eventually, fifteen were agreed, and were sworn in batches, to seek truth by God himself, and by their part in Paradise, and as they would answer to God upon the dreadful day of doom.

Robert Crichton then addressed the jury, and put the fear of God in them, by threatening them with *wilful error on assize*, if they dared acquit the panel; then Richard Cunningham addressed them, threatening the same, if they should dare convict him.

These formalities concluded, Crichton began with his probation, which proved short enough, since it depended on the confession that Pettigrew denied. Crichton had the clerk read out the statement Simon Pettigrew had made before the magistrate, confessing to the murder of his wife.

"Did you make this statement?" he demanded of the merchant. Pettigrew supposed that he had.

"Then do you own it now?"

"No, sir, I retract it. It was made in error, when I was distracted, by the recent death and burial of my wife."

"Then perhaps you will explain how you came to confess to a crime that you now say you did not commit?" Crichton countered dryly.

Richard Cunningham was on his feet, at once alert and watchful. "Master Pettigrew will *not*," he objected, "for as the lord advocate knows full well, the accused may not give evidence, save what he confesses or denies. Master Pettigrew *denies*. And there must be an end to it."

"Now that is true, you know," the judge admonished seriously. "We cannot allow the defendant to speak, for fear he may perjure himself. And we cannot allow him to perjure himself, for fear of eternal damnation. It is for your own good, Master Pettigrew," he exhorted kindly. "I do not mean to say that you are lying now, or that you lied before."

"But since he must be lying now, or else he lied before," Crichton argued smoothly, "then it would appear he is already perjured. Therefore, let him speak."

"As you well know, my lord, the law does not allow that," the judge replied severely. "And, since he is so muddled, he had better hold his peace."

Crichton was exasperated. "Will you not rule," he appealed again to the judge, "that this man's confession must stand?"

"No," replied the judge. "For unless he will acknowledge it, here before this inquest, his confession is not proved. You can advise the jury to accept it on presumption, but presumption by itself is insufficient proof. Have you no witnesses?"

"Aye, my lord," Crichton sighed. "I call the pursuer, George Barr."

Richard rose to his feet. "I object to that witness," he remarked lazily.

The justice peered at him suspiciously. "Indeed? On what possible ground?"

"On the grounds of . . . feeble-mindedness?" ventured Richard.

"George Barr is the pursuer," Crichton answered wearily. "If he were feeble-minded, we should not have had the case."

"That is correct. We should not," Richard confirmed.

Richard was overruled, and Elspet Barr's father was brought to the bar, where he swore on oath that Simon was a consummate, unconscionable rogue, a whoremonger, swingeour, fanatic and thief. But beyond that, he had proof of no specifics, and Richard soon established that he had not seen his son-in-law in years. What he knew beyond a doubt, beyond a doubt, he could not prove.

Since Crichton had no further proof, Richard addressed the jury:

"Good men of inquest, you have heard my lord Crichton put forward as probation a confession, which you have heard the defendant disown. I ask you to disregard this confession, for it was not made in your hearing, nor, in your presence, has the panel owned to it; therefore, the confession is not proved, and to admit it as probation of the charge were *wilful error on assize*. You have heard, too, the testimony of a witness put forward as probation, yet that witness told you nothing of what happened on the stairs. He cannot tell you what did happen, for he was not there. Therefore, the evidence he gives was mere presumption, and you cannot convict on presumption alone; to do so would be error on assize. Now my lord Crichton here will try to intimidate you, and to convince you that the opposite is true; that because you may presume guilt here, then you must convict. But I would bid you ask yourselves, where are the proofs? My lord Crichton will say, the proof is Simon Pettigrew's confession, that he made before the magistrate. Ask yourselves, though, has he confessed to *you*? The answer must be: he has not. Ask yourselves, then, has he owned his confession? The answer must be: he has not. And whatever you may think of this, whatever you *presume*, ask yourselves, did my lord Crichton *prove* the panel killed his wife. And, if he did not, you must acquit."

Robert Crichton stood up heavily. "Good men of assize," he stated, "this man has confessed, and you heard his confession. And that he has confessed, and then retracted his confession, is a ploy made by his advocate, to baffle and confuse. You know this man. You know his guilt. And to determine otherwise were error on assize."

The justice smiled. "Now, we're done. Unless there is a question?" He glanced at the assize, with a blankness of expression that suggested "Surely not." A stout man in leggings began to raise his hand, before he caught the judge's eye, and quickly put it down. The justice nodded sagely. "Well and good. The inquest may retire."

As the jury trooped out, Richard joined Hew at the side of the bench. "Now we must wait in hope of a sensible verdict," he whispered. "That lies in the jury's hands, for every case is lost or won, in the moment of selection of assize. The jury is the advocate's best ally, and his greatest threat. The most important thing is to learn to read the jury, and to understand their minds before they are sworn in," he went on to explain. "Take great care in making objections. They are not formalities to delay the trial, but often form the key to a defence. Of those summonsed, you may turn away two thirds, without giving a cause."

"Are there always fifteen jurors?" Hew inquired.

"There may be several more or less. But an odd number is preferred, ensuring a majority. A single vote is sufficient to convict or acquit. The verdict of each man is recorded against his name, and he must own to it. In case of wilful error, each man is accountable, and may not hide his face among the crowd. As to what you look for, in objecting to your jury, that will vary case by case. For sometimes you require them to be stupid, easily bamboozled and perplexed, and at other times you want a careful jury, that will comprehend your subtleties and follow through the process of the law. At all times, you will want a jury partial to your client. In this, the defence is at a disadvantage, since the lord advocate draws up the list, and he, in his turn, will object to those who appear to favour your client, even as you are objecting to those who seem to favour his. And, in as much as the pursuer must pay their expenses, they are in his pocket even before it begins."

"Then there can be no impartial juries," Hew objected.

"Indeed not. Their position is a strange one, straddling judge and witness. On the one hand, the role of the assize is to hear probation, and to assess, on the basis of the law, whether what it hears is proved. But on the other, the assize is called from those who have foreknowledge of the case; they know both parties, and are predetermined of the panel's innocence or guilt. I have seen trials, where the defence has sought permission to examine witnesses, and the justice has refused, on the grounds that the jury are quite adequate as witnesses themselves, for they already know the panel as a rogue. Therefore, our role as defence is to preclude those jurors who are set against our client, in so far as we can, and if we are not able to, then to bypass their prejudice, convincing them that they must listen to probation, and that what is stated is not proved, or, failing that, to offset their prejudice, with threats and promises, or bribes. It is a hazardous path, and one that takes some years to circumvent, learning how to read the jury — who remains resolute, who is impressionable."

Before Hew could reply, the jury reappeared, and Richard returned to the bar. The justice peered down from his stage. "Have you a verdict?"

"Aye, my lord," replied their chancellor. "By majority, of nine to six, the panel is acquit."

Richard gave a quick tight smile. "A bottle won of gascon wine, I think," he muttered quietly to Hew. He bowed to Robert Crichton, who reciprocated stiffly, as they left the court.

"I do not often take to drinking claret in the middle of the day," he excused himself, "yet we shall allow ourselves a cup or two, as testimony to our small success. I know a place, not far from the netherbow, where we can drink in private, the better to unpick our triumphs and replay them."

They walked towards the netherbow port, near to Christian's printing house, stopping at a close upon the north side, just before the gate.

157

"The taverner is Robert Fletcher, that keeps the caichpule for Master Patrick Fleming, of Patrick Fleming's close," Richard explained. "Fletcher has a chamber at the back of his house that overlooks the tennis play, likely to be quiet at this hour."

The caichpular seemed to know Richard well, for he received them warmly. "The room is empty for an hour, sir, and the court. Will you play?"

"No, alas, another time," Richard said regrettably. "We have business to conclude. May I ask you do not let the court this present hour? You know my terms. And we would like a jug of gascon wine, your very best."

Fletcher nodded. "It will be sent up to you, sir."

"Do you keep the caichpule, for your private use?" Hew asked, amused, as they settled on their stools. The room was small and dark, no more than a closet enclosed, at the top and the back of the house, but it had the advantage of a long partition opening downwards, that overlooked the tennis court, behind the service end, allowing full view of the play.

"I have an understanding with Fletcher," Richard smiled. "The caichpule is my passion, though I have so little time to play, with work, and family life, both of which, you know, are close and dear to me. I come to practise here on Sunday afternoons. Fletcher is a pillar of the kirk, and most devout; he will not hire the tennis court on Sundays, and his tavern doors are closed, most properly, through the hours of prayer. Yet though he will not hire the court, he is not averse to profit, and so we are come to an arrangement. He locks the court on Sunday, and goes to evening service, knowing all the while, of course, I have a key. He leaves the balls in place below the net. Thus, I have my practice on a Sunday afternoon, and Fletcher's conscience is not troubled by my play. For this, I pay him a retainer through the week, which allows me private access to this room. Pray, do not tell Eleanor. She thinks I spend the hours in religious meditation."

Fletcher returned with a lantern, two cups and a flagon of wine, and Richard poured their drinks. "The most difficult part," he explained to Hew, "was persuading Simon Pettigrew that he should confess."

Hew sipped his wine, shaking his head. "What I do not understand is why he needed to confess. If Robert Crichton had no proof . . ."

"You miss the point. Crichton had no proof because Pettigrew confessed. And because he had confessed, Crichton saw no need to look for proof. After all, he knew that Pettigrew was guilty of the crime. If Pettigrew had not confessed, then Crichton would have called for witnesses. It's likely that he would have found them. The turnpike is a common stairway, in a busy close."

"You mean to say . . ."

"Pettigrew was guilty, Hew. He killed his wife. And everyone there knew it; or rather, they presumed it so. Crichton knew it, and he knew that Pettigrew had confessed, and so he did not bother to look for further proof. He is an old man, at the close of his career, and his concerns are now with bigger things. He is fixed upon the Morton trial. He did not care so much about this little case. He was complacent, and he let his eye slip from the ball, so oftentimes returned without a thought; he did not read the angle when it came."

"Will Crichton not indict the jury, to assize of error?" questioned Hew.

"I think that unlikely. The truth is that he failed to prove the case. He will not care to have his failings held to scrutiny. Nor, since his probation was negligent, would he be likely to win. Those members of assize who voted in our favour were aware of this. I had convinced them that their actions were most proper to the law. Crichton knows it too. He has fallen to the simplest trick, and will hope to keep it quiet. In any case, even if the jury were indicted, and convicted, of assize of error, the verdict would still stand, and Pettigrew go free. But you are very quiet, Hew. I'm afraid you disapprove," Richard said perceptively.

Hew hesitated. "May I speak plainly?" he asked.

"I wish that you would." Richard smiled.

"I am conscious of your kindness, and am more than grateful for it. You have taken me into your home, and extended every courtesy. I would not offend you for the world."

"There is nothing that you cannot say to me. I am your friend."

"I am your pupil, sir."

Richard burst out laughing. "And a more reluctant one I have not seen. Peace, I will not have you whipped! What is on your mind?"

"It is the case," Hew confessed. "I understand its subtleties, and I applaud your cleverness, and yet that case was everything that I detest about the law. It is a game of tricks, playing with men's lives."

Richard was silent a moment. Then he answered gravely, "You are right, of course."

"I am sorry," Hew said simply.

"No, not at all. You cause me no offence. But I confess, I am to blame in showing you this case, where by my subtlety a guilty man walks free."

"I do not blame you," whispered Hew. "In truth, I admired you, and that makes me ashamed."

"It was a thoughtless case to pick. And I allowed my vanity to overcome good sense, in showing it to you. The truth is, I had hoped to right a wrong," Richard answered seriously, "but with another wrong, and that was simply pride. You are correct, this is a game of tricks. And I have waited for a long while to use that particular trick. Do you know who told it to me?"

Hew shook his head, knowing that he did not want to know. Richard went on gently, "But I think you do. It was your father. I have waited in the shade for twenty years, to see it work on Robert Crichton. Therefore, though I understand your scruples and applaud them — believe me, I do understand them — you must understand my satisfaction."

"Forgive me, sir, I do admire your skill."

"But not my pride," Richard answered dryly. "I think you may be right, in that you are not well suited to the law. Yet for your reservations in this case, I blame myself; the trial was not well chosen. There is something about you, Hew, I know not what it is, that makes me want to show you my worse side."

"You have shown me nothing but kindness," Hew protested.

"That was my intention. Do you play tennis?" Richard put in suddenly.

"Aye, when I can."

"Then you and I shall play a game sometime. I warn you, though, I may not be so gracious in defeat." Richard gave a sigh. "Ah, well, I must return to work. I can spare you for an hour or two, till suppertime. Will you return to the printing house? It is close to here, I think."

"Aye, across the street. Do you not mind it, sir?" Hew replied politely.

"Of course I do not mind. I am afraid I misled you into thinking that I disapproved of Matthew's book. But I was merely curious. I should be very glad to see it. I suppose it is now in the grip of the press?"

"They have begun to work on it. It will take a little time, for the manuscript was damaged in the Forth," acknowledged Hew.

"Then I must wish you luck with it. And the printer, Christian Hall. You say she is a widow. Do you know how Matthew came to know her husband?"

"No, that is a mystery. I hope that the goldsmith, George Urquhart, will be able to explain it."

"That is more than possible," Richard answered thoughtfully. "When you have your letters, I will introduce you."

Family Ties

In the collating room, Christian had removed the damaged papers from their binding and set them out in order on the floor. Where the pages were stuck together she had slit them apart with a blade and in part had managed to keep the letters intact: the iron gall ink was waterproof, and could only be removed by shearing with a knife. But in places, the top surface of the paper had been damaged and the letters had transferred onto the other side. These parts Hew was forced to reconstruct, to supply the missing words as best he could. With Christian's help, he began to make some progress and they worked together on the manuscript until the light began to fade. Hew was conscious of the business in the main shop, where a constant flow of visitors appeared to come and go, and once or twice they were interrupted by the week boy, Michael, or by Walter, with a stack of pages from the press to be hung up to dry. But for the main part, they were alone. And Hew discovered he quite liked the work, tedious and slow, in Christian's gentle company.

At last Christian said, "It is almost dark. Nonetheless, we have made a start. Can you come tomorrow, and go on with it?"

"I hope so," answered Hew. "It depends on Master Cunningham. I am beholden to him now, and if he wants me to attend him, then I must."

"I understand." She smiled at him. "And do you like the courts?"

"Not at all. The courts are tainted and corrupt. In truth," he confided recklessly, "I would much rather be here."

"Truly? That is strange." Christian looked surprised. "For we are working on a law book, after all. And though I can know little of such things, I confess, it seems a little dull to me. I should have thought the courts were more diverting."

Hew broke into a grin. "Though it pains me to say so, the book appears blindingly dull. It's true the practice is a little more engaging than the text. My father was an eloquent and most persuasive advocate. And yet he had a way with words that wrung the life from them whenever he committed them to ink. Yet, I have enjoyed the last few hours more than I can say. It is the company."

Christian blushed, unused to compliment. "If you like it here," she ventured, "then perhaps you'll stay awhile. It is our custom, at the close of day, to have a little supper in the shop, in what printers call the chapel. Would you like to share it with us? It's nothing grand."

Hew was touched. "I should like to very much."

He followed her back into the main part of the printing house, where Walter was rinsing off forms in the trough, and Phillip distributed type, newly washed, in his cases to dry overnight. The week boy unpicked the ink balls, leaving the leather to soak. Hew leant against the wall and watched their preparations as they put the press to bed. Finally, Phillip lit the lamps and said politely to Hew. "I will lock up the shop now, and say our goodnights to you, sir."

"Master Cullan will stay," Christian contradicted, "and share a bite with us."

"Indeed?" Phillip looked alarmed. "Ah, that is a pity . . . no, I do not mean that, sir . . . only there is something I had wanted to discuss."

Christian bit her lip. "If it is a matter for the chapel, then you may speak freely. Hew is our friend. In truth, he owns us, Phillip."

"Aye, I had forgotten that," the compositor allowed. "I must beg your pardon, sir. Lady Catherine Douglas called. We are to print her poems, and they are almost ready for the press. And," he added quietly to Christian, "I have made your feelings plain to Allan Chapman. He will not trouble you again."

Christian coloured. She was so very fair, reflected Hew, that the slightest hint of awkwardness showed clearly in her face. He found her openness appealing. "We must hope so," she said quickly. "Thank you, Phillip. Will you go upstairs, and see if Alison is home with William? They went walking by the burgh loch."

"He is a little too protective," she remarked to Hew as Phillip left. "He keeps our secrets close."

"It is a mark of good intent; he cares for you," acknowledged Hew.

"He is a loyal friend. And also, to speak truth, he has cause for his suspicions." Christian blushed. "Things

165

have not gone well for us of late. There is someone in this town who wants us out."

"Truly? Who is that?"

"The printer, Master Chapman," she admitted.

"Whose attentions Phillip has discouraged?" Hew said shrewdly.

"Aye," she looked away, "he says he wants to marry me."

"Which is not quite the same," Hew pointed out, "as wanting you out."

"It is the same," insisted Christian. "It's the press he wants, not me."

"Then he has poor judgement," Hew said lightly, "and will not make a go of it."

Christian flushed. "It is not a jest, Hew. I did think he meant well. But Chapman has done us great harm. You know I told you we were frozen out? We have fallen behind with our work. In particular, a large order of tracts we were printing for Henry Charteris; one of which you saw the other day. Charteris is a bailie on the burgh council, and he has been good to us since William died. But he is a man of business nonetheless, and he expects his work on time. Chapman offered to help out. He had an old press, in the laich house of his printing shop, that was little used, and he offered us the use of it, for it was warm and dry. His own press had escaped the worst effects of frost. And so we set up shop there for a day or two. He even lent a journeyman, to help complete the work. As you will understand, the laich house was quite dark, and not well placed for printing. Still, with lanterns and by candlelight, we managed it. Phillip and Walter were careful, as always, to put out the lanterns at night, and extinguish every flame. But there was a fire. Someone left a candle burning in the night, and the press caught light. All our forms and letters were engulfed, and the pages we had printed turned to ash, together with the copy. Strange to say, the fire was contained in the cellar. Chapman's own house was untouched."

"You mean to say he set the fire deliberately? But that is murderous! Was there no redress?"

"I am convinced he did," Christian nodded. "Yet we have no proof. Chapman blamed the fire on Phillip. He almost had him charged with it. We could not prove we had not left our candles burning in the night. I know Phillip," she concluded quietly, "as I know myself. And I am quite certain he was not responsible. It was Chapman's boy who set the fire. Chapman was solicitous — aye, quite solicitous. He went straight to Henry Charteris, and told him he would do the work himself, for half the fee. And so we lost that portion of the contract, though Charteris has allowed us to fulfil the rest. Since then, Chapman has pursued me like the plague. Each day he comes and makes another offer, more insistent and insulting than the last: I will have to marry him, or else sell him the press, for tis clear I cannot manage on my own."

"There must be some recourse to justice," protested Hew.

"I do not have the money to pursue it. And I do not have the time. Phillip says, that it were better to make good our loss ourselves, and carry on."

"I cannot think that that is good advice. You must consult a man of law."

Christian pulled a face. "And you are the one who was telling me, that the law is tainted and corrupt."

"Let me think on this," Hew persisted thoughtfully. "I'm sure that I can help. And, as you say, I have a proper interest in the press."

Christian shook her head. "It's best to leave it, Hew. We can manage it alone. You do not understand the workings of the council."

"Aye, I had a glimpse of them," admitted Hew, "and did not much like what I saw."

"Then let us hope our fortunes change," Christian answered, "with your father's book."

Phillip had returned with Alison, the nurse, and William, who was gnawing on an apple. Christian exclaimed, "Where did you get that?"

"*Man*," said the child elliptically, and took another bite. The apple was wizened and dry.

"What man? Alison, you must not let him take things," Christian remonstrated.

The nursemaid pouted. "The fruitman gave it to him. The bairn was girning on the street, and he had an apple rotten on one side — he cut the bad bit off. William has been fretful all the day," she returned defensively.

"For a bairn to have an apple," Phillip said to Christian, "surely does no harm. You're as bad as he is, for you fret too much."

"I do not like that Alison consorts so much with strangers," Christian asserted. But she relaxed a little, reassured, and lifted up the little boy to sit him in her lap. "Put aside your apple now, for here is Michael with the cheese."

Hew watched as Alison and Michael made a picnic table out of the correcting stone. They took a pair of cording quires — the outer sheets of waste that bound the reams of paper — to set down as a cloth, and prepared a little meal of oatcakes and crowdie, bannocks and salt fish, with green ale for the grownups and small beer for the child. Hew was passed a cup and a trencher cut from bread as Walter toasted stale crusts on the fire. It was not the finest supper Hew had eaten in his life, but in many ways, it seemed the sweetest, eaten on the floor in the faltering candlelight. Phillip fetched a fiddle and began to play a jig, fast and furious at first, then mellowing to medleys sad and slow. Michael's lips were dripping as he listened open-mouthed, and Hew exclaimed, "That boy is eating ink!"

Christian laughed, "It's the linseed oil. He likes it."

The boy grinned, wiping his mouth with the back of his hand, smearing his whole face with black. But the spell was broken. The compositor set down his bow. "Michael likes to look the part." He returned the fiddle to its box and left the room.

Hew had forgotten that the Cunninghams expected him for supper. He was not used to family life, and found it hard, though not for want of kindness on their part. As a small child, he had lived with his parents on the Cowgate. He went, once or twice, to look at the

169

house, but his mother's face remained blurred; she had died when Meg was born and Hew was Grace's age.

Hew found Grace disconcerting, for the child had taken to him, with a clear and steady trust he felt was undeserved. She missed her older brother James, an ally in her daily battles against Roger. Roger was fretful and taut, and Hew could not quite fathom him; though in his anger with his father, he sensed something of himself. When Hew was Roger's age, Matthew had retired to Kenly Green, leaving Hew behind to lodge with his high master, a man Hew still remembered with alarm, and no great lasting fondness. At fourteen, he had moved up to St Andrews, to the university; for four years among boys and men, he saw little of his family. Then he had gone to France. And coming home at last, he found an old man and a grave young woman, secretive and strange, where he had left a father and a little sister, and had had to get to know them once again. Therefore, but for snatches, he had never known his sister as a child.

Richard, though he sparred with Roger, doted on his children, with a fierce and partial pride. Outside the hours of court, he was devoted to his wife and family, and their happiness and comfort was his main concern. It was a mark of his generosity, and that of all his family, that he extended this concern to Hew. Hew's place in their home was accepted and assured, and it was only this unwonted kindness that left him feeling awkward, in a house where he was never left a stranger, nor ever felt that he was out of place.

170

★ ★ ★

Richard kept a small buith on the north side of the high street, in Leche's close, a little further eastwards of the cross, where he received his clients, and where he liked to sit in the quiet hours of morning, preparing for the clamour of the day. It was there that Hew found him as the sun began to lift, a little after six. Richard closed his book.

"I do not expect you to keep the hours that I do."

"I wanted some advice," explained Hew, "but I fear I am disturbing you."

"Not at all. My habits are my own, and peculiarly entrenched. In the early mornings you will find me here, and the early evening hours are reserved to share with family. All the other hours, I am at work. But all my time is placed at your disposal, if I am of use to you."

Hew shook his head. "I thank, you, sir. I do not deserve your kindness."

"Don't you?" Richard looked amused. "We must wait and see. Sit down there, and tell me what is troubling you." He stretched and stood up, walking to the window. "This is my favourite part of the day," he confided. "I like to see the world unfolding. There are no carts, no hucksters, in the early hours. I like it when the lanterns snuff out in the darkness, and a gradual waking creeps across the sky; the noisy, dirty, smoky city stirring, like a phantom in the loch, before the hungry monster roars."

"I had not quite considered it that way," reflected Hew. "It is dirty, certainly; noisy, thick and foul."

"But even the stench from the loch has its charm, don't you think? Perhaps not . . ." Richard mused.

"Do you ever spend the night here?" Hew asked.

"Sometimes, before a particularly difficult case. But Eleanor does not like it. I confess, I may not come as late or early as I like."

Hew nodded. "My brother-in-law, Giles, has a similar problem. He sometimes falls asleep in his consulting rooms. Though he is only lately married, which is worse."

"Indeed. Eleanor has grown patient, or else worn out of complaints, after all these years." Richard smiled gently. "What can I do for you?"

Hew sat in the chair reserved for clients and explained, "I wondered what you knew about the burgh courts? Specifically, what rights the printer has, and how he might protect his trade, when others seek to damage it."

Richard scratched his head. "I confess, not much. That falls within the burgh council who license and take action as required. It is, I understand, well regulated though. As far as I can see, there are many petty jealousies among the printing trade. By the day, buiths and stalls are appearing in the crames, with all manner of pamphlets, books and playing cards — Eleanor bought a packet just the other day — and few of them are licensed by the burgh council. Some will pay their fines and stake their claims, and within a month or two are trading with the freemen, when last month they were foreigners, and complaining about the next load of foreigners, who impinge upon their trade.

In general, the burgh welcomes printers, and is happy to encourage them, providing what they print is not scurrilous or scandalous or treasonous or troublesome, and does not upset the clergy or the king.

"The man who could tell you more is the printer Henry Charteris. Or the first bailie, Thomas Wishart. You have met him once before. He is the man who arrested you when you arrived."

Hew pulled a face. "I may give that a miss."

"I understand your qualms. They are a most officious crowd," said Richard, sympathetically. "What did you require, specifically?"

"It is Christian Hall. It appears that another printer has a grudge against her, and has tried to close her down."

"She is a widow, who took on her husband's press," Richard remarked.

"Aye, she is."

"And therefore she is vulnerable. The likelihood is that this man — for, of course, it is a man — hopes to put her out of business, or to make her trade so hard she is obliged to sell."

"It looks that way." Hew told Richard about the fire. "But fire-raising, surely, is a matter for the justice court, and not the burgh," he concluded.

"For certain, a plea of the Crown. But can it be proved? To leave a candle burning, though it may be careless, does not constitute a crime."

"But is Christian not entitled to some reparation, in as much as this occurred on Chapman's premises?" Hew persisted.

"As to that, I cannot say. It is a matter for the burgh court. I hazard, though, it will be thought an accident, and Chapman cleared of any blame, and any debt to her."

"Well then, is there a way to stop his intimidation of her?"

"How is it manifest?"

"He claims he wants to marry her."

Richard burst out laughing. "I do not think the courts would count that a threat to her. You mentioned that she had a child?"

Hew nodded. "Aye, a little boy."

"Then I imagine that the council would encourage her to take up Chapman's offer. It is difficult enough do the work, without a child. Therefore it is hard to prove that there is any ill intent. May I ask you something?"

"Aye, of course."

"You seem a little too . . . *involved* with Christian Hall. Do you think it wise?"

Hew coloured. "My father invested deeply in her press; I feel connected to her," he explained.

"That I understand," said Richard thoughtfully. "Have you made much progress with the book?"

"We have started the first chapter. But the work is very long. And, if I dare to say it, rather tedious. It will take a little time to restore the damaged parts. With your permission, I will go this afternoon, and return to it."

"You could, perhaps, bring the manuscript here, where there are fewer — shall we say — distractions," suggested Richard.

"I thank you, but the book has been broken in parts, and takes up a great deal of space. And if I make corrections in the printing house, they can be set more quickly, as I go along," Hew answered hurriedly. It was a poor excuse, and one that scarcely hid the truth: he wanted to see Christian. Richard looked displeased for a moment, and then smiled. Hew recognised his mood, and his control of it.

"I am afraid you may be falling in too deep," Richard answered thoughtfully. "And I think that as your friend I ought to find out more of this. Who is Christian Hall? For I confess, I do not know the press, and I know nothing of her husband. There is a tale attached to the premises she has; for they belonged to someone else before."

"Another printer?" queried Hew.

"Another printer, aye, that went away. But that is not my point. Where did Christian come from? And how did she know your father? Her house is somewhat far from Kenly Green, and somewhat close to mine, yet I had never heard of it. And since her press prints books about the law, I should perhaps have heard of it."

"I think that this is a new departure," Hew explained. "I have the impression, that it was a small and private press; printing bills and leaflets, pamphlets and so on, and not so many books. It seems my father financed it. Perhaps, after all, it was an old man's foolishness: he wanted to make sure they would take on his book. It is unlike him, certainly. I never thought him vain. But it is evident his interest in the press ran deep, for he went so far as choosing the device. It was the

175

mark that confused me, at the start, for I had supposed it was Christian's, though in fact it was her husband's. He was William Hall."

"If he was William Hall," Richard mused, "then who was she?"

"That the strangest thing. She does not seem to know, or else she does not want to tell me. I thought perhaps the goldsmith, Urquhart, might know more."

Richard was silent for a moment. Then he said thoughtfully, "I think it very likely that he does. Urquhart is a great repository of facts. He keeps his secrets close. He is the most elusive man, for he has no curiosity. And people tell him things, because he does not care. Well then, we must sound him out, before you fall in love with her."

Hew was startled. "I do not mean to fall in love with her!" he protested.

Richard laughed, "As to that, it is quite clear that you do, and that nothing I can say has hope of dissuading you. Therefore, I suggest that we find out who she is."

He walked towards the window, looking out. "The streets begin to fill. It is never still for long," he said. "Already I can hear the hucksters, practising their cries, though the markets do not properly begin till noon. The restless monster does not sleep for long. You mentioned a device. What was that?"

"The letter H entwined about a cross, for Christian and for Hall."

"I thought you said it was the husband's mark?"

"Aye, it was. It makes no sense. The H was for him, and the cross was meant for her, and so it seems the

176

press belonged to both of them. And above this is the tree of knowledge, that is often found on books, and sitting in the tree there is a black bird, like a raven or a crow, and no one seems to know what that might mean, but Christian says, it was my father's wish to have the corbie."

"A corbie?" Richard murmured. "That is strange. You don't know, I suppose, what that signified to him?"

"I confess, I can't imagine," answered Hew. "It is another mystery."

A Corbie Messenger

"We are running out of ink," Richard remarked, poking his head round the door, "and the clerk is at the council house. Perhaps you would be good enough to fetch some from the stationer, and to call at home, where I have left a letter I shall have to answer presently. It is from a distant cousin of my wife, and bears the Preston seal. You will find it in the writing desk, in my private closet." He handed Hew a key.

Hew accepted gladly, grateful for the air. He was pleased at Richard's trust, for Richard had been occupied all morning with a stream of personal clients that showed no sign of slowing, none of whom would let him listen in. Hew had spent the hours in the servant's cubicle, feeling stiff and bored. He left Richard to his work and wandered through the town, prepared to take his time. The stationer kept shop across the street, at the east end of the luckenbooths, the row of shops that stretched down from the tolbooth, along the northern aspect of St Giles. They occupied the space of seven tenements, with over buiths above, and further storeys in the process of construction, in keeping with the upward progress of the town. They had narrowed the street on the north side to a tight little lane, known as the buith raw, squeezing out the light from every house. In the middle of the luckenbooths an arched passage led through to the kirk stile, the porch of the kirk of St Giles. More commonly referred to as the stinking stile, this passageway collected all the debris from the shops, thrown from upper windows to the backside of the street. Behind it, between luckenbooths and kirk, were makeshift stalls set out against the north wall of the church, spilling from each buttress, nook and cranny. Hew walked now among these chapmen, watching as they opened out their stalls. He was astonished at how much they could fit in so small a place. Some sold haberdashery, silks and linens, buttons, lace and threads. Others offered silverware or pewter spoons and cups. There were vinegars and oil, cinnamon and cloves, and every type of metalwork, from knife and pot handles to buckles and locks, from scissors to purses and pins. There were chess sets too, and playing cards, and tiny painted horses made of lead or wood. All the trappings and effects of an inner world were found among the crames, the small essential fragments that made up domestic life. And yet the merchants were ephemeral, locking up their secrets when the markets closed. Hew thought he recognised a figure at the far side of the lane, but by the time he made his way there, the man had disappeared. And that was the sense that he had of the cramers, like Egyptian story-tellers, fugitive from law, they could come and go as easily as dreams.

Hew bought the ink and continued to the house for Richard's letter. He found the children playing in the hall and paused to watch, for Grace was building cards into a house.

"Those are pretty," Hew observed, as the card tower tumbled down. "Where did you get them?"

"Minnie bought them from a man in town. She thought that they might help me learn." The child pulled a face. "My father has sent away the nurse, and engaged a mistress. She speaks to me in French."

"She was once a maid," explained Roger, "that belonged to the old queen, Mary. Father thought she might teach Grace some better manners. I think that unlikely, though."

"I have good manners, don't I?" the little girl appealed to Hew.

"Certainly, you do."

"I don't like Jehanne," she pouted. "She is old, and smells of garlic."

"My sister, you recall, has a most discerning nose," Roger said unpleasantly to Hew.

His sister scowled. "Is he making fun of me?"

"I might suspect he mocked us both," Hew told her solemnly, "if I believed, he could be so discourteous." Roger had the grace to blush.

"Are you not at school today?" asked Hew.

"Roger has the cough, and the master finds it tiresome," Grace answered for him. "*Actually*, so do we."

Hew laughed. "Poor Roger! We must hope he will be better soon."

"Do you speak French?" Grace went on.

"A little," Hew admitted.

Roger said, "French is for girls and dancing masters," and Hew ignored him. Grace replied, "I should like a dancing master. But we don't have dancing here. Who was it taught you French?"

"A French girl called Colette," Hew answered gravely.

"Was she bonny?"

"Aye, she was," he smiled at her.

"Jehanne is fat and ugly. And she does not know how to dance. I think that was why the queen left her behind, when she went away."

"How stupid you are," Roger sneered.

Hew said hurriedly, "May I see the cards? I have a pack like this at home."

"Aye, very well," Grace sighed. "I cannot make them stand up, anyway. They keep on falling down. Look, I do know the names. This one is the sun, *le soleil*, and this one is *le roy*, the king; and here is the devil," she made a little shiver, "*le diable*; and this one," she screwed up her face, "is . . . *le pen-du* . . ."

"The hanged man," said Roger, looking over her shoulder.

"I *know* that, he's the hanging man. Why is he upside down?"

"Because he is a traitor," Roger said maliciously, "the worst type of thief. Tis likely that before they hanged him they would —"

"Likely, aye, but not for little girls," Hew interrupted hurriedly. Roger grinned.

"They make up a game of triumphs. Do you know how to play it?" he asked Hew.

"Certainly, I do."

"Then will you teach it to us?" Grace implored.

"If your mother will allow it — though I fear that means no. Meantime, let us try again to build your tower."

Hew was thoughtful as he handed back the cards. He had seen the pack before, or one very like it, in St Andrews on the stall of Marten Voet.

Hew fell into a pattern of attending Richard in the morning, either in the court house or his buith in Leche's close. When the courts were not in session, his afternoons were free. Most of them he spent in Christian's shop, correcting Matthew's copy, or reading out to Phillip as he set the type. Hew came to admire the compositor's skill, and the speed with which he set the type by touch, without looking down to the letters, and he learned to stand where he did not block the light, and not to touch the formes before they were locked into the chases. Walter and Phillip worked in curious harmony, each regulated by the motions of the other, each goading on the other to increase his speed. Michael meanwhile ran between them, and fetched and carried as required, while Christian collected and collated the texts, prepared the sheets for binding, and dealt with any customers. And Hew began to learn the printer's cant and customs, which amused him with their quaintness; how each new year they made fresh paper windows, to protect the pages from the sun; how

Walter was a *horse* and Phillip was a *galley slave*, though to say so in their hearing resulted in a solace, or a fine. These solaces, for transgressions of the printing house, were collected at the week's end and translated into liquor, for the little suppers that the chapel shared. And Hew began to look forward to those evenings most of all, when Christian would pull off her apron and cap, shake loose her hair and sit down by the fire, and Phillip would take out his fiddle and play, while William spun himself dizzy and chased round the room, flushed from his walks on the muir.

On Thursday next, unusually, the pattern was reversed, for Richard had some private business in the late hours of the morning, and excused Hew from his office till the afternoon. Hew arrived at Christian's shop a little after ten, to find the place in sombre mood. Walter and Phillip were both working furiously, while Michael and Christian were nowhere to be seen.

"What has happened?" Hew inquired of Phillip, who simply replied with a shrug, without taking his eyes from the frame. It was Walter who answered, "Christian has dismissed Michael."

"Whatever for?" asked Hew.

"He made a mistake," muttered Phillip. "One of his tricks missed its mark."

"I should say, rather, it hit it. It was not proper to dismiss him though," reasoned Walter. "And it was not reasonable. For what are we to do without a week boy? We are hard enough pressed at it is."

Hew smiled at the pun, but clearly no jest was intended.

Phillip warned, "Since that is the case, more work, less talk, must be the remedy here."

"But what has Michael done?" persisted Hew.

Walter jerked an elbow to the door of the collating room. "Look over there."

Pushing open the door, Hew saw nothing amiss. The uncorrected parts of Matthew's manuscript were stacked in a pile on the table to the right, next to the corrected copy and a stack of folded sheets for Henry Charteris. There was nothing out of place. Then he noticed a small packet on the floor, lying careless in a corner, as though someone had dropped it there, incongruous in the neatly ordered room. He placed it on the table and unwrapped it. Inside he found the carcass of a bird, a blue-black ball of feathers on a brittle stack of bones. A translucent eye protruded limply from its socket. Pinned to the breast was a white scrap of paper, printed with the words "Ane corbie messenger."

Hew took the parcel back into the printing house. "What's this?" He dropped the bird on the correcting stone.

"God's truth, but not on there!" objected Phillip. "The wretched boy has played a trick and Christian has dismissed him for it. He has gone too far."

"What can he have meant by it?" asked Hew.

Phillip shrugged. "Who knows?"

"He will not admit to it," interjected Walter. "He claims, the packet was already in the shop, when he came in with the ink this morning. Plainly, he was lying."

184

"Is it so plain?" Hew wondered quietly. He folded the dead crow back in its packet. "Where's Christian?" he demanded.

"It is not convenient for you to be here," Phillip said tersely. "We are too busy. And Christian is not well today. She has no time to help you with your father's book. Go and worry some poor debtor, or whatever else you do."

As he spoke, Christian appeared from upstairs. "I heard voices. Is something amiss?" she inquired anxiously. Then she saw the package in Hew's hands.

"I told the boy to take that with him," she said tonelessly. "Since he has not done so, Walter must dispose of it."

"I can take it with me, if you like," offered Hew.

Christian answered coldly, "Put it down."

"I would like to call a meeting," Phillip said abruptly.

"Call it now, we are all here," Christian replied. "And if you can call it without stopping work, then so much the better. We are behind enough."

Phillip sighed. "If you will leave the work a moment, but to hear me out, it would oblige me. The matter is of some importance."

"If you would pick up your letter, and go on with it, it would oblige me, Phillip. Or Walter will stand idle, and it will fall to you to make good his losses."

"This wants reason!" Phillip countered crossly, "though I know the bird upset you —"

"How is that?" Christian turned on him. "A child's trick! How should that upset me?"

"It should not," he told her earnestly, "for that is all it was. Michael at his tricks and afraid to own it. He has gone too far. But was it proper to dismiss him, for a childish jape? And besides, we want a week boy. Who will fetch and carry? Let me speak with him, and Walter here will bring him to a state of right contrition. Let him say he's sorry, and allow him back."

"I will correct him," Walter promised cheerfully, "on the correcting stone." He winked humorously at Hew, who was sickened.

"You think it *was* Michael?" Christian hesitated.

"I am convinced of it," Phillip assured her. "He is still a bairn, and did not understand that it would fright you. Let me put it right."

"As you will," she conceded quietly. "I pray you, do not mention this again."

Hew spent the afternoon in conference with Richard, who wanted to discuss the finer points of spuilzie, and the hours passed slowly. But excused at last, while Richard had some business in the court house, he came by the printing house to see the week boy emerge, red-eyed, with the crow held out in front of him, swinging by its feet, like a leper's bell, or the heretic's indictment of his sin. On impulse, Hew caught up with him.

"Where do you go with that, I wonder?"

"I am to drown it in the loch," the boy mumbled, in a voice suggesting he had not long dried his tears. "Not *drown it*, for tis dead already, but to be rid of it there," he corrected, unnecessarily.

186

"The north loch is foul enough without that, don't you think? Why not bury it upon the shore. I will help you find a place." Hew took advantage of the boy's hesitation, leaning forward to relieve him of the bird, and walked along beside him till they reached the loch. Michael sniffed a little, but did not demur.

"Here's a likely spot, now. Make a grave," suggested Hew.

The act of digging seemed to cheer the boy, as it was meant to; and when they had a chasm they judged big enough to hold the bird, Hew placed it in the hole and crossed its wings, with a grave solemnity well-judged to make him grin, in shared and secret sacrilege. Michael smiled a little wanly, and was brave enough to lift the paper from the corpse, and venture timidly. "*Ane corbie messenger.* What does that mean?"

"The raven that Noah sent forth from the ark, in the story of the flood; it signifies false messenger, or one that comes late, or comes not at all." Hew looked at him curiously. "You did not write it, then?"

The boy shook his head. "I cannot write, sir. Phillip has been teaching me my letters," he said simply. "But we have little time for it. I can read a little, though," he added proudly.

"And you did not kill the crow?"

The boy looked close to tears. He shook his head. "I never saw the bird, before Christian found the parcel. And I never brought the parcel. It was lying in the shop, when we opened up."

"Then why did you confess to it?" Hew persisted gently.

187

"Phillip said I must." The boy wiped his nose on his sleeve.

"I think that you like Phillip very much."

"I admire him, sir. He is teaching me my letters," Michael answered desperately, "which will help me set good copy. I would wish to be like him, if I can."

"And you do not like Christian," Hew concluded.

Michael said judiciously, "I do not mind her much. She is a woman."

Hew laughed. "Aye, then, there's the rub. You do not mind her when you should."

"How can a woman be master, sir, over a man like Phillip!" the boy burst out. "It is not right!"

"Is that what Phillip says?"

"No, sir. Phillip likes her," the boy admitted grudgingly.

"So Phillip told you to confess?"

"Aye, sir, and he said, if I did own it as a jest, he would makes things right with Christian, and I should keep my place. Which he did, sir."

Hew did not mistake the pleading in his voice. "But surely," he said softly, "Christian must know you cannot write."

"We telt her I made copy of the letters from a book, it was a trick to tease her."

"Then you have been punished unjustly," Hew pointed out.

The boy shook his head. "No, sir, I have kept my place. And had I not confessed, I should have lost my place. Phillip said, I must confess to Christian, or

188

she would dismiss me. He said that it was what she wished to hear."

Meeting Richard later at the tolbooth, Hew saw something that eclipsed these strange affairs. Marten Voet the card seller, escorted by two bailies, passed him by the entrance to the turnpike stair.

"What is happening here?" he inquired of Richard.

"Burgh council business that does not concern us. Nonetheless," said Richard thoughtfully, "it does involve your printer, in some sense."

"In what sense?" Hew asked him urgently.

"In as much as this is one of the unfree printers I was telling you about. He is a maker, not of books, but of playing cards."

"Aye, I know," Hew exclaimed impatiently. "What is he doing here?"

Richard regarded him for a moment, with a look of grave amusement. "You are a little forward in your form of question," he admonished mildly, "If I were you, I'd keep that tone of voice for court."

Hew muttered, "Pardon," barely masking his frustration.

"Granted," Richard smiled. "It appears he has been brought in for illicit trading. He's a Frenchmen, if you please! Though it may be hypocritical to judge. My own wife bought a packet of his cards. As I understand, he does a roaring trade. All of which is of no consequence to us; the council will dismiss him with a fine."

"I know the man," repeated Hew. "He is not French."

Richard, plainly, had grown weary of the argument. "French, English, Turk, it's all the same. If he came here from the Canongate, he still would be a stranger — and, of all the printers, they're the worse. He came, and made a nuisance, and will presently be gone, as, my friend, will we. There's work to do tonight."

Hew ignored him, crying out, "Marten, Marten Voet!"

The card seller did not respond. But as he paid his fine and motioned to depart, Hew blocked his way. "You are Marten Voet, from Antwerp. We met in St Andrews, at the senzie fair," he asserted bluntly.

Only then did Marten stop to look at him. "You are mistaken, sir. My name is Luc Martin, and I am French. I have not been at the fair, nor in the place you mention, but am newly docked at Leith, having come from Rouen."

"Let the poor man pass, Hew, and be gone about his way," Richard called out sharply, "unless you want a pack of playing cards. I cannot have you making such a scene."

Reluctantly, Hew stepped aside. "He is Marten Voet, I'm sure of it," he said again to Richard.

"And what if he is? These dustyfutes have many secret lives. They live by their wits. What matters is that they move on, and do not make a nuisance of themselves. Your friend Martin — that I think we may conclude to be his name, with some degree of certainty — has made his moonlight sales and paid his dues."

"No doubt you are right," Hew sighed. "I bow to your experience."

190

"I'm very glad to hear it, Hew! At last you have begun to learn!" Richard clapped him on the back. "You are the most perverse and wayward pupil I have had. Now here are some very dull writs that will keep you busy for the next few days, and leave you no time free for pursuing mysteries."

Lines of Inquiry

Returning home for supper later in the day, Richard and Hew were startled by the rumble of a deep, familiar voice. It seemed to fill the hall, booming from the windows in the upper gallery. Sitting in a gossip chair, in Richard's favourite spot above the street, was Doctor Giles Locke. Hew's first thoughts were for Meg, while Richard asked alarmed, "Is someone sick?"

"Not at all," beamed Giles. "I was explaining to your son why it is not well-advised to eat green plums. He has the makings of a fine anatomist."

"That does not surprise me," Richard answered dryly. "Roger is the sort of boy who likes to tear the wings from flies."

Roger scowled, and the doctor looked taken aback. "A little harsh, I think," he commented.

"But Giles," protested Hew, "whatever are you doing here? Has something happened to Meg?"

"Your sister is quite well, though exhausted by the journey. I left her in the lodging house, with Paul. She is under strict instruction to lie down and rest. She does not take too kindly to instruction," Giles admitted.

"Like another from her family," Richard laughed. "Good doctor, you are welcome in my house."

"Aye, tis good to see you. But what are you doing here?" persisted Hew.

"Doctor Locke has been explaining to us how our use of fruits impacts upon the humours," Eleanor said weakly. Her usual calm politeness seemed a little strained. "And why we should not eat green pippins. I sent Grace upstairs, when the narrative became a little too *direct*."

"The consequence of poor digestion," Giles asserted, "cannot be too forcefully impressed upon the young. I have seen a bairn bloat like a hog's bladder, after a surfeit of pears."

"We apprehend the risk, and will remember it," Richard said politely, "when the apple trees are once again in fruit."

"Now that you are come home, I will take Roger upstairs. Will you stay to supper, Doctor Locke?" Eleanor offered. "We have nothing green."

"*Cowcumbers*," Giles remonstrated sternly, "are by far the worst, to a windy constitution, being cold and wet. Indeed, I thank you, madam, but we are lodged without the city walls, and my wife will be expecting me. I must be gone before they close the gates."

"A pity, then, another time," Eleanor said, evidently relieved.

Giles bowed to her. "I shall look forward to it. I pray you, take no trouble, for a little leg of mutton will suffice. With perhaps an egg or two," he added wistfully.

193

"I will send up some wine," Eleanor answered, somewhat at a loss. "Come, Roger, let's go and find Grace."

Roger resisted. "I should like to stay. Doctor Locke was telling us of hard fruits in the belly. They are very cold and windy, and corrupt the blood. I especially liked the part," he said to Giles, "about the stinking vomits and the flux."

Giles gave a little cough, "Ah yes, good boy, go to," he murmured awkwardly.

"Aye, Roger, go, this is men's talk," Richard said impatiently. Roger glowered at him as he allowed his mother to escort him from the room.

"Giles, for the last time, what's your business here?" demanded Hew. "And why have you brought Meg?"

"That is no kind of welcome. I have brought you letters from your man of law."

"But surely," Hew exclaimed, "you did not have to bring them here yourself."

"That's true enough," conceded Giles. "But I have had no peace from Meg since she read your letter. And since I have some business here in town, we thought to make a journey of it. I am here on a matter which, as Richard well inferred, is not fit for mention before wives and bairns. You will recall, before you left, I found myself much exercised in trying to control the verol — what the vulgar call," he said to Richard, confidentially, "the Spanish fleas or pox."

Richard blanched. "I am well glad," he muttered, "that you concealed your purpose from my wife and children."

"For which purpose," Giles went on to Hew, "I have come for conference with my good friend Doctor Dow, who has a practice here on the Cowgate. Doctor Dow is an expert in the *morbus gallicus*, and our council desired that I should consult with him. So I have taken leave of absence for a while. Your sister has been most vexatious, and would not be left behind. As I understand," he turned to Richard, "the disease is as rife in Edinburgh as it is across the water."

"So I am told," Richard answered seriously, "and the worst is in the Canongate, where the gudemen cannot keep their tails within their breeks."

"Quite so," murmured Giles.

"How long do you mean to stay here?" Hew inquired.

"As long as it will take for me to conclude my inquiries, and for Meg to recover from the ride. Though, I should say, we made a good journey. We came from Pettycur to Newhaven, and found a smooth crossing, that passed without incident. Now I have taken rooms in a tavern on the outskirts of the city, for the town itself is noisome and foul, and not at all convenient for Meg. I fear though," he continued fretfully, that once she is rested there will be no staying her, for she will want to see you, and to go to shops and such, and all such silly vanities."

"More likely she will want to help you in your conference," Hew pointed out.

"That is what I fear," Giles admitted gloomily. "It really would be preferable, that she had stayed at home."

"Eleanor will be pleased to take her," offered Richard, "while you are engaged with Doctor Dow."

"And she shall come to the print shop and meet Christian," suggested Hew.

Giles looked a little doubtful. "The printer? Is that a likely place for her?"

"Aye, for certain. Christian is most gentle and refined. Meg will like her very much."

"Then your printer is a woman!" Giles exclaimed, amused. "Ah, we should have guessed it! Christian is a woman's name, for sure. Though you and I, who lived abroad, might be excused for not remembering it."

"I confess, that it never occurred to me," admitted Hew. "Christian is a widow, and has qualities that will endear her to Meg."

"Then *Christian* is your little bird. A match for Doctor Dow, I doubt."

"What do you mean?" Hew frowned.

"The corbie and the doo — the raven and the dove," Giles explained.

"Whisht, no, he won't like *that*!" Richard put in, laughing, "for he wants the little printer to himself."

"Then I begin to understand," the doctor winked at Richard, "why he has not come home."

"There is no way of warning him, and no way of restraining him. Trust me, I have tried," Richard grimaced.

"This is most utter piffle!" Hew protested.

"I think I know your Doctor Dow," Richard turned to Giles. "Is he not our visitor?"

196

"He is indeed," Giles agreed, "A most accomplished man."

"What do you mean, your *visitor*?" asked Hew.

"The visitor is appointed by the burgh council to investigate suspicious deaths," Richard elucidated, "due to infectious sickness or foul play. Doctor Dow has given evidence, once or twice, in cases of suspected slaughter, poison, and the like. He was called to Elspet Barr, when she was found dead on the turnpike. It was fortunate for us, perhaps, he was not called in court. He is a fair practitioner, remarkably good at his task."

"We could do with the position in St Andrews," Giles reflected.

Hew looked up, startled. "The girl on the beach!" he exclaimed. "What happened to her, Giles? But how could I have forgotten her?"

"That is not so very strange," Giles assuredly him kindly, "given all that has happened to you since. To come so close to drowning has a purgative effect upon the wits. Not to mention — for we will not deign to mention — the time that you spent stinking in the gaol. There is nothing like a little degradation to refine one's point of view."

"You are saying that I thought too much about myself?"

"I'm saying it is natural you forgot the girl."

"You will excuse me," interrupted Richard, "for I do not follow this. Who is the girl on the beach?"

Hew replied bleakly, "A dead lass was found on the shore at St Andrews, two or three days before I rode south. Giles and I were made to see her by the coroner.

197

She had been smothered and raped. I found out her name," he added, to Giles, "she was Jess Reekie of Largo."

Giles nodded. "Her mother came, too late. The poor lass was already in the ground."

Hew fell silent, staring at the fire. Richard placed a hand upon his young friend's shoulder, saying with compassion, "This *mattered* to you, Hew. And yet you never said. You keep your secrets close."

"It mattered that she had a name. I could not give her justice," Hew said quietly. "For Jess, and for people like her, the law does not serve."

"The way things are, that may be so," Richard confirmed. "Yet we have a young king, and the world is changing. So the law will change. Pursue the law, and you may find your justice after all. How else will you discover it? An eye for an eye? In revenge?" He turned away abruptly. He was clearly moved. "Gentlemen, you must excuse me. I have left some papers in my chamber, that I wished to read tonight. I shall wish you goodnight, Doctor Locke. If there is any assistance you require while you are here, pray don't hesitate to ask. I should be glad to show you the town."

"That is most kind," Giles enthused. "I have a whim to play a game of caich. Perhaps you could direct me to a court?"

"But certainly. I should be delighted to play with you myself."

"Giles does not play," Hew qualified quickly. Richard looked perplexed.

"I am in the early stages, of beginning to begin to play the game," Giles contradicted, "and am keen to learn. Perhaps we might play doubles, with your bright boy Roger making up the four?"

Richard laughed sardonically. "That is not a good idea. Though Roger is a quick and subtle boy, at any kind of sport he is curiously inept. In truth, were his mother not above suspicion, there are times I should wonder that he is my son."

Giles looked a little thoughtful. Later, he remarked to Hew, "That was a cruel thing that Richard said about his son. If I were a father, then I cannot think I would express myself so pointedly."

"They have a strange relationship," reflected Hew. "Though Roger's mother tells me they are close, I confess, I see no sign of it. Richard goads his son, who seems to spark the worst in him. But Roger is a difficult boy."

Early the next morning, Hew called upon the goldsmith, George Urquhart, with the letters Giles had brought. Unlocking Urquhart's secrets, Richard had explained, called for subtle questioning. "He is as close as any man I've met," he confided, "and if he came as witness to the court I would not care to see him on the other side." He insisted on accompanying Hew, as curator of his interests and affairs. And Hew, as it turned out, was well advised to have brought along a friend. Urquhart kept his shop in the heart of the luckenbooths, adjacent to the kirk or stinking stile. In appearance, it was little different from the other shops, apart from the windows, which were fitted with iron bars. Inside, there was a vaulted chamber, stifling in the close heat of the forge, where Urquhart welcomed customers. The young King James himself, so Richard claimed, was sometimes to be found there, perched upon a stool, drinking sack with George Urquhart on some private business of his own. Beyond this entrance cell, that held the goldsmith's tools of trade, it was supposed he kept enough in gold to make secure the commonwealth. But this was supposition, for no stranger ever passed there; James himself had never glimpsed what lay within those vaults. Whatever streams of fortune Urquhart dammed and banked there, he released, by strict appointment, in disappointing drips.

Urquhart himself was equally impenetrable. Each evening on the stroke of eight, he closed his shop and made his way along the stinking stile, sidestepping the muck that lined the street. The crowds would part to let him pass. And though he let his shop keys jangle from his belt, no one dared to cross him as he sauntered to the Cowgate where he kept his house. The crames ran with thieves, like a garden full of weeds, and once a dead body had been found slumped in the stile, doubled in a puddle of its own congealing blood. Yet Urquhart walked untroubled, without a second glance, or the slightest qualm or quickening of his step.

This goldsmith now subjected Hew to careful scrutiny before he would admit him to the shop. "Matthew Cullan's heir, you say? And yet I do not know you," he remarked.

200

"You know *me*," said Richard firmly.

"Aye, for certain," Urquhart said at last. "You had best come in."

"I know you, Master Cunningham," he said cunningly to Richard, "as a connoisseur of rings. I have a pair of diamonds you may care to look at while you're here."

"When our business is concluded," Richard winked at Hew. "For the present, I am here with Master Cullan."

Urquhart motioned them to sit upon the stools, in the fierce heat of his fire, while he looked upon the letters, leaving them to sweat. He examined Hew's documents though a diamond cutter's eyeglass, for any mark of swindle, forgery or theft.

Hew grew impatient, and was about to speak, when Richard hushed him with a smile. "George will not be rushed."

"Quite right." Urquhart looked at them astutely. "Master Cunningham here knows, as well as most, the danger of false letters."

"It is a risk I meet," the advocate observed, "from time to time, in my profession. Yet it is less common, than you may suppose."

"In my profession, I assure you," Urquhart answered smoothly, "false letters are more common, than you may suppose. Never, ever, underestimate the threat of forgery." He folded up the letters, returning them to Hew. "I know your lawman in St Andrews, and I am convinced that this is his hand. I will accept that you are Matthew Cullan's heir. A gentle and an honest man, I have not seen him for some years. I am sorry to hear of his death."

He turned towards a cupboard in the wall, and returned to pour three thimblefuls of sack, as carefully as cups of molten gold.

"Gentlemen," he stated as they drank his toast, "I am at your service, for whatever service you require."

"I understand my father had deposits here," said Hew.

"He left a little gold secured within my vaults. If you wish to have it you must make an appointment with my servant, at a more convenient time. Meanwhile, I can advance you monies on account, if you so wish."

"Master Cullan will have monies on account," Richard put in quickly. "For which, since you hold his capital, there will be no charge."

"That goes without saying," Urquhart replied. He unlocked a box and took out a small purse of gold. "This may do you for the while. Was there something else?"

"I understand I have inherited a printing press, run by Christian Hall. Can you explain the terms?" asked Hew.

"Indeed, I remember the transaction," Urquhart nodded. "The documents are in my deed box." He rummaged awhile at the back of the room, and returned with a paper. "Aye, here it is. You are misinformed, however, for you have no interest in the press. It belongs, out and out, to Christian Hall. It was your father's gift to her, upon her marriage."

Hew exchanged glances with Richard, who frowned and shook his head.

"But Christian said her husband borrowed money from my father," Hew exclaimed. "I do not understand."

Urquhart coughed discreetly. "Christian Hall . . ." he looked at the paper again, "was the daughter of a woman called Ann Ballantyne, who made her living as a seamstress.

"Your father has supported her from childhood. William Hall was Christian's tutor. He was engaged, by Matthew, to teach her to read and write. When her mother died, and William married her, your father gave William the money to set up a printing press, but the stipulation was that it belonged to Christian, not to him. William Hall was her curator, Christian being under age. And William was a good man, as I understand. She took his name," he added delicately, "because she had no other. Sadly, two or three years ago, her husband died of smallpox. She took on the business, unaware it was already hers. That was your father's wish; my part in this was simply to oversee the transaction."

"Does it say who her father was?" Richard interrupted.

Urquhart looked at him coldly a moment, as though he did not care for his tone. Hew was too confused to speak.

"I regret," Urquhart answered stiffly, "that the father's name is not recorded here. However, Ann Ballantyne lived with her daughter in a cottage at the north back of the Canongate, beneath the Calton crags." He turned once more to Hew. "The cottage is presently vacant, since the last tenant has left. I welcome your instructions on disposing of it; I can find another tenant, or it can be sold."

Hew found his voice at last. "And what is that to me?" he answered hoarsely.

"Did I not say? The house belonged to your father. I'm sorry if this information has unsettled you," Urquhart concluded, folding up the paper. "Let me know what you decide about the property."

"Did you know about this?" Hew turned to Richard as they left.

Richard wrestled for a moment with his conscience. Then he said, "I'm ashamed to say, that I suspected something of the sort. I knew that Matthew had a friend that he visited at Calton crags. But he did not confide in me. I swear to you, I had no notion that there was a child."

"Christian is twenty-two. Then this was while my mother was alive."

"I'm afraid it must have been," Richard agreed reluctantly. "I am so very sorry, Hew. I know you do not wish to hear this."

"Why sorry? What is to regret?" Hew answered wretchedly. "In every way, in every sense, my father was not the man I thought he was."

Richard looked distressed. "What will you do? Will you go home?"

"Go home! You were so keen to have me here, to learn my father's trade!" exclaimed Hew bitterly.

"But by your own admission, you were not well-suited to it. And with this new impediment . . . It can only cause you grief."

"I see no reason to abandon Christian now," objected Hew. "The least that I can do, is to make good Matthew's debt."

Richard shook his head. "I cannot think that wise, when you have feelings for her," he said gently.

"What feelings?" Hew said savagely. "I concede it possible, that I felt a connection with her; that is no surprise, since we *are* connected. I assure you, that I have no *feelings* that are not proper between friends."

Richard shook his head. "I can read you too well, and know that nothing I can say will change your mind. But I beg you, reconsider. You are troubled and confused."

"I thank you, Richard, and I know that you mean well. But I have nothing to go home for. Christian has done nothing wrong and, beyond a doubt, she has a deeper claim on me than I supposed. Therefore, I will stay, and see her through her troubles now. It is surely less than she deserves."

"Then I applaud your courage, though I count it foolishness. What will you tell her? The truth?"

"I will tell her nothing. Keep this secret. Do not tell a soul."

"Of that, you are assured. I pray to God you both may not be hurt by this," Richard answered grimly.

Hew stared at him. "How should this hurt us?"

"That much is clear. You have fallen in love."

Catherine

Richard's fears for Hew were proved unfounded. For the next time he came to the printing house, he found another woman to distract him, dressed in widow's weeds. The veil and feathered gown of blue-black silk gave her from behind the semblance of a crow. But when she turned, he saw the sculptured beauty of her face, perfectly composed, the pale, translucent skin of the natural redhead, full dark lips and solemn eyes, quizzical and searching. The sharp folds of her skirts were studded with a thousand beads, that shivered as she moved and caught the light, and the thick coif of hair curled beneath her cap was bound with black silk ribbon dressed with pearls. "Shall I read it once again?" she was asking Phillip, in a voice fraught with mischief.

"Aye, once through." Phillip had already set the type, and Hew watched him run his thumb across the rows of letter, pressing down or prising out a character out of line, while the stranger spoke in lilting tones. "It is called simply *Song*.

"In the place he drew for me
My lord's bright pencil turned to dust

The fruits that clustered on the tree
In this garden left in trust
Rosy pippins by the pound
Fleshy peaches plump and round
Ripe plums drooping to the ground
Wracked and ruined by his lust."

"That is a pretty song," said Hew.

The widow started, for a moment discomposed. "Gentlemen do not eavesdrop. I did not see you there."

Phillip sighed. "This is Hew Cullan, a student of the law. Pray, do not mind him. He is often here, and is a friend of Christian's.

"Lady Catherine Douglas," he observed to Hew.

Hew bowed to Catherine. "It seemed more polite to listen than to interrupt. I am sorry if I startled you. Please go on."

The lady Catherine had recovered her composure. She replied disdainfully, "I do not care to read in front of strangers."

"Then that is a pity," Hew said gravely. "I should like to know what happens in the end."

"The lady is deceived by her true love, and everything he touches turns to dust. She pines away and dies for him. He is the very essence of your sex."

"If that is so, then I will abjure it straight away, and beg to be a girl," Hew answered solemnly. "And, yet, I would protest, her peaches are not yet so fully blown that she may not share them with another."

Catherine stared at him. "You are impertinent."

"Not at all. I merely state, there is a way your song might have a happy ending. Not all men are so treacherous."

"Aye, perhaps," conceded Catherine. "But a good song should be sad, don't you think?"

"A sad song should be sad. But a good song should make the heart soar."

"Are we done with the quibbling?" asked Phillip. "Because, if we are, I should like to have the second verse, before Walter falls asleep in the press."

"Aye, in a moment," Catherine said absently. She had let the paper fall.

"So you are you a student of the law?" she inquired of Hew. "Then should I be afraid?" She looked at him through eyes that promised laughter, with the smallest creasing of the corners of the mouth.

Hew made another bow. "Aye, madam, you should be afraid."

Phillip spluttered, "Very likely!"

"You do not look like a scholar," Catherine observed. "A student of the law must be very dry and dull."

"I confess it," Hew said smiling, "dry as dust."

"Let me see." She took up Hew's hand and pulled off his glove.

"These fingers are quite moist and soft, not all at dry," she observed. "I think you are a gentleman, though you do not behave like one."

"A moist hand in a man is no good thing," muttered Phillip.

"Do you think not?" demanded Catherine, "then let me see your hands," and she grasped the compositor by

208

the hand, so sudden that he dropped his composing stick, cursing in annoyance.

"That is a solace," called Christian severely, coming into the room, "and worse, in front of Lady Catherine Douglas. Phillip, I'm surprised at you."

Phillip swore again.

Christian glared at him, and turned to Catherine. "Please forgive our want of manners," she said quickly. "Have you met Master Cullan?"

"The scholar? Aye, I have. And he is warm and moist, that signifies good humour. The typesetter is dull and dry. Your hands are rough," Catherine complained to Phillip, wrinkling up her nose.

"Madam, they are rough because I work with them," Phillip answered shortly. "I have to handle letter, that is rinsed in lye."

"Truly?" Catherine mocked. "How loathsome!"

"It really is not fair to tease him," interjected Hew, "when he has work to do."

"Then I am rebuked."

For Phillip's sake, Hew took his leave. "I see I am disturbing you. I will retire to work upon my script," he offered gallantly.

"Are you a makar, then?" persisted Catherine.

"Sadly, no. It is my father's book, a treatise on the law."

"How very dull."

"It is, to speak truth, unremittingly dull. We are now come to the second chapter, which deals, in inexorable detail, with the laws of reset."

"There are times," reflected Catherine, serious for once, "when it may serve us well to know the law, and times indeed, when even justice cannot help us. Nonetheless, if I require a lawman, I shall send for you."

Hew bowed again. "I shall be at your service. And, in the meantime, leave you to decide your lady's fate. May I put in a word for a moment's happiness?"

"You may not. You really are impertinent." Catherine tossed her head. But she did not seem displeased.

"Catherine is a tease," Christian said to Hew in the collating room. "You must not mind her."

"I do not mind her in the least," he assured her. "Is she by any chance related to James Douglas, earl of Morton?"

"I know not? Why do you ask?"

"It was what she said about the law. There is a darkness there below the jest. And Morton, who was once above the law, who was himself the law, now stands accused, and helpless in its face."

"Doubtless, the earl has blood on his hands," Christian considered.

"Doubtless he has, but doubtless also he is blameless of the charge that will prove his downfall."

"Aye, perhaps. But Catherine's bitterness has quite another source. Her husband died at court, in another woman's arms, and for a while she could not bear to show her face. If she seems hard and mocking, then it is an act, to cover up her hurt."

"You seem to know a great deal about her," Hew remarked.

"For certain, we are printers, and the world brings us its news. Catherine's poems, in some sad sense, are an answer to a world that treats her badly. She has joined a little group of makars that amuse the king, and some of them have had their verses printed, for their private use, or gifts to friends. Because I am a woman, she has brought her poems to me, and trusts me to protect them from the crowd. They satirise the minor players of the court, such as her husband, and are often cruel and savage in exposing indiscretions. However, they amuse the king, which is why she is allowed to circulate them to her friends."

"A pity she should be so bitter. She is so very beautiful," reflected Hew.

"Do you think so?" Christian looked sceptical. "But she is very old, I'd hazard, almost thirty. Her looks will not last long."

Female friendship, Hew reflected, only went so far.

When next he met his sister Meg, Hew felt ill at ease. He could not discuss their father's indiscretions. Like a closet door, the subject hung between them, for Meg could read him well, and was sensitive to mood. His sister, in her turn, was not herself. He found her sad and strained, as he had left her in St Andrews, and the change of place and air did nothing to provoke a change of mood. She was grieving, still, at their father's death, and she had not resolved her differences with Giles. There was a distance still between them that it troubled Hew to see, and Giles left her often to her own devices while he was in conference with his good friend Doctor Dow. With some reservations, Hew brought her to meet Christian, and he was not reassured to see how well they liked each other. They could have been sisters, he concluded bitterly. Though they were not alike — Meg was dark like the raven, while Christian was fair — there was a close affinity between them that confirmed his deepest fears. And there was worse to come, for it turned out they had known each other once as children. Matthew had taken Meg to play at Carlton crags. "Then I must have met your father!" Christian cried, in innocence, "and I never knew it, Hew! How strange!" Hew felt lost for words, and looked away. He turned his attentions more openly to Catherine, for whom Meg had formed a consummate dislike. She thought Catherine artful, proud and haughty, and complained as much to Hew. To which her brother said merely, "Things may not be as they seem."

Catherine was a clear distraction, and a welcome one for Hew. In honesty, he admitted to himself that it was not just her company he relished but the friction that she caused within the printing house. Phillip did not approve of her. He resented her dry mockery, her hauteur and her wealth, and he disliked the vicious candour of her poems. Catherine became a lure, and Hew began to plan his visits to coincide with hers. Catherine let it slip that she was growing fond of him. She hoped their friendship would not finish with the printing of her poems. Hew assured her it would not.

He came to chapel suppers still, though, for Christian's sake, he often stayed away. It saddened him to watch her sitting by the fire, stitching ribbons to the sleeves of William's frocks, unaware that she was Matthew's child. And William was a Cullan through and through. Invariably, the ribbons were torn off in his adventures with the nursemaid on the muir. The small boy charged around the shop, and had to be restrained from tumbling in the press. Once, he pulled the drawers that lay in the correcting stone, and scattered Phillip's flourishes and blocks. When Phillip retrieved him, and turned him upside down, by way of a distraction, an apple core came tumbling from his smock. Christian picked it up and frowned. "What's this?"

"*Pippin,*" William said obligingly. He took the pippin from his mother and began to gnaw on it.

"He's teething," Alison said defensively.

"Aye, for sure. Who gave him it?" Christian asked quietly. "Was it the fruitman again?"

William said, "It was *Davie,*" and Alison blushed.

"And who is Davie?" queried Christian.

"Alison's friend," the little boy answered. "He walks with us on the muir."

The nurse flushed deeper and stuttered, "It is a man we met. There is no harm in it."

"Alison has a sweetheart," Michael sniggered. Phillip glared at him.

Alison looked stricken, and Hew felt sorry for her. She was a foolish, gentle girl, whose face, though never handsome, had been scabbed by pox. She had caught the smallpox nursing William Hall, while Christian and her infant had been kept away. Her chances of a sweetheart, in her present state, seemed poor enough.

Christian said quietly, "Alison, I do not want you to take William on the muir again."

The girl looked up and bit her lip, mutinous behind the threatening tears. "The air by the park is good for the bairn."

"Understand me, Alison; you are not to take him there. And I will not have him given things by strangers, as I told you once before."

Reluctantly, Alison nodded. Christian said nothing more, but took the apple core from William and threw it on the fire.

Later, as Hew said goodnight to Christian at the door, he asked, "Is it so very wrong for the child to have an apple? I know my brother Giles is set against them, but I'm sure a pippin never did me any harm."

Christian shook her head. "It is not the apple, Hew. I do not like them talking to strangers."

"Can it really hurt that Alison has found a friend?"

"What friend?" Christian challenged. "She is so very trusting, that I fear she is misused. Alison is poor and simple, and she does not understand the ways of men. How likely is it that this man will want to marry her?"

"Not very," Hew admitted. "But everyone may have a little happiness, don't you think?"

"I used to think so. Now, I'm not so sure. But perhaps you're right; I am too hard on her. I cannot always bind her to my will. The truth is," Christian sighed, "I am afraid. And though I know that fear has blinded reason, still I feel the need to keep them safe."

Unconsciously, Hew took her hand. "What is it you are so afraid of?" he asked gently.

Christian whispered, "Someone has been coming here at night."

"What makes you say that?"

"Odd things have been happening. When I open the shop in the morning, things have been moved. Small things that are not significant. Yet taken together, they begin to look strange."

"What sort of things?" Hew probed

"We have lost the proofs to Catherine's poems. It does not really matter; they have been corrected. Phillip left them lying on the stone. In the morning, they were gone."

"The proofs were waste," Hew reasoned. "Why should it matter, then, if someone threw them out?"

"It matters," Christian answered seriously, "that no one did."

"Then is it not quite possible that Catherine took the poems herself?"

"More than likely," she agreed. "That is my hope. Catherine looked over the proof copy, and made the corrections with Phillip. The trouble is, I dare not ask her, for I dare not let her know that we have lost her poems. When she brought them to us, she gave us her absolute trust.

"In the wrong hands," Christian went on, "they could do us incalculable harm. It is forbidden to print ballads, verses and the like without a licence. Catherine's poems are for private circulation, and are not intended for the common eye. We are printing them without a name, and without our mark, which is itself a crime. Therefore we must be careful that we leave no trace. Phillip will check the count," she broke into a smile, albeit a little weak. "He says Walter has nine and a half fingers — the half he lost eight years ago when he first used a press — and therefore we are fortunate that he can count to ten. Beyond that is beyond him, and beyond our hopes."

"Aye, that sounds like Phillip. Nonetheless, he may be right. Perhaps it was Walter who threw out the proofs?"

"I do not think so, Hew. Also, there was ink spilled on the floor, where the day before there was no ink, I'm sure of it."

"Well . . . as you say, they are small things. And you are busy here. It is not hard for things to be misplaced. It is hard to say, how these things in themselves might constitute a mischief," Hew said reasonably.

"But suppose that someone came here in the dark, to look for Catherine's poems, and spilled the ink, not seeing it?"

Hew laughed. "Were there footprints in the ink?"

"Do not mock me. I am serious."

"And seriously, I apprehend your fears. But I do think these are trivial matters. In a busy printer's shop, there may be many accidents. I think it very likely Catherine took the proofs. It is the sort of thing that she would do. As for the ink, I expect Michael spilt it, and did not care to own up to it," Hew reassured her.

"No, do not blame Michael. I will not have him become the common whipping boy. In my heart, I knew he did not bring the corbie. I ought not to have allowed the men to punish him."

"The shop is locked," Hew pointed out, "therefore it is hard to see how anyone could come here in the night. Who sleeps above? Walter and Phillip?"

Christian shook her head. "Walter has a wife; they live at Pocketclief. And Phillip rents a room across the street. Only Alison and William sleep upstairs with me. But I have asked Phillip to remain here to keep watch, for the next night or two. He does not seem to mind too much."

"Aye, for sure," muttered Hew. Christian frowned at him. "He is a good man, Hew. And though he has not said so, I think his lodging house is somewhat mean and low. He takes no one there, and on Sundays is reluctant to go home."

"He is paid well enough, for the setting of my book," Hew remarked.

Christian gave a drawn-out look, under which he grew a little hot. "The terms were fair. Phillip is saving to buy his own press."

"I suppose you still trust him?" he wondered.

Christian said quietly, "Aye, with my life."

Blackfriars Wynd

Hew did not return to Christian's shop for several days, for he was watching Richard in the courtroom. He amused himself in trying to predict who Richard would object to from the jury. In several cases, he was wrong; then he became more subtle and more accurate. Richard was a careful tutor, who shared his inner thoughts as frankly as his influence. As Hew began to learn, he found, to his confusion, that the law appealed to him. He wanted to ask questions and put arguments, to counter with objections on his own. Richard had to quell him with a look when he became too vocal in the court. In the morning, they shared breakfast on the wooden gallery, and discussed the case. Richard nurtured and encouraged Hew, allowing him expression of his thoughts, pointing out the flaws with amused and gentle patience, teasing out the subtleties. And Hew became drawn in to Richard's inner world.

On the third day of the trial, as they left for court, they were met by Meg and Giles coming up the stair.

"How sad you look, in black," his sister smiled. "It suits you, Hew. I never thought to see you look so serious."

"Hew is growing up," the doctor diagnosed. "That may be no bad thing."

"Do not confuse me with my coat," Hew countered. "When I am myself, I prefer the gooseturd green."

Giles slipped his arm around Hew's shoulder. "I am in conference this morning, with my good friend Doctor Dow, while Meg is come to spend the day with Eleanor," he murmured. "I thought that you and I could dine together, after our exertions. I have found a little place."

"Why don't we all dine here?" suggested Richard generously. "Doctor Dow would be most welcome."

"Doctor Dow is shy of company," Giles excused him quickly. "And I hoped to speak with Hew upon a private matter. Therefore, though I mark the kindness, I regret we must decline."

Richard shrugged. "Another time."

"I do not quite believe in your good friend Doctor Dow," teased Hew. "Since I have never met him."

"Nor have I," Meg interjected pointedly. "For all there is, as I am told, a gudewife Doctor Dow, that accompanies him. In truth, I sometimes wonder whether they exist."

"But that is preposterous!" Giles exclaimed. "Of course there is a mistress Doctor Dow! And no one who has met his wife could ever be in doubt of her existence."

"That is my point," Meg said archly, "that I have not met her."

"Aye well, another time," Giles muttered vaguely. "This morning we have business, very dull and bloody."

"Dull *and* bloody?" Richard queried. "Surely, never both?"

"In my profession, sad to say, almost always both. Doctor Dow has made a study of the grandgore. And this morning, he proposes that we make a new experiment, upon a patient he has staying in his house. The remedy is somewhat rigorous, alas."

"Poor man," Meg said compassionately. "Then I may bring some comfort to him."

Giles looked helpless for a moment.

"I think it may not suit you, Meg," her brother rescued hurriedly.

"You are quite wrong," insisted Meg. "You know I am not squeamish when it comes to physic. You are the one of us faintest of heart."

"And as I recall," Giles countered cunningly, "you were the one that wanted me to have that private talk with Hew."

"Aye, very well," Meg gave in reluctantly. "You must tell me how it turns out." It was not clear to what they referred, and Hew felt a little unnerved.

"I know a brave little brewster called Bessie, on Blackfriars wynd, who bakes a rare pie, and who is a little muddled about fish days," the doctor confided, "Meet me at the high school a little after twelve."

The trial was done by noon, and Hew met Giles as arranged, at the dinner hour. He waited at the foot of Blackfriars wynd, where it met the Cowgate, close to the town school. There were no signs for taverner or cookshop, and he was surprised when Giles appeared and led him to a kitchen on the corner of the street.

In the centre of the kitchen stood a wooden barrel, laid out like a table with a cloth and set for two, with trenchers, cups and spoons, so close between the fireplace and the brewing vat that Hew could taste the liquor from the mash. The air was thick and heady with the smell of toasted malt. After a morning's concentration in the court house, he began to feel a little sleepy.

"Bessie is the brewster for the kirk, and since the session do not stint themselves, you may be assured that is a mark of quality," Giles explained. "Moreover, she sells herbs and spices, some of which, in truth, have been proscribed. Her physic brings some comfort to our patients on the Cowgate. And for a place to talk, there is none more close or private. We may be assured of her discretion."

"Is the business private, then?" Hew asked, a little alarmed.

Giles coughed discreetly. "Rather, I may say, a little delicate. Now, are you hungry? Bessie has an oven here for drying out the grain, and has ventured into coffin crusts, by way of a sideline. The flavour of the malt imparts a curious savour to the pasties that is quite beyond compare."

Bessie had arrived, with a frothing pitcher and a glistening slab of pastry on a plate.

Giles took out his pocket knife and wiped it on the table cloth. Hew's stomach gave a lurch. He did not care to hazard what had soiled the blade.

"Do your researches go well?" he ventured.

"Doctor Dow shows some success in remitting the excesses of disease," Giles answered cautiously.

"In the hie town and the kirk they say that pox is rampant in the Canongate, and has its roots at Holyrood, in our royal court," Hew persisted.

"There is truth in that." The doctor sliced a slab of pie, unwilling to be drawn.

"Truly, I confess, I give it little credence. Such rumour is the bastard of a lax and free regime, the rise of Esme Stewart, and the threat of papacy, of all things French and foreign, driving fear and loathing through the town. This city is a closed, suspicious place, whose frank mistrust of foreigners is bordered at the netherbow. I counted it the hatred of lascivious excess."

"A moral apoplexy. There is truth in that," Giles smiled. "Nonetheless, be assured, there is grandgore in the Canongate. Though I concede that rumour overplays the threat. When I see poor wretches suffer, I am bound to take it seriously."

"And yet you say that Doctor Dow has some success in treating it."

Giles took a sip of ale. "He has had success in moderating symptoms, with a herbal remedy procured from Bessie here. I remain unconvinced that the sickness has been stifled at its root. My fear is that the pox lies dormant, and will rear its head again, but after many years. Its legacy appears in babes unborn," he added gloomily.

"A sad prognostication," Hew observed. "I heard tell of prisoners who had lost their noses. Would it be the grandgore?" he wondered.

"More than likely."

"I have heard it said that the late King Henry Darnley had the grand-gore, not the smallpox, when he came to lie at Kirk o' Fields."

"I have heard the same," admitted Giles.

"Our present young king is weak-limbed and bowed."

Giles grinned. "Now you are the one who makes rumour," he pointed out. "So scandals spread more quickly than the plague. Though he may be indifferently formed, his defects are not typical of pox. I think it is some other ill afflicts our present king."

Hew fell silent, staring in his cup. Presently he said, "You speak of sickness passing through the generations. Meg has the epilepsie."

"Aye, what of it?" Giles said calmly.

"My cousin Robin Flett, his sister died of falling sickness."

"He was your mother's cousin, as I understand."

"Then if Meg had a child, the child might have it too?"

Giles sat thoughtful for a moment. Then he answered quietly. "It is a possibility. I do not count the risk. It does not pass directly to the child."

"And if *I* had a child?"

"It is a possibility."

"And this does not . . . deter you, I suppose?" questioned Hew.

"It is as I say. I do not count the risk."

"My mother died in childbirth," Hew reflected.

"That, too, I have noted. And since the risk to Meg outweighs the danger to the child, I cannot give it countenance."

"What is it you are saying? That she cannot have a child?"

"That I do not wish to speak of it," Giles replied emphatically. "Come, this is not why we are here. I am charged to speak with you, on a matter of some delicacy."

"Aye, so you said. What can be so delicate, you do not wish to speak of it?"

The doctor sighed. "It is your sister wanted me to mention this to you," he explained at last. "She thinks you are not kind to Christian. There, the thing is said. Though I count it little of my business, I come merely as Meg's messenger. She thinks also . . . that you are too reckless in your friendship with Catherine Douglas, who is wanton and not to be trusted. According to Meg."

After this awkward speech, he cleared his throat, and stared uncomfortably into his cup.

Hew was still for a moment. Then he said quietly, "Meg is quite wrong on both counts."

Giles looked up. "Dearly, I should like to tell her so. Though I confess that what I have seen looks rather to confirm it. It is plain to us all that there is a bond between you and Christian, and yet, to her face, you are flirting with Catherine, to whom I sense you have no real attachment, and that causes Christian hurt."

"As I say, you are wrong on both counts," Hew repeated. "I do not deny there is a strong connection between myself and Christian, and it is no surprise that Christian has sensed it. No doubt, Meg feels it too, though she cannot know why. Christian is our father's child. Therefore, my regard for her may not be more than that."

224

Giles exclaimed, "But surely, that cannot be true!"

"I only wish that it were not," Hew answered sadly. He told what he had learned from Urquhart. "If you can find some other explanation," he concluded, "then I should be more than glad to hear it."

Giles shook his head. "Though I did not know Matthew long, I would not have expected this of him. And he kept it secret all that time?"

"Aye, and from Christian herself. I have not felt able to tell her. In my father's defence, he made provision for her. He has watched over her for all these years."

"Then when he sent you with the manuscript . . ."

Hew nodded. "He must have meant me to find out. And finding her in trouble, I determined to protect her. For she is my sister, nothing less, and nothing more."

"You must not tell Meg. For Matthew was the world to her. This would break her heart," Giles declared decisively.

"I know it. Nor would she believe it. But she and Christian met when they were bairns. He took Meg to the house at Calton crags. Aye, he was that open, Giles. He let them play together."

"Dear, dear, then I am sorry for it. This is hard on Christian," Giles reflected. "It is plain she likes you, Hew."

"And I like her. But it cannot be helped."

Giles shook his head. "It is a muddle and a mess. Where does Catherine come in this? She is your consolation, I suppose, a mere distraction?"

"Not at all," Hew replied seriously. "To say so were to underrate her charms, and insult her. Catherine's flippancy and wit are a pretence, that masks a hurt and tender soul, and I am quite honest in my regard for her. I like her very much."

Giles pursed his lips. "You do not count her a risk?"

"If she is a risk, then I am prepared to take it. All my life, I have been treated as a child, cosseted and guided, given good advice. Now, even now, though I am of age, and come into my inheritance, I am once again a pupil in someone else's house. I am tired of it, Giles. Trust me, for once, to know my own mind," Hew insisted.

"Then I suppose there can be little point in warning you against her," Giles agreed at last. "Aye, go where you will. I wish you happiness. In any case, I shall not interfere."

Hew returned to Christian's shop, hoping to see Catherine once again. The talk with Giles had strengthened his resolve: he wanted to make love to her. He wanted to prolong the friendship, knowing there was nothing in the way. Coming to the printing house, he was aghast at what he found. At first he thought of William, run amok, and yet he knew the damage went beyond what could have been inflicted by a child: he met a scene of devastation. Walter's press had been wrenched off from its brace, and a bare hole marked the floor where it had stood. The paper in the windows had been stripped and torn, and all the locks were broken, while the door swung open on its hinges to the gawping street. Phillip knelt with Christian in the middle of the shop, picking over fragments in the dust. "All of this, ruined," he said starkly.

"What has happened here?" Hew cried.

Christian answered calmly. "We have had a visit from the burgh council."

"I do not understand."

"They closed us down." She waved her hand towards the door, to which was pinned a paper: "Closed, by order of the magistrates."

Phillip stood up. "The council have impounded all the letter and press — save what they have scattered on the floor."

"Is is broken?" Christian asked him softly.

"Most of this is chipped. But it is not ours. It was left by the printer who was here before us, and is very old and worn. Look, these are musical notes, of which we have none of our own."

"He left nothing, I suppose, to do us harm?"

"Only worn out letter. I will wrap it up, and return it to the store. It was copy they were looking for, and they have taken all our formes and manuscripts and all the wrought-off sheets.

"They took your father's book. I'm sorry, Hew," said Christian sadly.

"Catherine's poems?" he questioned, with a flooding dread.

Christian shook her head. "All of them were sent to her, the copy too. And Phillip has distributed the type. We left no trace."

"Thank God for that!" To his shame, Hew felt regret; for if Catherine's poems were printed she would not come again.

"Then what were they looking for?" He struggled to dismiss the thought of Catherine, focusing on Christian.

Phillip shrugged. "They had word, they said, of illicit printing on these premises. They have taken away the copy in their search for evidence. When they do not find it — be assured, they will not find it," he said fiercely to Christian, "then they will absolve us and return it. All this means is that someone has complained of us. As to who, we need not ask. It was Allan Chapman."

"Can you be sure?" Hew frowned.

"It is most likely, Hew," Christian confirmed. "Do not be alarmed. Though this may slow us down, it will not stop us. It is a hazard of our trade. The press will be restored."

Hew left them to their clearing up, and walked down to the Cowgate, coming back to Blackfriars wynd. For close to Bessie Brewster's, by the school, he had noticed Allan Chapman's printing house. He stood outside a moment, looking at the wares that Chapman had displayed on a counter folding out towards the street: inkhorns for schoolboys, penners and quills, and a small stack of pamphlets and books. He took a moment to compose himself before he pushed open the door. He found the master printer folding paper at his counter, at the forefront of his shop, a man in his late forties with a sly, suspicious smile. The printer gave a cautious welcome: "Can I help you, sir? You are, perhaps, a master at the school?" He had noticed Hew's black coat.

"Indeed not," Hew said pleasantly, without elaboration. "I have a book that I am hoping to have printed."

"Oh aye?" Chapman watched him narrowly. "What kind of book?"

"It is a text book, for students of the law, written by my father. He was an advocate in the justice court, some years ago."

The printer looked cunning, counting the cost. "I know not, if we are the place for such a venture," he replied at last.

"My father left sufficient funds to see it through the press," Hew mentioned carelessly.

"Then that may be different. Let me take a look at it."

"Unfortunately, I do not have it here. It was at the press of Christian Hall, and was seized by the council this morning, along with the type. Perhaps you had heard?"

"Really? Ah, really?" Chapman looked amused, and, unless he acted well, quite pleasantly surprised. "Indeed, I had not heard," he commented. "So Christian had the bailies in." Though clearly welcomed, Hew felt sure this came as news. "Dear, dear! Was there something in your book to cause offence?"

"I confess, I do not know; I have not read it," Hew admitted. "What would they be looking for? Should I be concerned?"

"In general, Catholic tracts," the printer answered thoughtfully, "or anything thought likely to offend the kirk or king. Which is not always easy to predict," he smiled, a little sourly, "since what pleases one, invariably is poison to the other. I am afraid that sudden closure is a hazard of the press. We all are in perpetual thrall and censure of the council. Christian's closing down may not be permanent. Though if it is, of course," he added, "she may find herself in gaol. Which only goes to prove what I have always said, that printing is no business for a woman. Least of all, a woman with a bairn."

"I cannot think my father's book could cause offence," reflected Hew. "It was a simple textbook, somewhat sad and serious."

"Then the script will be returned to you, when it has been passed. By all means, when you have it, bring it here to us, and we will talk on terms. You are prepared, I suppose, to take on the full cost?" Chapman persisted greedily.

"That was the general idea," Hew agreed. "There are, of course, some other printers in the town. Such as Henry Charteris."

"Charteris does not take piecework," Chapman countered. "I have no doubt, we can meet you on fair terms."

"What I cannot understand," Hew returned, "is why Christian Hall's press has been singled out for censure? When yours, for example, has been left unscathed."

"They may come to us in time," the printer grimaced. "But it is more likely that the council were informed by someone where to look. Most often, that is the way of it."

"Then who might inform them? A rival, perhaps, in the trade?" suggested Hew.

Chapman looked at him shrewdly. "If we did *that* sir, we would none of us stay open longer than a week. Let us hope the information received was false, and that Christian does not languish in the gaol like Robert Lekprevik."

"We must hope not," agreed Hew. "Meanwhile, since we may assume the script will be restored to us, may I look around your shop, and see some examples of your work?" He had no real sense of what he should be looking for, yet he wanted to know more of Allan Chapman.

"You may sir, if you do not stop the work," Chapman nodded. "I will show you round. We have three presses here, which means our capacity is far greater than Christian's. Each press can produce up to fifteen hundred sheets in a twelve-hour day. To which end, we employ five pressmen, and the occasional extra hand, as this man here, who is working in two colours," he droned on, as they began their tour. "The black ink we buy in, in barrels, but the red is vermillion, bought as pigment and made up by the week boy on the premises. Two-colour printing is skilled work, and if you required it, would cost a little more. Alternatively, you can have the book coloured by hand, after it is printed. Do you wish for illustrations?"

Hew was no longer listening. He was staring at the beater who applied the ink in quick, deft circles to the forme locked in the press. "But I know you!" he exclaimed. "You are Marten Voet, the card seller."

Marten placed a sheet of paper down upon the forme and turned back to face them as the pressman pulled. "You are mistaken, sir," he answered quietly. "My name is Luc Martin. We have never met."

"Indeed, I am certain of it," insisted Hew. He confronted Allan Chapman. "This man is a card maker from Antwerp. I have met him once before, in St Andrews at the senzie fair, and he has lately been selling his wares in the hie gate, where he was fined for unfree trading."

Chapman shrugged. "That was not the tale I heard, though he is an itinerant. As far as I know, he is Luc Martin, a Frenchman, lately crossed from Rouen to Leith. Here, this will not do," he roared at Martin, "the ink is far too thick, and you have taken up too much of it. The paper has rubbed. Take care, man! Paper may come cheap to you in France, but they sell it dear enough to us; we cannot afford to waste it."

"Will you lose me my place, sir?" Marten whispered to Hew, as he took up a waste sheet of paper. "For pity, why would you do that?" He dabbed off the excess ink. Hew heard the desperation in his voice, and stepped back in confusion. He was certain, after all, that this was Marten Voet. Yet why should he expose him? He told a desperate tale of fear and persecution, living by his wits. Who could blame him if he chose to change his name?

"Then I am mistaken," Hew conceded awkwardly, "And I beg your pardon."

Marten muttered, "*Thank* you," turning quickly back towards the press.

"Now then, sir," Chapman said reproachfully, "you promised not to stop the work. If they fall behind, the men will lose their pay, and that is not fair to them. The puller, now, is out of time, through no fault of his own.

You have seen, besides, all there is to see here. Come back into the shop. If you wish to look at books, then we have some on the counter. You will have to pay for binding at additional cost. Gibson is a good man, near the tron. Now, what was it you were saying, about the Frenchman, Luc Martin? He is an itinerant journeyman, and I confess, I know little about him. Do you say that he cannot be trusted?"

"Not at all," Hew capitulated hurriedly. "I fear I was misled. I took him for another man."

"Aye?" Chapman sounded sceptical. "In any case, I will not keep him long. His work is careless, and wants finish. He came opportunely, when we wanted a man, but since he does not satisfy, I'll let him go at the end of the week."

"I should not like to think I cost him his place," protested Hew, "by cause of an honest mistake."

"Not at all," Chapman said politely. "I am much obliged to you. I never cared for foreigners. They are a menace and a pest, a very plague."

"You offered to wed Christian, did you not?" Hew asked him at the door.

The printer regarded him curiously. "Aye, I did," he admitted, after a moment. "It was meant for a kindness. It is a hard thing for a woman to run a printing house. The offer was refused, and I was turned away, most unkindly. I shall not venture help to her again. But I think, sir, you are implying something other in your question. I do not like your tone."

"I meant nothing," Hew said thoughtfully, "save that I admired your wish to help her. I heard that you were kind enough to offer her a press, when she was frozen out."

"Aye, in our laich house," Chapman answered warily. "Regrettably, someone left his candle burning, and it caused a fire."

"I understood it was a boy of yours?" probed Hew.

"Did you, now? Ah, I see the way of it," Chapman stared at him. "Then ask yourself this: what sort of man sets light to his own premises? If any boy of mine had left his candle burning, then you would not find him here to tell the tale. If you want to know who threatens Christian's business, look to Phillip Ramsey. That is all I'll say. And now, good day to you. When you have your manuscript for printing, I'll be glad to see it." Angrily, he closed the door.

The Hanging Man

Hew found Richard at the tolbooth, where he broke the news. Richard listened gravely. "Damn the burgh council! They have taken all the papers? And your father's too?"

"Aye, and all the formes and letter. They have closed the press."

"Then we must use what influence we have to bring the matter to a close."

"It is good of you," Hew answered, gratefully.

"Not at all. Your interests are mine," Richard promised.

They found the council clerk at his office in St Giles. Richard quizzed him for a moment, and then groaned and turned to Hew. "The burgh court is still sitting upstairs; it cannot help our case if we burst in. The bad news is it was your old friend Wishart who brought in the manuscript. He is ever over-zealous, and he always goes a step too far. Though the clerk will go to fetch him, he will doubtless make us wait. He will enjoy the little power that he has over us." He sighed. "I have scant patience with these councillors. And yet I fear we must allow their petty rule, and swallow it. God did not make me well for such humility."

"This is kind; you need not wait," Hew said apologetically.

"Not at all. I will not leave you in their thrall. If we must squirm, then we shall squirm together," his friend insisted.

Wishart made them wait for the best part of an hour before he came to meet them, smiling unctuously. "What business do you have, sirs, with the burgh council?"

"Good sir," Richard answered smoothly, "we are come on behalf of the printer Christian Hall, whose press you have impounded. We beg to ask, upon what charge?"

"There is no charge," the bailie said, "as yet. The press is under investigation, for illicit printing. If we find evidence of such, and a charge is brought, you will be informed."

"You have taken, sir, among the matter of her press, a manuscript that belongs to my friend here. Since it is his property, and not that of Christian Hall, I ask that you return it."

"Ah, yes, I do recall," the bailie smiled unpleasantly, "that this is your wild prentis lad, the erstwhile vagabond. Rest assured your manuscript is in safe hands. It will be examined by the censor, and when he is assured that it has nothing to offend, it will be returned to you."

"This is ridiculous," Richard said crossly. "The work is a legal textbook; it contains nothing untoward. If the court has doubts, then I suggest that you release the manuscript to me, since I am better qualified than any in your council to examine its contents, and assess whether or not there is malice in them."

"That may well be, sir, but the fact is," said the bailie firmly, "this is a matter for our jurisdiction, not for yours. These effects will remain here until they are examined, when, if they are harmless, they will be returned to Christian Hall, whence they were removed. If they prove malignant, sir, and you wish to represent her, then, in due course, you will hear from us."

"But what is it you are looking for?" asked Hew.

"That I am not at liberty to tell you. You may have no fear, sir, if, in truth, there is nothing to offend there. But we are informed that something foul has issued from the press and we are bound to follow up the information."

"Your information was malicious, then, and I must doubt its source," Hew complained.

"As to that, our source was impeccable," Wishart answered loftily.

"And, I doubt, you are not free to divulge it," Richard sneered.

"On the contrary. Because it was impeccable, and made most frank and freely, I can see no reason why it should not be disclosed. The complaint was made by the minister of the kirk of St Giles, Walter Balcanquall. So you will understand why we have to take it seriously."

"The minister! Then we must go to him, Richard, and demand to know what he meant by it," Hew exclaimed.

Richard frowned. "Stay," he advised, placing a hand on Hew's arm. "This puts a different complexion on things.

"Step aside a moment," he said softly. "This may be more serious than I thought. Walter Balcanquall is an honest man, who is not fearful of controversy. He would not bring this charge without due cause. We must move more cautiously. Let me speak with him on Sunday, after kirk, and meantime wait to see what transpires. Take a moment to reflect. I know the man, Hew. He would not make an accusation out of malice."

"Then he has made a mistake," Hew answered hotly.

"That is very likely. Nonetheless, these are dangerous waters. Therefore let us be circumspect, and not jump in headlong. It is likely, while we wait, the press will be restored, and we will have no cause to trouble Balcanquall. I must confess I do not like this, Hew."

"Do not make your noises in our court," the bailie interrupted smugly, "and we may not have to trouble you in yours. The sooner you are gone, sir, the sooner we may see to Christian Hall."

Richard bowed stiffly. "I am disappointed, that you do not see fit to return my friend's possession to him."

"We shall take good care of it. And if the work is blameless, he shall have it in due course. And if, of course, it isn't, he shall share the blame," the bailie winked, "since he has made a claim to it."

"Let us come away now," Richard muttered, "for I fear we do more harm than good. Does it not enrage you, Hew?" he demanded, in a sudden show of temper, from the safety of the street, "that he should have such power? That little man sits swaddled in his own smug suit of lard. No sooner had you come within the city than he had you thrown in gaol, and took away your liberty. Now he lays his greasy hands on Matthew's book. Dearly, I should like to wrench it from him."

"To speak truth, I care less for the book than for the effect on Christian's business," Hew replied more reasonably.

"Aye, we must secure the press," Richard agreed. "But since you are my friend, and in some sense my dependant, then my first concern is for you. There was nothing, I suppose, in Matthew's book to do you harm?"

"Not that I know. Though most of it I have not read," admitted Hew. "And part of it is damaged still. I cannot think the censor will make much of it."

Richard nodded. "Then we must wait, and hope that you are right. No, we shall not wait. There must be something more. I will not let that man defeat us. I will speak to the provost, and look to a higher authority," he promised.

It appeared, against all odds, that Richard's petition to the provost had some influence, for the following day, all Christian's possessions were returned to her, together with Hew's manuscript, and her licence to print was restored. "But why?" she asked the bailies, baffled, and was told they had not found what they were looking for. "And what was that?" she asked in vain. The answer came when they went next to kirk, from Walter Balcanquall.

★   ★   ★

239

The kirk was a great leveller, at least upon the surface; though it was a place where paupers mixed with kings, the rich had stools and settles in the choir while the poor had to stand and huddle in the dust, crowded at the back or on the floor. There were sermons daily in the great kirk of St Giles, but the Sunday service was the main attraction, looked forward to by many through the week. The reformers had partitioned off the church, dividing it in sections, and there were several ministers straining to be heard, proclaiming doom from different sides and slants. Among them was the tolbooth kirk, where malefactors were exposed on Sundays; and members of the great kirk often strayed to see them; given choice of sermon, they attended both. Parts of the church had been pressed into secular use, as council rooms and meeting places, with a second thieves' hole underneath an aisle, closer to the graveyard than to God. In the glory days before the reformation the high altar of the kirk had been the haunt of money changers; now this landmark had been swept away and they conducted business at the regent Moray's tomb, and the far aisles rang with the chink of passing coins. The cramers, for their part, had continued to expand, and clung like barnacles to all the outer reaches of the walls. It would be hard to conceive of a part of human life that was not represented there, the traffic of the world, from birth to death, and if there was no actual copulation in the kirk, it was amply represented in the text. For since the great days of John Knox, now mouldering peaceful in St Giles' kirkyard, the congregations had enjoyed a blistering succession of attacks. The present incumbent,

240

Walter Balcanquall, could be relied upon to carry on the form. He did not spare the people or their sins the full and scathing censure of a scornful God. Nor did he balk at touching on controversy, or fear the wrath of council or of king. His sermons were looked forward to, with hope and trepidation, as the thrilling climax to a dreary week.

Hew took his place among the crowd, seated between Richard and the children, on the family settle near the front. The service began with a psalm and a sequence of readings that warmed a restless audience up for the main event. Finally, when all was calm, and the coughs and sneezing done with, Walter Balcanquall appeared. Balcanquall was a man of great authority, and a popular preacher. He had the presence to wait until the audience were entirely still before he deigned to speak, beginning only then in a low and quiet voice, which rose to a crescendo, once they were absorbed. He could lull or stir a crowd of thousands, at the height of his powers. Now, as the chamber hushed, he began to speak.

"Some of you no doubt recall that I spoke to you four months ago of the depravities and evils in our royal court." Balcanquall paused for a moment, looking round, as though to ascertain the presence of the king, and Hew strained his neck towards the royal platform, but the box was empty; James was absent at the abbey kirk at Holyrood. The minister gave a sigh, though whether of disappointment or relief was hard to tell. He had his congregation with him, from his mention of the court. A quiver of anticipation flickered round the kirk.

"For which," the minister went on, into the heady silence, "I was called to answer to the Privy Council. And as you will know, I made good my account, and had the full support there of the kirk assembly, as was right and just. For I was not afeared to speak the truth. I spoke to you of whoredom and adultery, and of the wicked converse of the French at court, that led to that disease so aptly called the French pox, or the *morbus gallicus*, that is the outward marker of a filthie soul."

From the corner of his eye, Hew saw Richard smile to Eleanor, who was glancing somewhat anxiously at Grace. Roger, for his part, was grinning broadly, though he had grumbled roundly as they left the house. Hew could feel the crowd around him, taut with expectation, hushed in the fear that they might miss a word.

"And that disease, I telt ye," Balcanquall was thundering, "was rife throughout the Canongate, and in the precincts of Holyrood house. Now, I have to tell ye, that pernicious evil creeps upon the high town, and its filth is spread to our own houses. And did I not warn ye, that unless we rid ourselves of this filth, and unless we repent, and make clean the king's house, then all of us are likely to be damned? And for that cause, I was not afeared to stand up here before ye and decrie the king his evil, for the vanity and licence that pollutes the royal house. And I am not afeared to say to ye again, the wickedness that taints that house continues still. For here, in my hands, I have the proof of it, a set of verses foul enough to make ye blush, yet part of which, I read to you, as a warning of the muck that issues still from that unhappy court. It is a poem called *Morbus Gallicus*, or otherwise, *The French Disease*, that begins in wanton pleasure, ending in destruction, of the body and the soul."

Balcanquall unfurled his paper, his hands shaking with emotion, and made low his voice again as he began to read:

"The French Monsieur at court
Is of a waggish sort
That likes to prank and sport
And to prick and quibble with his tongue
That all the girls and boys
Who care for tinselled toys
May learn his antic ploys
While they are young.

"The French Monsieur has lips of gold
For framing secrets sweet and bold
Before bright lassies grow too old
He teaches them their part.
Yet they won't care for aught
His silver tongue has bought
When the lessons he has taught
They ken by heart.

"The French Monsieur with all his charm
That sounds no warning or alarm
Can surely mean no lasting harm
To all those shining girls and boys?
And so I cannot say

Why at the close of day
The brave lads leave their play
And the lasses fall to weeping at the tinsel of their
toys."

This reading was so rare and provocative a treat that
the people took a moment to digest it. They waited
patiently in hope of explication. Balcanquall let the
silence drift a full two minutes before he began again.
"Aye, ye are speechless, are you not, in the face of such
depravity? Now this has come from that same court,
and lest ye did not follow it, I will make it plain to you."

At Richard's side, Hew saw Eleanor send up a silent
prayer that he would not.

"Tinsel, as you know, is the utter devastation, of a
property, and more than that, in sight of God, it is
damnation, or the devastation of the soul. Now I read
this as a warning to ye all, where these worldly vanities
will take ye, if ye do not keep your houses clean; then
set aside your longings and your lusts, your filthy toys
and vanities, your cravings for embroidered cloths and
costly foreign fripperies, your wasted hours at dice
and gaming, cards and other sports, your long nights at
the tavern, when ye ought to be at prayer; Or else your
own destruction soon awaits ye, here, and hereafter,
body and soul."

The congregation gave a great, collective sigh, letting
out its breath, and proving the sermon a success.
This was grand entertainment, for most were barely
coloured by this shame that shone its full harsh glare
upon their king.

244

Richard leant towards Hew. "Are we to infer, those verses came from Christian's shop?" he murmured.

Hew nodded dumbly.

"Then let me speak to Balcanquall, and find out what he knows. Have no fear," Richard promised, "I will be discreet."

As he made his way out through the crowd, Hew looked for Christian. He found her in the doorway, looking pale and anxious. She held William by the hand.

"That was Catherine's poem," she whispered.

"I guessed," Hew answered grimly. "Now we know what they were looking for."

"Thank God, we left no trace of it."

"Thanks rather, to your prescience. I'm sorry that I doubted it," admitted Hew. "What we must know is how this came to Balcanquall. Was it one of Catherine's copies, or the missing proof?"

"We cannot ask him where he got them, without owning that we knew about the poems," Christian answered fearfully.

"Richard has gone to talk to Balcanquall. He will be both subtle and discreet. Do you think it possible that Catherine sent the poems herself? She is perverse enough to do it, don't you think?"

Christian shook her head. "She would not put herself at such a risk. Besides, I do not think that Catherine would betray us, by giving out our name. For all that she pretends, she has a good and faithful heart."

"You do not know how glad I am to hear you say that," Hew told her earnestly.

Christian flushed unhappily. "We must go home," she murmured. "William finds the sermons tedious and long." The little boy stood straining at her hand, like a terrier on the leash.

Hew caught up with Richard in the street. He had already despatched his wife and children, and was making his way cautiously down towards the netherbow. "I am going to the caichpule," he confided. "Would you like to come?"

"I promised Meg that I would call in at the west port after kirk, to dine with her and Giles," Hew excused himself. "Though there is little to be had there in the way of dinner."

"Well and good — another time. I had a word with Balcanquall, and asked him how he came by Lady Catherine's verse. It turns out that her poems were sent to him, unsigned, in a letter that decried the printer, Christian Hall. It was this that he showed to the council, that caused them to shut down the press. He meant no malice to the printer, but he felt it was his duty. He was relieved to hear the council found no proofs."

"For sure, they did not, for Balcanquall had them," Hew replied thoughtfully. "Who told you it was Catherine's poem? I do not think I mentioned it."

Richard looked taken aback. "Well, I suppose Balcanquall."

"And yet you said the verses were unsigned."

"Ah, you have mistaken me. The letter was not signed. Balcanquall does not know who sent it. But the poet and the printer were both named. In truth, the

246

lady Catherine and her predilections are well known to anyone with influence at court."

"Then Catherine too may be at risk," Hew frowned.

"I fear that may be possible. Though Catherine Douglas is a favourite of the king, she has few other friends at court. It is possible that someone there has done this mischief to her."

"Is that likely," Hew objected, "when, exposing her, they do more damage to themselves?"

"You are a little animated, Hew." Richard looked amused. "Do I detect a softness now for Lady Catherine Douglas? Is she another of your conquests? Be warned, she will devour you."

"Catherine is a friend. The world acquits her badly. And her wild demeanour is a brave defence," Hew replied abruptly.

Richard grinned. "You are the most contentious boy. As always, you lack judgement, and will not be told. You want good sense, and discipline, and more appropriate friends."

It was a relief to leave the town, and come into the west port, where Hew was expected for dinner at the inn. He was surprised to find his sister sitting on her own, red-eyed, in the taproom.

"Where is Giles?" queried Hew.

"He has gone for a walk in the fields." Meg blew her nose. "And gave no hint or warning when he might return. I hoped that coming here to town . . . that we might make a holiday. And yet he spends his days in conference with Doctor Dow. He seems distant and distracted."

"I'll talk to him," Hew promised, moved by her distress. He hurried out into the fields but saw no sign of Giles. There was no one else in sight. Hew walked on a little, pulling at the grasses on the way, until he came across a courtyard of dilapidated buildings, leading to an ancient barn. There he heard a noise, a deep and throaty rasping. Curious, he opened the barn door. A little to his right, neatly folded on the floor, he found the doctor's coat and hat, on top of which were placed a pair of shoes. The gasping came again, a low and mournful moan, and as he peered into the darkness of the barn he saw a sight that chilled him to the bowel. Hanging from the rafters by a rope, naked in his shirt tails with his face tight and purple, hung the heavy carcass of Giles Locke. Hew did not take pause to stop and think, but launched himself wildly at the body, catching hold of the legs, that swung two or three feet from the ground. The combined effect of this precipitation, and of Giles' colluding weight, caused the rope to break, and the two of them fell tumbling to the ground.

"Oh my dear friend, surely nothing is quite bad enough to risk damnation. And besides, have you thought about Meg!" Hew cried. At the same time, Giles sat up and spluttered, "God save us, Hew, have you gone mad?"

"I, mad? I am not the one who tried to take his own life, against the laws of nature and of God!" remonstrated Hew.

Giles burst out laughing. "Oh my poor dear fool! Look at the rope! Was it round my neck?"

Hew looked at the rope ends, frayed in the straw, and had to concede it was not.

"Whatever were you doing, then?"

"An exercise," Giles answered, just a touch defensively. "That much any one with half an eye can see."

"An exercise?" echoed Hew, incredulous.

"As prescribed in the book, of health for magistrates." Giles stood up heavily and retrieved his clothes, extracting a small volume from the pile. "Such are part of my regimen for healthful exercise. 'Tie and make fast a strong rope to some beam or post, and through the same rope put a good big wooden cudgel . . . and taking hold with your hands at both ends of the cudgel, lift up your body so that your feet touch not the ground and move your legs to and fro hanging still by your hands.' It is designed, as you may well see, to draw down the humours."

"Dear God," muttered Hew, shaking his head.

They were disturbed, at that moment, by the farmer, who was standing in the doorway, with a pitchfork in his hand. "What do you think you are doing there? Ah, I see the way of it, ye filthie sodomites . . ."

Hew scrambled to his feet. "I have another exercise to recommend to you," he murmured to his friend.

Giles put on his coat. "Aye, and what is that?" he queried pleasantly.

"*Running!*"

★ ★ ★

They took refuge, giving way to tears of laughter, in Bessie Brewster's kitchen. After several stoups of ale, as Giles recovered his colour and his breath, Hew demanded, "Well, then, what is this about?"

Giles darkened again. "It is a little delicate," he answered miserably.

"Giles, we have long been friends."

"Aye, that's true enough." Giles took another swig of ale and sighed. "You promise not to laugh?"

"In truth, no," Hew admitted cheerfully, "though I promise not to taunt you with it."

"Then that must suffice," Giles accepted gloomily. "The truth is that your sister Meg ... her falling sickness for a while grew out of hand, and we could not control the fits. I feared it was the marriage brought it on, when she was used to be more calm and constant."

"She is recovered now, though?" Hew asked anxiously.

"Aye, with medicines, we have come to manage it. As you see, she is quite well. But the matter is this. Since her sickness, I have found myself unable ... to ... to converse with her."

Hew stared at him. "Then the marriage is not consummated?"

"At first it was," admitted Giles. "In truth, her sickness is no bar to it; only I have formed a fear ... a pressing fear, of harming her. Since your father's illness and our separation ... since the coming of the grandgore, resolution fails. I find myself ... inhibited. It is a fear, in part, that I may cause her hurt. And then there is the risk — the real risk, you must see — that she may fall with child, and that may pose a risk to her, that I cannot calculate. And to lose her — let me say, I cannot contemplate it. Together with these fears, I daily come across more cases of the pox."

"Surely, though, you're not afraid of that," protested Hew.

"Not for ourselves," admitted Giles. "Yet in my mind it sullies and pollutes the act, and in my heart I see her fragile and so pure I know not how to broach her. In truth, I cannot broach her, and I fail. Or else I fear to fail."

"I understand. It is this wretched sickness has polluted reason, and perverts good sense. Do you still desire her?"

"More than ever, aye," Giles answered wretchedly. "It is for that reason I have taken up this course of manly exercise."

"To strengthen your . . . resolve?"

"To distract from it. To channel all those energies, and frustrations, I would spend on her."

Hew shook his head. "You need to tell her, Giles," he told him gently.

"How could I? She is pure and good, and can have no notion of such things."

"I think you are mistaken, in her expectations. Giles, you are a man of much experience."

"I know it. It has never failed before."

"Yet you are shy and blushing like the greenest boy. Meg is your wife."

"That may be the trouble," Giles conceded gloomily.

Hew felt at a loss. "Well, I can say no more. This will not resolve unless you talk to her."

"Of what? Of her sickness? Of childbirth? Of grandgore? The marital act? You must see how hopeless that is! I am resigned to circumvent it in this way rather than distress her by approaching it."

"She is distressed, as it is, by your circumvention," Hew pointed out. "She thinks you do not care for her. And so it's clear your strategy has failed."

"That is the rub," admitted Giles. "The closer I become to her, the more I do desire her; thus, the more I want her, the more I am determined to avoid her."

"Then the solution is simple enough. Do not avoid her. Give in to the desire," Hew advised.

"But the greater the desire, the more my inhibition. I am closed in a circle that I cannot break."

The Borough Muir

Later that same week, Hew and Richard were at work together in their chambers when a messenger arrived with a letter for Hew. It was delivered first to Richard, who broke the seal, observing dryly, "It seems you have a client."

Hew looked up from his desk. "Truly? Yet I am not qualified."

"For this case, in particular, I fear that may be true. Yet the client asks for you by name, and is most emphatic. It is Lady Catherine Douglas."

"Catherine!" Hew felt his heart leap. "Is it about her poems?"

"Your question proves my point; you are not qualified to cope with her. Though I concede, it may be about the poems," Richard answered with a smile, "I do not think that likely. She claims she wishes to consult you on a personal matter. She wants you at her house, at five o'clock this afternoon. Her house is on the Canongate. Do not be late.

"It is a pity," he reflected, "for I have to go to Craigmillar this afternoon, to see Sir David Preston. I meant to take you with me. You would like his tower house. It is rare and grand. He has made a fish pond in the shape of letter P." Since Richard was in a particularly good humour, it was far from clear whether he was being serious. "It is very likely I shall stay for supper; I shall have to leave you here," he went on. "No matter, then, another time. Since these people are too grand to come to us, we must go to them. Yet it may prove diverting for us both." He peered out of the window. "Do you think it looks like rain?"

"It is a little dark," admitted Hew.

"I fear it. I shall set out now, before the storm. I wish you every fortune with your conquest." Richard bowed.

Though Richard left behind a pile of case notes, Hew could not settle to the work. He yawned and fidgeted, stretched his legs and wandered round the room, playing with the ink and quills. He took a stack of textbooks from the shelves and put them back again. The clerk began to irk him with the scratching of his pen. He considered, and dismissed, a visit to the printing house: it felt like infidelity. The afternoon dragged on. Presently, it began to rain; he watched the water puddle darkly in the close, and became more restless at the greyness of the sky, that made the day seem later than it was. He had no cause to go back home and change, for he wore a brand new suit that the tailor had made ready just the day before. It would be ruined, he realised gloomily. At last he judged it almost five, and set off to the Canongate. It was raining heavily, and by the time he arrived he was soaked.

Catherine's house was at the bottom of the street, close to the abbey of Holyrood house, a tall land with a garden, and fine windows cased and glazed. As he shook the water from his boots, Hew rapped at the door. The servant took a while to answer, calling out at last, "Lady Catherine is unwell."

Hew felt the rush of disappointment. "Then I'll call another time, and wish her well," he answered miserably.

"Nay, not at all, sir. I'm to take your cloak and show you in. She insisted on it, sir. Go now, it is the door there by the right. I'll set your things here by the fire to dry. Tis a damp enough night of it now."

It was, Hew conceded wryly, a damp enough night; his green cloak hung a sodden black, and reeking like the dun ewe's pelt, his cap wrung limp and shapeless. He allowed himself to be relieved of them, and knocked on Catherine's door.

"Is it you, Hew? Come then, I have wanted you." Her voice came oddly raw, as if she had a cold. Inside, the room was ablaze. A great fire raged upon the hearth, beneath the flaring of a dozen candles. The furnishings and drapes were coloured red. The board was set with scarlet cloth, upon which stood a jug of claret, burnished in the flame. The chamber was private and enclosed, and there was little else to catch the light, except the stand bed boxed in red, its crimson curtains drawn. Perhaps from the fire, or the effect of the furniture, Hew felt himself perspiring, his wet breeches awkwardly starting to steam.

"Pull aside the curtain, do. It is hot in here. And I want see you, Hew!" Lady Catherine croaked.

He did so, folding the fabric back to the post, and gazed at her.

"Sit by me on the bed. I swear, you are blushing."

"It's warm in here." Hew looked away.

She lay there on her pillows, naked to the hips, where modesty, or fickleness, had draped a sheet. Her hands were linked behind her head, a pose designed to tilt and tip her breasts, which winked at him becomingly, beneath her tumbling curls. She was laughing at him.

"Then you must take off your coat," she counselled.

"I heard that you were indisposed. Did you expect the surgeon?" he retorted dryly. Nonetheless, he had undone the buttons on his coat. With slow deliberation, and his back to her, he folded it and placed it on the floor.

"I expected *you*. Poor Hew! I fear that I have shocked you!"

"You wanted to consult me, on a legal matter. Then perhaps you wish to make your will?" he answered gravely.

"Ah, you're so dry!" Lazily, she shifted in the bed. Still he did not turn.

"I think it is the scholar's life. It *desiccates* you," Catherine teased. "Is it true, they sprinkle herbs among the college oats, to shrivel up the ardour of the rampant boy, that all his longings turn to dust, and he is good for nothing but the kirk? The pity of it! All those years!"

"I know not. I have always eaten out."

He turned to face her then, damp in his silk hose and shirt, and sat upon the corner of the bed, looking down at her.

"Be careful!" Catherine taunted him. "Lest looking at a woman turns your wits!"

"Against that risk," he informed her seriously, "I have made a plan."

"What are you doing?" she demanded.

He had gathered back her hair, exposing her shoulders and neck. With delicate fingers he circled her throat, tracing a line to her breast.

"Cartography," he teased. "'Tis what we scholars do when we are come upon new worlds. Surely you have heard of it? We are intent on mapping them. Now then," he frowned a little, studiously, at the crescent scar he fingered on her breast, "what might we call these? A pair of earthly dunnocks or twin celestial spheres?"

"Impudence!" She slapped him, sinking back at once to submit to exploration. Hew continued with his survey. Presently he said, "In order to complete the map, I must fold back the counterpane. This piece of cloth is an impediment."

"Is it, though? To what?"

"*Excavations*," he said solemnly.

"Ah, I think not! It's your turn!"

Nimbly, she slipped out from under him and pushed him back upon the pillows where she sat astride, triumphant, unbuttoning his britches and shirt. Laughing, he allowed her access.

"I see virgin lands!" Catherine cried in triumph.

"You are mistaken, alas. *That* is a well-trodden path."

257

"Whisht will you, insolent boy! Or I will mark it out for you!" She trailed her fingers down his chest. "Aye, these are forests . . . *oh!*"

Finding out the place, she whispered to him softly, "Here be dragons, though . . ."

At that moment, which was not the most convenient place to pause, there came a sharp rap on the door. The servant had returned, and gazed at Hew with a look of bored contempt that plainly stated he was not the first sad loun laid bare in Catherine's bed. "There's a woman down below that wants you. And she will not be deterred, sir," she declared, her tone implying this was usual too. "It is the printer, Christian Hall," she added carelessly.

Hew was already dressing, fumbling with his strings, as Catherine lay back in the sheets. She said a little ruefully, "Tis plain to see where your allegiance lies."

"You are mistaken," mumbled Hew, his shirt above his head. "It is not like that. There must be something wrong, else Christian would not come here. I'll be back."

"Aye, aye," she was laughing at him, more amused than cross, "though you may fool yourself, I am less easily deceived. Go, play the printer's prentis, if you will."

He ignored her, already at the door, and took the turret stairs two at a time until he reached the hall, where Christian stood waiting. Twin spots of colour marked her pale cheeks when she saw him, his coat still half-unbuttoned and his shirt untucked.

"My doublet was soaked," he muttered, and felt himself blush.

"Of course," she said bleakly. "Forgive me, I disturb you. I ought not to have come. Richard's servant told me you were here on business."

He caught at her sleeve. "What is it? Something's wrong."

Christian hesitated, on the edge of tears. "You will think it foolish. Only William and the maid have not returned. She went out on the muir, after all I told her."

Is that all, he found himself thinking, and bit back the words. He felt angry with her, not for intruding, but for the confusion she had wrought in him. He knew it was unreasonable. "Is it not likely," he forced himself to say calmly, "that they have taken shelter from the rain?"

"That is what everyone says. But with all that has happened . . . these strange events . . . I cannot help but fear some evil has afflicted them," she answered miserably. And he knew, to his shame as he stood in his unbuttoned coat, that it was fear for William that had brought her there, and only fear for William, desperation that drove out all proper feeling, that could make her bear to stand there in the face of his delinquency.

"Phillip is making lanterns to take out upon the moor, to make a search before it grows dark. We hoped you might make up the party," Christian whispered.

It was all but dark already, in the wrenching wind and rain. "For sure . . . but in a moment . . . I must fetch my cloak."

She shook her head; she had already given up. "The party is about to leave. I must go ahead. But if you are engaged —"

"You cannot think it! I will come." He watched her leave, hopeless and silent a moment, and then returned upstairs to Catherine. He felt relieved to see her dressed, in a shirt of sorts, and perched upon a stool, combing out her hair, that fell in thick red curls upon the linen of her shift.

"I have to go."

"Of course you do. Printer's boy," she taunted him.

"You are mistaken, madam," he said stiffly. "I do not answer to Christian. But her child has gone missing, on the borough muir. A search party has been raised. I have promised to join it."

"Is that so?" She made her eyes wide. "Her little child? He is so very small, the muir so very large. And is he there alone?"

"He went there with his nursemaid," he informed her shortly. Her questions had begun to annoy him; still, he felt attracted to her. Coming close to gather up his clothes, he could smell the perfume on her hair.

"Then no doubt the nurse has sought for shelter, and will stay there till the rain has passed," she answered quietly. "There is an ancient chapel on the muir; I expect you'll find them there. It's madness to attempt a search tonight."

"I quite agree."

"Well, then, stay?" she tempted, setting down the comb.

260

He swallowed. "Though, dearly, I would like to, I cannot."

"As you will. You should know though, that if you go now, the offer will not come again."

"What!" he demanded. "You would turn me away, because I helped to look for Christian's child?"

"Aye, because of that," she answered oddly.

There was no time for argument; in any case, he scarcely took her seriously. He kissed her on the cheek, a mere formality, and took his leave.

The rain had not ceased in its intensity; the whole of the high street was grey, the mud track beginning to puddle, running down the slabs in streaks like beggars' tears. Hew's cloak and hat, already sodden, gave up all vestige of shape. It was madness, certainly, to venture on the moor in such weather, and yet Hew met the party at the printer's shop already setting out, with a sombre urgency that made him feel ashamed. Giles and Meg were there; Meg had her arms around Christian, holding her back. "We must wait here, in case they return. Where have you been, Hew?" his sister demanded, and he blushed afresh beneath her glare.

"Go to, go to, no time to lose," Giles put in briskly. He was wearing a fisherman's jerkin, and a pair of wool breeks stiff with tanning, with waxed boots ballooned to the thigh, topped with a cope of oiled cloth, his wardrobe never ceasing to surprise. In his hand he carried one of Phillip Ramsey's lanterns, mounted on a stick, a cone of waxed paper, shielding a candle. It gave off little light, already faltering in the wind, and its flimsiness appeared to underline the hopeless nature of their expedition. Nonetheless, there was a certain sturdy comfort seeing Giles there in his raincloths, and Hew was about to ally himself with his party when Phillip appeared, and shot him a murderous look.

"We will split up," he announced. "The physician goes with Walter to the wester hie gate . . . and you, no you don't," he took Hew's elbow grimly, "you will come with me, and search the east side by the gibbet."

"Why on earth there?" Hew asked nervously. Phillip stood brooding and angry, and he wondered for a moment whether he was mad. He glanced across at Giles, who appeared not to have noticed, busily adjusting an enormous hat which Meg tied to the buttons of his cloak with bonnet strings.

"You were at the house of Catherine Douglas?" Phillip demanded.

"And if I was?" retorted Hew.

Phillip glowered at him. "At another time, and in another place, I should strike you down. For now, I should be grateful to you."

"Whatever do you mean?"

"You really don't know? Then you're more of a fool than I thought."

Phillip was deranged, decided Hew. He had given up the warmth of Catherine's bed to spend the evening with a madman, traipsing in the mud upon the borough muir, doomed to make his search among the sodden corpses, where the wild dogs gathered, howling out the storm. Gloomily, he followed, with the flicker of the lanterns in the wind no brighter than the prick of fireflies dying out, and tried not to think of Catherine in her linen shift, combing out her hair before the fire.

Though it was early still, the skies were thick with cloud. They lost sight of the path as they made their way deeper onto the moor. Phillip stumbled in the darkness, crying, "Sweet Christ Jesus, help me! I have lost the light!"

"What is it, do you fear the dark?" Hew called out dryly. "A solace, too, if Christian heard you curse."

Phillip screamed, "God's light! Where is the *light!*"

"What have you found?" Hew swung round with the lantern, lighting Phillip's face.

She was not long dead. For Hew could smell the blood still, a thin metallic stream that seeped into the earth, sweet and sticky at her throat. It was smeared and sticky too on Phillip's face, like a bairn's face gorged on sweetmeats. And in horror he was scrubbing it, furious with blades of grass, scraping clean until it bled. He had fallen across her, deep in her belly, where she was torn to show her innards, spilling from the pale white flesh.

She was not long dead. For Hew had seen her that same morning, setting out, her scrubbed and cheerful face pinched pink to hide the pock marks, smiling, round and foolish, when the birds were singing, and the sky was blue. Had he spoken to her, then? Or spoken to the child? "I saw her but this morning, surely, she cannot be dead," he whispered idiotically. "I saw her only yesterday; then she can *not* be dead."

She was not long dead. Yet already the land had begun to claim her. The rain had smudged her face, and muddied her like tears, knitting her drab hair into the greasy earth. It puddled in the places she had spilled, the grass lank and dark with her blood.

"Jesu, I fell into her," Phillip was sobbing, wiping his mouth.

Into her cavernous flesh, sticky and soft. Alison was not long dead, yet the land had already reclaimed her, carrion for sodden earth, seeping through the ground.

Hew took out his handkerchief and handed it to Phillip, who continued scrubbing at his face until all trace was gone.

"I can *taste* her," he moaned.

"You imagine it." Hew moved a little further back, as Phillip called out fearfully. "Do not go! Where are you going?" He remained upon his knees.

"Hush. To find the light." Hew found the lantern where Phillip had dropped it, all too close to Alison, and lit the candle from his own. He gave the lamp to Phillip. "Stand up. Hold it high, and shout. We must alert the rest."

"Stay!" Phillip called out desperately, "Pray, do not go!"

"Stand up and hold it high," Hew ordered, not without compassion. He began to edge away, methodically to search the fence at its perimeter, and with his boot to kick aside the clumps of moss and leaves, searching, with a calm cold dread, for the body of the child.

A world appeared to pass before they saw the lights, and heard the others come towards them, tiny pricks of firelight answering their cries. And then, in a moment, it seemed Giles was there, assuming grim and clear command, and his vast oiled cape was pressed into service — perhaps one always meant for it — and made a dry shroud for Alison's corpse. And Giles could lift her gently, like a sleeping child, and rest her in its folds, and though he frowned a little, he did not remark the blood that stained his coat and hands. And he tucked back her hair, and brushed away the crumbs, and covered up her nakedness, that went beyond the flesh into the spilling of her bowels.

"You must take her to the house of Doctor Laurence Dow, at the Cowgate," he instructed. "And he will take the course of action proper to his office."

"Was it the dogs?" Phillip demanded suddenly. "Was it the dogs, did *that* to her."

Giles regarded him curiously. "A little brandy, I think," he said after a moment, "would serve the case well."

"I can taste her in my mouth," Phillip told him desperately.

Giles tutted. "Brandy, as I said." He walked off in search of Hew, who was poking at the damp earth with a stick.

"We must take the lassie back now to the town. Tomorrow, we shall mount a proper search. But now it's growing dark, the clouds obscure the moon."

Hew rounded on him. "Suppose he is alive! We cannot leave him here!"

Giles answered patiently. "The muir is five miles square; you cannot find him on your own, and in the dark."

265

"Then fetch men with torches. Light fires! Call out the watch! Wake up the town! We cannot go back."

The doctor sighed. "It shall be done. You will not want for reinforcements. I must go now, with the body. Truth will out, *post mortem*."

Hew strode over to Phillip, who stood shivering, miserable and drenched, and seized him by the throat. "How did you know where to find her?" he cried hysterically.

Phillip crumpled, sobbing, to his knees. "I swear, I did not know. I took you to the gibbet for I meant to frighten you."

Giles came between them, taking hold of Hew and shaking him. "Who does this help?" he asked him quietly. "It is not Phillip. Let him go."

The Bairn's Part

It was Richard, in the end, who persuaded Hew to leave the muir, arriving with the watch. Hew never found out who had called them, whether it was Giles, or his good friend Doctor Dow, who had sufficient presence to arouse the soldiers and recruit them in the search for a missing printer's child. The muir became a blaze of light, and Richard took Hew by the arm. "Come home with me. For it is almost night, and the gates will soon be locked. There is nothing more that we can do tonight."

Hew obeyed him numbly. Drenched with rain and cold, he had lost all feeling. He allowed his friend to take him home. By the fireside, it was Richard who brought towels and called for possets, and for brandy-wine: "You have had a shock." Hew could not stop shivering. And it was Richard who sat with him all the night, when Eleanor had gone to bed, to keep the fire alight and listen to the horror of his tale.

At last, the rain had stopped, and a wary, bloodshot dawn began to streak across the sky, watery and tentative. Richard opened up the shutters to the gallery. "It's almost light."

"I must go back," Hew murmured.

"In an hour or two. It can do no good when you have not slept. The soldiers will pick up the search. Rest awhile, Hew, it will help. If there is news, I will wake you."

"William was my father's grandson, and my flesh and blood," Hew cried. "I cannot leave him on the muir."

"I understand," Richard sighed. He returned to the window, looking out upon the street. Already, a small handcart rumbled through the marketplace. Across the square, doors and shutters opened; someone emptied water down into the close.

"I think you must prepare yourself to face the worst," Richard told him gently.

"There are outlaws and Egyptians in the forests on the muir. I am very much afraid that they have killed the nurse to take the child."

Hew shook his head. "That is a nursery tale, to frighten bairns," he answered fiercely. "I do not believe the gypsies steal our children. Why should they?"

"Why would they not," asked Richard, sadly, "when we take theirs? The imps you saw on Dysart Muir were tinklars' bairns, the lot of them."

But the soldiers had flushed out the woods, setting light to ramshackle houses, and had driven out the gypsies from the muir. Hew was sickened to see families forced into the glare, routed from their homes. The muir was cleared of outlaws, and the prisons filled, without news of William. The little boy was lost without a trace. Hew returned, several times a day, to Christian's printing house, and yet he could not bring himself to speak to her. She remained upstairs, in the care of Meg, while Hew hung about the workshop, quarrelling with Phillip. Walter printed notices about the missing child, and they posted them in every tavern, shop and kirk within the boundaries of the town, to no effect. On the third day, Hew said desperately to Richard, "I think that I may venture further south, in hope of hearing news."

Richard sighed. "Why not? In truth, you are no use to me, in your present mood. And though there is small hope, the air will do you good. You may take my horse," he added generously.

Richard's courser was a light red roan, of calm and gentle temperament. Hew took the easter hie gate, to Dalkeith, passing by the gibbet where they had found the corpse. In sunshine and a brisk light wind, the place had lost its terror, though the creaking gibbet and the circling crows were eerie still. Riding south, Hew felt the air clear a little as he left behind the oppression of the town. He was running, he was too aware, from Christian, for he could not face the anguish of her grief. The last time they had spoken was at Catherine's house; his dereliction haunted him. It helped to have a purpose, to be riding out with leaflets, looking for the child, to pursue inquiries, anywhere but here. It helped to ride eastwards, in the open air. He knew, however, he was running away. Unless he found her child, he could not bear to look on Christian's face.

Three miles south east of the town, Hew arrived at Craigmillar, the family seat of the Prestons. Sir David was at home and received Hew kindly, coming out to meet him in the gardens of a castle that overlooked the town on every side from the summit of its tower. There was indeed a fishpond, Hew noticed sadly, that shaped the letter P. Sir David was magnanimous. "I knew your father," he professed, "when we kept a house in town. My father was the provost, and knew Matthew well. And now you are prenticed to the lawman Richard Cunningham. Well, well, he has done work for us. Eleanor, his wife, is our distant cousin. You are welcome here."

These credentials well established, Sir David took Hew into the tower house to show him the view. From the top of the tower, he could see the whole, from the castle on its rock to the park at Holyrood, the hollows and high crags and hills, and beyond to Leith, and across the estuary. Below him, laid out like a counterpane, he saw the borough muir, its wildness interspersed with little lands and settlements between the clumps of trees. Somewhere among them, he thought with a pang, must be William.

Sir David was staring at him. "I fear the height up here has made you giddy," he said sympathetically. "On some, it has that effect. A grand enough view, is it not?"

"Beyond compare," Hew assured him. "And yet it brings a heavy sadness. I am looking for a bairn who was lost upon the muir, and I cannot help but think he must be buried in those trees. If I look hard enough, and long enough, I might find him. Yet I do not want to find him in his grave." He felt himself grow hot, and rubbed his face.

"You are faint," Sir David said perceptively, "and must sit down and drink. Tell me about your lost bairn. The muir is no place for children. By the burgh loch, or the king's park, may be safe enough. Beyond, I would not walk myself without a guard."

"The boy was lost by the gibbet, on the easter road."

"By the gibbet! Why would he be there?" the laird exclaimed.

"He went walking with his nurse, whose body was found murdered on that spot."

Hew handed him a leaflet. "Can you show this paper, and explain its contents, to your people and your friends?"

"For sure." Sir David glanced at the letter and furrowed his brow. "What age is the child?"

"A little more than two, and less than three."

"Then I do wonder . . ." Preston went on thoughtfully. "A day or so ago, I heard a tale . . . It may be nothing, though. Have you left this notice at the parish kirk at Liberton?"

"No, not yet," admitted Hew. "Tell me, is there news?"

Preston shook his head. "I cannot say. From what I heard, I recommend you try Kirk Liberton. Ask for John Davidson, the minister there. He is an interesting man."

"That is not the John Davidson that was regent at St Andrews, and that was expelled for his contentious verses?" wondered Hew.

"The very same," Sir David smiled. "He has been, to some degree, rehabilitated, though he remains a thorn in the monarch's side. Ask him what he knows of this."

271

"I thank you, sir. Is there something you suspect? Can you not give a hint of it?" Hew demanded eagerly.

The laird shook his head. "I would not raise false hopes. But I wish you fortune in your search. When you return to town there is a service you can do for me, and I should be obliged to you. Ask Richard Cunningham to call on us. I have waited on him for the last three days."

"Has he not been to see you?" queried Hew, surprised.

"Not unless he came when I was out," Preston answered dryly. "We expected him at supper. It is a matter of some moment, which must shortly be attended to. Pray you, do remind him. He will understand."

"I am training for the bar, if you wanted some advice," Hew ventured.

"Thank you. That is kind. But this is a personal matter. Richard will attend to it," Preston answered vaguely. "Godspeed, then. I will see you on your way."

Hew took the next path west towards Kirk Liberton. The old church here was crumbled and worn, for the parish was a poor one, yet the minister received him with a gentle grace. John Davidson had turned a little grey, and grown a little thinner than the regent Hew remembered; nonetheless, his eyes were bright and keen. Hew introduced himself. "I know you from St Leonard's; you were regent there while I was still a student."

"Cut short, I fear," the minister said sadly. "It was always my deepest regret that I was forced to leave my place, and abandon my scholars halfway through their course. By the look of it, you have done well. What did you say your name was? Ah, now I remember you! A subtle and ingenious boy, well-disposed to argument. Perhaps, in truth," he twinkled, "a little too disposed. You had, I think, a somewhat serious friend."

"Nicholas Colp," supplied Hew.

"Aye, Nicholas. Is he now ordained? He was well fitted to the kirk."

"I fear not. Fortune did not treat him kindly. We are friends, still, nonetheless."

"Friendship is a blessing," Davidson observed. "As for fortune, that may turn against us. You, I think, were never destined for the church, nor ever apt to prove a good disciple. Yet you had courage, and some wit. To what end have you put them?"

"I am training for the law."

"Ah, the *law*," the minister said scornfully.

"Though I am not quite convinced of it," admitted Hew.

"There is hope for you yet, then," Davidson approved. "If I could give you some advice, it should be to be true to yourself; it may cause you anguish, in the piercing glare of day, but in the small hours of the night, there is a deeper comfort that will come to you. We are not put in this world for our ease."

"You say that, yet you fled to England," Hew objected recklessly, "at the whiff of danger."

Davidson looked startled a moment, and then broke into a smile. "Aye, so I did," he conceded gently. "You always were a most contentious boy. And what you say is true enough. It felt like dereliction, and my heart was set against it, lest it hurt the courage of my friends. But my friends counselled me to ask God what I should do, and so I did. I knelt there for a long time praying, where at length God told me that he wanted me to flee."

"How came you back to Liberton?" Hew changed the subject tactfully.

"The earl of Morton relented at last, and permitted me this living, that I have held these past three years. Now fortune has turned against him," Davidson continued without rancour. "God willing, I may bring some comfort in his final hours. Now," he went on, clearly moved. "What is it I can do for you?"

When Hew had told his story, Davidson exclaimed, "Now there is a strange tale!"

"And one that bears repeating," Hew assured him. "I urge you, spread the word."

"I doubt . . . I do fear, to do better than that." The minister seemed troubled. "Forgive me, I fear we have made a mistake."

"What do you mean?" challenged Hew, half daring to hope.

Davidson sighed. "Three nights ago, a stranger called here at the kirk. He brought a little child. He claimed he came upon him wandering by the muir, a gypsy bairn, he said. The bairn was threadbare and bloodied, soaking in the rain. He wanted us to take him as a foundling."

"Then you have him here?" Hew demanded anxiously.

274

The minister shook his head. "Peace, I regret, we do not have the child. The kirk session was convinced his story was a lie, and sent them on their way. The man was a packman, some sort of cadger. He would not have been the first to offer up his bairn, for the nurture of the parish, once his wife had died. As you must understand, the parish here is sorely overstretched. We have suffered famine now for several years. The soil is poor; our oats and barley seldom thrive. We cannot fill our own mouths, let alone a stranger's bairn."

"Where did you send them? Which way did they go?" Hew asked abruptly.

"We set them on the Dalkeith road, and that with no good grace," Davidson admitted. "They were going south."

"Then you will excuse me. I must take my leave."

"I understand your haste. But consider that this may not be your child, but the cadger's own true bairn, as we supposed."

Hew shook his head. "A child of two or three, and wandering on the muir, is too much a coincidence. It must be William."

"Pray God, then, that you find them. There is one more thing, "the minister said delicately, "that you do not seem to notice on this paper here. Was William an idiot child?"

Hew stopped in his tracks. "An *idiot*?" He stared. "No, you are mistaken. He is not an idiot."

"Then you must consider this is not your child. The chapman brought a blabbering bairn, that whimpered when we questioned it, and could not speak its name. It was a factor we considered when we thought to take him in. An idiot bairn may fail to earn a living, and may yet live long."

"Thank God for Christian charity!" Hew answered bitterly.

The minister smiled ruefully. "The little that we have does not go far."

As they came towards Dalkeith, Richard's horse began to flag and Hew left him at the stables of the nearest inn, to be fed and watered. He walked to the parish church of St Nicholas, close by Dalkeith palace: the earl of Morton's seat, he remembered wryly. To his great surprise, his inquiries here were fruitful. A bairn had been found the day before, abandoned in the kirk. Since no one had come forth to claim him, the infant was to be fostered, pending fresh inquiry. At Hew's request, the child was brought back to the church, clinging to his foster mother's skirts.

"Is this the bairn?" the minister inquired.

For the first time, Hew felt hope and certainty give way to sudden fear. He had been sure, beyond a doubt, the infant must be William. With the little boy in front of him, he no longer felt so certain.

"Hercules, do you ken this man?" the woman asked the child.

"Hercules?" echoed Hew, incredulous.

"We did not ken his name," the woman said defensively.

"My own good lady wife," the minister explained, "likes to name the orphan bairns. She can be a little fanciful. Tis likely, if we keep him, we shall plump for George."

Hew knelt to the floor, level with the child. "Do you know me, William?" he asked gently. He looked into the small, closed face, for some small spark of Christian, in the wide grey eyes, in the soft curve of the mouth, and met with blankness.

"He does not speak, no, not a word. It is an idiot child," the foster mother said, almost with a touch of pride. "But he is douce and brave; he disna greet."

"Is this not your nephew, then?" the minister inquired, perplexed.

"I confess," Hew answered helplessly. "I cannot tell." It did not sound like William, he reflected. He looked at the gude wife. "Have you cut his hair?"

She nodded. "Aye, we always do. For lice."

"And you have changed his clothes?"

She pursed her lips. "We had to burn his clothes. For they were torn to rags and thick with blood, and we were fearful of infection. It was not the bairn's blood, though. There was not a mark on him."

Hew had an image in his mind, of Christian sewing ribbons to the sleeves of William's gown. It must be William, surely, he convinced himself, if the clothes were stained with blood.

"I have come to take you home," he whispered to the child. "Home to . . . *Minnie*, who has missed you." He had struggled to recall the baby name. On impulse, he picked up the little boy and held him close. The child did not resist, but in a moment placed his head upon

Hew's shoulder, and with a sigh clutched two small fists into the velvet of Hew's cloak and closed his eyes.

"He likes you, anyway," the minister observed, in clear relief.

"Aye, I will take him." Hew fished in his pocket. "Here is something for the poor box, for his keep."

He could feel the child's breath, hot on his neck, and the grip of the small fist assured him he was still awake, yet the little boy clung to him, motionless, a thin scrap of rags, hot in his hands.

"Let us hope that you are William," he murmured to the child. "Or else, God help us both."

It was now too late to set off to Edinburgh; the gates would be locked before they could reach them. Hew returned to the inn where he had left the horse, and took a room for the night, with a *lit de camp* for himself and a small cot for William, no more than a blanket thrown over rags. The premises were neither clean nor comfortable, and with a sense of misgiving he took the little boy into the taproom. It was early still, yet the place was crowded, and a raucous game of dice was in progress by the bar. Hew found a quiet corner where he set the child upon a stool. He ordered a bowl of boiled mutton in broth and a cup of small beer for the child. Somehow, he persuaded the tapster to produce a jug of claret, bread and cheese, and a plate of roasted beef. The food was surprisingly good. William seemed content enough, for he drank down his broth, gazing all the while at Hew's cup and plate, till Hew gave in and fed him scraps of beef, washed down with the rough watered wine. "Do not tell your mother, though," he

278

winked at him. The child stared back solemnly, and Hew was in no doubt, he was no fool. William, full at last, wiped his smeary mouth upon his sleeve and slipped down from his stool towards the gaming tables, where the men were playing cards. Alarmed, Hew went after him, reaching for his hand. "You must not run off!"

As he spoke, the dealer of the cards looked up, and catching sight of William, gave a start. The man turned round wildly, looking for escape. Hew caught his eye. It was Marten Voet, the card seller. And since the gaming tables, and the crowd of players, and Hew Cullan and the little boy stood between him and the door, he had no choice but to confront them. William stood, impassive, like a little ghost, his small hand resting quietly in Hew's. And had he been a ghost, Marten Voet could not have been more terrified.

"No, no, no," he cried at last. "You will *not* do that to me. I swear, he is not mine!"

"You left him in the kirk," Hew answered quietly.

"What else could I have done? Without I left him there, the parish would not take him. I am no monster. I have stayed to see him settled," Marten cried.

"Then you are the cadger, who brought him to Kirk Liberton."

"What can I say, sir?" the card seller whimpered. "I found him on the muir, and wish to God I'd left him there. He is the devil's child."

He was afraid of William, so it seemed, yet William, clearly, had no fear of him. He had flopped down on

279

the floor and was playing with a card that had been dropped.

"He is my nephew," Hew said coldly.

Marten crumpled in relief. "Your nephew? Thank the lord! Then you have him, sir. I found him at the roadside by the muir. And, God help me, I should have left him there if I had known the trouble he would cause."

"You do well enough without him," Hew observed shrewdly. A heap of coins lay on the table, close to the card seller's hand.

Marten's opponent, who was drunk and losing heavily, took advantage of this fresh diversion to demand of Hew, "Do you know this man, sir? What do you say? Is he a cheat?"

Hew rubbed his chin. "Indeed, I thought I knew him," he said thoughtfully, "and his name was Marten Voet. Now, it seems, he has a different name, and another set of lies."

"What's that?" The man staggered to his feet, swaying dangerously, "Are you a card jak? A swingeour?"

The card seller gazed at Hew imploringly. "Do not do this, sir. Why do you hound me? If the bairn is your nephew, then I saved his life."

"I reserve judgement on that." Hew placed his hand on his sword. "Meanwhile, there is something we must settle. Perhaps you will return this man's money, and share a quiet drink with me, where we are not overheard."

Marten saw no other way. Miserably, he pushed the pile of coins towards his opponent, who protested, "What are you, the law?"

"Aye, I am the law," Hew answered smoothly. "And I am the kirk, where gaming is prohibited, as I'm sure you know. Take your losses, sir; your wife will thank you for them." He steered Marten back to their table in the corner, where he settled William firmly on his stool. "You will sit there," he instructed. "And *you*, sir, will sit there," he said to Marten Voet, pushing him down on a bench. "If you think of fighting, know that I am armed."

"Why should I want to fight you?" Marten asked, bewildered. "I am a printer. I sell playing cards."

"Tell me what happened to the nurse," demanded Hew.

"What nurse?"

"The child went walking with his nursemaid on the borough muir. The nurse was killed," Hew said abruptly.

"Dear God, is that what happened?" Marten cried, aghast. "I swear, I saw no nurse. Do you think I would have taken him, if there had been a nurse? I found him wandering by the muir. And he was soaked and bloodied and his clothes were torn. It was the foulest night you ever saw, and I took him to the nearest church. They would not take him in. Can you imagine that? The bairn was soaked and starving and they would not take him in! What was I to do? I could not leave the child. I could not keep him."

"And so you left him here, abandoned in the church," reflected Hew.

"They did not see us coming," Marten answered hopelessly. "It was all that I could do."

Marten's tale rang true. "Aye, I believe you," Hew sighed at last. "Why did you change your name?"

"I am deep in debt, sir," the card seller confessed. "There is a warrant in the name of Marten Voet, from Middelburg. And since Campvere is your staple overseas, they would send me back, and I would be imprisoned, if they caught me. When I saw you at the senzie fair, I swear, I did not lie to you. I told the truth about the inquisition. All my life, I have been running, hounded on from place to place. The last thing I should want — the very last thing, sir, would be a child."

"Aye, fair enough," acknowledged Hew.

"Then you believe me, sir?"

"Why not? It is a desperate tale. Where will you go now?"

Marten looked incredulous. "You mean to let me go, sir?"

"I see no reason not. You saved the child. And if you had not brought him from the roadside, in all probability he would have died. Here is money for your pains."

"I thank you more than I can tell you, sir." Marten seized the purse. He hesitated. "You think he saw it, then? The thing that you described?"

"I think it very likely," Hew conceded grimly. "The boy is not a natural idiot. I fear he saw the slaughter, and it turned his wits."

"God save us," Marten muttered.

"You should thank the Lord that William seems to like you."

"He is more at ease with me than I should like," the card seller owned ruefully. "I am well glad, in truth, to see the back of him."

A Pack of Lies

Hew stripped the boy of his clothes and tucked him into the small bed of blankets. William made no objection, his head already drooping as his eyes began to close. It took Hew a little longer to find rest on the nearby pallet bed. He listened to the breathing of the child, soft and sighing by his side. Through the thin straw mattress he could feel the bare slats of the bed. The room felt cold, and he took the thickest blanket from his bed and tucked it over William. "What horrors have you seen?" he asked the sleeping child. William gave no answer, sleeping on in silence, watered, warmed and fed. At last, Hew fell asleep, and as the morning broke he drifted into dreaming, closed in bed with Catherine, where their love was consummated, lapped in linen sheets. He awoke to a warm sweet wetness, and lay blissful in its comfort, sated and content, until a small limb thrust against his belly caught and winded him, and he realised that William had crept in beside him and had wet the bed.

At breakfast, Hew considered the child, who was swallowing oatcakes and milk. His clothes were grubby and soiled, and his face was caked with last night's broth, and what looked like the beginnings of a cold. He seemed a little rough around the edges, in a poor enough state to return to his mother. Since the alewife had two little daughters, Hew offered them a shilling each to make William more presentable. Meanwhile, he settled his account. Returning to the stable to saddle up his horse, he was startled by a wail, and saw William in the rain butt in a flood of tears. The little boy stood naked in all but his shirt, as the small girls drubbed and scolded, determined to have him come clean. Hew felt a pang of remorse. The coldness and indignity did not sit well with William, and his howls were fierce enough to scare the horses from their hay. Hew ran to his rescue, snatching up the child. William, still wet, heaved a sigh, and laid a damp head on Hew's shoulder, grasping his coat with his fists. "We men must stick together," Hew advised him guiltily. The little girls tutted like fishwives, their hands on incipient hips.

With William dried and dressed, Hew collected the red roan and prepared to mount. The child struggled fiercely, and refused to sit, until the alewife pointed out that he was clearly frightened of the horse. She brought out a length of woollen plaid, which she wrapped around the bairn, tying him to Hew, so that Hew could hold him safely in his lap without dropping his hands from the reins. Hew could feel the small boy tense and quiver, and the small, tight beating of his heart. He hoped, sincerely, William would not feel the urge to piss on him.

"Now we are going home," he told the little boy, "and you will see Minnie again. You remember

Michael, Phillip, and the shop? You remember Walter?" *Alison*, he almost said, *do you remember Alison, raped and murdered on the muir?* "Minnie will be waiting for you," he went on. "She will be so happy to see you, that you can't imagine. It will make her cry. But you mustn't mind that, because . . ."

The little boy was looking up, with solemn grey eyes that showed no understanding. If he remembered Minnie, it did not show in his face. Hew felt at a loss. "You must remember Minnie. She is slight and fair, with narrow feet and hands. Her eyes are grey, like yours, that in a certain lamplight turn to palest blue; she has fine, unruly hair, that will not stay inside its cap but is always falling down; and a light dust of freckles, sprinkling her nose, like a shaking of spice, and a low, sweet voice, that will sing you to sleep with lullabies, and tell you stories by the fireside when the day draws dark and you both are tired; and her tread is firm, yet light and soft, and she has the sweetest scent and smile . . ."

And so he spoke on softly, and disclosed his inner thoughts, unconscious and unheard, not knowing what he said. William had fallen asleep, lulled by the sway of the horse.

Coming to the city's gates, Hew began to feel afraid. The little boy stirred. What if he were wrong, and the bairn was not William? *What if he were wrong?*

He dismounted at the west port and left the horse outside, where Richard kept him stabled, lifting the child in his arms. William murmured sleepily. Still wrapped in the plaid, he carried the child along the Cowgate, and up Blackfriars wynd towards the netherbow. He did not go into the shop, but turned instead into the stairway that led up the house, pushing open the door. Christian was lying on a bed before the fire, with Meg at her side. They both looked up, startled at the sound. Hew let the child slip gently to the floor, where he stood unsteadily, blinking at the light. Meg began to speak as Christian screamed.

Christian screamed, and Hew knew at once that he had been mistaken, that the small boy was not William. He stepped back in a chasm of darkness. What he had done, no mother could forgive: the child was not William. Then he saw Christian laugh and cry, crying, laughing, all at once, the small boy fiercely clutching at her flaxen hair, the little face washed with wet kisses and tears. As Hew drew back, his sister cried, "However did you find him, Hew?"

"Is it the right bairn?" he said foolishly. "Is it William?"

Meg stared at him. "Of course it is! Surely, you knew him! For pity though!" She realised, smiling, "You didn't, did you? You're a *man*."

Hew told his story. Yet he did not stay for Christian's thanks. By the time she remembered him, and looked up from her dizzy tears of laughter, he was gone.

He walked alone awhile, too drained for company. At last, as it grew dark, he made his way to Richard's house. He could see the lamplight flicker in the street, and hear the laughter of the children in the hall, yet still he longed for solitude. Richard, when he saw the shadow on Hew's face, assumed the worst, and took him to his closet room, where he called for brandy. "What has happened now?" he questioned gently.

Hew sunk in a gossip chair and closed his eyes. "I found the bairn," he whispered.

"I understand. I am so very sorry."

"You do not understand. William is alive."

"Alive?" Richard breathed, "God be thanked!"

"He has witnessed horrors, though. He cannot speak."

"You can barely speak yourself," Richard said compassionately. "This has worn you out. Your tale can wait."

Hew demurred, "I want to tell it."

Richard heard him out. At last he said a little sceptically, "This man Marten Voet; you let him go? You did not warn the provost of Dalkeith?"

"Aye, I let him go. For he was not a threat."

"I wonder you are sure of that," Richard answered quietly.

"I believed him."

"You will forgive my saying, but I fear that that was rash. You did a grand thing in finding the boy, and returning him safe to his mother. Yet I am afraid you made a grave mistake when you let the card seller go. You are too green and soft, and too easily taken in by a tale. I fear that villain saw your weakness, and exploited it."

"Why do you say that?" Hew asked him curiously. "Marten saved William's life."

"Was that it, do you think?" queried Richard. "Or was it that he could not bring himself to kill him? Marten Voet was in St Andrews when your fisher lass was raped and smothered. Now another lass is raped and murdered on the muir, and Marten Voet was there. You cannot count that mere coincidence."

Hew was silent for a moment. Then he said. "That is a lawyer's argument, based on presumption. Which you must allow, accounts for nothing."

"I allow it does not count for proof. But surely, it must be enough to have him held for questioning. I am afraid that you have let your pity for this man betray you into making a mistake. Well, it may not matter. I do not mean to alarm you. You have recovered the child, and Marten Voet doubtless is long gone. Let us hope he takes his chance to flee to England, and we hear no more of him."

Hew hesitated. "Do you think I should go after him?" he asked uncertainly.

"Aye, perhaps; or else leave it. Hew, I do not know." Richard seemed perplexed, and a little agitated. "Why not send word in letters to the provosts of the towns that he is like to come to, warning them of him, as fugitive from justice? We shall put him to the horn; someone else will apprehend him."

"But we have no evidence," objected Hew.

"The evidence is circumstantial. It might be enough. Consider, Hew; you are so keen for justice for these lasses. Will you wait for him to rape and kill again?"

"I will send the letters," Hew agreed unhappily. "God help me, I forgot the fisher lass. And Marten Voet was there! I *believed* him, Richard!"

"Your greenness does you credit, I confess. I will be almost sad to see it clouded by experience," Richard answered. "Nonetheless, you want to lose a little of that trust."

"As you say." Hew felt confused and upset. "I saw Sir David Preston," he remembered suddenly. "He bids you call on him, as soon as possible."

Richard exclaimed. "Sir David! I forgot! I doubt these strange events have moved me too. I must go tomorrow, at first light."

"I thought that you had gone, the day that William disappeared."

"Was it that same day? But I suppose that it was. You are quite right," Richard mused. "I turned back, when it began to rain. And I had quite forgotten it! Did Preston tell you what the matter was?"

"He was most close and secretive," remembered Hew.

"Then I should go to him alone. No matter, I will go tomorrow, once my horse is rested. I suspect this is to do with Morton's trial. Sir David's father was a loyalist ally of the queen; Craigmillar was her second home. It is said that the plot to murder Henry Darnley was contrived in that house, and that the house itself was to be the setting for it, had not Darnley gone instead to Kirk o'Fields. The Prestons have a knack of turning with the tide, and are fiercely allied now to our young King James. There may be some secret Morton is apprised of, that David Preston fears will now come out. While I am gone, I shall make inquiries after Marten Voet. If he is on the road, he may be apprehended still. You should take some rest. Try not to worry. Let us pray that you did the right thing."

★   ★   ★

Hew slept long and late. By the time that he awoke, Richard had already left for Craigmillar, and he found himself free for the day. He ate breakfast by the window looking on the land market. A low and bitter wind blew across the gallery, the sky above the tenements was gunshot grey, and the landscape, as ever, loomed cold. Even at this height, the huddle of the high town seemed oppressive, and Hew felt starved of light and air. He decided he would walk to Calton crags, to find a fresh perspective on the town. But as he made his way towards the netherbow, he saw his sister Meg. She was struggling, so it seemed, with a beggar in the street, for a woman dressed in ragged drabs stood clutching at her gown. Hew hurried to her side. As he began to remonstrate, Meg stilled him with a look. "This is Annie, Hew," she forewarned him quickly. "Have you met?"

"I do not think that I have had that pleasure," Hew admitted gravely.

"She is Alison's mother."

"Oh, my dear God!" Hew was appalled.

"Alison goes home on Sundays," Meg explained. "And Annie came to ask why yesterday her daughter did not come."

"Dear God," Hew swore again, "Had no one told her?"

"It seems, with William missing, it was overlooked. Annie does not walk well, and she does not go to kirk without her daughter's help. Their parish is St Cuthbert's, at the west side of the town. I understand they live near the west bow. Annie has struggled to come out today, to look for Alison."

"Mistress — Annie — I am so very sorry," Hew said bleakly.

The old woman looked at him blankly, through eyes so thickly clouded he could not tell if she could see.

"Does she not understand?" he whispered to Meg.

Meg nodded sadly. "It has been explained to her." She steadied her grip on the old lady's arm. "I have given her a sleeping draught; it was one I had made up for Christian. Now we must help her home, before it takes effect."

Hew took Annie's arm upon the other side. "Did you have to poison her?" he hissed.

"She was so greatly exercised," Meg replied defensively, "we feared that it would do her harm. The draught will give her ease, but for a little while. Do not argue, Hew. Help me take her home."

Annie's lodgings were a small low chamber underneath a tinsmith's shop, and chimed from dawn to dusk with the ringing of the hammermen. Meg helped the old lady into her bed. "She's settled now," she mouthed above the din. "The tinsmith's wife has promised she will sit with her awhile, until she wakes."

"Were there no other children?" Hew found himself shouting, to make himself heard.

His sister shook her head. "Alison was a late and only child. A gift from God, as Annie said. Her husband has been dead for eighteen years."

Escaping from the heat and noise, Meg asked Hew to walk her to the west port inn. She looked tired and strained, and Hew began to fear her weakness had returned. They were grateful to come landward, back into the countryside, away from the sick hurry and the clamour. "It is a little quieter," Meg reflected gratefully, as they passed the port. "There is something I must tell you. Something Annie said."

"Aye, what was that?" Hew answered warily.

"Alison had met a man, and they were to marry."

"Aye, a man called Davie," he recalled. "Then Davie must be told about her death. Did Annie tell you where to find him?"

Meg shook her head. "She does not know. They never met. But she said he was a printer and a man of means. He sent Annie gifts — food and blankets, and a cooking pot, when her old one had a hole. Annie was delighted with the match."

"It is more likely that her daughter bought those things," reflected Hew, "knowing that her mother wanted them."

"Aye, but it was Davie, surely, who gave her the money. But he was a printer, Hew! She said this before Christian, and Phillip, and Walter, and none of them knew of a printer called Davie, much less of one with money to spare."

"What is it you are saying?" Hew asked her slowly.

"That Davie is your printer, Marten Voet. Do you not think it possible, that they are the same?"

"I think it more than possible, that Annie is confused," objected Hew. "Her daughter worked for a printer, after all. It is quite likely Davie has another trade entirely."

"No, you are wrong, for there is more. Alison was much enamoured, Annie said. And Annie is a sad, simple soul, whose trust can be bought for a cooking pot or blanket, and yet she let it slip, that Alison was not quite well at ease. This printer wanted her to help him in his trade, by bringing him some things from Christian's shop."

"What things?"

"Annie does not know, or did not understand it. She said that it was waste and of little consequence. But Christian confirms that papers have gone missing."

"Aye, that's true," admitted Hew, "the proofs of Catherine's poems."

"Whatever Davie had, he wanted more, so Annie said. And Alison was not convinced. She confided in her mother that she feared to lose her place, if she went on to help him. But Annie said she would not want the place when she had a man to marry her. She advised her not to risk the wrath of a good man, by refusing him her help, that could do no hurt to Christian."

"That is poor enough advice, from a mother," criticised Hew.

"It is *advice*, from a *poor* mother," Meg corrected sadly, "who saw in this the faint chance of prosperity, for her daughter and herself. The rub is that she advised Alison to give him what he wanted. Do you not think it possible, that Alison was killed for what she gave him?"

"Even if she was," conceded Hew, "it does not place the blame on Marten Voet. Marten has no money for the like of cooking pots."

"Yet he was on the muir, and he found the little boy. And he is a printer, and a stranger to the town. Surely, that cannot be mere coincidence," persisted Meg.

"I do not believe it," Hew declared. "For William went with Marten and he had no fear of him."

"You cannot tell," Meg said earnestly, "what William knows or fears. What horrors he has locked up in his heart, he has forgotten them. We have no way of knowing what they are. I hazard that he does not know himself."

"You think it possible that he has shut them out?"

"I think it more than likely, Hew. Such horrors can distort our memories, and make them false, like dreams. We may believe on waking, or we may forget."

"I know that you are wrong," Hew asserted desperately. "Marten Voet is not the killer. He is of a class of men, like gypsies on the muir, who are used as scapegoats, for they have no place or purpose in this world. All his life he wanders, and is everywhere suspected. It does not make him guilty of a crime."

"It does not make him innocent," Meg countered gently.

They had arrived at the inn, where Meg began to faint. Hew caught her as she fell, and was relieved when Giles appeared. "All this has been too much for her," he scolded, lifting her to bed. "She is not strong."

"I am quite well," Meg murmured, coming round. "In truth, I do not like the town. The people live so close, and packed in layers, like a pie."

Giles tsked. "Far too much excitement," he said sternly.

Hew took solace in the taproom, reluctant to return to town, and to the closed-in world that Meg described. He had drunk almost a pint of watered wine by the time that Giles returned.

"Still here, Hew? Meg has gone to sleep. I will join you for a drink or two."

"Is she quite well?" Hew asked anxiously.

"For certain, only tired," Giles confirmed, with unusual conviction. "The last days have been taxing for us all. Doctor Dow has concluded his report on Alison. It is a sad affair."

"Do you think that is possible that the same man killed Alison that killed Jess Reekie?" Hew blurted out.

"Now why do you ask that, I wonder?" pondered Giles, as he poured a cup of wine.

"Meg thinks that Marten Voet is the printer Davie. And it seems likely it was Davie who killed Alison. Marten Voet was in St Andrews when the fisher lass was killed. Richard says both girls were raped and smothered," Hew explained his chain of thought.

"Ah, did he say that?" Giles answered thoughtfully. "Then he has been talking to my good friend Doctor Dow. On which point, we have found a difference of opinion. Nonetheless, there is a grain of truth in it. Do you wish for the convolute answer, or the straight one?"

"Giles, you have never given a straight answer in your life," Hew said wryly, "so I do not imagine you mean to start now. I am prepared to be circumspect."

"I think, in this case, you require the answer that best suits your theory," Giles replied perceptively. "No matter, I shall give you both. And as you well observe, the straight answer is Doctor Dow's, and the more intricate one, mine. Since Doctor Dow is the visitor here, his report has precedence. It is no surprise, though a little disappointing, that his account has already reached the notice of the courts.

"Doctor Dow has concluded, in his post mortem, that Alison was raped and smothered — there were clear signs of sexual congress, and of compression to her face and throat — and that her corpse was savaged by the wild dogs on the muir. In which case, there are clear similarities with the corpus of Jess Reekie, who was smothered and raped, and left in another open space — it is the difference in the habitat that accounts for the apparent difference in the bodies. In this case, since Marten Voet was there, or very close, on both occasions, he becomes a suspect."

"That is what I feared," Hew admitted gloomily.

"On the second account, which is the one I favour, it becomes less plausible," continued Giles, "that the crimes are connected. I am qualified to say this, even more, perhaps, than Doctor Dow, for I have seen both corpses and am not convinced they are alike. To be more precise, I do not concur with the report on Alison. I think we need to be a little circumspect."

"For once, that is something I'm willing to hear," owned Hew.

"It is unlike you to insist on gory detail," Giles remarked. "You are wont to be meticulous."

"Do not quibble, Giles," Hew countered sharply. "Tell me your account, of how she died."

"Well, as you know, I do not like to be pinned down, absolutely. And I allow it possible, that Doctor's Dow's account, that she was smothered and then torn apart by dogs, can be forced upon the facts. But forcing on the facts is not my favoured manner of approaching things."

"*Please*, Giles, to the point."

Giles would not be hurried, and he looked a little pained. "Well, if I were pressed, I should say that Alison died from her wounds. In short, she bled to death. There was a little too much blood, and too little time, to support the notion that the dogs had made a meal of her. I think the slashes to her body and the tearing at her throat were inflicted with a knife; the cuts were not the jagged marks of teeth but the slashings of a man who showed no care or skill. The compression to her face, when he tried to smother her, was not enough to kill her."

"Then surely, he was mad?" Hew exclaimed.

"So it would appear," Giles nodded. "Such a frenzied attack implies complete loss of control. As to the rape, I would rather say that Alison showed signs of sexual congress. Clearly, she was not a maid. Yet there was a difference between her and Jess Reekie. There is no doubt that Jess was raped; the violence that the lass sustained, was concentrated, shall we say, upon the nether parts. As for Alison, she endured an attack of the most horrific violence, and had recently had intercourse, but I cannot find a link between the two. In conclusion, if you were to ask Doctor Dow whether the same man committed both crimes — allowing, of course, that he has not had access to Jess Reekie — he would tell you, *probably*. If you put the same question to me, I would answer you, *probably not*. Does that help?"

"A little," Hew conceded, miserably. "Though the truth is, since that is what I did want to hear, I dare not fully trust it."

"You are hard on yourself," Giles said gently. "Even if you were mistaken in letting Marten go, you brought the bairn back safely. Is that not enough? What is the matter, Hew?"

"It is the fear, that I was wrong. And I have a deeper fear, that makes no kind of sense," Hew answered desperately. "For I am more afraid of being right."

Devil's Advocate

Richard did not return home until late that evening, and, when he came, was quiet and distracted. At breakfast the next morning he instructed Hew to go to their chamber and wait for him there.

"I have business with the college of justice, and may be some time. If a client comes, you may perhaps advise him. You are, I think, far enough advanced to do so alone."

"Is the business to do with Sir David Preston?" inquired Hew.

"What's that . . .? No, it is a private matter," Richard answered absently, "that you may hear of presently. If there are no clients, then you may consider on what certain grounds a wife may claim oppression, for our current case. I have left some notes."

Hew went alone to the chamber, and was obediently leafing though the case notes when he heard a commotion at the door, and Meg appeared, trailing William by the hand.

"They have arrested Christian!" she cried. "And Phillip and Walter! They came this morning, and ransacked the shop. Not the bailies, Hew, but *soldiers*!"

At the panic in her voice, the child began to cry. Hew sprang to his feet.

"Dear God, what now! What for?"

"They would not say," Meg sniffed. She lifted William into her arms. "They dragged Christian out in front of her child. They were both distraught."

"I will find out," Hew assured her. "Take William back home and wait for me there."

To the astonishment of Richard's clerk, he ran out without closing the door. At the old tolbooth, he hammered and swore until the gudeman appeared. "Be quiet, sir! Where is the fire?"

"Where is Christian Hall?" Hew demanded. "Take me to her!"

"That is no manner for a gentleman to ask," the gudeman answered crossly. "Since, as I recall, you are supposed to be a gentleman, and not, as some may take you for, a thief. Who is Christian Hall? I do not ken the name."

"Do not play games!" snarled Hew. "Open up, and let me see the iron house."

"You will see it soon enough, and presently, if you persist in taking such a tone. Desist, sir, and speak plainly. What is the matter?"

"What in God's name are you doing, Hew?" A cool voice spoke behind them. Richard Cunningham was fast approaching from the nether tolbooth. He walked between the justice general and the king's advocate, Robert Crichton. Hew shot them a glance, and continued with his ranting undeterred.

Crichton said, amused, "This is your young pup, is it not, Richard? He is exceedingly loose."

"Surely, this cannot be your prentis," the justice general frowned, "that makes a row and clamour in the street. I'll warrant he wants discipline."

"He is, and he does," Richard answered grimly. "With your leave, I will amend it."

He grasped Hew by the arm and muttered, "Have you quite taken leave of your senses?"

"They have taken Christian, Richard, and they will not let me see her!" Hew cried wildly.

Richard sighed. "Aye, I have just heard. Do not berate the gudeman. She is not here."

"Where is she?"

"*Not here*," Richard warned. He bowed stiffly to the justice. "My lord, please excuse me. For there is a matter that I must attend to."

"So it seems," sniggered Crichton. "You have your hands full there."

The justice peered disapprovingly at Hew. "Young man, if you hope to be an advocate, then you must learn a little self-control. Brangling in the market like a fishwife will do not at all."

"We are right sorry," Richard answered firmly. He propelled Hew down the street, and did not let go of his arm until they reached the safety of their buith on Leche's close, and he had firmly shut the door.

"Now, sir, you have some explaining to do."

"Where have they taken her?" Hew cried, unrepentant.

Richard sighed. "They are at the castle," he admitted. "I must warn you they are charged with a most serious crime. Christian and her men are accused of leasing-making; it is the slander of the king's person, and akin to treason."

"But this is madness, Richard! Who is it that persecutes her so? As if the killing of her maid and kidnap of her child were not enough! What is she supposed to have done?"

"A scandalous tract has fallen into the hands of the justiciar, defaming the king. It bears Christian's signature and stamp."

"Aye, very like! And if she were to print a paper that defamed the king, then think you she would sign her name to it!" exclaimed Hew. "This is but another attempt to discredit her. Surely you must see that."

Richard said oddly, "We may not discuss this further. I shall overlook your wild behaviour in the street, though it might be apposite to write a letter of contrition to the justice general. You made a poor impression there."

"May not? Why not! Richard, you have ever been most free with your advice; do not desert me now, by failing to defend her. Surely, you must speak for her, for surely, you must see, how wrong this is," cried Hew.

"I regret, I cannot."

"You cannot? You will not! How can this be possible?"

"I regret I may not speak with you further on this. I am engaged to speak against her for the Crown."

"What! You are appointed pursuer? That was precipitous, Richard! Arrested but this morning, and you are already set against her! Your eagerness betrays

303

you; if the charge is treason, as you say, then properly it belongs to the king's advocate, or failing him, his depute. Did you have to beg for it?" Hew accused him bitterly.

Richard said quietly, "You know well enough that I am powerless to refuse, if the Crown demands it. Crichton cannot take the case, because he is engaged with Morton's. Therefore it devolves to me. Understand, it gives me no great pleasure to harangue a helpless woman to her death. Since I understand you are upset, I will forgive this gross discourtesy. Now, you and I will have no further discourse on this matter, the case is *sub judice*, and the subject closed between us."

"The subject is not closed. For I shall conduct her defence," Hew promised hotly.

"Now that really would be a mistake," Richard frowned. "I counsel you most strongly against it. If you speak for Christian, you will lose. And you will lose not because I am the better advocate or have the more experience, but because of your own fatal weakness; your lack of detachment. If you stand against me, then I can promise you, Christian and her friends will hang."

"I assure you, I intend to speak for Christian," Hew asserted.

"I urge you, do not set your wits against me, for I do not want this argument."

"There is no other course," Hew answered coldly. "Understand, I am determined."

Richard nodded curtly. "Then we are opposed. I will leave you now, to reconsider. I have work to do."

Hew sat alone for a while, allowing this new horror to sink in. At last he took his coat, and returned to the printing house. The door stood open. He was startled to see Richard there before him, looking through a pile of papers. Richard looked up. "I trust you are disposed to be a little more temperate, than when we last met," he ventured mildly.

"What are *you* doing here?" Hew demanded.

Richard sighed. "Alas, not more temperate. Your passion will undo you. Specifically, in this case. As to what I am doing here, I will make no secret of it. I have come to look for proof. Since Christian's trial is to be precipitate, in about ten days, there is little time to lose."

Hew blanched. "As soon as that?"

"Aye, as soon as that. You should be grateful that she will not suffer long."

Meg had appeared from upstairs. "William is asleep," she said to Hew, "worn out by his tears. I let Richard in. I hoped that he might help us."

"That he will not," Hew retorted tersely. "He is acting for the prosecution."

Meg looked aghast. "Surely —"

"It is a matter in which I have no choice," Richard answered quickly, "as your brother must well know, though he fails to understand it. Though I do not expect you to see it, I had hoped for some sympathy from him."

"Is it true?" Meg whispered to Hew. "Can he really not help it?"

"It is true," Hew admitted reluctantly, "that it is the law. If he is appointed, he cannot turn it down."

"I thank you," Richard nodded, "at least for that. I can assure you," he said softly to Meg, "this brings me no pleasure. I wonder, what is this?" He changed the subject quickly, pulling out a paper from the pile.

"It is the title page of my father's book," replied Hew. "To be more accurate, it is a proof copy."

"That is very good," Richard answered thoughtfully. "Did you see this printed on the press?"

"Aye," Hew admitted.

"Excellent. But where is the rest of the book?"

"That is all that was printed," Hew explained. "Christian was not happy with the proof. There was too much broken letter, and the printer's block was worn. She has ordered more, and a new plate has been made, but with recent events, you must know, the press has been at a standstill."

"I understand. But where is the manuscript?"

"Is it not here?" Hew looked surprised. "Then I do not know."

"Suppression of evidence is misguided, to say the least," Richard commented.

"I have not suppressed it. The last time I saw it, it was here. You were here before me," Hew pointed out. "You cannot think I took it."

"Aye, maybe not." Richard looked displeased. "Though this will be enough.

"I tell you, as a friend, that you have lost your case. This is the paper that will hang Christian Hall."

Hew stared at him. "What do you mean?"

"It bears a strong resemblance to the offending document. The letter and devices are the same. They have come from the same press."

"That is not possible!"

"I have expert witnesses will swear to it. I am so sorry, Hew. But you know I cannot throw away the prosecution case. However, since you have become more reasonable, I will explain the charge. Christian has been charged with leasing-making, that is the crime of spreading false report, or slanders of the king. A scandalous tract was found pinned upon the market cross, that bore the signature and device of Christian's press. You will see the tract in court, where it will appear as evidence."

"May I not see it now?"

"I'm afraid not. The matter is so sensitive it cannot be disclosed. In point of fact, the man who found it pinned there on the cross and reported it to the magistrate is now in gaol, for reading it."

"That is madness!" Hew exclaimed.

"Quite so," conceded Richard dryly. "However, the magistrates have examined the tract, taking due precautions to protect themselves, and conclude that the contents are both treacherous and scandalous. That is all you need to know. This paper is the proof it came from Christian's press."

"No printer, in his right mind, would defame the king, and put his name to it," insisted Hew.

"You would think that, wouldn't you?" Richard smiled sardonically. "But juries are much harder to convince. They prefer the simplest option, for it does not tax their wits. If a man's name is inscribed upon a paper, then they will assume he wrote it there. It is the common position, from which you will find it hard to deflect them. You will not find it simple to convince them this was forgery. I have, besides, two expert witnesses to swear that it was not."

"May I know their names?" inquired Hew coldly.

"I see no harm in it. I believe you know them both. They are Master Allan Chapman, printer of this town, and Phillip Ramsey, Christian's compositor."

"Phillip!" Hew exclaimed. "I thought he had been charged with the same crime."

"He may well be complicit," Richard nodded. "He is a strange man, I think."

"Both he and Chapman are suspect in this," declared Hew.

Richard looked more sceptical. "Ah, if you say so," he agreed politely. "I will leave that up to you. But I have said too much. When we talk of this again, it will be in court.

"How is the little boy?" he inquired of Meg. "I understand, he does not speak?"

Meg shook her head. "This new distraction does not help. He is lost and scared. He will not talk to us. I will go and wake him now," she turned to Hew. "It is his dinner time."

"Poor bairn!" Richard took his leave. "His mother and his nurse! Life can be cruel."

Hew followed Meg upstairs, and watched her wake the little boy and sit him at the table, where she fed him broth from a spoon. He opened up his mouth, mechanical and urgent, like a baby bird. It seemed he had forgotten Christian, for he did not look for her.

"Still no words?" sighed Hew. "Does he run about and play?"

Meg shook her head. "He does nothing." She wiped the child's face with a cloth. "You may get down, and go and find your ball." The little boy slid wordless from his stool.

"He understands," Meg asserted. "He will not play with the ball, but he will go to fetch it if required. I will take him to the west port inn, to see the horses."

"Aye? He's feared of horses," Hew mentioned absently.

"Really? That is strange, for I had not remarked it. He has a wooden hobby by his cot. No matter, though. We'll feed the ducks. Ducks, William?" Meg asked brightly. The little boy looked blank.

"There has been no change," Meg sighed, "since you first brought him home. Giles and I will move into the shop. I am convinced that locked inside there is the same bright little boy, if only we could find the key."

"If anyone can reach him," Hew declared, "it will be you and Giles. I could not think of a kinder pair of foster parents."

His sister flushed. "Paul has gone to Doctor Dow's, to ask for Giles. He is in the midst," she sighed, "of one of his interminable conferences. But I'm sure he will come when he hears. Hew . . . I have done something that is perhaps a little foolish. I have hidden father's manuscript."

Hew held up his hand. "Stop! Say no more! Do not tell me where. Whatever instinct led you to do that?"

"I do not know. But Phillip had been working on it when the soldiers came. And when I saw it lying there, and thought what it had been through, something made me take it — it was ours, our father's. Then I heard Richard asking for it, and he was not pleased to find it gone."

"Aye, you're right, he was not pleased," Hew said thoughtfully. "You have suppressed the evidence."

"Did I do wrong?

He shook his head. "I do not know. But since Richard wants it, let us keep it hidden. Fortune is against us; we must take our chances where they come."

The next few days were uncomfortable for Hew. Since he could not ask for Richard's help, he had to make his case alone, and he made little progress. The charge against the pressman had been dropped, on the grounds that Walter could not read. But Walter threw no light upon the mystery. He knew nothing of the paper on the market cross. Hew was working blindly, in the dark. He came often to the door of Richard's buith, and stopped. He felt a desperate sadness: in his fear for Christian he had lost a tutor and a friend. He missed Richard sorely, on both counts. At home with the Cunninghams, the atmosphere was strained. Hew took refuge in the company of Grace, and as he watched her play, he gave thought to William. Privately, he spoke to Eleanor.

"May Meg bring William here to play with Grace?"

Eleanor looked taken aback. "The printer's bairn? I do not think so, Hew. Richard would not like it. In truth, he has asked me not to speak with Meg, until the trial is done. It is a very serious charge. He is anxious that we are not tainted by it."

"I understand. Then there is no chance, I suppose, of going there with Grace?" Hew ventured hopefully.

Eleanor shook her head. "None at all. You know that Richard does not speak about these things, but he has said enough to make it clear the case is awkward for him. He is embarrassed by your opposition, while you live here in this house. I wish that you would drop it."

"I'm afraid that I cannot. Perhaps you would prefer it if I left?"

"You were always welcomed in this house," Eleanor protested warmly, "and are welcome still. I hope you have no doubt of Richard's love for you."

"I do not doubt it. And I bitterly regret that I must stand against him."

"I cannot pretend to understand it," Eleanor said sadly. "We must hope and pray it will be over soon. Why did you want the little boy to play with Grace?"

"He is remote, and will not speak. I hoped the solace of another child might draw him out."

"As well it might. There are other children, surely, near his age?"

"Aye, there must be, surely. But I do not know of any."

Hew did not entirely let the matter drop, for it came to him again, when Grace was prattling on the stairway to her dolls. Grace possessed two poppets, known to the selected few as Arabella and Celeste. Arabella had a head of German clay and a linen body stuffed with rags; her wardrobe, made by Eleanor, was a replica of Grace's own. She was said to be long-suffering, sweet-natured and content. Celeste was a Flanders baby, and a wooden fashion doll, discarded by a lady Richard knew at court, when her outfit was no longer *à la mode*. This sense of second best had left her snide and cross. Despite her Flemish origins, she spoke a faltering French, in the manner of the spiteful and despised Jehanne. With these two poppets, Grace rehearsed her daily tribulations; while Arabella listened sympathetically, Celeste was cruel and withering.

"Arabella is good at keeping secrets," Hew observed.

The child looked at him suspiciously, assessing whether he was making fun of her. Deciding he was serious, she nodded. "She understands everything."

"That must be a great comfort. May I borrow her?"

An expression of alarm came fleetingly across Grace's face. She clutched the doll closely towards her. "Why?"

"A little boy I know is very sad," Hew explained. "Both his mother and his nurse have had to go away. And he has no baby, like Arabella, to talk to. In truth, he is so sad he does not talk at all."

Grace struggled to make sense of this. She was a kindly child, and she well understood what it was to have a nurse who went away. To lose a mother also must be worse. And she was fond of Hew, and dearly wished to please him. But her love for Arabella must come first. "He might have Celeste," she offered doubtfully.

Hew considered this. Celeste, for all her finery, was brittle as her nature; her clothes were hung on a tight wire frame, and there was little in her pointed pouting features to attract a two year old. "Celeste is not as kind as Arabella," he said gently, "and I do not think that she would understand as well."

"Well then . . ." Grace was struggling, "you might find a baby in the crames."

"What I have in mind requires a special sort of person," he said softly, "and a special kind of baby, such as Arabella. If you do not want to share her, then I understand."

"It is not that . . ." She could not bear to disappoint him, and he felt a pang of guilt as he saw the look of anguish in her eyes. "It is only . . . is the little boy so very sad?"

"He is very, very, sad," he told her solemnly.

"Then if he has Arabella, it will make him more sad when she has to go away. He will want to keep her," Grace said desperately.

"I will make him understand, that he cannot," Hew assured her. "I promise you, that I will bring her back. I want her only for a day and a night, to see if he will speak to her. Then whether he does or does not, I will bring her back to you."

"Only one day?"

"You have my solemn word. And perhaps," he enticed her, "Arabella would like a new gown, for her outing."

Grace shook her head. "She wouldn't. She likes the ones she has," she said emphatically. She held out the doll. "But *I* would."

From the savour on the stair, Hew knew at once that Meg was cooking. He found Giles at home, and observed a closeness between husband and wife he had not noticed since his father's funeral. Perhaps it was the cooking after all, for Meg did not care to be cooked for, while Giles cared very much to be cooked for by his wife. The pot that bubbled now on Christian's hearth made up for the deficiencies of the west port inn, eclipsing even Bessie Brewster's pies. "You are just in time for dinner," Meg smiled up at him. "Will you join us? I'm afraid the stew is low on herbs," she pulled a face, "for there is little to be found here in the town. The spices are not fresh, and there are no proper rigs. I miss the gardens back at Kenly Green."

"Doctor Dow has a physic garden at his house on the Cowgate. I will take you there sometime," Giles offered. He dipped a finger quickly in the pot and licked it clean. "At least you have some meat. We say *pish* to fish," he said solemnly to William, who was sitting by the fire.

"Whisht," scolded Meg, "you will teach the bairn bad habits. What will his mother say?"

"He pays no heed," protested Giles.

"You are wrong there, for he follows every word. William, come and wash your face and hands." She poured water from a jug into a bowl. "It is nearly dinner time."

314

"I have something for him," Hew remarked. He brought out Arabella from behind his back. "Now I know that you may think it somewhat strange," he said hastily to Giles, "but it is an experiment, just for a day or two. I hoped it might encourage him to play."

"On the contrary," said Giles unexpectedly, "I see nothing that's unmanly in a poppet. Provided that he uses it in active play — *active*, mind — and does not mother it, that is a sound idea. Collecting poppets is a manly sport: the kings of France, or so I'm told, keep cabinets full of mannikins."

"The kings of France have cabinets full of living ladies," Meg said disapprovingly. "Nonetheless, it cannot harm. It is a good idea."

Hew knelt on the floor beside the child. "There is someone come to see you," he said gravely, "and her name is Arabella. She is very good at keeping secrets. I had her from a friend of mine, a little girl called Grace, who wanted very much to come and play with you. Since she may not, she has sent you Arabella in her place."

The little boy stared at him, considering, before thrusting out his arms to take the doll.

"Excellent," beamed Giles. "Now leave him to his play, and come and have some wine. He will do much better if he is not watched."

He pulled three wooden goblets from the press and began to pour the claret. Meg set up a trestle board, laying down a cloth. From behind them by the fire, they heard a wrenching sound. All three turned at once, to see William shake the doll, so fiercely that the head tore

315

from the cloth. As Meg cried out, he threw the mangled poppet to the ground, and taking up the poker from the fire, smashed it with full force into Arabella's face. Giles was the first to recover, and to stride across the floor to seize the poker from the child. "Now that is quite wrong," he advised him sternly, "and it will not do at all. When I said *active* play, that was not at all what I meant."

"That was naughty, William," reinforced Meg. William looked up, his eyes filled with terror, confusion and doubt. Then he spoke out clearly, "*It was Davie did it!*" bursting into sobs. He buried his head in Meg's skirts.

There was silence for a moment, before Giles summed up quietly. "Well, then, now we know. Poor desperate little bairn. And poor old Arabella," he observed to Hew.

Morbus Gallicus

As counsel, Hew was permitted to see Christian and to take her clean blankets and clothes. He climbed up to the castle, to what appeared the coldest place on earth, standing stark and rigid in the wind. Its bleakness had long since seen off the royal court, to make a warmer palace in the house of Holyrood. The prison was impenetrable as the rock on which it stood. Each outer door that opened with yet another set of keys led deeper down to darkness and despair.

Christian was kept within a holding cell, quite clean and dry, equipped with bed and candle. She had access to a bible, left by Walter Balcanquall, with bread and water daily, and a little ale and broth. Hew found her lying quiet on the bed; she rose to greet him calmly, asking for her child.

"William is quite well," he promised her, taking her cold hands in his. "Meg is looking after him. He is almost his old self, and has begun to speak again. He misses you."

Christian persisted, "Who will look after him when I am gone?"

"Well . . ." Hew hesitated, "It is to be hoped, that he will be an old man then, and capable of fending for

317

himself. Unless," he tried to make her smile, "you mean to see him grow into his dotage."

Christian shook her head. "Do not try to humour me. For myself, I am no longer afraid. Walter Balcanquall came today, to pray with me. He was very kind. He says that that he will come again before . . . After the trial."

"You must not talk like this," urged Hew. "You must be strong. Tell me you have not confessed!"

"I have not confessed," she answered quietly. "I do not understand the charge."

"The charge is leasing-making," he explained to her. "That is a form of *lèse-majesté*. You are accused of slandering the Crown."

"I understand the crime, as any printer should," Christian qualified, "but not why we are charged with it. What have we done? For we have printed nothing untoward, except for Catherine's poems."

"It was not the poems. A paper was pinned up upon the market cross that bore your mark, and spoke scandals of the king."

"What did it say?"

"I cannot find that out. We are working in the dark," admitted Hew.

"We did not print any such paper," Christian stated. "It must be a forgery."

"So I believe. Then the essential thing is that you do not confess," Hew assured her. "Not even to Balcanquall."

"The minister said that I was very brave," Christian answered wryly. "He assumed we made the paper, to

318

expose the weakness of the king. It is a thing that he would do himself, and he admires us for it. He says . . ." she faltered, "he says that God will look more kindly on our sins. He knows I am to die for it."

"Then he is wrong," Hew insisted fiercely.

"The strange thing is," she went on, disregarding this, "we spoke of Catherine's poems. And though he told the council who had printed them, he swears he never meant us harm. He said there was fire in his belly and rage, against corruption in the royal court, he wished to stop the channels that gave credence to their lusts. He did not stop to think what it might mean for us. Nor did he mean such hurt to Catherine. He did not even know who she was."

"Catherine brought her sorrows on herself," Hew answered quietly. "But there is malice lies behind this charge, and we must trace it to its source, and face it as we can."

"They will not let me speak to Phillip, or to Walter," Christian told him sadly.

"Walter is released, on the grounds he cannot read. On which count, Michael also is excused," Hew explained. "Phillip is a different matter. He is cited as a witness for the Crown."

"That cannot be true," Christian flushed. "Phillip would not speak against me."

"I'm afraid it is true."

"Then he has been made to. They are most persuasive here." She turned to face the window. "I have heard the cries."

"Have you any notion what he might say?"

"There is nothing," she asserted, close to tears, "that he can say to hurt me, unless it is lies."

"Then he will be committing perjury and we shall have to break him. I am so sorry," Hew said simply. "Yet you must have trust. The good thing is, your trial is very soon, which leaves less time to weaken your resolve. When you come to court, you must not confess. Answer what is put to you, and I will do the rest. Do not confess, but think of William. And, I promise you, all will be well."

"I have thought of William often, in the last few days," Christian answered softly. "I mean my husband, not my son. I think I will be glad to have the chance to see him once again."

"Stop this now," Hew told her sternly. "For you must not think like this." He sat down beside her on the bed. "Fight this and be strong. You have done nothing wrong."

"You said yourself the courts were tainted and corrupt. The world was set against us from the start. I am so very tired. But tell me, if the case goes badly, what becomes of William? Tell me, I must know," she pleaded.

"I will not indulge this."

"*Please*. I cannot sleep, for thinking on it."

"Aye, very well," he sighed. "If the case goes badly — and I promise it will not — then I will take him home with me to Kenly Green."

"Why would you do you that?"

"*Because he is a Cullan*," Hew almost answered, biting back the words. "Because it is a grand place for a

320

child. And if he does not care to live with me, then Giles and Meg will take him to St Andrews. They are very fond of him, and he will like it there."

"What is it like?" she whispered. "I have never been."

"St Andrews? It lies by the ocean, sheltered in its bay. And there are four main streets, that meet at the cathedral, and the castle on its cliff looks down on all. The thoroughfares are grand and wide. And on the south street, where the merchants have their houses, everything is fair and brightly painted and the street is lined with trees. And all the lands have rigs and gardens, falling out behind. The air is fresh and clear, and the harbour filled with boats, and sometimes, when the waves are high, a light spray showers the city walls, like snow."

"That sounds grand. Has every house a garden?" she said drowsily.

"Every one," he answered solemnly. "Then there are yellow sands, that lie between the castle and the pier, and eastwards to the kinkell braes and west towards the links, where a little child can run and play, and a pool to bathe in by the rocks."

"William would like that."

"Aye, he would. And then, when he is grown, we'll send him to the grammar school, and when he is a little older, to the university. And he will learn to speak his mind, and be the match of kings."

Christian smiled. "I cannot imagine it."

"Well then, come and see it," Hew declared. "When all this is over, why not bring your press, and you and

William both shall start afresh. St Andrews wants a printer."

"Aye, perhaps." She gave a little sigh and closed her eyes.

The guard stood at the door, and motioned Hew to leave. As he went through the gates and heard the last lock click, he saw the lands and tenements that lined the castle hill, the ever upward spiral to the sky. The prison closed around him as he stepped into the air.

Hew had asked Giles to meet him in Christian's shop. "Do you think you could work a printing press?" he inquired. "I could ask Walter, but I dare not trust him. Though he is a good man, he is not one of the sharpest, sad to say."

"I should think so," Giles agreed cheerfully. "What does it require? A little strength? You will find my regimen of exercise has been most beneficial, after all."

"Aye, well and good," muttered Hew. "It is only one sheet. I have learned enough from Phillip to set type, though I will do so slowly."

"Splendid! What are we making?"

"A forgery. But we shall want the help of your good friend Doctor Dow. For he is well known, and above suspicion." Hew explained his plan. "Will he help us?"

"Aye, beyond a doubt. He is a player," Giles assured him. "Do you think the plan will work?"

"We must hope so. It depends upon the jury. Richard says the jury will accept the simplest explanation."

"Very true," nodded Giles. "And very reasonable."

"I never heard you put that case before," objected Hew, "and I do not want to hear it now; we must prove to them the plainest facts are false. We must make them doubt what they know to be true, and question the evidence before their very eyes."

"That will be difficult," suggested Giles.

"It will be hard enough. And even if we do succeed, we will be faced with Phillip. I have no notion what the man will say. And if he swears that Christian made the paper on the cross, our case is lost, before it has begun."

They worked on in silence a while, and after three or four attempts produced a sheet that satisfied.

"That's good," accepted Hew. "Now can you do the rest with Doctor Dow?"

"Assuredly. But there is a matter that I wanted to discuss. I fear it will alarm you," Giles said gravely.

Hew was disturbed by his tone. "So serious! Has there been another death?"

Giles shook his head. "This is private . . . Did you lie with Lady Catherine Douglas?"

Hew gaped in astonishment. "Not this again! Giles, when will you stop? You are not my keeper," he protested.

"This is not a jest. That I am prepared to break my oath is a measure of my strong regard for you. I have never in my life betrayed a patient's secrets. Therefore I pray you understand the severity of this. I ask you again, did you lie with her?"

"Not in the sense that you mean. The truth is, we flirted, and I was beguiled by her, but she quickly tired of me. There was no consummation," Hew retorted. "Now, let that content you!"

"It contents me well. Then there is nothing more to say."

"Stay, you don't leave it at that!" Hew was angry now. "You go too far, Giles, even for a brother, even for a friend. You cannot leave it there! Explain yourself!"

Giles stared at him for a moment. At last he said, "Aye, very well. Lady Catherine Douglas was arrested yesterday and taken to the castle gaol, where my good friend Doctor Dow was called in to examine her. He found her riddled with disease. She has the *morbus gallicus*."

"God save us!" Hew exclaimed.

"*You*, in particular," his friend replied dryly. "Catherine is condemned to exile overseas, until her pollution is spent. Doctor Dow has hopes that she will find a cure."

"She is *banished* for the pox! Is sickness a crime? This is horrible, Giles!"

Giles nodded sadly. "The truth is Catherine caused offence when her poems were published, for it brought upon the court the censure of the kirk, which led to the displeasure of the king. Therefore Catherine Douglas has been made a scapegoat; her exile makes amends for the court's humiliation, punishing her for airing its secrets, while giving her up is a sop to the kirk; a proof that immoralities are sought out and oppressed."

"Is this the king's will?" Hew asked indignantly.

"The will of his council. These are powers we have no hope of overthrowing. Accept it, Hew, and do not lose your way. Catherine's cause is lost."

324

"I understand," Hew answered slowly. "Ah, but Giles, the cruelness of it! Doctor Dow has seen her, though; will he not take me to her?"

Giles shook his head. "That is impossible. In confiding this to you, I have betrayed his trust." He relented, at the anguish on Hew's face. "You have one hope of seeing her. Her ship sails tomorrow, at dawn, from the port of Leith. Be assured, she will be guarded well by soldiers. So stir up no mad plans for springing her release. But if you wish to say farewell, it may be possible."

"I thank you," Hew said soberly, "I do thank you, Giles. I understand what it must cost you to break faith."

"As to that," Giles replied, with a ghost of a smile, "you may have no doubt, I have debated it. And in conclusion find that there are many kinds of faith. It is not law but conscience that determines when they crack."

At Leith harbour, at first light, Hew could barely see the water for the creeping closeness of the haar. From the huddled smudge of ships a flank of pricking mastheads pierced the sky. He heard soldiers' voices, ringing clear and crisply through the fog. As they lifted kegs and barrels into boats, Hew saw Catherine brought amongst them, under watchful guard.

"Let me speak with her, a moment, please," he begged. The captain of the guard was ready to refuse, when something in him softened, for he saw his own lass waving from the shore. "Aye," he muttered gruffly, "only for a moment, then," and stood a little off, to supervise the loading of the boats.

Catherine gazed at Hew impassively. "So, you have found me out. I pray you, do not hate me," she said quietly.

Hew answered her hoarsely, "Why would I hate you?"

"For I took you to my bed, knowing that I was infectit with the pox."

"Catherine, *why*?"

"It was evident that you loved Christian, and that Christian loved you. And yet you were so easily lured from her, for all that you did love her, you were willing to betray her love, but for an hour of pleasure, on an empty afternoon. Because you were so easily corrupt, I felt it was no sin to have corrupted you. For your incontinence, I thought you must be equally to blame."

"You are wrong about Christian," Hew exclaimed fiercely.

"In the end, you chose Christian, when you left me to look for her child. That was what saved you. But you were willing to deceive her; like a bairn, you came scrabbling at my pockets, in the search for sweets. It grieved me, for I cared for you."

"That is hard to believe," he accused her.

Catherine sighed. "I loved my husband Robert, though he risked it all, to tumble in the sheets. I do not doubt he loved me too, as deep and fierce as I loved him, and yet he did allow himself to be lured, with promises of sticky sweets and comforts, and coming homewards to his wife, infected me."

"And you thought to pass on his gift?"

"You were so willing to accept it, Hew, so ready to forget her and her child," Catherine answered sadly.

"This sick revenge is skewed. And you know nothing of my love for Christian. Aye, I came to you, in spite of her. But I came with clear regard for you; and for your sweets, your wit, your charms, I could have loved you, Catherine, you must know, I *wanted* to."

"As you say, in spite of her."

"*Despite* her love. Christian is my sister. Therefore I may not be free to love her," Hew said quietly, "as I believed I was free to love you."

Catherine was silent for a moment. "I did not know. But though she is your sister that does not absolve you from your guilt. You used me for your comfort. Can you deny that you came hot and willing to my bed while thinking of another?"

Hew shook his head. "I wanted to make love to *you*."

"And yet when Christian called, you left me in my bed, without a second glance."

"She needed me. She needs me now," he answered helplessly.

"Of course she does. And have you given thought to me since? Or sent a note to tell me how things were? Or did you pause to wonder what became of me, the woman you left lonely in her bed?"

Hew fell silent then.

"You did not. You forgot me. And when the soldiers took me, you were nowhere to be found. The truth is, in the printer's shop or in my bed, you only saw and wanted Christian."

Hew cried out, "You blamed me, for betraying Christian; and you blame me now, for not betraying her! I liked you, aye, I liked you, for your humour and your wit and for your charms; I thought that they were yours to give, and mine to take as freely. If I forgot you, in the search for Christian's child, and in her present danger, then you must allow for circumstance. But Catherine, I am *here*; surely that must tell you something?"

At the sound of raised voices, the guard edged closer. "Enough! It's time to board."

"Aye. I am ready." Catherine lifted down her veil. Already wan and frail in sickness, she appeared to lose her step, and leant upon the soldier, who held out a hand to steady her. "Hew Cullan, some advice: do not give way to bitterness. It is more vicious than the pox, and infectious to the core."

There was nothing he could do but watch her go.

False Impressions

On the day of Christian's trial, Hew and Richard shared breakfast in the gallery above the street. It was not quite light, and the morning chill did little to dispel Hew's nerves. He felt sick with fear. Richard, by contrast, seemed calm and composed. As they broke their bread he mentioned curiously, "Grace told me the strangest tale. She claims you took her poppet, Arabella, and returned it broken. I think that that cannot be true. If Grace is lying, I will punish her."

"I am afraid that it is true," owned Hew. "Certainly, you have no cause to punish her. She was kind enough to lend her poppet, and unfortunately, it was broken. However, it has been repaired, and Grace has now forgiven me."

"Whatever did you want it for?"

"I wanted it for William, by way of an experiment. It proved a little too successful, at least for Grace's poppet."

"You mean the printer's boy? What sort of an experiment?" demanded Richard.

"I hoped that Grace's baby would unlock his silence. And so it did. William saw the murder of his

329

nursemaid, Alison. He showed it in his play with Grace's poppet. And he has begun to speak again. He named a man called Davie as the killer," Hew explained.

"This is outrageous!" Richard exploded. "How dare you implicate my daughter in your wild experiments? Have you no care to the risk!"

Hew stared at him. "There was no risk to Grace," he answered reasonably. "She was not there. Though, I must confess, I had not counted on the risk to Grace's poppet. I have made my peace with her, and she has now forgiven me. She gave up her baby, of her own free will."

"God help you, man, have you no sense at all? In truth, you know nothing of children! You cannot make a contract with a bairn of six! Grace gave up her baby, that is dearest to her heart, out of her regard for you. This is ill done, to take advantage of a child. She says you promised her a gown! Now do you think that proper, sir? I begin to think it is no longer fitting that you stay here in my house."

"No, Richard, you are over-wrought," Eleanor protested, coming up behind them with a pitcher of fresh milk.

"Richard is right," Hew replied quietly. "I have stayed too long. I will remove this evening, to the west port inn."

As they left for court, Hew found Grace in the doorway, tearfully clutching her doll. "Daddie has sent you away," she whispered. "Is it because of me?"

He shook his head gently. "It is because of the trial."

Richard was trying to rattle him; it would take little enough.

Hew was shaking as he came into the courtroom. And when he saw Christian, frightened and bewildered, standing at the bar, he almost lost his nerve. He wanted to hold her, to take her in his arms, and yet he knew he had to look at her remotely, and remain detached. It was the hardest thing that he had ever had to do.

The jurors were sworn in, and Hew looked at them in panic, searching for a sympathetic face. He could not read the inquest, or find any trace of their affiliations. Richard, meanwhile, seemed to know them all, and went through the jurors briskly and decisively, until he had them whittled down to his own exacting shape. Hew stood by, helpless, as they were sworn in.

Christian then made her plea, so quiet that the jury could not hear her, and she was forced to speak again. No sooner had she spoken, than the door to the outer chamber opened, and the king came in, with his favourite, Esme Stewart, and several of his council, to take their seats upon the stage.

"Since the charge is leasing-making, then we thought that we should hear it," James acknowledged languidly. "Now, pray, begin."

The judge peered out at Richard. "Will you set out the case, Master Cunningham? Who is it that the panel sets against you? Your young pup? Surely not?"

"Indeed, my lord, it is my prentis, Hew Cullan, who would try his wits today, in a momentous case," Richard answered gravely.

The king, leaning forward to observe, was heard to say aloud, "I know this man, Hew Cullan. We have met before. We may have some entertainment here today." Aware that the court had paused to wait on him, he waved his hand expansively, "Did I not say, begin?"

He was so very young, thought Hew, and so assured, and yet he seemed overshadowed by the lords that flanked him. The young king shifted nervously, and did not sit still. His taut and watchful presence set the court on edge.

"I thank you, your grace," Richard bowed. "My lords, I call as my first witness, Allan Chapman." Chapman shuffled forward to the stand.

"Are you Allan Chapman, master printer, of the netherbow?"

"I am."

"And you have been in business there for how long?"

"Nine years, come Michaelmas."

"Then you must be fully master of your trade," Cunningham remarked.

"And if I am not, sir, I would like to meet the man who is my master at it," Chapman replied, with a hint of smugness.

"Tis well, for you are well placed to advise us. I have in my hand, a piece of printed paper, that, in deference to his majesty," Cunningham bowed to the king, "I may not read out in open court. Suffice it to say, that it is slanderous to the majestie's dear person, and were it not required in evidence, then it should have been destroyed; and presently we shall consign it to the flame. But though we like it not, we must preserve it for a while, only in this place, as evidence."

Here Hew interrupted, looking to the justice general, "For the jury's sake, should it not be read out?"

The justice shuddered. "I think not. The assessors have seen this paper, and that it defames our sovereign lord is not the matter in dispute here. Surely, you do not contend that?"

"Not at all," Hew answered quickly, "But I thought perhaps the jury —"

"The jury have been told the document is slander," said the judge severely. "Since that question is resolved beyond dispute, there is no cause for them to hear its content."

Richard winked at Hew. "You show your greenness now," he whispered. "Have a care!" And he turned back to the printer.

"Master Chapman, I pray you to look at this paper, without looking at its content, which you need not know, and will not be asked of you. But pay particular attention, if you will, to the print, and tell us, coming with a printer's knowledge, what you see there on the page. I pray you, look upon the letter and the block, and do not divulge the matter." Richard passed the paper to Chapman, who studied it closely. "Tell me, what do you see?"

"I see thirty lines of copy, set as verse, and below it a signature and device, such as printers use."

"Can you describe the device?"

"It is of a black bird, like a raven or corbie, and the bird is atop a tree, that we call the tree of knowledge, for it often represents the matter in a book, and below the tree entwined the letter H pierced through with a cross, that signifies —"

Richard interrupted, "but for a moment, do not tell us what it signifies; tell the court, merely, do you recognise the device?"

"Certainly. It is the device of . . . should I say the name?" Richard nodded. "It is the device of . . . of her," he jutted a thumb towards Christian, "I mean the panel, Christian Hall."

"One moment," Richard turned to Christian. "Do you admit this bird and tree and letters, to be your device?"

"You do not have leave to question her," objected Hew.

"My lord," Richard said to the judge, "it will save us all a lot of time if the panel will say now if her device consists of letter H, a cross, a raven and a tree. The point is not contentious."

The justice looked at Christian. "You do not have to answer this," he advised, "however, if you choose to do so, it will save us time." His tone made clear which he considered the expedient choice. Christian glanced at Hew, who nodded cautiously.

"It is my device," she said, in a small voice, "or one very like it."

"I thank you. May I put to you one further question? You need not answer," Richard continued hurriedly, as Hew rose to object again, "but if you will not, it may hurt you. This is a paper taken from your shop. Can you look at this paper and tell the court if you recognise it? Is it from your press?"

He showed the page briefly to Hew as he passed it across. It was the title page from Matthew's law book. Christian took it, trembling. Once again, she glanced at Hew, who nodded his assent.

"Do you recognise it?" Richard asked her gently, in a voice made low with pity and respect.

"It is a page from a law book we are printing," Christian whispered.

"From your press, beyond a doubt?"

"Beyond a doubt."

"Specifically, what page?"

"The title page."

"And the picture we see on that page, of the bird and the tree and the H and cross, that is your mark or device?"

"It is," Christian admitted.

"Then I thank you. You have been most helpful. We need trouble you no more."

Richard plucked the paper from her hands. Unsure of herself, Christian looked again at Hew. He gave her what he hoped was a reassuring smile. But he was thinking rapidly. Richard had returned to Chapman.

"Now, sir, if you will, consider this paper. Set the two there, side by side. Pray take your time."

Richard remained silent while the printer examined the two sheets of paper, eyes screwed in concentration, and did not speak again until Chapman looked up to meet his gaze.

"In your opinion, as a master printer, were these two papers produced on the same press?"

Chapman said stoutly, "Beyond a doubt, they were."

Hew leant forward a little, his eyes upon Chapman. He gave no answering smile to Christian's imploring looks across the court.

Richard continued, "You seem very certain of that. Perhaps you could explain to us, who are not expert in the field of printing, how you come to be so sure?"

"Well sir, if you would look here first at the device, you will see that the ink is not distributed quite evenly upon the page; at the righthand side of this tree the leaves are quite marked and distinct, while on the left, the leaves are blurred, and in one place do not show at all, and that place is left blank on the page. This device has been block printed, quite cheaply. That is to say, it has been carved from wood, rather than engraved in copper, in the new style, and in consequence the wood has become somewhat worn, and in places, the original engravings have smoothed out. On both these papers, the ink has failed to take in exactly the same way, in exactly the same part of the design. Therefore it is proved beyond a doubt that the same block was used to print both pages."

"It is not possible, I suppose, that another block could be constructed — what my friend here will call a forgery — to mimic the same sort of wear?" Richard suggested.

"It is not possible. That wear is the result of many, many presses; and its distribution is due perhaps to the peculiarity of a particular pressman. It is like . . . it is

336

like, sir, a pair of boots that wears down in a particular place; another man who had the same pair of boots could never wear the sole down quite the same. And even the same man, when he had another pair of boots, and in his same peculiarity of walking wore them down in about the same place, would never wear them quite as thin, unless he wore them exactly the same, for the same length of time and in the same places, and for the same number of days."

Richard allowed another smile. "Indeed, I have a pair of boots that show such particular wear. You explain it very well. Tell me, though; is it not possible, that though the same block were used on both these papers, they were printed on different presses?"

"I would stake my reputation, sir, that that is not the case. The letter is the same in both."

"Can you explain?"

"In several places, the characters are broken — here, on the upper case T, and there the lower case a, and here the O, that looks more like a C. These are what we call naughty letter, sir, and in a proper printers ought to be discarded. But these broken letters appear on both papers."

"The same?"

"The same."

"And it is not likely that a different set of letter should appear, by coincidence, to be broken in just the same places?"

"It is inconceivable, sir."

"I thank you. You have been most helpful. And I have no further questions. Perhaps these two papers might be passed around the jury," Richard appealed to the judge, "that they might compare the broken letters and the smudging of the trees — without, of course," he qualified, "attending to the matter of the slander."

The justice nodded. "Master Chapman, don't step down. For Master Cullan may have questions."

"I do have one or two," Hew answered pleasantly. "Master Chapman, I must thank you for your clear and full account. It has been most illuminating."

Chapman grinned complacently.

"You have been printer here for nine years now?"

"As I said."

"And in that time, you have made, as I understand, no less than thirteen complaints against printers, stationers, bookbinders and booksellers, here in the town. Is that correct?"

"I have made some complaints, against unfreemen and strangers, who did unlawfully trade in the town. I couldna tell you how many."

"I can tell you, Master Chapman, for they were recorded in the burgh records, that there were thirteen. How many of those were upheld?"

"Since you have seen the burgh records, no doubt you can tell me yersel," Chapman retorted. "For I don't remember."

"Since you don't remember, happily, I can. Two were upheld; one was a French merchant, selling Catholic tracts, and the other, just the other week, was a playing card seller, to whom you subsequently gave employment in your shop."

"Aye? Well, he was unlicensed," Chapman answered.

338

"Indeed he was."

"I do not see where this is going," interrupted Richard.

"My lord, I come to it. Do you think it fair to say you do not care for competition?" Hew enquired of Chapman. But before he could reply, Hew hurried on. "Did you, on William Hall's death, attempt to take his press from Christian Hall? Have you, in the past two years, made several such attempts? In short, Master Chapman, have you in the months since William Hall's death made such a noisome nuisance in her shop that she was forced to bar her doors against you, and on one occasion, her pressman was obliged to remove you bodily?"

Richard rose to his feet.

"I take it amiss," Chapman answered huffily, "that you construe my interest so. The truth is," he appealed to the jury, "that I offered her my help, and the use of my premises, when she was frozen out. Is it widow's work to run a press? Of course it is not. The work is hard, and not fit for a woman. Least of all, a woman who has lately had a child."

The jury, stout body of brave men and true, nodded its agreement to a man, and Richard sat back down again. "My lord," he muttered wearily, "but to the matter, now. May we not press on?"

"Aye, the matter," Hew returned. "Your expert advice. Tell me, Master Chapman, if you were to print a paper that spoke slander to the king, would you put your mark to it?"

"The case would not arise," Chapman told him loftily.

"I do not suppose it would. But don't you think it odd, that Christian Hall, if she did defame the king, would set her name to it?"

"If and should and were and would," Richard mimicked genially, "Dear, dear!"

The justice appeared to have fallen asleep.

"I imagine," Chapman replied, "that, being a mere woman, she did not fully understand what she was doing. It is one of the hazards of printing, and one of the reasons, of which there are many, that a woman is unsuited to the press."

There was a murmur of agreement from the jury. Hew realised he had lost them and moved swiftly on.

"You have given us the benefit of your experience. Pray, will you look at *this* paper, very carefully, and give it to us again. Tell me, do you recognise it?"

Chapman looked at the paper, a little surprised. "Aye, that I do. Where did you get it?"

"That I will come to in a moment. But first, will you tell the jury what this paper is, and how you know it?"

"It is a proof copy of a notice we printed three or four days ago, for Doctor Laurence Dow."

"Then it came from your press?"

"Aye, it did."

"Can you tell the court a little more? What the paper says, and how you came to print it?"

"I can, for it caused quite a stir. Three or four days ago there came into the shop two physicians, the one was Doctor Dow, that is well known here, and the other one a stranger. They brought with them a notice of some pestilence brought by a sailor to Leith, which they wanted to be copied and distributed throughout the burgh here and in the Canongate. It was most urgent, they said, and must be done at once. Which because we have several presses and one kept standing for proofs, we were able to do straight away, while they waited. Doctor Dow hastened the procedure by reading over the copy to the compositor while he set the text."

"Tell me, was it printed copy that they brought to you, or manuscript?"

"It was printed copy, sir, I dare say an old notice, of which there were no more copies."

"Even so. Then how can you be sure that this copy I have shown you came from your press, and was not the original notice that the doctor brought to you, or another copy of the same?"

"Because, as I say, it was a proof copy. Do you see this H sir, in this word? The middle bar is missing, and part of the first leg is gone, so that it looks more like an *i* and an *l* than a capital *H*. The character is broken. Doctor Dow himself remarked upon it, and he said it would not do, for the word could be mistaken. And I was most vexed with the compositor, that he did not spot it, and that it was his carelessness that caused the sort to be broken, for he must have dropped it on its head, for it to be so badly damaged."

"What do you do?" inquired Hew, "with sorts that are so badly damaged they may not be used again?"

"We call them naughty letter, sir, and prise them out, and set them in a tray apart, that they do not find their way back into the cases. And when the tray is full the boy takes it to the foundry to be melted down."

"And this was done here?"

"It was. The naughty letter was removed, and a good one inserted. That is the foul proof you have, sir. Only one was printed. I thought we had disposed of it."

"Therefore you can swear it came from your press?"

"I can, sir, and I do, sir, for I know it did, beyond a doubt."

"Because, as you said before, it is not possible that two sorts should break, in just the same place."

"As I said before."

"Then it would surprise you to hear that the particular notice, which you hold in your hand, was not printed on your press, but on the press of Christian Hall?"

"It would astound me, sir. It is not possible."

"It is not possible. And yet," Hew turned to the jury, "I can prove it to be so."

There was silence now. Richard sat straight, listening intently.

"There is a boy outside," continued Hew, "Master Chapman's week boy, who will testify that he destroyed the foul copy you made on your press, on the day you printed it, having no more use for it; and there is a doctor, one Giles Locke, a friend of mine, who presently will testify that he and I did print that paper in your hand, on Christian Hall's press, on Tuesday afternoon; and if you will come to her shop, I can show you the press, with the forme still in place, and locked in the forme, is the same broken H, and here, in fact, I have another copy," he drew out a sheet of paper, "and another and another, aye, sir, look, and pass them round, all of them the same."

"Is this a question?" Richard tried. "I have not heard a question." But he turned a little pale.

"Here is a question for you, Master Chapman," Hew said smoothly. "Would you like to know how this was done?"

"Aye, I would," Chapman spluttered.

"This is how: Doctor Locke and I made a notice warning of the pestilence, on Christian Hall's press. To emphasise the urgency of this report, we used a great many capital letters. There was another reason for that, as you will shortly see. When we were finished, and the work was printed off, we prised out a letter H, and chipped it with a chisel, and Doctor Locke ensconced it in his pocket. When once the print was dry, Doctor Locke and his good friend Doctor Dow came to your shop, in a great degree of urgency and agitation, requiring copies of the notice to be made at haste. To expedite this task, they stayed to help, as often authors do, though some are more a hindrance than a help. I will leave you to conclude which sort my friends best fit. They stood over the compositor, offering advice as he set out his tray, and while Doctor Dow rattled on about the graveness of the task, Doctor Locke slipped the broken sort into the case, with the nib uppermost, as I had showed him. For in the past weeks I have spent a good deal of time at the printing house, and I have watched the compositor at his work, marvelling at his sleight of hand, and though I lack the skill to do it, I

343

have learned how this is done. And we chose upper case letter, knowing he would have far fewer of them; if we slipped it in his case, then he was bound to take them up, having just enough. And just in case the poor man did notice it was broken, there was Doctor Dow, to hurry and distract him, and suffice to say, he did not notice it, until the proof was made. And when the proof was made, in case you did not notice it, then there was Doctor Dow to make another fuss and point it out. And so the compositor prised it out and dropped it in the naughty tray, where Giles scooped it out and dropped it in his pocket once again. And we took it back to Christian's press, and put it back into the space where it had been, and printed out these pages, with the naughty H intact. That is to say, *broken*, of course. The forme is still there, if you care to see it."

Chapman shook his head. "I do not understand what all this proves," he answered hopelessly. "It is just a trick."

"Aye. It's a trick," Hew said gently. "That is what forgery is."

Richard stood up. "One last question, Master Chapman. Surely, all this trickery cannot have changed your mind. You swore that you were sure, you were quite certain, that the papers I showed you were both from the same press. Surely, you do not retract that."

"I . . . I know not, sir," the man confessed miserably. "I cannot swear it . . . for I thought the proof was mine, no, more than that, I *knew* it was . . . and yet I am proved wrong. In conscience, sir, I cannot swear it; I am feared to swear."

"You were so sure . . . so sure . . ." Richard trailed off. "Aye, my lord, I'm done," he finished curtly.

Hew knew that his opponent was unnerved. Yet the case was far from won. He could not rely on the jury; he feared he had merely perplexed them. As if to illustrate his doubts, the judge leant forward.

"Master Cullan, I'm a mite bumbaised. Is there some sort of pestilence broken out at Leith? Ought we to be alarmed?"

"No, my lord," Hew answered, with a sinking heart. He glanced up at the king, who was grinning, though this scarcely reassured. "I understand the notices were made as a precaution. Doctor Dow is ever cautious, and he likes to be prepared."

"How very reassuring," said the justice. "Is it dinner time?"

Fast and Loose

When the trial resumed Richard Cunningham called Phillip Ramsay to compear. The compositor appeared so meek and cowed, so broken in demeanour, that Hew wondered what pressures had been wrought to induce him to bear witness for the Crown.

"You are Phillip Ramsay, compositor, employed by Christian Hall, in her shop upon the hie gate on the south side near the netherbow," Richard put to him.

"I am, sir," Phillip whispered, with a hoarse and fearful deference Hew had never heard from him before. He heard it with a sinking heart. He looked for hope and confidence, not this sad dejection and defeat.

"How long have you worked there?" Richard asked.

"For about five years," answered Phillip. "I was employed by her husband, William Hall."

"Then at the time of William Hall's death, had you completed your apprenticeship?"

"I had, sir; and was working for him as compositor."

"You remained there when he died. Why was that?"

"The chapel, sir — that's what we call the printer's shop — had become my family," Phillip answered simply. "I would be loath to leave it."

346

"I understand," said Richard sympathetically. "Now, Master Allan Chapman here has offered his opinion on some papers, alleged to have been printed at Christian Hall's press. I ask you to do the same. Will you look at these papers, and inform the court whether you have seen them before?"

Richard handed the witness the scandalous tract, and the title page from Matthew's book, which Chapman had examined in the court that morning. Phillip considered. "This I have seen," he said at last, holding up the page. "It is a proof copy of the title page of a book we are printing, and is taken from our shop. This other," he indicated the scandalous tract, "I have never seen before."

"Look at the devices on each page. Are they quite the same?" Richard pressed.

Phillip scrutinised them carefully. Finally he owned, with a hint of reluctance, "I confess, that they do appear the same."

"Very like, or quite the same," persisted Richard.

"I would have to say . . . the same."

"Such as could only have been printed, with the self-same block?"

"I would say so, aye," Phillip said unhappily.

"I thank you. Then I have no further questions."

"If I may keep you for a moment more?" proceeded Hew. "Can you tell us something about the block, which printed the device upon the proof that you identify as coming from your shop?"

"It is an old wooden block, cut down from one that was used by William Hall. Originally, it had his signature upon the bottom there," Phillip pointed with his finger to a line beneath the printed tree. "When he died, to save money, we cut off the signature, so that the device would serve equally well for Christian. Christian kept the piece," Phillip added poignantly, "in the hope that one day it would serve again for her son."

"Was this block the only one you had made?" asked Hew.

"Aye, it was. Since we have only one press, and only one compositor, we can set one book only at a time, and scarcely had the need for two. But just recently, Christian has had a fresh one engraved, in copper, for the old wooden block has become too worn to take the ink well. We mean to use the new plate in setting the book — of which this worn one is the proof — that presently is ready for the press . . . or would be, were we free to print it," Phillip added quietly.

"Then when this proof was made, and Christian saw the impression, she decided that it would not do, and had the fresh plate made?"

"That is correct."

"Then what became of the old plate? Was it cast into the waste tray, with the naughty letter?"

Phillip shook his head. "It was made of wood, and could not be melted down. I cleaned it, and returned it to its place. It is kept in the drawer under the correcting stone, because it is not part of any font. I thought it might provide a pattern, or prove useful if the copper plate became scratched. Besides which, William's signature, that was its other half, remained there still. It did not seem quite proper to throw them both away."

"And is it still in that drawer, to this day?" wondered Hew.

Phillip hesitated. "In truth, sir, no. It went missing."

"It went missing." Hew repeated carefully. His heart leapt at the news. And yet he knew that he must put the proper questions. He could not rely on Phillip. "Can you say when?"

"Not with certainty," the compositor confessed. "So much has happened lately that more ordinary events have been eclipsed. I can tell you when I noticed it was gone."

Hew nodded, "Aye, go on."

"The sequence of events was this. After I had set the proof copy, and we had looked at the proofs, Christian ordered the new plate. That took several days to come. In the meantime, I made the other corrections to the forme."

"That would include, for example, taking out the naughty letter and replacing it with good?" Hew inquired.

"Aye, that is so. I am afraid we have a good deal of broken letter, for times have been hard since William died, and we cannot afford new, so we have to make the best of what we have. But for this particular book, Christian was most particular to amend its faults as best we could. And so, as far as I was able, I took out the broken sorts."

"Then did you put the broken letter in the waste, or redistribute it?"

"I put it in the waste tray to be melted down. Christian was determined to have new. She believed that with the printing of this book we should see our fortunes change. And so we have," Phillip said wryly, with a bitter stab at his accustomed wit.

"And so what happened next?"

"The new plate arrived, and I began to set the work again." Phillip turned towards the jury. "The manuscript had fallen into water, and was very hard to read. And the work was going well when we were overtaken by events. Christian's little son went missing with his nursemaid on the muir; the nurse was found dead, and the child was lost for several days. During this crisis, no one did work on the press. But after several days, the child was found, and I returned to work, thinking to make up the time we had lost. Coming to the end of a large section in the copy, I considered that it wanted an embellishment, some sort of flourish, to mark where it closed. Such embellishments, together with strange characters and astrological signs, that are not unique to one sort of letter, are kept together in the drawer, with the printer's block. When I opened the drawer, I noticed that the printer's block was gone. It was the largest of the blocks, and had its own place at the front of the drawer, being most frequent in use."

"And always it was kept here in its place?"

"Always. It is not possible to compose, with any degree of accuracy or speed, if everything is not kept in its proper place."

"Then you were surprised to find it gone?"

"I was vexed, sir. For it meant that someone else had meddled with the blocks that only the compositor

350

should touch. But in the event, we did not need the block, and everything else had remained in its place, so I continued with my work, and for a time forgot about it. I was working on the copy when the guards came to arrest us."

"A printer's shop is a very busy place, is it not?" mused Hew.

"Aye, sir, it is," Phillip agreed.

"And in the course of a day, several people come and go; and authors come in to check proofs and copy, and customers to place orders, and binders to collect work for binding, and ink makers and paper makers, and messengers who come and go, changing by the week. There is a good deal of traffic, is there not, of fetch and carry, back and forth, and to and fro, on any working day?"

"There is."

"Then it would not be difficult, I think, for any one of these said bookmen, week boys, ink sellers, authors or messengers, if he should choose, to pocket a handful of the naughty letter you had cast into the tray?"

"Not difficult at all. The sorts would not be missed."

"That is interesting. Because I have the tray here, with some naughty letter in it. It was taken from the shop yesterday. Will you take a moment now to look through the tray, and see if you can find the sorts that printed on the title page. The upper case T, and the a and the O?"

"Aye, sir, but surely —"

"Pray do as I say."

Phillip examined the sorts in the tray, turning them over carefully. "They are not here," he concluded sulkily.

"They are not there. That's strange. Yet they appear, do they not, in the print of that scandalous tract, that same broken T, and a, and the O, that are broken on the title page?"

"They appear to, aye."

"They appear to, aye. Master Chapman has told us that the chance of two sets of letters being broken in just the same places, are so slight as to be quite impossible. Do you concur with that?"

"I would have to, aye."

"Indeed. Then tell us, in the scandalous tract, do you see any other letters broken, but for these three?"

"No sir. They are all intact."

"How very curious. I have no further questions."

"But sir," protested Phillip, "I do not understand. For those broken sorts could not be in the tray. The week boy took them to the foundry. They were melted down."

At a stroke, he had blown apart Hew's case. And Hew saw Richard Cunningham allow himself to smile.

"Now then," Richard countered, quickly on his feet, "you are very loyal, are you not, to your employer Christian Hall? Some might say, devoted."

"Our chapel is a close one," Phillip said defensively.

"Aye, as I say, you are close. Now, you stated, did you not, that only the compositor has access to the case?"

"Aye, in general, that is true."

"And only the compositor would know the layout of the case, and where to find the letters and the blocks. Is it conceivable, do you think, that a messenger, or a week boy, or an author or — what was it now, an *ink man*, with a pocketful of letters pilfered from your tray," Richard went on mockingly, "might come into the shop, and go into that case, that you did guard so jealously, and remove the block, without your knowing it?"

"No sir, not a stranger," agreed Phillip.

"*Not a stranger.* Then if the block was removed from the drawer, the only person who could have removed it was someone who knew where it was; someone who had access to the case when you were not there in attendance; someone, in short, who came from the shop."

"I suppose it must be so."

"I suppose it must be so," Richard echoed crisply. "I thank you for your help. I have no further questions."

Phillip stood helpless, the title page still in his hand. He had begun to sweat. His hands were dirty from the gaol. There was a sordid, hopeless shabbiness about him as he fumbled with the sheet. Hew was struck by the bitterness of irony; it was Matthew Cullan's proof that he was holding in his hand, Matthew Cullan's book that he was setting when they took him; Matthew Cullan's manuscript that had fallen in the firth and was all but rubbed away when Phillip took such pains to resurrect it. The warmth of the courtroom began to close in, and Hew was aware he had lost.

"May I have a cup of water?" he asked suddenly. The palest flame of hope began to flicker through his mind.

"It is not usual," said the judge, "yet may do no harm."

The cup was brought, and as Hew accepted it he caught sight of Phillip Ramsay's face, grey and unhappy in the fading light. He stood still in the box, for no one had advised him to stand down.

"Take it to the witness," Hew told the clerk. The cup was set down beside Phillip, who looked at it as if he had not seen such a thing before.

"Do you have a handkerchief?" Hew asked him quietly.

"A *handkercher?*" This was so ridiculous that for a moment it allowed the briefest glimpse of Phillip's scorn to filter through. "Sir, I have been in the castle gaol these past ten days. And even when I went, I did not have a handkercher."

"I suppose not. Then you must take mine." Hew removed it from his sleeve and handed it to Phillip at the witness stand.

"Dip the end in water, and rub it on the printed tree upon that paper in your hand. Make it somewhat wet, but do not rub too hard. I wish to see what happens," he explained.

Phillip stared at him. "Nothing will happen, sir." His voice revealed hopelessness, too raw for pity.

"Do it," Hew commanded.

Richard yawned. "More games."

Phillip wet the cloth, and wiped the page. He held it up. "It is a little wet, sir, nothing more."

Hew nodded. "Now do the same to the scandalous tract. Wet the cloth, and rub it in the same place, by the branches of the tree."

Phillip did so, "Why, sir, that is strange. The ink is smudged."

"Hold the page aloft, for the court to see." Indeed, the ink had smudged. "What do you conclude from that?"

"That it is not printers' ink."

"And what do you conclude from that?"

"That this was not made in any printer's shop."

"Can you tell us, what sort of ink it might be?"

"I know not . . . not iron gall, that is used in quills . . . but wait . . ." Phillip wiped again with the cloth, cleaning off the black. "It is iron gall, here, underneath. But gall is too loose and thin for printing, so this has been mixed with something else . . . something that would give it weight and substance, and the right amount of blackness. Something that dissolves in water. I would say . . ." he licked the corner of the handkerchief, "I would say carbon, or soot."

"Then this ink has been made to look like printers ink, from common writing ink, mixed with common household soot, for colour and consistency, for printing from the block."

"I should say so, sir. But the person who made this, understanding not the properties of ink, did not know how to make it permanent. When it gets wet, it separates."

"From which we should conclude?" Hew prompted gently.

"That the paper is a forgery."

★   ★   ★

355

It was enough. The jury were convinced, by this magic fast and loose, and Christian was acquitted. To Hew's relief, Richard took it with surprising grace. "Well played, indeed," he murmured. "Let me take you to Robert Fletcher's and buy you a flagon of wine. You look as though you need it."

But before they could depart, the court clerk informed them that the king required their company, in the council room. Richard grimaced ruefully. "And now for the reprisals. Alas, they will have to be endured." He ushered Hew before him. "Victor's spoils," he teased, magnanimous.

James had grown a little since his visit to St Andrews. In essence though, he had not changed. He was walking round the council room, restless and alert as ever, in the company of several watchful lords. As soon as they had made their bows, and the king had deigned to let them kiss his hand, James demanded bluntly, "How does it feel to be beaten, Richard Cunningham? And by a novice too!"

Richard bowed. If the barb had stuck, he did not show it. "Majestie, there are two occasions only when it does not shame a man to lose: when he's beaten by his pupil, and when he's beaten by his son. Master Cullan here has been my pupil at the bar these past few weeks, and in dearness, I confess, is almost like a son to me. There have been times, of late, that I despaired that he would ever make an advocate. Therefore, I protest this loss has made me proud."

The king laughed. "A pretty speech. I almost could believe it, if I had not watched you play at tennis with

356

your son. Believe me, Master Cullan, Richard does not like to lose. Do you play caich?"

"Majestie, I like to, when I have the time," admitted Hew.

"Then you shall play with me sometime. You and I have met before. Perhaps you don't remember it?"

Hew suppressed a smile. "I could hardly have forgotten it, your grace."

"Indeed? But I was a boy then, and now I am grown," observed the king, with such an air of false humility that Hew hardly knew what to say. They had met the previous year, when James was still thirteen. The boy was playing games with him.

"We met at St Andrews," James remarked to Richard Cunningham, "where Master Cullan here involved himself with mysteries, in putting on a play, that well did entertain us; and here he is again, amusing us once more, with all his tricks. I confess I am surprised to see him here, for like yourself I had my doubts that he would ever make an advocate. Yet here you are again, Master Cullan, aye, and once again, you court controversy, for I find you defending a charge, of slandering our name."

"Tis not the crime that I defended, sire, but the accused," Hew explained hurriedly.

"What did it say, this scandalous tract?" demanded James.

"I beg your pardon, majestie?"

"This slander that was written of our name. What did it say of us?"

"I confess, I do not know. I was not allowed to see it."

"Truly? Master Cunningham, do you know what it was?"

Richard bowed again. "Your grace, when the trial concluded, the paper was destroyed. And with it we obliterate its memory."

"And yet the crime has not been solved. That paper was the evidence."

"Some things are best forgotten, sire."

"I do not think so. For there was a crime," objected James.

"Beyond a doubt," conceded Hew.

"I don't suppose you know who did commit this crime?"

"I cannot say, as yet. But I wish to find that out."

"I too should like to find it out. So you may take it as your charge, to find it out," the king said seriously, "and when you do, to let me know."

"I shall make it my best endeavour," Hew promised.

"Then you will succeed. For I know you excel in finding things out."

"Sire . . . I do not think that you have any cause to fear."

It was the wrong word, for James started, fretfully. "Fear? What should I fear?"

"I meant, I do not think this crime was aimed at you. It was a crime intended to implicate Christian Hall," Hew explained.

The king stared at him. "I think you will find that the charge was one of leasing-making, and against our

358

proper person. If Christian Hall did not commit this crime, then we wish to know who did. And *that is all*."

"You cannot win against him," Richard said, taking Hew's arm as the king left the room. "That much, even I have accepted. Dear Hew, you're so very young!"

"Am I forgiven, then?"

"As to what I said this morning, I pray you think no more on it. Grace would be distraught if I sent you from the house. And if she is stout enough to forgive the hurt to Arabella, I can only follow her example. In truth, what I said to the king was no exaggeration. I was proud of you today. For you have shown that sharpness and detachment that were sadly lacking. Besides which, what you said was true. Christian Hall did not commit the crime. But there your case must end. It is not in your scope, to find out who did. Do not heed the king; he will forget this soon enough when Morton comes to trial."

"You are full of sound advice," reflected Hew.

"And you are fresh and raw, and plumped up with success, that comes before a fall. I pray that you will listen and accept it," Richard smiled.

Calton Crags

Meg had taken William through the barley fields to collect the morning dew. They dropped it into potions, restorative for restless eyes, and into may butter, to strengthen and soothe. Meg gathered boughs of hawthorn blossom, crab apple and broom, and William picked posies of violets and primroses, clenched in his fat little fists. The tight yellow buds of the broom were pickled in verjuice, and the violets distilled into syrups to calm a fractious child. They built a bower of light pink blossoms, trailing over troughs of blackened lye. The printing house became a vale of flowers. Meg baked biscuit breads of aniseed and clove, and roasted capons on the fire to welcome Christian home. As Christian wept, her small son whispered shyly, "I picked flowers for you."

The little chapel was restored, all except for Alison, whose name hung heavy in the air, unsaid. Hew brought wine to the party, yet he did not drink. He sat remote at the fireside, thoughtfully watching the crowd. Christian held William sheltered in her lap as Phillip found his fiddle and begin to play. Meg was baking oatcakes on a skillet. Hew saw the week boy snatch one from the pan. "A word, if you please," he said quietly. Michael sucked his fingers as he followed to the corner by the press.

"If you dip your fingers in the fire then you will burn them," Hew observed.

Michael started guiltily.

"There is something I must ask you," Hew continued. "And you must answer truthfully, though you are afraid. Can you do that, do you think?"

The boy considered. "Yes, sir," he agreed at last.

"Good lad. You know that bad things have been happening. Alison was killed, and Christian went to gaol. And all of it began with the corbie messenger, for which I know that you were not responsible."

"I *wasn't* sir," the boy insisted.

"Therefore you must tell the truth," Hew answered kindly, "as you did to me before about the bird. You must tell it, even if to do so seems wrong, even if it appears to hurt Phillip. Do you understand?"

Michael nodded.

"When Phillip was in court," Hew put to him, "he said that when he set the copy for my father's title page, he gave you the broken letter and you took it to the foundry. Is that correct? Was he telling the truth?"

"Yes, sir," Michael muttered. He did not look up at Hew.

"Are you quite sure?"

"Phillip was not lying, sir," the boy blurted desperately, "when he said he gave it to me . . . only . . ."

"*Only* . . . ?" prompted Hew.

"Only that . . . I did not take it. I was going to . . ."

"You were *going* to," Hew repeated softly. "What happened that prevented you?"

"I gave the type to Alison," the boy admitted, "she was going to the hammerman, to buy a cooking pot. She promised she would take it on her way. It saved a journey," he put in defensively. "But does it matter, sir? You do not think that Alison was killed because I gave her broken type?"

Hew could not answer him, since that was what he thought. Instead he asked, "Do you think that Alison could have taken the device — I mean the printing block? Did she know where it was kept?"

"I do not know, sir . . . Aye, she did," the boy reflected. "William pulled the drawers, and scattered all the blocks, and Alison helped Phillip pick them up. It put Phillip in a bad temper, for he hates us touching things."

"Aye, I remember that. Thank you," Hew said thoughtfully. "You have told me what I need to know."

He returned to the fireside, where William sat still in Christian's lap, far distant from the little boy who caused havoc through the shop. Hew ruffled William's hair. "He is quiet still," he noticed. Christian smiled at him. "He is not quite himself. And yet he is much better now. Meg tells me he has nightmares, and relives his terrors in his dreams. It is a sign, the doctor thinks, that the horrors have worked loose, and that he may be rid of them in time. He does not speak of Alison. I hope he may forget her," she admitted sadly. "Hew, I have not thanked you properly for all that you have done."

"It's nothing," Hew said absently.

Christian looked down to hide her tears. "It's everything, to me," she assured him. William gave a whimper, and she forced a brighter smile. "Have you said thank you to Hew, for sending you the apples?" she asked the little boy.

"Apples?" queried Hew.

"Aye, that was kind of you. Meg said they came this morning, by the fruitman's boy."

"I had forgotten," Hew said, frowning. "May I see them?"

"They are on the board beside the flowers."

Giles stood at the table, with a pie from Bessie Brewster he was setting in a dish. "A pastry to add substance to the feast." As Meg approached, he cleared his throat and frowned. "Apples, Hew! I really can't approve your gift to William. The child is of a windy disposition, and you know my thoughts on fruit."

"I did not send them," murmured Hew.

Meg exclaimed, "We felt certain it was you! The fruitman said a gentleman had bought them for the little boy, who had lost his mother and his nurse."

"Is it likely that I would say that?" Hew demanded grimly. "This is a threat," he confided to Giles.

The music had stopped. Christian stood, wild-eyed, with William in her arms and Phillip by her side. "Then it is not over? It begins again!" She shuddered, clutching close her child.

"Someone meant it for a kindness," Phillip reassured her. "Do not fret."

"It is not kindness," Christian cried. "Do you not see? *Davie* gave him apples. It is like the corbie messenger. Someone wants to harm us. And it *does not end*."

"You are overwrought," Meg soothed. But Hew said gravely. "Christian is right. It does not end." He took Giles aside. "They cannot stay here. It is no longer safe."

"There is Doctor Dow's house on the Cowgate," Giles suggested.

"That is not far enough. I know a better place. I will need your help, and that of Doctor Dow."

Hew explained his plan.

"It is too dangerous," objected Giles.

"If you play your part, and Doctor Dow's good wife agrees to hers, it will prove safe enough," Hew assured him. "Can you take them safely there, tomorrow at first light?"

"Aye. That is the simple part," Giles agreed reluctantly.

"Write to me a letter, when the thing is done. I will do the rest. On Sunday, I will come to Doctor Dow's. Meanwhile, I must speak with Walter Balcanquall. I counsel you, tell no one where they've gone."

As the little group dispersed, the flowers began to wilt.

On Saturday, Eleanor prepared a supper once the children were in bed. "Sir David Preston has sent two fat cunings from his estate," she explained to Hew, "and I thought that we should celebrate the closing of your case. I have not liked to see you so at odds."

"In truth, we were never opposed," Richard said genially, "except in the courtroom. Which is no more a quarrel, than a game of caich, when all is said and done. And yet there is real cause to celebrate. For I have spoken to the justice general, who agrees that Hew is ready to be entered for the bar. I have been thinking it is time you were admitted to the faculty," he turned to Hew. "For certain, you have proved yourself, and your probation is complete."

"I thank you, sir," Hew answered miserably.

Richard looked amused. "You do not seem very pleased about it. I may tell you, it takes most of us a year or more to achieve what you have done in several weeks. Now that you have leave to prosecute, I promise you, our battles will begin in earnest."

Before Hew could frame a reply, they heard a knocking at the door, and Eleanor frowned. "Who can that be at this hour?" Presently the servant appeared with a letter for Hew.

"A little late for correspondence," noted Richard.

Hew read his letter carefully, and told the servant, "No reply," as he placed it in his pocket. There followed an awkward silence, eventually broken by Eleanor.

"Properly, of course, it is a fish day, and yet I think it possible to be too nice about such things. Your brother Giles, for certain, is quite exercised upon the benefits of meat."

"Aye," Hew allowed grimly, "on that, at least, he is always unequivocal."

Eleanor had served the rabbits, one fat and roasted, with his belly stuffed with herbs, the other stewed and jointed in a broth. In spite of the dark, meaty fragrance, Hew found little appetite. He pushed a listless fork around his bowl. Richard watched him closely. "Do we have more bread?" he asked his wife, "to soak up this liquor? It is a shame to waste it."

"We may want it for tomorrow," Eleanor replied, "I will have to ask the maid."

"Are we become so frugal, that we cannot have fresh bread?" Richard said, a little sharply.

"Tomorrow is the Sabbath," Eleanor reminded him. "I will see what I can do."

"And was there not a bottle left of good canary wine, locked up in the laich house? Do not send the lass. I do not trust her with the key," Richard added pointedly.

"Aye, very well," sighed Eleanor. "I'll go and look."

"She will be gone a while," Richard winked at Hew. "I finished it last week. Sometimes she is slow to take the hint. Now, I know you well enough to know that there is something on your mind, and you know me well enough, to trust that you can talk to me. Was it something in the letter?"

"Aye, it was." Hew took out the paper and handed it to Richard. "It is from Walter Balcanquall. He has heard from John Knox."

"Then it is no wonder you are so disturbed," Richard quipped. "When Balcanquall begins to summon forth the dead, we all must be afraid."

Hew did not smile. "Ah, not that John Knox. John Knox is the minister of the parish kirk at Lauder. I asked Balcanquall to write to him, and several ministers along the London road, for news of Marten Voet. Voet has been apprehended, on the old Roman Dere Road, near Lauder, and is held in the kirk steeple there."

"Aye, so I see," Richard read the letter. "But that is good news, is it not?"

"They will not keep him long, without good cause to hold him. I must go there tomorrow, to explain the charge," said Hew.

"Then why so sad? At last you have the villain in your hands, and may have your justice for those two poor murdered lasses, that has meant so much to you. Surely, you do not still have a qualm for Marten Voet?" Richard reasoned.

"In truth," admitted Hew, "it is no more than vanity. I am unhappy that I got it wrong."

"Well then, put it right," his friend encouraged him. "When do you leave?"

"At first light. I will take Giles with me, to support my claim."

"That's fair enough. Now that the trial is done, you can happily be spared for several days."

"As to that," Hew said seriously, "I still have fears for Christian and her child. However, I have moved them to a place of rest, where they may be safe while I am gone."

"Aye, very sound," Richard nodded. He helped himself to the last portion of the rabbit. "Are they at the west port, with your sister?"

"No, that would not do. Meg is quite worn out. She is not suited to the dizzy turmoil of a child. I have found a better place, where Christian feels at home: her childhood cottage, at the foot of Carlton crags."

"I think that very apposite. Then you can catch your villain, with a clear and open conscience," Richard said approvingly.

"That is what I hope," admitted Hew. His sprits did not lift, and he said little else before Eleanor returned, with a barley bannock and a bottle on a tray. "No manchet loaves, and no canary wine, but I have found some claret."

Richard seized the bottle, blowing off the dust. "Now this is rare indeed! I had it from a merchant who avoided import duties. I had quite forgotten it!"

As Richard and his family came to church that Sunday, Hew walked east along the Cowgate to the house of Doctor Dow. The doctor and his wife were already gone to kirk and Hew was met by Giles, in a strange array of clothes, suggesting some peculiar experiment. "Is it ready?" Hew inquired.

"Doctor Dow's good wife has made what you required. And we have tried it out, as best we can," Giles confirmed. "Will you change here?"

Hew nodded briskly, taking off his coat. "God willing, it will not be put to test."

"I pray not," Giles answered seriously. "Are you quite sure about this?"

"Not sure at all. Indeed, I hope I am wrong. Were they delivered safely?" Hew asked anxiously.

"I took them there myself," Giles assured him. "And Meg went too, for company. You were quite right about

368

the people, Hew. I cannot overstate the kindness they have met there."

"And you told no one where they are? Not even Phillip?"

Giles snorted. "Especially not Phillip, who made himself most disagreeable. I told no one, and I swear that no one followed us. I would not have left them had I thought there was a risk. Hew . . . I cannot let you go alone."

Hew was silent for a moment. Then he said quietly, "You know I understand the risk, and have taken all precautions. This is something that I have to do alone."

"I understand you feel responsible. But Meg would not forgive me, if you came to harm," protested Giles.

"I cannot take you with me, Giles. For you are scarcely inconspicuous. Whatever are you wearing?"

"My dissecting outfit," Giles admitted. "It is the matter of a moment, though, to change."

"Peace, Giles, I am gone," smiled Hew. "You have not seen me."

"Take Paul," his friend insisted. "He is armed, and primed, and somewhat drably dressed."

"Aye, very well," conceded Hew at last.

"Is it some sort of espionage?" Paul inquired excitedly.

"Something of the sort," Hew answered wryly. "Can you bring a tinderbox? The cottage has been empty for some months, and may be cold and dark."

They made their way up to the netherbow, where they turned north to Calton hill. The servant chattered on the way. "Is there likely to be bloodshed, sir? In faith, I am prepared for it. My work with Doctor Locke has overcome my squeamishness. I am not that callow boy that you once knew."

"I am relieved to hear it. But I hope there will be no cause for the spilling of blood. What is required here is caution, Paul, and vigilance, and above all quietness," Hew warned him. "Can you hold your tongue?"

"I can sir, and I will, sir. I can be silent as the grave, and hot irons would not force your secrets from me. The doctor's work is close, and confidential. He has taught me . . . oh!" Paul caught the drift. "You wish me to be quiet, now, sir?"

"That is the gist," Hew confirmed. "I wanted space to think."

"Then I can be quiet, as the smallest mouse." Paul said confidently.

They had come to the cottage, on the outskirts of the Flodden wall, and Hew unlocked the door.

"What should I do, sir?" Paul asked, in a loud stage whisper. "Do I stand and watch?"

"Aye, a little further off." Hew looked around. Behind the cottage ran the ruin of the old town wall. "Crouch there," Hew instructed, "and keep watch."

"Aye, that I will," Paul accepted eagerly. Then he hesitated. "What is it I am watching for?" he wondered.

"To see if anyone comes in," Hew answered patiently.

"And if they do, I should pounce on them, and prick them with my blade?" suggested Paul.

"No, you should do nothing," Hew assured him, "until I give a sign."

"Aye, very well. But what sort of sign?"

"I know not — a whistle. I will whistle if I want you, Paul. Unless you hear the whistle, do not show yourself."

"Aye, well and good," the servant answered happily. "What tune will you whistle, sir?"

"Oh, dear God!" Hew swore, and checked himself. "No tune. Just a whistle, long and low, like this." He gave a long low whistle, and Paul nodded, satisfied. "We should practise it indoors, in case I do not hear."

"No, we should not," retorted Hew. He pushed Paul firmly in his place behind the wall. "If you do not heed the whistle, I shall scream."

Hew entered the house and let the door close behind him, leaving the key in the lock. He left the shutters closed, and lit the lamp, looking through the rooms. The cottage had been empty over winter, yet the doors were solid and the walls and windows watertight, the place was clean and dry, beneath a layer of dust. The light oak furniture, half tester bed and press, were scaled to fit, and the fabrics of the bed were finest silk, out of keeping with a small and modest house. The entrance hall led back into a second chamber, with a kitchen and a closet below stairs. The cottage backed on to a long strip of land, sloping to the hills, and flanked with plum and apple trees, the new leaf already in bud. A chicken coop, and garden beds of vegetables and herbs, were visible beneath the straggling weeds; a secret garden hidden in the hills, a stone's throw from the bustle of the town. A meeting place for lovers, Hew thought bitterly. It was cold in the cottage, and he lit a fire, trailing smoke against the pale blue sky. He sat thoughtful in the gloom, prepared to wait. It would be a while yet, for the sermon at the kirk had just begun. So he did not expect the rapping at the door. He started to his feet. It was doubtless Paul, he reassured himself. Then he heard the rattle of the lock, and a voice calling loudly, "Christian, are you here?"

Hew cursed as he climbed the low steps from the kitchen, throwing open the door into the hall. Full square on the hearth, glaring and glowering, stood Phillip.

Without pausing to speak, Phillip lunged at him. Hew was prepared, and caught him with a blow upon his shoulder that send him staggering against the wall. As he stood up again, Hew drew his sword. "I do not recommend it," he said coldly.

Phillip rubbed his shoulder, sulking like a bairn. "Where is she?" he demanded.

Hew ignored the question. "How did you know to come here?" he returned.

"Christian told me. This was her home as a child."

"Aye, I was afraid that she might tell you," Hew admitted. "Therefore it is fortunate they are no longer here."

"Villain! Where is she?" screamed Phillip.

"Don't you mean, where are they? Did you forget little William?" Hew taunted. "Or does he not fit with your plan?"

"I will kill you," swore Phillip.

"How do you mean to do that? When you are unarmed, and I have a sword? With which, I can assure you, I am quite adept."

"You think you are so very subtle," Phillip sneered, "That you can have and hurt her, when you do not even want her, that you can have her at your beck and call. Be assured, you swingeour, that she is not yours."

"You are mistaken, if you think I make a claim to her," Hew countered coldly.

"I know you don't," said Phillip. "That makes it all the worse."

Hew sighed. "It is infernal luck, to set a snare and catch a rabbit, when I want the fox," he remarked. "Phillip, you can see that Christian is not here. Now go away, or I will have to hurt you."

There was a sudden clatter at the door, and the servant Paul appeared, alarmed and breathless. "I went off for a piss, and missed your whistle. Is all well?"

Hew groaned aloud. "God's truth! Are you armed, Paul?" he asked wearily.

"Aye, sir, armed and ready." Paul drew his dagger with a flourish.

"This man is not wanted here. May I trouble you to take him back to town?"

Phillip scowled. "Since Christian is not here, I'm going anyway. There's no need for that."

Paul looked disappointed. "Then the danger is averted, sir?"

"Aye, then, it is," agreed Hew. "If you will see him out of sight and earshot, I shall have no further need for you. Stop to talk to no one on the way."

He watched as Paul escorted Phillip from the house and prodded him, protesting, down towards the water port. Having dealt with these distractions, Hew settled down to wait.

It was several hours before he heard the lifting of the latch, and the visitor at last came in, so quietly that he thought perhaps it was the wind. The shutters were still closed. Hew had allowed his lamp to burn out, leaving only the soft smudge of candlelight in the corner by the window and the last sooty embers of the fire. He listened, taut among the shadows. The visitor removed a bundle from his back, and slid it softly to the floor. He stood for a moment, considering. Then he took the candle from the sill and let it cast its light around the room. Hew stepped out into its glow. "They are not here."

"Aye, so I see," the answer came soft, with a trace of amusement. "And yet you sit here in the dark. May we light the lamp?"

"By all means." Hew took the flame and applied it to the lamp. He held the lantern high to show his face.

Richard smiled wryly. "Not gone to Lauder, Hew? Then what about the letter?"

"The letter was a forgery, written by Giles Locke."

"How singular. Your brother has become adept in forgeries, I think."

"I doubt he has," Hew agreed. "He learned his trade from you."

"Then I suppose the minister at Lauder isn't called John Knox?"

"Curiously, he is," admitted Hew. "I have learned, also from you, that the best way to lie is to build the lie on truths. I did go to Balcanquall, and he did write to

Lauder, though his friend John Knox has not replied. But Balcanquall was helpful to me in another way. He told me Catherine's poems were brought to him by you. He said that you had had them from a friend, though he was somewhat shy of breaking confidence. He is a proper man."

Richard grimaced. "Never trust the kirk, Hew."

Hew ignored this. "So I did not care to leave Christian on her own."

"That I understand. I felt the same."

"Ah, did you now?"

"And so I resolved to look in on them, on my way to the tennis court," Richard said smoothly. "May I inquire where they are?"

"Far from here."

"You are secretive indeed," noticed Richard, smiling. "Yet we were once so close. Is there no one that you trust?"

"Certainly, not you," acknowledged Hew.

"Surely, you do not suspect me, on the word of Walter Balcanquall? Well then, that's a pity." Richard made a move towards his bag. "For I thought that we were friends."

"Why did you have to come here?" Hew asked him softly. He could not mask the note of sadness in his voice.

"Much like yourself, I wanted to make sure they were quite safe."

"And what is in your bag?"

Richard stared at him. "My tennis things." Suddenly, he laughed, and opened up his sack. "Racquets for the caichpule, apples, and a knife. The apples, I confess, were a present for the child. I thought that he might like them. Was I wrong?"

"You sent apples to the house."

"I know that Giles insists they are the devil's shitting potion, but you cannot think I meant to harm the bairn," objected Richard, buckling up his bag. "You have read too many nursery tales. Now, I should like a game, before it grows too dark. Since I have no partner, will you play with me?"

Hew blew out the lamp. "You wish to play a game of chases," he said slowly.

Richard smiled indulgently. "I do."

A Game of Chases

Patrick Fleming's caichpule had been built into a courtyard overlooked in every sense, enclosed by lands and tenements that turned their backs upon an accidental space. Within this space, a timber frame was lined with panels painted black. The caichpule was left open to the elements, to make the best use of the light. A gutter in the centre of its floor allowed collected rainfall to escape into a drain, channelled to the entrance of the close. The steep slope was levelled, to fall gently to the centre from both ends, and the floor was paved with stone. It was smaller than the courts that Hew had played upon in France, perhaps seventy feet long, by twenty feet wide, running slightly angled, north to south. The tenements that flanked it on all sides extended far above the penthouse roofs, and kept high curving services from landing in the street. Of the surrounding lands, only Robert Fletcher's on the south side had windows that looked out onto the court, with a small timbered gallery high above the service end recklessly exposed to flying balls.

Since it was the Sabbath, both the court and Fletcher's gallery were closed. Richard led Hew through a passageway in Patrick Fleming's close, opening to the caichpule from the west. He unlocked a little doorway in the galleries, upon the penthouse side, and locked this door behind them as they entered, securing the key in his pocket. At first he did not speak, but strode out to the centre of the court to inspect the net, a loose rope strung with tassels, hanging to the floor. The trough beneath the net was clean and dry, for it had not rained for several days. This inspection complete, Richard opened up his bag and removed a pair of racquets, which he examined thoughtfully, before handing one to Hew. "I always play with racquets," he remarked. "I never have much cared to use my hands."

At the other side of the net, the caichpuler had left a large basket of balls, covered with a canvas cloth. Richard removed the cloth and inspected the balls with the same exaggerated care he had focused on the racquets, before he made his choice.

"I wonder," he reflected next, "what should be the stakes?"

"The stakes are high," Hew assured him.

Richard smiled. "Incalculably. May I propose," he went on politely, "that we spin your sword, to determine who has service? Then, for safety's sake, we'll place it in the trough, for fear that you may fall on it, in the Roman style. And against that same risk, I shall lay down my dagger."

Cautiously, Hew removed his weapon, handing it to Richard, who spun it lightly on the court. The handle fell to Hew, upon the service side.

Richard bowed. "There you have won the advantage." He placed his dagger in the dip below the net and Hew placed his own sword beside it, stepping back to take his serve. The court was a simple *jeu quarré* with four winning openings on the service side, and a wooden *ais* or target strip behind him to the left, and a grille upon the hazard side, which Richard stood defending. The floor was drawn with lines to mark the chases.

Richard called out, "Since we have no boy to mark us, we must note the chases where they fall, and trust ourselves, as gentlemen, to keep each other's score."

They watched each other warily, like strangers. The timber walls distorted sound, holding in the dull thud of the balls, and their voices echoed oddly, forced and strained. At the same time, the panelling muffled and confused the noises from the street, enhancing the impression of enclosure. For a while, they played in silence, focused on the game, until Richard laid a chase and called out, "Worse than four, I think."

Hew picked up the ball, but did not return it. He turned it over in his hand. "How did you mean to do it?" he asked softly.

"Do you wish to rest? I should say *pause*. It always makes me smile that we describe as *rests* the moments when the ball's in play," Richard observed. "Will you rest awhile, or play the rest?"

Hew shook his head, fingering the ball. "Did you mean to cut their throats? To kill Christian first, and then the child?"

Richard winced a little. "I suppose you will not believe me when I say I did not want to kill the child," he protested mildly.

"I do not believe it." Hew stepped back to take his serve. It clipped the penthouse roof above the door and spun down to bounce a second time, halfway between the net and the back wall. Hew grimaced. "Hazard half a yard?"

"I'm afraid so," Richard nodded. "That's the second chase." He took a ball out of his pocket, preparing to change ends.

"What I told you was the truth," he went on, as Hew assumed the hazard end. The service took Hew by surprise.

"Ah, pardon, for you were not ready," Richard offered generously. "I will play the shot again. I did not seek them out, intent on killing. The apples were a gift, a present for the child. But the intention was to let him see my face, to see if he remembered it. If the child had screamed — and only if he screamed — then I meant to kill them both. If not, you will allow, I did not mean to hurt them. The apples must be proof of that."

Chilled by Richard's calmness, Hew mirrored the cool frankness of his tone. "*You* will allow, though, surely, that it would not have been enough that William did not scream. He knew you as the printer Davie. You could not have risked him calling you that name," he pointed out.

"Ah, that is true. Still, I must protest, I did not want to hurt the child. I prayed to God I need not do it. Still, I hope," Richard whispered, almost to himself, "I may not need to do it." Suddenly, he took his serve, and lunged too late for Hew's return.

Hew cried, "Won it!" He had bettered Richard's chase.

Richard pulled a face. "Forty:thirty, then, to you. You must allow though," he reflected, delaying the service once more, "that I did not kill the child upon the moor. That signifies for something, surely?" He let the ball spin, and embarked on a rest that went on for several minutes, until Hew lured him to the net and won the second chase.

"It signifies for nothing," Hew replied, as Richard caught his breath. "You left him there to die."

Richard said indifferently, "Perhaps." He served into the grille and called out, "Fifteen:love."

Hew wiped his face with his sleeve. His shirt was streaked with sweat, yet he felt cold. The light in the court was beginning to fade.

"Are you ready to play on?" Richard called abruptly. "It's growing dark."

Hew had lost his concentration, and they played several games before another chase was laid. At last, when they changed ends, they did not speak. Then Richard said again, "The apples were intended as a gift. I did not wish to harm the child."

Hew shook his head. "You left the child exposed, assuming he would die. Do not dress as pity, what was simple cowardice."

"Aye, you are right," Richard conceded. "I could not bring myself to kill him. Yet I'm glad I do not have his death upon my conscience now."

"You speak of conscience, like a proper man, with human thoughts and feelings," Hew said bitterly.

"You know me, Hew. We have been good friends, and I have made you welcome in my house. How can you doubt my proper thoughts and feeling?" Richard sighed.

"You forget I found the body of that girl, that you left torn and ravaged on the moor. It looked as though the wild dogs had dismembered her, and made their savage banquet in her heart. What sort of man is capable of that?"

Richard let the ball drop. "Dead," he answered quietly.

"What did you say?"

"It is a *dead* ball, no longer in play. You cannot understand," his tone was more defensive now, "how *difficult* it was, to make her die." He stood for a moment, reflecting, and then observed, "I find I cannot talk and play."

"Which would you prefer to do?"

"Talk, I think. Then play."

Richard lay against the wall and closed his eyes. For a while, he seemed to be asleep, and then he murmured dreamily, "When I brought you to my house, I had no idea you were the devil's instrument. I loved you like a brother, almost as a son."

"What do you mean?" Hew asked uneasily.

Richard smiled. "I see that the familiar terms disturb you. Do not be alarmed, for we are not related. I had no notion then that you were the corbie messenger."

"How was I the messenger? You sent the bird," objected Hew.

"That was a little crude," his friend allowed. "But I could not resist it. Roger killed the corbie with his bow; a single arrow through the eye. He is the most ingenious boy. He wanted to dissect it, and was vexed to find it gone. Aye, you were the messenger, late by twenty years."

"I do not understand."

"You are precipitate. Listen, and I shall explain. Show a little grace, and do not interrupt, until the tale is done. You have played a part in this, and you must share the blame. At your father's funeral, I mentioned my first case. Perhaps you will remember it? It concerned a writer in our close. His name was David Corbie, and he died a traitor's death — I notice you remark the name, though you did not ask it then. He was hanged for the making of false letters, in the forging of a pardon for a prisoner at Blackness. A crime, I can assure you, he did not commit."

"How can you be certain?" murmured Hew.

Richard smiled. "Poor fool! Don't you see it yet? I stole the writer's seal, and made the forgery myself. Ah, do not judge me, till you know the whole. I was very young. The prisoner was a kinsman of my father, like to name my father as accomplice to his crime. Not without cause, I may say. If he had spoken out, my family would be ruined; my mother would be destitute, my father would have hanged. Everything I did, I did for them.

"I did not think, you understand, that Corbie would be blamed. I did not *think*. For I am not the monster you suppose. And when he was, I tried to save him, on my life. Well, not quite my life," he conceded wryly, "*that* I could not spare. But all else I possessed, I placed at his disposal. Your father found me out. He knew the truth."

"I do not believe you!" Hew objected hotly, "for my father would never have colluded in your crime."

"He came to it too late for David Corbie," Richard sighed. "Matthew was distracted by your mother's death, for which he blamed himself. He found the way to show me he suspected, when he made me witness Corbie's execution. I think I did not mention, how *unkindly* Corbie died. They struck off his right hand, and nailed it to the cross, where he could look on it before he hanged. And since he was a traitor, they did violence to his corpse, and tore it into four. The body on the muir disgusted you, yet Alison was ravaged in the savage heat of passion; David's flesh was wrenched by the iron cold grip of law. You may wonder which was worse."

"You can excuse neither one by the other," argued Hew.

"Aye, perhaps not. Yet hear me out. After Corbie died, my training was complete," Richard went on, with a touch of irony, "and Matthew's own career fell in decline. Six years later, he retired, to your house in Kenly Green, and our paths no longer crossed. Yet all the while, I sensed he knew my secret. When I saw him last, before he died, I came ready to confess. If he had

384

given any hint, in gesture, word, or look, then I should have wept, and knelt before him, pouring out my conscience, making clean my sin. And yet he gave no sign; he received me civilly, and kindly, and with hopes that I might act as tutor to his son."

"Then you can be sure, he did not know. It was the fevered product of your guilt, that made you think it," Hew assured him.

"So I believed," said Richard sadly. "Something lifted from my heart. When your father died, I felt a peace I had not known for twenty years. I asked you to my house, in open friendship, with a glad full heart, out of love for Matthew. I might as well have asked the devil in to sup with me, for I did not foresee that Matthew had designed in you my end."

"This is madness," Hew protested.

"Do you not see, that from the start, he meant you for his instrument? He sent you with a book of his old cases. And I made you welcome in my house, not knowing you brought hell and fury in your wake. For where did he send his book? To David Corbie's child."

"Dear God! I thought —"

"Of course you did," Richard nodded sympathetically. "For that was what I wanted you to think. Christian Hall is not your sister. What Matthew did for her, he did from pity, and perhaps, in part, from guilt. He took my dereliction on himself, and sought to make amends for it. I did not know, at first, who Christian was. I was as much perplexed as you, until you told me her device, and that Matthew had selected it. And then I knew the book must prove my guilt."

Hew shook his head. "You are mistaken. Alison has died for nought, for there was nothing there."

"You underestimate your father's subtlety. Matthew planned this from the start. I had to have that manuscript. I began to watch the shop, from Robert Fletcher's tavern. I saw the nursemaid in the street, playing with the child. Later, I saw Catherine come and go. I knew Catherine well. She gave Grace a poppet once, that strumpet called Celeste. But I digress," Richard smiled. "I meant to speak of Alison. I followed her upon the muir, and became her friend. Such simple souls are cheap to buy. I knew that she would help me. She knew me as the printer, Davie. We were sweethearts, she supposed. I met her in the afternoons when you were in the printing house. I changed at the tennis court, into workman's clothes. A strange thing, is it not, how men judge us by our dress? You will remark this most of all, for when you came in boatman's rags they cast you in the prison house. Likewise, in the law courts, none may speak, without the proper clothes. My fear was that this would not work so well upon the child, that he would know me by my face, because he does not understand the ordering of rank. To Alison, I was her Davie, and a printer. I persuaded her to bring me printed papers from the shop, by way of an exemplar, that I promised to return. I wanted, in particular a textbook on the law. The silly girl had no notion what I wanted, for she could not read. She brought me Catherine's poems. And though they were not quite what I was looking for, I realised I could make good use of them. I passed them on to

Balcanquall, in the hope of closing Christian's press. I hold no grudge against Catherine," he paused to reflect. "Her husband was one of my clients, whose heart stopped in the throes of passion with a whore. Robert gave Catherine the grandgore. I expect she has passed it to you."

"I did not lie with her," Hew answered shortly.

Richard looked amused. "Then you showed more restraint than I supposed.

"What I did not anticipate, foolishly, was that the burgh council would impound your father's book. No one was more relieved than I to see it safely back in Christian's hands. And yet I was no further forward, for I did not have the manuscript. And I could not have it, for the book was charmed."

"This is madness, Richard, nursery tales! The burden of your guilt has turned your wits!"

"Is it, though? It came through flood, and God knows what; when all else was destroyed, it remained unharmed. What else could it mean, but that Matthew had bewitched it? Then I became obsessed with Christian Hall. I would her destroy her absolutely, wipe her out, as I had done her father, and remove all trace of proof. I would make a forgery that she could not deny. It took some time to persuade Alison to steal the block and type. She had disobeyed her mistress and she feared the bairn would tell; I bribed the bairn with fruit. I had not brought back the papers I had promised; I persuaded her that they were waste, the block and letter too, would not be missed. She was afraid that she would lose her place; I promised her a better one. And, you will allow, I sent her to a better one," he pleaded, chillingly. "I knew I had to kill her, even then. For even little Alison, foolish as she was, would not have held her tongue when Christian came to trial. So I arranged to meet her for the last time on the moor. I brought a banquet in a napkin, sweetmeats for the child. And, while William played, I offered to make love to her."

"Then it was not a rape," muttered Hew.

"It was not a rape," Richard agreed. "Later, it made sense to let you think it was, to tie the crime to Marten Voet, and the murder in St Andrews. Though you cannot think," he gave a shudder of disgust, "I wanted her. Whatever you will think of me, I pray, do not think that."

Hew fell silent, sickened. Then he said at last, "Did you have your horse with you?"

"Aye, as it happens. He was tethered to a tree stump on the moor."

"Then William's fear is not of horses," Hew concluded thoughtfully. "He was afraid, but of a particular horse."

"Is that so?" Richard laughed. "I once saw a horse hanged, for murder of its master when it trampled him to death. But I do not think my poor red roan will stand up in the witness box. No matter. You must know what happened next. I teased and chased her through the wood; we fetched up by the gibbet, where I led her back into the trees. It is a lonely spot, where no one likes to linger long. And it began to rain. Alison was laughing, wild and soaked, upon our bed of leaves. I tried to cut her throat, but my hands were shaking, and I could not cut deep enough. I tried to smother her; my hands were thick with blood," he shuddered in distaste, "and still she would not die; she struggled, even screamed — how could she go on screaming, when her throat was cut? Then you must see, how *difficult* it was. And though I cut and cut at her I could not stop her crying, close her eyes and silence her. And when at last she stilled, I could not stop, until I fell exhausted in her arms and both of us were spent, soaked in rain and blood. And then . . . when I came to again, I saw the little child. I had quite forgotten him. And he was peeping from the trees, where he had run to shelter from the rain, quite still and blank with horror. I reached out towards him — I swear it was to comfort him — but he fled back through the wood. And though it was the simplest thing to follow him, a weariness took over me. I let him go. I trusted that the storm would seal his fate. I had clean clothes in my bags, for I had thought of that. Beneath my coat and bonnet, I had worn your boatman's rags. I buried them in mud and rode back through the rain. The block was in my pocket, and I felt a curious calm."

Richard stood up and stretched. "It is a relief to confess," he admitted, "like one of Giles Locke's laxatives. I feel lightened and refreshed. Shall we play again?"

"And if we do, what happens next?" asked Hew.

"Allow me one last game," Richard answered quietly, "after which, I shall concede that I have lost."

Richard played erratically and closely to the net. To Hew's astonishment, he left the court behind him undefended, losing three points in succession to Hew's serve. The fourth serve he returned and embarked upon a rest, returning to the net where best he could. Hew did not understand this strategy. Richard seemed resolved to throw away the game. And though he saw him coming to the rope, he was ill-prepared for Richard's final stroke. Richard caught his volley at the net and played the shot backhand. Masking the direction, he took up the ball in flight and rammed it home. Instead of glancing off the side wall, as Hew had expected, it struck him full force in the face. As the court turned to blackness he felt himself crumple, parting his lips to mouth his surprise, and heard the clatter of his racket on the ground.

"I thought you were dead," Richard observed; almost, Hew thought, with a hint of reproach. The walls of the court seemed to spin and close in, and Hew was hit with motion sickness in a sudden wave.

"Pray, do not try to move. Let's see what we can do to help you."

Richard knelt by his side. He had taken off his coat, and rolled it into a pillow, slipping it under Hew's head.

"Lie still for a moment," he urged.

Dizziness spilled over to confusion. Hew could no longer see. A red haze had covered his eyes. He lifted his hand to the side of his head and heard himself murmur, "A surgeon."

"Aye, in a while," agreed Richard. "Dead ball. The score is now forty: fifteen. Though I'm afraid, the game is done."

Hew fought for consciousness. He struggled to regain his sight, and failed, the red haze returning to black as he felt his eyes close. But he could hear, still, Richard's quiet voice, and another noise outside. He forced his mouth open, framing a cry, but the sound did not come.

"Do you hear that? There are people outside in the street," Richard noticed. "Shall we call to them, and tell them of your accident? The pity is, you did not die. Well then, let us both be quiet; they will soon be gone."

He began to move, softly, back to the net.

"You know," he said a moment later, "this was not what I had planned. And it will be harder to account for. But nonetheless . . . Have you noticed that the slabs that pave the caichpule have a pinkish tinge? The floor is washed with oxblood. Perhaps you wonder why? It gives colour, so the greyness of the balls shows up, and provides a hardness that improves the drop. And for this purpose, bulls are sometimes brought alive and slaughtered in the tennis court, on their way to the fleshmarkets. Nothing so strange, then, to mark it with blood, for this place where we play has been a slaughterhouse. I think you did not know that — not so many people do — but you may think it fitting after all, to lend a little colour to the chase." And reflecting in this way, he drew his knife and drove it deep and deftly into Hew, pulling back to watch his lifeblood spilling to the floor.

Last Will and Testament

Hew groaned, with surprising conviction. A dull and thudding thickness filled his head. He felt his temple throbbing, bulging like a tennis ball. He was lying on a mattress in the house of Doctor Dow. The place had a whiff of the consulting room, with rows of white bottles, specimens and jars. Someone pressed a bandage to his chest. A sticky trickle marked the edges of the hurt; as the rag was tightened it began to sting. Hew moaned again, experimentally, and struggled to sit up.

"Be still a moment. You have taken quite a blow," Giles advised him cheerfully. He tied the bandage neatly. "How do you feel?"

"Terrified. There are two of you." Two anatomists loomed over him, poised for their dissections.

Giles chuckled, "Peace, you are not seeing double. This is my good friend, Doctor Dow."

"Then I am pleased to meet him," Hew said feelingly, "and I should be more pleased, to see his wife. Her stitching held; the jerkin saved my life."

"She is an expert sempstar. She made good your wounds, neat as any surgeon, saving us considerable expense," Giles acknowledged. "There is nothing like a woman's touch. The jacket though," he nodded to Hew's jerkin, darkly stained with blood, "was inspired. What made you think of lining it?"

"Dun Scottis, when he kicked me in the estuary," Hew admitted ruefully. "Though his force was tempered by the flow of water, still I caught his glance, and the padding in my britches saved me from grave hurt. The pity is, I did not line my hat."

"Aye, we had not reckoned Richard to be quite so good at caich," conceded Giles. "It was madness, Hew, to face the man alone, knowing he had killed in such a frenzy."

"Hence the precautions," argued Hew. A sudden wave of giddiness subsumed him. He closed his eyes. "What has become of Richard, Giles?" he whispered.

"Peace," the doctor soothed him, "he was taken into ward. They caught him in the act, with his knife in hand. Howsoever he may twist, he cannot turn from that."

"How did you find us?" murmured Hew, who no longer had a proper grip on things. He wanted to be sick.

"No thanks to Paul, who proved quite useless as a spy," tutted Giles.

"To be fair," Hew acknowledged, "I dismissed him."

"Then you are a madman and a fool, and you deserve a flaying," Giles said sternly, "never mind these cuts."

"I know now why I do not choose you for my doctor," Hew said wryly. "Your bedside manner lacks finesse."

"I'm serious, Hew. Had you been killed, you would not have been the one explaining it to Meg. I knew that it was madness to send Paul. I should have gone myself."

"But you, Giles, lack the subtlety that this sort of subterfuge requires. In any case, how *did* you find us?"

"It was Phillip," Giles admitted, unexpectedly. "It turns out he has lodgings underneath the tennis court. A dark and incommodious set of rooms. Apparently, he has them for a pittance. Though they serve ill for him, they turned out well for you. He saw you come into the court with Richard Cunningham, and raised a hue and cry that you were playing tennis on the Sabbath, forcing Fletcher into giving up the key. They found a little more than they expected; Fletcher called the watch. As to Phillip, he was not best pleased he saved your life. He does not seem to like you very much."

"Poor Phillip. I have treated him badly. Yet he almost spoiled the plan," reflected Hew.

"He was its saving grace," Giles contradicted. "I confess, when I saw you, I felt my heart stop. We thought you were dead, Hew."

"I thank you for your rescue," Hew said awkwardly. "And for all your care."

"You are most welcome to it. Though you once swore you would not be my patient, while you lived."

"Did I say that? Then I repent it, freely. Have you finished with the bandaging? I must go to Richard."

Giles shook his head. "Do not even think of making his defence. You will have to stand against him, as witness for the Crown."

Hew lay back again and closed his eyes. "What will I say to Eleanor and Roger, Giles? What will I say to Grace?" he whispered desperately. "It was bad enough that I broke Arabella."

The doctor took his hand. "That was not your doing," he said kindly. "Nor was this."

When Hew felt well enough to ride, he hired a horse and left the city, turning west. The path was smooth and dry, and before the sun rose high he made his crossing to North Queensferrie, arriving at the boatman's cottage shortly before noon. There among the flotsam, he found Christian, Meg and William, sharing bread and milk. And leaving Meg with Jonet and the child he took Christian to the shore, where as they walked he told his story, carefully and tenderly. Christian did not weep, but gazed at him, asking, "Then William is safe? We are all of us, safe?"

"Aye, it is over," he assured her. "You are both quite safe."

"Will there be a trial?"

"Richard will confess to killing Alison. He knows, if he does not, that I will press the charge of treason. Then the king will have his say, and he will suffer more. As it is, he will hang. And though there is no hope for him, his family will be spared from disgrace."

"Is it no disgrace, that he killed a girl?"

"*That* they will recover from. It is the lesser charge," Hew sighed. "Though it should not be. Yet, it is enough."

"You sound as though you pity him," Christian observed.

"He was mad, I think. Made mad by the guilt of his first crime. And that, the greater treason, was the one crime I can almost understand, though it is the worse one in the law. The deception of the desperate boy, I almost could excuse, but not what followed it. His conscience drove him deeper into sin. If he had confided in me, then I have no doubt, I should have kept his secret for him. Alison should not have had to die," Hew concluded sadly.

"But that," Christian said wisely, "was not for you to say. He brought it all upon himself."

"Aye, he did. I am afraid that it may take a little while," reflected Hew, "to clear your father's name."

"It is a name I never heard before today." Christian looked out across the estuary, where seabirds flocked upon Inchgarvie, and the ferry boat rolled on into the distance, to the southern shore. Hew broke in to her sadness, taking both her hands in his to ask impulsively, "Will you stay with me, always? Marry me?"

She pulled away her hands. "I cannot," she said simply.

"I could not ever speak of my regard for you," Hew persisted, "when I thought it wrong. Then let me speak it now!"

Christian shook her head. "It is too late. You went with *her*."

"With Catherine? I swear to you, that Catherine —"

"Ah, do not say that she meant nothing to you. Do not say that," she pleaded.

"I cannot, for it is not true. But Catherine knew, far better than myself, where my true heart lay. Our love was never consummated," Hew said bleakly, "because of you."

"It does not *matter*, Hew."

"Can you not forgive me?"

"I am betrothed to Phillip," she explained. "For after our release from gaol, I felt so very tired of being alone. Phillip knows the press, and has always been my friend. He will take on William as his own. I do not think that you would care to be a printer, Hew, and have a little child; and yet that is my life. It may be hard, at times, but it is all I know."

Hew shook his head. "It is really what you want?"

She was silent, for a long time thoughtful, before she answered, "Aye."

"Then I wish you happiness," he told her quietly.

"We shall make a fresh start," she gave a wan smile. "Phillip thought perhaps that we might go to London. And the press must have a new name. The corbie has brought us nothing but bad luck."

"It was your father's name," Hew reminded her.

"Aye, poor man. It is time that he was laid to rest. We shall have a ram's head, after Phillip Ramsay."

"Was that his idea?" demanded Hew.

"No, he would not hear of it," Christian demurred. "Yet I shall insist upon it. The idea was mine."

"Well, it's a good one," Hew allowed. "And for the first work of the Ram's Head Press, I know the very thing. My friend Nicholas Colp is at this moment finishing his book on Ramus. I will have it sent to you."

"Ramus?" Christian echoed doubtfully. "Is that likely to prove popular?"

"Incalculably. And, especially now. For I have heard it rumoured Edinburgh is soon to have a university. Though it can never hope to be the equal of St Andrews, this bastard institute is sure to want a printer. The Ramus will declare good faith, and ensure you are considered for the place."

"I'm not sure that is quite what we were looking for," said Christian, unconvinced. "Your father's book is worthy, and we shall finish printing as contracted, yet we do not live in hope of selling many copies. In truth, it is a little dull. Phillip thought that we should start to look to profit: Psalters and cheap prayer books, and the people's favourite sermons — leaving out the ones by Walter Balcanquall. Then ballad sheets and picture books, and tales of travels overseas . . ."

"And monstrous babies with two heads," Hew put in humorously.

"Aye, precisely," Christian nodded. "That's the sort of thing. Do you know of any?"

"I confess, I have no friends who write that sort of book."

"A pity. If you hear of one, be sure to let me know."

She turned towards the water. "I should like to walk alone here, for a while. Would you mind too much?"

LAST WILL AND TESTAMENT

Hew hesitated, as though about to speak, then changed his mind, and made his way slowly back to the house.

"If you had told me at the start," Meg accused, "I could have told you at the start, how ridiculous it was. Christian could not have been our sister. For our father was not that sort of man."

"I know well enough, you would have said so, for you could not bear to think ill of him. Therefore, your saying so would never have convinced me, and my saying so to you, could only cause you hurt," reasoned Hew.

"Which only goes to prove that you are wrong, and I am right," argued Meg. "William, do not touch that knife. It's used for gutting fish. It's very sharp. How could you have thought it, Hew?"

"Giles believed it too," Hew said, a touch defensively.

"And he is more foolish than you," Meg said fondly. "Why, do you know, he thought that . . . Ah, never mind. It is so very curious, how men and women do not talk. Did you know that Jonet and her man had not discussed the drowning of their son for twenty years? What madness, Hew! Christian and I soon sorted that."

Hew laughed. "God love you both! I am thankful, after all, that she is not my sister. One of you is quite enough."

Meg took his hand. "I was wrong about Marten," she admitted. "And I thought you were too trusting. I am sorry for it, Hew."

"In truth, I doubted it myself. Or rather, I did not want the alternative. It was Richard who tied Marten to the crime. About the things that mattered, Marten told the truth. Marten was at Antwerp when the Spanish came. There were horrors in his face that cannot lie."

"Then he did not kill the fisher lass?"

Hew shook his head. "Giles broke the link between the crimes. Once again, it was Richard that proposed it. There was nothing to tie Marten to the killing of the fisher lass, save he was at the senzie fair, and was a likely scapegoat. Richard played a dangerous game: he was also in Fife when Jess Reekie died."

"You do not mean that Richard killed that girl?" Meg exclaimed.

"Peace, rest assured, the murders are quite separate. I think that justice for poor Jessie lies among the fishermen, in Largo Bay, God rest her soul."

"Then what is Marten's part in this?"

"He has no part; that is his part. But Marten is a foreigner, and so a natural suspect. He came passing through, for that is what he does. He came here in search of fortune. Edinburgh, as we know, is a cold, inhospitable place that does not take kindly to strangers. Marten found scant comfort, and moved on. But then, by chance, he found William on the muir, and playing into Richard's hands, brought on Richard's destruction. In implicating Marten, Richard gave himself away, for he told us over much about his crime. Besides, you know my ways," Hew smiled. "I never care to follow where I'm led."

400

"Then Marten, almost, became Richard's fate? Like the coloured cards he sells?" suggested Meg.

Hew snorted. "*That* is fanciful. I will allow, though, Marten Voet is something of a mystery."

"What happens to him now?"

"I left him on the road to London, selling cards and tales. It is a desperate life. And yet, I almost envy him." Hew answered thoughtfully.

"Envy him? Are you mad! Suspected and shunned wherever he goes!"

"You are right, of course," conceded Hew. "It is a fickle madness. Sometimes, though, I think, to be without the boundaries would be grand."

"You are a fool, Hew," Meg answered fondly. "You ought to settle down. Christian loves you, and you let her go."

"It is for the best. Phillip loves her. And I do not want to run a press."

Hew leant forward and removed the knife from William, who let out a howl. "And I am not prepared to be a father yet. I barely know myself, let alone a child. Christian will be happier with Phillip. She liked Phillip first, and will like him better when I've gone."

"And what about you?" Meg asked perceptively.

Hew stood up and went to the door. "I can hear Minnie coming back from her walk," he said to William. "And she has been walking right next to the sea; her cheeks are all wet with the spray." He swung the little boy up in his arms. "Call to her! Tell her, it's time to go home."

★ ★ ★

Since Richard had been caught red-hand, he was convicted of malicious wounding, without the need for trial. At the same time, he confessed to the murder of Alison. He was sentenced to be hanged, at the market cross. And the day before this sentence was to be carried out, Hew returned to Richard's land to speak with Eleanor. He met Roger on the turnpike stair, who stared at him with hatred, pushing grim and silent past him to the street. At the entrance to the close he turned and spat. "You are a traitor. And I hope that when they hang you, they will cut your heart out and throw it to the dogs."

Hew watched the boy go trailing off to school, his shoulders tight and hunched. Eleanor received him more graciously, in the dim glow of the shuttered hall that had lost its heart.

"I do not blame you," she said sadly. "Richard must be mad, I think. I can make no other sense of it."

"Have you been to see him?" Hew inquired.

"Once," she admitted, "but I will not go again. The worst was, his saying, 'I did it all for you.' He slaughtered that poor girl, believing all the while, that he was doing it for me, and for the children. That is hard to bear. And Richard says his one regret — *his one regret* — is that he will not live to see the earl of Morton's trial. He hoped to lead the prosecution. That will fall to Robert Crichton, after all. For myself, I confess I am grateful that Morton's downfall will eclipse our own. For in a day or two, Richard will be hanged and all will be forgiven. Except," she added quietly, "by the mother of that girl." Eleanor began to cry. "How did you find him out?"

"He was subtle," Hew admitted, "and I was not sure until the last. I set a trap for him. He was my tutor, and I loved him for it, yet I saw that he controlled and directed me too much."

"You are a wilful boy," Eleanor said tearfully.

"I do confess, when pointed, I am apt to turn the other way. I suspected Richard, yet I could not know the whole. He was often kind, and he was always plausible. He buried all his lies among the truth. Small things betrayed him in the end. For though he had my confidence, he knew a little more than he was told. He knew that Balcanquall had Catherine's poems, when Balcanquall himself did not; he said that Alison . . ." *was raped*, he thought, and checked himself. "He knew the details of her death before they were released by Doctor Dow, and he was absent, often; and never where he should have been. On the day she died, he was expected at Craigmillar, and did not arrive. I never did find out," he said in afterthought, "what that business was."

"That I can tell you," Eleanor said unexpectedly, as she blew her nose. "For he made no secret of it. My cousin has a mind to build a caichpule at Craigmillar, and he wanted Richard's advice. I do not suppose that he will know us now."

"Eleanor, though it is no consolation, you will be well looked after," Hew promised her. "The boys will have their education. Grace will go on with her French."

Eleanor forced out a smile. "Then she may not thank you. Jehanne is old and cross, and though I scolded Grace for saying so, she does reek of garlic. I am ashamed to say, it is a consolation. I have been troubled with the fear we should be destitute. Was that wrong?"

"It is natural for a mother to be anxious for her children. That fear, at least, I may take from you."

"You are kind. The boys will take it hard."

"Roger, I think, will not forgive me," Hew observed.

"I believe he will, in time. Though it was not apparent, Roger and his father loved each other. Aye, they loved each other . . . *fiercely* is the word."

Hew left Eleanor among her thoughts, and called in to the tolbooth, where he bribed the gudeman with a purse of gold. Richard was in fetters in an upper room that at least allowed the light. He smiled at Hew, half-mocking, from his chains.

"Did you want me to make it easier for you?" he asked ironically. "I cannot do that, I'm afraid. You must play the devil, to the end. Yet, you will allow, I taught you well."

Hew gazed at him steadily. "I came to tell you that I have made arrangements for your family. Eleanor shall keep her house, and the children will continue with their education. Giles thinks that Roger has the makings of a fine physician. We shall see it done."

Richard smiled sardonically. "Then you shall see him snuff out more lives than his father. At least he will not hang for it. You realise, of course, that you are merely doing what your father did? For you have been his puppet all along. He sent you as my nemesis."

"I do not believe that," Hew replied. "There is nothing in the manuscript that suggests he knew. This you have built in your own mind, perverted by guilt. You read conspiracies, where there were none."

"You are wrong," Richard swore. "Matthew knew. "Why else would he send you?"

"You brought me here yourself," Hew reminded him. "And it was your own infected mind that saw threat where there was none. The pity is, I might have kept your secret, had I known. But you were driven deep and deeper into guilt, and to commit a crime that nothing could excuse."

"Do you not see, it was fear for my family? Fear for my family that compelled me from the start!" Richard cried.

Hew said gently, "Then you need not fear. For they will want for nothing, and they need not live in shame. Your children will not know the full scale of your treachery. And in the end, they will remember you as a man they knew and loved. That little you denied to Christian."

Richard was silent for a moment. Then he said, "It is a strange thing. Now I know I am to die, I feel almost resigned to it, almost, I might say, at peace. That jacket you had made," he looked up suddenly and smiled, "was most ingenious. I am almost glad it saved your life. But supposing I had cut your throat?" he teased.

"There was a metal collar, hidden in the ruff," Hew admitted.

"Ingenious. Such a thing might serve well in a hanging. I do not suppose . . .?"

"Alas, not."

"Ah, well. It was worth a try. However, I do have one last request; I hope you will not refuse me. Dearly now, before I die, I should like to look at Matthew's book. May I have it now, to see me through the night? I think it likely that I may not sleep."

Hew nodded. "Aye, for sure. I'll see what I can do."

He took the script from Christian, and returned it to the gudeman, who received it doubtfully. "Suppose he sets the place alight, and burns it with his candle?"

"And suppose he does," Hew answered patiently. "His cell is made of stone. He cannot burn it down. Since he will hang tomorrow, let him have his wish."

"Then I suppose he shall," the gudeman mused, "for old times' sake."

Returned to the west port inn, where he had taken lodging, Hew found Meg and Giles preparing to depart, Giles upon a sturdy bay, and Meg upon Grey Gillat. Paul and the baggage formed the vanguard, on a chestnut mare. "We are going home today. Come with us, Hew," Meg pleaded.

"Aye, but in a day or two. I'll catch you up. Tis likely I will overtake you, on my fine dun horse," Hew smiled a little absently. "Though it will cost me dear enough to pay his ransom."

The lightness of his tone rang hollow, and he looked away. "You do not have to do this," Giles said, understanding. Hew answered quietly, "I think I do."

At daybreak the next morning, he returned to town. He found a place upon a forestair that looked out upon the market cross. Further up the street, Eleanor had closed the shutters, yet the house could not escape the clamour and the glare. He thought of Grace and Roger, huddled in its hall. And through the jostling crowd, Hew saw Richard walking with the gudeman, a little tired and strained, yet with that spark of cautious brightness he was wont to show before a testing trial, an exhilarated nervousness. And as he climbed upon the scaffold he looked out, mocking, at the crowd, and his eyes met Hew's, resting for a moment. Then Richard's gaze dissolved into a smile, and he gave way to laughter as the hangman placed the noose around his neck.

Hew stood without a sound, and did not look away until the last. And even then, when all the crowd were gone, and Richard was cut down and taken to his grave, he did not stir, until the gudeman hailed him from the street below. "I doubt you want your book sir, then I doubt you will be vexed," he called out cheerfully. "I telt you it was dangerous to leave it. Though he did not burn us down, he tore it into shreds." The gudeman dropped a sack, that opened as it fell, and a thousand scraps of paper scattered to the wind.

The Lion House

Hew did not return to Christian's printing house, but made one last journey through the netherbow to the palace of Holyrood house. He passed by Catherine's lodging in the Canongate, and looked up to see the sun glance off the shuttered windows, resolutely closed. He saw no sign of life. At the foot of the hie gate, he came at last to the king's palace, sheltered in the hills. Since James was expecting him, he was admitted at the gate, and passed into the north west tower, where he was left to wait in a chamber lined with tapestries. He stood there for a while, ignored by sundry guards, until the entrance to the inner chamber opened and the goldsmith, George Urquhart emerged, bowing retrospectively to the young king. Urquhart closed the door behind him and gazed at Hew benignly as he passed. "Master Cullan! You are come to see the king. You will find him in a curious mood. Yet you are well met," he remarked.

"Well met, indeed," Hew bowed stiffly, "since I am going home and want some money."

"That can be arranged," Urquhart acquiesced. "Have you decided what to do with Christian Corbie's cottage?"

"I would like to make it over, as a gift, to Annie Forrester, widow of the west bow, whose daughter Alison was murdered on the muir; in truth . . ." Hew stopped short. "You said, Christian *Corbie's* cottage."

"Aye, well noted," Urquhart nodded. "For so your father always cried it, though of course it was not hers. It is a generous gift. I wonder whether you have given it much thought?"

"But you said you did not know her father's name!" objected Hew.

Urquhart shifted slyly. "If you recall, I said his name was not inscribed within the deeds. I never said I did not know it. They are not the same," he pointed out.

"But you withheld it," Hew exploded, "If you had spoken out, then Alison need not have died."

"You can hardly suppose that I had the knowledge to prevent it," the goldsmith answered smoothly. "I knew who Christian was, I do confess. I did not know that Richard meant to kill her maid. Do not confuse science, with prescience."

"Then what of Christian? Would you have let her hang?" Hew countered angrily.

"That was no concern of mine. Why do you suppose your father came to me?" the goldsmith replied.

"I cannot imagine, since you clearly have no scruples and no morals."

"That did not come into it. It was a matter of absolute trust. The key to holding secrets is to keep them," Urquhart smiled. "Since your father did not leave instruction to inform you of the name, I kept it close. It was not, in, fact, his choice. The name was kept

409

secret on the wish of Ann Ballantyne, Christian's mother, who did not wish her daughter to be sullied with the shame of it. You may infer that Matthew wanted it remembered, by the device that he constructed for the press."

"Yet you allowed me to believe the worst of him," Hew accused him bitterly.

Urquhart regarded him closely. "Have a care to what you say," he advised at length. "I *allowed* you? It seems to me that you were well prepared to think the worst of him; that I must think deficient in a son. Though to be somewhat circumspect, you were guided and misled by Richard Cunningham. You did not notice how he framed your questions for you. He was a skilful advocate. It is indeed a pity that he proved to be insane. He was also, I regret to say, a most valued customer. I have in my shop a pair of diamond rings, that he is, alas, no longer able to collect. I don't suppose that I can interest you in them?"

"You cannot," snapped Hew.

"Then that is a shame. But never mind, they will make a trinket for the king, if I thin them out a little. Richard had unusually fine fingers, very slim, almost like a girl."

"I think it a marvel," Hew observed grimly, "that Richard did not kill you, and that no one else has slit your throat on some dark winter night."

"It is no marvel;" Urquhart answered solemnly, "my life is charmed."

"Aye, it would seem so."

410

"No, I mean it *is*. I paid a wise man forty pounds, for magic prophylactics." Urquhart tapped his nose. "Do not tell the king."

Hew was shaken by this revelation, and was unprepared for the coming of the king, who appeared at his side, as though by stealth, gazing at him curiously. Hurriedly, Hew bowed. "Majestie, I was distracted, for a moment, by George Urquhart."

James regarded him keenly. "So I see. We are about to take a turn about the gardens. Follow!" he commanded. Then he changed his mind. "Ah, do not follow, walk ahead. We are going to the lion house."

Hew bowed again, perplexed, "As you will, your grace." He made his way down to the gardens. The king had a menagerie, where he kept a sad collection of wild beasts and royal pets, the lion and the lynx, and brightly coloured birds, whose plumes began to fade like summer flowers, for want of light and air. Hew waited nervously outside the lion house. And in a while, the king appeared, a small and fluffed up fledgling flanked by crows, with his lords and council flocked around him, in their silks and chains. He waved them off, "stand a little back, my lords. They do not like the stink," he remarked to Hew, smiling imperceptibly, the merest ghost.

"It is pungent, majestie," Hew noticed.

"It keeps the mice away," James returned thoughtfully. "And the rats. Another of our lions died this winter," he went on. "They do not live long."

"Perhaps it is too cold for them," suggested Hew.

The young king shivered in the bright spring air; the sun was high, and he was finely dressed, in cloth of gold and silk, yet he had come without a cloak. Hew slipped his own from his shoulders, "Will you take my cloak, your grace?"

James looked startled and amused. "No thank you, Hew Cullan," he said gravely. He paced back and forth, while Hew stood still respectfully, and bowed his head as James prepared to speak. "I have no doubt it is too cold for them," he allowed at last, returning to the lion house. "They are not suited to these climes. And yet, I do not think that is why they die. We keep them warm and well, and they have meat and drink, and all that they require. And yet they pine. They are a royal beast, and do not care to be shut up in a house. It is a pity," he said sadly, "for they are the emblem of our Crown; we want them as our pets, yet they persist in dying."

"It is vexatious of them," Hew agreed. The king glanced at him sharply.

"We have read your letter," he retorted, "which was why we sent for you. So it was Richard Cunningham that wrote slandering our name. We should not have guessed it."

"Majestie, I must point out, that you were not the object of his crime," protested Hew.

"You said that before. Though you will accept that every crime, in as much as it offends our person and estate, is a crime against the king. It is unfortunate, that you allowed this man to hang, before he could be made accountable for his acts against the Crown," James observed.

"It is a pity, sire. That was an oversight," excused Hew.

"Was it though, I wonder?" James asked shrewdly. "Is it not possible, still, to exact revenge upon his corpse?"

"The body was cut down, your grace, and returned to Richard's family for burial."

"A pity. He has got away with it." James said, regretfully, as though Richard had been one of his pet lions, who had died to spite the tyranny of his affections. "Still, you know the law. May we not prosecute his family for his treasons, and seize his land and tenement? He amassed some wealth, I understand?"

"The law allows it," Hew admitted. "Though his wife and children are quite innocent of any part in this. In such a case, I should expect them to come in the king's will, and a just monarch, doubtless, would extend his mercy, and allow them to live peaceful in his realm."

"Aye, perhaps so," James considered. "It seems to me that you have power to circumvent the law, which may serve you well, if it does not see you hanged. You have taken Richard Cunningham beyond our reach. I hope that does not mean that you collude in treason."

"Not at all, your grace. Though Cunningham is dead, he never was a threat to you. My only wish was to protect the innocent. It is to be regretted that his crimes have led to Lady Catherine's exile."

"Aye, that it true." As Hew had hoped, James was distracted. "And I was sorry for it, for I liked Catherine Douglas." The king's imperiousness began to slip, and Hew saw a glimpse, for a second, of the boy. James had not yet reached his fifteenth birthday.

"I wondered, whether your majestie might allow her to return?" Hew ventured.

"I am afraid that it cannot be done," James admitted. "You know, it was through my intervention that Catherine was allowed to sail for France. She was destined for the prison at Inchgarvie. Have you seen the place? It is a living grave. Catherine has been spared that, and so far my mercy has extended; I may not do more. The kirk here is a constant itch, and Catherine's sin inflames it. Were I to recall her, we should have no peace."

"That is a pity, sire."

James stared ahead, reflecting. Presently, he said, "You had a jacket made, I think, that defended you from harm."

"Aye, Majestie. It was made by the wife of Laurence Dow, to his specific pattern, to protect the vital spots."

"That is ingenious," the king observed. "I must have the pattern."

"It shall be arranged."

"Aye, it shall. They want to take my power from me," James blurted suddenly. "They all of them want power."

"Who do, majestie?" Hew asked him curiously.

"*All of them.*" The boy looked away as he struggled to compose himself. In a moment he had overcome his terror, and turned back. Hew saw the lords glance up, alert to each nuance and movement, shadowing their king.

"Would you like to be king's advocate, Hew Cullan?" James demanded.

"No," retorted Hew.

The king laughed. "Ah, but you are blunt. And that is not the answer I expected. Richard Cunningham did want to be king's advocate. Aye, dearly, he did want it. But you beat him after all. It must give you satisfaction, to have beaten your old master, to have routed him so soundly, in the end."

"It gives me none at all," Hew answered soberly. "In truth, it breaks my heart."

"It breaks your heart! How strange you are! For in your place, if I had such a master, it would please me well to best him," James declared. "Well, forget Richard Cunningham, for though I should have liked to see his head upon a spike, we are to have a bigger prize, that dwarfs his petty treacheries. I mean, the earl of Morton. Should I expect to find you at his trial?"

Hew shook his head. "No, your grace, I shall be gone by then. I'm going home."

"Home to St Andrews?" the king echoed thoughtfully. "Then you may be gone. But when I have want of you — and be assured I shall have want of you, Hew Cullan — I expect you to come."

Before he left the town, Hew bought a horse from the west port inn. And though it was a fine quick horse, of grave and placid temperament, and did not shy or falter at the boat, he exchanged it for Dun Scottis at the Inverkeithing stable, where the taverner appeared delighted with the deal. Dun Scottis, for his part, remained unmoved, trotting onwards placidly through Fife, as leisurely and slow as if he pulled a plough. At

Pettycur, they met a group of travellers coming from the ferry, and kept pace with them, moving landward on the path to Kennoway and on to Ceres, which brought them to St Andrews from the west, north of Kenly Green. Hew's heart began to quicken as he turned on to the south street, through the west port of his own beloved town, and rode his horse along the clear wide thoroughfare that led to the cathedral, past the kirk of Holy Trinity and the south side colleges, St Mary's and St Leonard's, down towards the harbour and the pier. Turning at the abbey walls, he urged Dun Scottis home to Kenly Green. On his left he saw the clear blue stretch of water and the quiver of the barley fields, leafy flecks of yellow where the corn began to colour in the sun. He saw the white tipped seagulls resting on the rocks, specks upon the hazy layers of grey and blue. He reined the horse closer, hard by the shore, where they could taste the salt air on their cheeks. And riding through the marram grass that trailed the water's edge they came at last to Kenly Green, to find the trees in blossom, and the woods pricked out in violets, peeping from the trees. Hew dismounted long before he reached the gate, and let Dun Scottis loose to graze among the fields. Nicholas stood waiting in Meg's garden.

"I saw you coming from the tower," he called. "So you are home at last! Have you brought the books?"

"Books?" Hew stopped short in his tracks.

"Aye, Hew, the books we wanted for the library. But surely you did not forget them? All that distance, all those weeks, spent working in a printer's shop, and not a book to show for it!"

"I confess, I had forgotten it. I had more pressing matters on my mind," admitted Hew.

"Aye, I know. Giles told me all. I meant to tease you, Hew. But you have had some strange adventures."

"It is a traveller's tale," Hew smiled, "and I am done with travelling, for a while."

"'Tis not like you to jest. You are not very good at it. And yet I am right glad to see you quite so well."

"Aye, it is a miracle," Nicholas said cheerfully, "I am quite well. Giles has brought a potion that brings great relief to the aching in my bones. He has given Meg the receipt, and she is making more for me. It is not quite approved by the apothecaries."

"Did it come from Doctor Dow, then?" wondered Hew.

His friend shook his head. "It appears not. Giles claimed that he had it from a brewster, a purveyor, so he says, of the deepest darkest secrets. He says we are not to tell Meg."

"Well and good. Were you tending to her garden?"

"I was thinking on it," Nicholas said seriously. "You do not think it has grown rather wild? I think that it might benefit from order and restraint."

Hew considered the fresh cicely, the chervil, dill and chives that pushed their straggled shoots into the late spring air. Emphatically, he shook his head. "Absolutely not. Let them grow free."

Hew fell silent then, and became a little thoughtful, in a manner that suggested he no longer wished for company. Nicholas stood back to watch him make his way towards the house. He entered there alone, and barely spoke a word as the servant took his hat, but explored the walls and passages, the cool, familiar contours of the stone, and wall by wall took in the fabrics and the furniture, the turning of the stair, the scent of burning candles, the sweet array of flowers. And presently he came up to the library, where he began to search through Matthew's books, methodically at first, and then with fierce intent, so that when his friend discovered him, he was buried deep in papers, wrenched out from the shelves and scattered round the room.

"Dear God! Have you any idea how long it took to arrange those books? If you had told me what you wanted, we might have found it in the catalogue," Nicholas objected mildly.

Hew cried out, distraught, "There must be something more! I have to know!"

"What would you know?" Nicholas asked gently, kindly as he might address a child.

"Did he plan it all the while?" demanded Hew. "Was I made the puppet, of his last revenge?"

Nicholas was quiet for a moment. Then he said, "Giles thought that Richard brought his end upon himself. It was the sad disorder of a fevered conscience. He willed his own destruction, in his search for peace."

"Since he destroyed the manuscript, I can never know," Hew answered bleakly.

"I will tell you what I think," Nicholas began. "Though I did not know your father well, or long, I knew him in the last months of his life, and helped him with his book. And though I do not like to say so to his son, it was the deadest, dullest sort of book that I have ever seen. If he wrote his secrets there, then rest assured, it was as safe a place to leave them as the grave. And yet, I am convinced, he never was aware of Richard's guilt. Matthew was a kind and careful man, who looked after Corbie's family out of pity, nothing more. If he felt regret, it was that he did not take on the case himself, and not because he was complicit in the crime. Your mother's death and sister's sickness turned him from a path that he well loved, and all his life he mourned its loss, and hoped to see his old ambitions realised in you. His book was an offering to a son, to persuade him to a course a father once had loved and lost. Yet in his heart, he knew that you were never meant for it. Trust me, for I saw him die, and he was not a man with something on his mind. Matthew was a good man, and he loved you well. You must be content with that."

"He died," Hew whispered wretchedly, "and I did not know him."

"And perhaps you never will," his friend allowed. "Yet we may judge a man as much by how he dies, as how he lives. And a good death, in part, is measured not by how we die, but by what we leave behind."

Hew glanced wildly round the room. "Aye, then what is left? Books, land, a country house? What did he leave behind him, after all, of any worth?"

Nicholas said simply, "He left his children. He left you."

★ ★ ★

On a bright windswept morning in the last week of June, Hew walked to St Andrews by the shore from Kinkell Braes. He stopped at the harbour to look at the boats, before climbing the kirk heugh north of the cathedral and turning into North Street, where he stopped at Giles Locke's tower. He found his friend in his consulting room.

"Just in time," beamed Giles. "I was just about to go back home for dinner. Will you join us?

"I have a letter in my pocket here from Laurence Dow," Giles remarked, as they turned into the Castlegait. They paused at the corner, looking at the cliffs, where the white gulls dipped and circled, carried on the wind. The doctor pursed his lips. "Fish day," he remembered sadly. "Nonetheless, we have a salmon."

"What news from your friend?" asked Hew.

Giles brought out the letter and put on his spectacles. "He sends Meg a receipt for a water for the dropsy, made from nettle tops . . . the earl of Morton's head is placed upon a spike outside the tolbooth where the corbies pick it clean . . ."

Hew shuddered. "I thank God I am not there to see it."

"*Amen* to that. So are the mighty fallen. Doctor Dow makes good report of Morton's death. The earl confessed to foreknowledge, but not to the killing of Darnley. I dare say he had blood enough upon his hands; though it were not King Henry's, yet the king's undid him. So our pasts are wont to haunt us."

"Must we speak of this?" objected Hew.

"Ah, pardon, it was badly judged. Then this perhaps is not the time . . . but I will broach it anyway. I never had much judgement," Giles excused himself. "I made my report to the burgh council, on the *morbus gallicus*, you know, and it was well received. Moreover, there have been few cases in the past four weeks. I dare to hope the sickness runs its course. Meanwhile, I have spoken of the role of visitor: I have been asked to take it on here in the town."

"That is excellent news!"

"Which means I may conclude my studies on the grandgore, and apply myself to other, more suspicious deaths. I thought we could begin," Giles shot him a look, "with the sad case of Jess Reekie. Perhaps you will approve?"

"I do indeed. Did you say we?" inquired Hew.

"That is the other part," admitted Giles. "I thought that with your knowledge of the law, you were well placed to join me. There is a vacancy at college for a reader in the law. I beg you to consider it, for you might meddle freely in its constitution yet have little obligation to the courts. You might even," he said dryly, "write a book on it."

Hew snorted. "Meddle! Is that what I do?"

"You scratch it like a sore," his friend affirmed, "that you cannot let alone, until you've rubbed it raw. In this position, you would have your liberty to catechise the law, and perhaps anon to mend it. Will you take it?"

"In faith, I might," considered Hew. "I have a mind to settle. I begin to understand my heart, Giles. I have fled from it too long. And I have gained little from my travels; I have been tossed upon storms, stripped of my rank, buffeted, bloodied and bruised; I have loved and lost, not once, but twice, yet neither woman shared the comfort of her bed with me. I am well glad to be returned among my friends. As to the law, if I can make it speak for those like Jess, who have no voice, I will be well content."

"That is what I hoped," Giles smiled. "In truth you are too loose to travel safely on your own. You want good steady counsel and a wife."

Hew snorted. "And a *wife?* You change your tune!"

"Not at all," insisted Giles, a little piqued. "Our brush with William has convinced me that your father's line must not die out. And since you make so little progress there, Meg and I are trying for a child."

"You do not say so, Giles!" cried Hew. "Then your problems are resolved!"

"Aye, God willing, or else are just begun," Giles grinned. "And, if I may say so, it is the direct result of that wholesome course of living you dismissed so scornfully."

"How so?" queried Hew. "I thought the purpose of that course was to suppress the carnal appetites."

"Aye, so it was, at first," his friend admitted cheerfully. "It came about like this. You know that I embarked upon a course of healthful exercise, devised by several learned authors, chief of which was Guglielmo Gratarolo . . ."

"Aye," said Hew facetiously, "you did it by the book."

422

Giles gave a little cough. "Quite so. And you are aware I worked my way down through these exercises . . ."

"To find they did conclude in carnal converse?"

"Need you be so crude, Hew? Of course they did not. Or that is to say, that happily they did, though that was not the purpose there intended."

"Aye, then to the point?"

"Peace, I come to it . . . Well, you know, I began with the golf . . ."

"For which you had no aptitude," Hew pointed out. Giles did not rise to this.

"And then progressed to tennis," he continued thoughtfully. "Now that you are home, we might perhaps reconsider taking lessons at the caich? For I feel I may have something there that could be nurtured out . . ."

"I think it not quite apposite," Hew retorted hurriedly, "to an expectant father."

"Oh! Think you not?" Giles said, disappointed. "I had not heard that. Well, no matter then. I next progressed to the gymnastics, as you know, and yet had not the build for it . . ."

He paused, preparing his defence, while Hew declined to comment.

"Well then, the next stage, as to more gentle exercise, was being rowed in boats," Giles went on.

"And being rowed in boats," Hew put in feelingly, "I do *not* recommend."

"Aye, though you must allow your own experiences were singular. According to Gratarolo, being rowed in boats is exercise gentlest and easiest of all others. And yet I find it somewhat jolting to the belly, for such a man as has a hearty appetite."

"And you are such a man."

"I do confess it freely. Well then, this takes us to the last and gentlest exercise of all, most suited to the aged and infirm, that is healthsome to all parts, and injurious to none."

"I cannot think what that might be. I trust it is not swimming?"

"Good God, man, no!" Giles started, horrified. "But let me read the proper words of the author Gratarolo, here Englished for convenience by the gracious Thomas Newton . . ."

"Giles, do get on with this," urged Hew.

"In his directions for the health of magistrates and students . . . what was that? Quite so." Giles turned a little pinker as he reached his climax.

"I have the passage here about, in my pocket, '. . . *fricasies and rubbings*, soft and hard. For fricasies and rubbings nourisheth and comfort the whole body . . .' to which end he most poignantly instructs, 'before thou arise out of thy bed, either to rub or else *make somebody else to rub* . . . thy back, breast and belly softly, and thy arms and legs hardily and strongly' . . . and so you catch his drift. Now Meg was most obliging in assisting with this exercise . . . wherefore you understand," Giles gave another cough, "I found my previous shyness was completely overcome. But you are laughing at me, Hew, I must protest!"

"In truth," Hew said fondly, "I do not laugh at you, but at the joyful outcome of this tale. Dear Giles! I am so very glad."

"Well," his friend replied gruffly. "I allow, I felt well satisfied. And since I have no further use for these exertions, I shall lend the book to you. It may keep you out of trouble for a while."

Also available in ISIS Large Print:

Nightshade

Paul Doherty

January 1304 and Hugh Corbett, devoted emissary of King Edward I, has been charged with another dangerous mission. Scrope, an unscrupulous manor lord, has reneged on his promise to hand over the Sanguis Christi, a priceless ornate cross he stole during the Crusades. Furthermore, he has massacred as heretics fourteen members of a travelling religious order, whose corpses now lie in the woods near Mistleham in Essex.

The King, determined to restore order and claim the treasure before the Templars demand its return, sends Corbett to Mistleham. But as Corbett reaches the troubled village, it becomes obvious that Scrope has other problems. A mysterious bowman has appeared, killing townspeople at random. Have the Templars arrived to wreak revenge?

As panic rises, can Corbett restore Mistleham to peace, and return the treasure to the King, before further blood is shed?

ISBN 978-0-7531-8320-5 (hb)
ISBN 978-0-7531-8321-2 (pb)

Michaelmas Tribute

Cora Harrison

It is 1509 and, for the people of the Burren in northwest Ireland, the Michaelmas Fair is a joyous time. A chance to buy and sell their wares and pay tribute to the lord of their clans. But this year is different. The steward of the MacNamara clan has decided to raise the tribute and it's not long before tempers are running high.

When the steward's body is found in the local churchyard, it falls upon Mara, the Burren's Brehon Judge, to piece the puzzle together. Was it revenge, greed or something more sinister that led to his murder?

When another body is discovered — allegedly suicide — Mara is not convinced and, despite the distraction of a surprising offer of marriage, it is up to her to bring the killer to justice before they can strike again . . .

ISBN 978-0-7531-8172-0 (hb)
ISBN 978-0-7531-8173-7 (pb)